GOLD COAST ANGELS: DOCTOR'S REDEMPTION

BY
MARION LENNOX

GOLD COAST ANGELS: TWO TINY HEARTBEATS

BY
FIONA McARTHUR

O MILLS

D1146625

GOLD COAST ANGELS

The hottest docs, the warmest hearts, the highest drama

Gold Coast City Hospital is located right in Australia's
Surfers Paradise, at the heart of the Gold Coast,
just a stone's throw away from the world famous beach.
The hospital has a reputation for some of the
finest doctors in their field, kind-hearted nurses
and cutting-edge treatments.

With their 'work hard and play hard' motto,
the staff form a warm, vibrant community
where rumours, passion and drama are never far away.
Especially when there is a new arrival—
fresh from Angel Mendez Hospital, NYC!

**When utterly gorgeous bad-boy-with-a-heart
Cade rolls into town, trouble is definitely
coming to Surfers Paradise!**

If you loved **NYC Angels**, you'll love the high drama
and passion of this irresistible four-book
Mills & Boon® Medical Romance™ series!

GOLD COAST ANGELS:
A DOCTOR'S REDEMPTION

BY
MARION LENNOX

First published in Great Britain 2013
by Mills & Boon, an imprint of Harlequin (UK) Limited.
Harlequin (UK) Limited, Eton House, 18-24 Paradise Road,
Richmond, Surrey TW9 1SR

© Harlequin Books S.A. 2013

Special thanks and acknowledgement are given to Marion Lennox
for her contribution to the *Gold Coast Angels* series

ISBN: 978 0 263 89916 0

Harlequin (UK) policy is to use papers that are natural, renewable
and recyclable products and made from wood grown in sustainable
forests. The logging and manufacturing process conform to the
legal environmental regulations of the country of origin.

Printed and bound in Spain
by Blackprint CPI, Barcelona

Dear Reader

It's autumn as I write this, and the weather's closing in on Southern Australia where I live, so right now I'm packing my togs and thongs (that's Aussie-speak for bathing costume and flip-flops) and heading for an extension to my summer. I'm flying up to the Australian Gold Coast. Why not? In Southern Queensland it's almost perennially summer, the beaches are superb, the surf's excellent—and there are lots of places that sell drinks with little umbrellas!

I'm sure the characters in Gold Coast City Hospital didn't have drinks with umbrellas in mind when they applied to work in the hospital we've set our stories in. Surely not! Our *Gold Coast Angels* are a dedicated team of young medics, whose every thought must be tuned to the medicine they live and breathe. But we've nobly allowed them some down time. We've thrown in a little surf, plus a touch of intrigue and drama, and we've definitely included romance. A *lot* of romance.

Your four dedicated Aussie authors have thus had a wonderful time playing on the Gold Coast, researching everything we needed to bring you four fantastic romances. But I've been away for too long, writing and not sun-soaking. Now there's a sun lounger with my name on it waiting up north. I can hear it calling. I can hear the surf calling. The Gold Coast's a wonderful place for lying on the sand and reading romance. Maybe I'll meet you there. I'll be the one with the umbrella.

Happy reading!

Marion Lennox

'Marion Lennox's RESCUE AT CRADLE LAKE
is simply magical, eliciting laughter and tears
in equal measure. A keeper.'
—*RT Book Reviews*

'Best of 2010: A very rewarding read. The characters are
believable, the setting is real, and the writing is terrific.'
—*Dear Author* on CHRISTMAS WITH HER BOSS

Marion Lennox is a country girl, born on an Australian dairy farm. She moved on—mostly because the cows just weren't interested in her stories! Married to a 'very special doctor', Marion writes Medical Romances™, as well as Mills & Boon® Romances. (She used a different name for each category for a while—if you're looking for her past Romances search for author Trisha David as well.) She's now had well over 90 novels accepted for publication.

In her non-writing life Marion cares for kids, cats, dogs, chooks and goldfish. She travels, she fights her rampant garden (she's losing) and her house dust (she's lost). Having spun in circles for the first part of her life, she's now stepped back from her 'other' career, which was teaching statistics at her local university. Finally she's reprioritised her life, figured out what's important, and discovered the joys of deep baths, romance and chocolate. Preferably all at the same time!

CHAPTER ONE

WHY DID ACCIDENTS seem to happen in slow motion?

There seemed all the time in the world to yell a warning, to run down the beach and haul the dog out of harm's way, to get the fool driving the beach buggy to change direction, but in reality Zoe Payne had time for nothing.

She'd been sitting admiring the sunset at the spectacular surf beach five minutes' drive from Gold Coast City Hospital. A tangerine hue tinged the white crests of the breaking waves, the warm sea air filled her senses and the scene was breathtakingly lovely.

She'd also been admiring a lone surfer, far out in the waves.

He was good. Very good. The surfable waves were few and far apart, but he had all the patience in the world. He waited for just the right wave, positioned himself before the rising swell with casual ease, then rode seamlessly in before the breaking line of white water.

The scene was poetry in motion, she'd decided, and the surfer wasn't bad either. When the wave brought him close to the shore she saw him up close. He was tall, sun-bleached, ripped, and the way he surfed said he was almost a part of the sea.

But she'd also been watching a dog. The dog was lying partly concealed among the dunes, closer to the shore than the place she sat. She wouldn't have known he was there, but every time the surfer neared the shore the big brown Labrador leaped from its hiding place and surged into the shallows. The surfer came in the extra distance to greet the dog, they exchanged exuberant man-dog hugs, and then the surfer returned to the sea and the dog to its hiding place.

She'd been thinking she'd kind of like to go and talk to the dog. This was her first week at Gold Coast City and she was feeling a bit homesick, but there was something about man and dog that said these two were a team that walked alone.

Only now they weren't alone. Now a beach buggy was screaming down from the road above.

There was no way a beach buggy should be on this beach. There were signs everywhere—protected beach, no bikes, no horses, no cars.

And this wasn't a local fisherman driving quietly down for an evening's fishing. This was a hoon driver, gunning his hired beach buggy—she could see the rental signs—for all he was worth.

He hit the dunes and the buggy became almost airborne.

The dog...

She was on her feet, yelling, running, but her feet wouldn't move fast enough, her voice wouldn't yell loud enough.

Oh, dear God, no!

For the buggy had hit the dune in front of the dog and hurled right over. It crashed down, hit the next dune, was gunned to further power and roared off along the beach, leaving whatever had happened behind it.

One minute Sam Webster was paddling idly on his board, waiting for the next wave. He was about to call it a day. Surfing after dark was dumb. He knew the risks of night-feeding marine life, and risk-taking was for fools. Besides, the waves were growing fewer, and the current was taking him out. If he couldn't catch a wave soon, he was faced with a ten-minute paddle to get back to shore.

It was time to head back to the beach, take Bonnie home and head for bed.

To sleep? Possibly not. Sam Webster didn't do much sleeping any more, but hard surfing morning and night helped. His job at the hospital was high-powered and demanding. He crammed his days to the point of exhaustion, but still sleep was elusive. Nights weren't his friend.

But Bonnie needed to be home. Where was a wave when you wanted one?

And then...

He heard the beach buggy before he saw it, roaring along the beach road, and then, unbelievably, veering hard across the dunes onto the beach.

The dunes...

'Bonnie!'

He was yelling now, paddling and yelling at the same time, but the tide was turning and he wasn't making headway.

Where was a wave? *Where was a wave?*

The buggy was freewheeling along the beach.

Bonnie!

And then the buggy hit the dune where Bonnie lay.

His eyes were locked on the hollow where Bonnie had dug herself a cool spot to lie. He was willing her to emerge. Willing her to show herself.

Nothing.

A figure was running from the grassy verge above the beach. A woman. He wasn't interested. All he was interested in was Bonnie.

Where was a wave?

For one appalling moment she thought it was dead. The great, chocolate-brown Labrador was lying sprawled on the sand, a pool of blood spreading ominously fast.

She was down on her knees.

'Hey,' she said. 'Hey.' She spoke softly. The last thing she wanted was to terrify the dog even more. The eyes that looked up at her were great pools of fear, shock and pain.

But not aggression. Fear, shock and pain sometimes made even the most placid animals vicious, but Zoe knew instinctively that this dog wouldn't snap.

She was beyond it?

Maybe.

The buggy looked as if it had landed on her hind quarters. Her head, chest and front legs looked relatively unscathed, but her left hind leg... Not unscathed.

There was a gash running almost its length.

So much blood...

She hauled off her shirt, ripping it, bundling part of it into a pad and using the rest to tie the pad so she got maximum pressure, talking to the dog as she did.

'Sorry, girl, I don't want to hurt you, but I need to stop the bleeding.'

Even if she stopped it… The blood on the sand…

She had to get this dog to help. She'd seen patients go into cardiac arrest through blood loss, and this dog was losing so much…

She glanced out to sea. The surfer was frantically paddling, but he was far out and there were no waves behind him.

It'd take him maybe five minutes to reach the beach—and this dog didn't have five minutes.

She'd slowed the blood flow. She hadn't stopped it.

There was a vet's surgery near the hospital. She'd seen it the day she'd arrived, when she'd been making her first exploratory forays, searching for a supermarket. It had a sign on it, 'All Hours, Emergency'.

That's what this was, she thought as she ripped and tied her shirt. Total emergency.

Her car was right by the beach. Could she lift the dog?

She glanced again out at the surfer. He was surely the dog's owner. She should wait.

And give him a dead dog?

There was no choice. She scrawled one word in the sand. She lifted the big dog into her arms, staggering with the weight, and then, despite its weight, she found the strength to run.

It was the longest paddle of Sam's life.

The long, low waves that had been giving him such pleasure all evening had disappeared. The sea looked millpond-smooth but the tide was surging and the current was almost stronger than he could paddle against.

In a normal situation he'd let the current take him along the beach, travelling sideways to the tidal tug and gradually reaching the beach without this fight. But this wasn't a normal situation.

Bonnie.

Emily's dog.

He remembered the day Emily had brought her home. 'Look, Sammy, isn't she adorable? She was in the pet-shop window and I couldn't go past her.'

They had been medical students and dirt poor, living in a one-room university apartment. Having a dog had meant moving house, taking on more rent than they could afford and juggling impossible study hours into caring for an active dog, but Em hadn't thought of that.

She'd seen a puppy and she'd bought it. She hadn't thought of consequences.

Which was why Emily was dead, and all he had left of her was her dog, *his dog*, and his dog had disappeared, carried by a stranger up over the sand dunes to the road beyond and he couldn't see her any more and he was going out of his mind.

And finally, when he reached the beach, things weren't any better.

He dumped his board and ran, but what he found made him feel cold and sick. The hollow where Bonnie had lain was almost awash with blood.

So much blood... How could she survive blood loss like this?

Where was she?

He turned and saw three letters scrawled in the sand, rough, as if done with a foot.

'VET.'

Sensible. Dear God, sensible. But where? Where was the closest vet?

Staring at Bonnie's blood... It was so hard to think.

Think.

There was a vet's surgery near the hospital, the one he normally took Bonnie to. It was the closest. Surely whoever it was knew that.

He was heading up the beach, ripping his wetsuit off as he ran.

So much blood... It was impossible that she would survive.

She had to survive. Without Bonnie he had nothing left.

The veterinary hospital was open and amazingly, wonderfully, a vet came out to meet her. Maybe it was the way she'd spun into the entrance, burning rubber. Medics were clued in to hints like that, she decided, because by the time she was out of her car, a middle-aged guy wearing a clinical coat was there to help her.

'Road trauma,' she said, wasting no words, somehow shifting into medical mode. What she must look like... She'd ripped off her shirt to stop the blood flow. She was wearing a lacy bra and jeans and sandals and she was smeared with blood from the neck down—or even higher, but she wasn't looking. But the vet was looking. He took her arm and hauled her round so he could see her face on, before he even looked at the dog.

'Are you hurt?' he demanded, and she caught herself, realising he needed reassurance. Triage dictated humans before animals, even for a vet, so she needed to waste a few words.

'A buggy hit her on the beach,' she said. 'I saw it happen but, no, I'm not hurt. This is all her blood. She's not my dog—her owner's out surfing but I didn't have time to wait for him to get back in. She's bleeding out from the back leg.'

'Not now she's not,' the vet said, and he was already leaning into the car. He could see the tourniquet she'd fashioned with her shirt and he cast her a glance of approval. 'She's Bonnie,' he said, flipping the name tag on her collar. 'I know her—she's one of the local docs' dogs. Sam Webster. You're not medical yourself, are you?'

'I'm a nurse.'

'Great. I'm the only one here and I'll need help. You up for it?'

'Of course,' she said, but he hadn't waited for a response. He was already carrying the dog through the entrance to his surgery beyond.

CHAPTER TWO

HE'D COME TO the right place. As soon as he pulled into the entrance to the veterinary surgery he could guess Bonnie had been brought here.

An ancient car was parked across the emergency entrance. It looked battered and rusty, it had obviously seen far better days, and right now the back door was swinging wide and all he could see on the back seat was blood.

There were spatters of blood on the ramp. There were spatters of blood leading to the entrance.

He felt sick.

He'd got rid of his wetsuit. He was wearing board shorts and nothing else, his feet were bare and so was his chest. He felt exposed, but the feeling was nothing to do with his lack of clothes.

Get a grip. You're a doctor, he told himself harshly. *Let's treat this as a medical emergency.*

At this time of night the vet surgery was deserted, apart from a cleaner attacking the floor with a look of disgust. He looked at Sam with even more disgust.

'Sand as well as blood. I've just cleaned this.'

'Where's my dog?'

'If you mean the half-dead Labrador the girl brought

in, Doc's got her in Theatre.' He motioned to the swing
doors at the end of Reception. 'Girl went in, too. You
want to sit down and wait? Hey, you can't go in there.
Wait…'

But Sam was gone, striding across the shiny wet
floor, through the green baize doors and to what lay
beyond.

He stopped as soon as the doors swung wide.

He might be an emotionally-distraught owner, he
might be going out of his mind with worry, but Sam
Webster was still a doctor. He was a cardiac surgeon,
with additional training in paediatric cardiology. The
theatres where he operated were so sterile that no bac-
teria would dare come within fifty feet, and he was
trained enough so that barging into an operating
theatre and heading straight for the dog on the table
wasn't going to happen. So he stood at the door and
took in the scene before him.

Bonnie was stretched out on the operating bench.
There was already a drip set up in her front leg and a
bag of saline hung above. The vet, Doug—he knew this
guy, he was the vet who gave Bonnie his yearly shots—
was filling a syringe.

There were paddles lying on the floor as if tossed
aside.

Paddles.

He had it in one. Catastrophic blood loss. Heart failure.

But the vet was inserting the syringe, the girl at the
head of the table was holding Bonnie's head and whispering to her and they wouldn't do that to a dead dog.

Doug glanced up and saw him. 'That'd be right,' he
growled. 'Doctor arriving after the hard work's done.

Isn't that right, Nurse?' He heard the tension in Doug's voice and he knew Bonnie wasn't out of the woods yet, but he also knew that this girl had got his dog here in time—or maybe not in time, but at least she stood a chance.

If she'd gone into cardiac arrest on the beach...

'How are you at anaesthetics?' Doug snapped, and he forced himself to focus on the question. Medical emergency. How many times had he had the rules drilled into him during training? Take the personal distress out of it until the crisis is over.

'I'm rusty but grounded,' he managed.

'Rusty but grounded is better than nothing. Humans, dogs, what's the difference? I'll give you the doses. I want her under and intubated and Zoe here doesn't have the skills. I've called for back-up but I can't get hold of my partner in time. You want to make yourself useful, scrub and help.'

'What's...what's the situation?' He was watching Bonnie, but he was also watching the girl—Zoe?—holding Bonnie still. They wouldn't have had time to knock her out yet, he thought. They'd have been too busy saving her life.

The girl looked...stunning. She was smeared in blood, her chestnut-brown curls were plastered across her face, she was wearing a lace bra and jeans and not much else.

She still looked stunning.

'Don't talk,' she said urgently. 'Not until you're scrubbed and can stay with her. She heard you then and she wants to get up.'

That hauled him back into medical mode. He nodded and moved to the sink, fast. He knew the last thing they needed was for Bonnie to struggle, even so much as raise her head.

'It's okay, girl, it's okay.' In the quiet he heard Zoe's whisper. She wasn't so much holding Bonnie down as caressing her down, her face inches from Bonnie's, her hands folding the great, silky ears.

He had no doubt that this was the woman who'd saved his dog's life. He'd seen her in the distance, picking Bonnie up and carrying her up the beach. From far out in the surf he hadn't realised how slight she was. And the blood... If she'd walked into Gold Coast Central's Emergency Department looking like that she'd have the whole department pushing Code Blue.

He glanced at the floor and saw the remains of her shirt, ripped and twisted into a pad and ties. That explained why she was only wearing a bra.

She'd done this for his dog?

Was she a vet nurse? If so, how lucky was he that she'd been on the beach?

Luck? He glanced again at Bonnie and thought he needed more.

Doug was injecting the anaesthetic. Sam dried, gloved, and took over the intubation. Zoe stood aside to give him room then moved seamlessly into assistance mode.

She was obviously a vet nurse, and a good one. She was watching Doug, anticipating his needs, often pre-empting his curt orders. Swift, sure and competent.

Doug was good, too. He'd met this guy before and thought he was a competent vet in a family vet practice. His work now said that he was more than competent to do whatever was needed.

They worked solidly. With fluid balance restored, Bonnie's vital signs settled. Doug had all the equipment needed to do a thorough assessment and a full set of X-rays revealed more luck.

Her left hind leg was badly broken and so were a couple of ribs, but apart from the mass of lacerations that seemed the extent of the major damage.

Her blood pressure was steadying, which meant major internal bleeding was unlikely. Amazingly, there seemed little more damage.

'I can plate that leg,' Doug said curtly. 'It's easier than trying to keep her off it for weeks. If you'll assist...'

Of course he'd assist. Sam was almost starting to hope.

He thought of the buggy crashing down on Bonnie, and he thought this outcome was either luck or a miracle. Either way he was very thankful.

And that this girl had been there as well...

She hardly spoke. She looked white-faced and shocked but her competence was never in question. Doug was a man of few words. He worked and Sam worked with him, and the white-faced girl worked as well.

They needed the full team of three. With Bonnie anaesthetised and seemingly stable, Doug decided to work on to do whatever was necessary.

'Otherwise I'll be hauling a team in to do this tomorrow,' Doug said. 'That's two doses of anaesthetic and with both of you here I don't see why I need to do that.'

Zoe wasn't asking questions. She must be desperate for a bath and a strong cup of tea with loads of sugar—

or something stronger, he thought—but she didn't falter. Sam hadn't seen her before, but he had only been at the Gold Coast for a year. He'd brought Bonnie to the vet twice in that time, for routine things. Two visits were hardly enough to know the staff.

He'd like to be able to tell her to go and have a wash, he thought, but she was needed. She'd scrubbed and gloved and was ignoring the fact that she was only in bra and jeans. She looked shocked and sick, but she was professional and capable.

And she still looked…stunning. It was the only word he could think of to describe her. A bit too thin. Huge eyes. A bit…frail?

Gorgeous.

What would she look like without the gore?

But he only had fragments of time to think about the woman beside him. Most of the time he forgot, too, that he was in board shorts and nothing else.

There was only Bonnie.

This was no simple break. Bonnie's leg would be plated for life.

Sam was no orthopaedic surgeon but he knew enough to be seriously impressed by Doug's skill. The fractured tibia was exposed and Doug took all the time he needed to remove free-floating fragments. He was encircling the remaining fragments with stainless steel, bending the plate to conform to the surface of the bone then drilling to fix bone screws. He checked and checked again, working towards maximum stability, examining placement of every bone fragment to ensure as much natural healing—bone melding to bone—as he could. Finally he started the long process of suturing the leg closed.

Which was just as well, Sam thought. Zoe looked close to the edge.

Bu they still needed her. She was doing the job of two nurses, assisting, preparing equipment, anticipating every need.

Bonnie was so lucky with her rescue team. The big dog lay under their hands and he thought he couldn't have asked for a more highly-skilled partnership.

He owed this girl so much. If there was back-up he'd stand her down now, but there was no one. She'd already done more than he could ever expect—and he was asking more.

But finally they were done. Doug stepped back from the table and wiped a sleeve over his forehead.

'I reckon she'll make it,' he said softly, and as he said it Sam saw Zoe's eyes close.

She was indeed done. She swayed and he moved instinctively to grab her—this wouldn't be the first time a nurse or doctor passed out after coping with a tense and bloody procedure. But then she had control of herself again, and was shaking him off and moving aside so Doug could remove the breathing tube.

'I… That's great,' she whispered. 'If it's okay with you, I might leave you to it.'

'Yeah, you look like a bomb site,' Doug said bluntly. 'Take her home, Sam, and then come back. Bonnie'll take a while to wake. I won't leave her and you can be back before she needs reassuring.'

'I have my car…' Zoe said.

'I've seen your car and I'm looking at you,' Doug said drily. 'You drive through town looking like that you'll have the entire Gold Coast police force thinking there's been an axe murder. Leave the keys here. I'll park it round the back and you can fetch it tomorrow. Where do you live?'

'The hospital apartments,' she said. 'They're only two blocks away. I can drive.'

'You tell me those legs aren't shaking,' Doug retorted. 'You've done a magnificent job, lass, but now you need help yourself. You have some great staff, Sam. You were damned lucky to have your colleague on the beach.'

'My colleague...?'

'You realise Bonnie arrested?' Doug went on. 'Heart stopped twice. With blood loss like that it's a wonder she made it. A miracle more like. If Zoe hadn't got her here... Well, if she cops a speeding fine for her trip here, I'm thinking you ought to pay it.'

'I'd pay for more,' Sam said, stunned—and confused. 'You're not a vet nurse?'

'I'm a nurse at Gold Coast City,' she managed. 'I'd rather go home by myself.'

A nurse. A human nurse. One of his *colleagues*?

'Take her home, Sam,' Doug told him. 'Now. Take a gown from the back room, Zoe, so you look less like a bomb victim, but go home now. You deserve a medal and if Sam doesn't give you one I'll give you one myself. Go.'

'I'll be giving her a medal,' Sam growled. 'I'll give her a truckload if she'll take it. What you've done...'

'It's okay,' Zoe managed. 'Enough with the medals. Doug's right, I just need to go home.'

She wanted to go home but she didn't want this man to take her.

She wanted, more than anything, to slide behind the

wheel of her car, drive back to Gold Coast Central, sneak in the back way and find a bath and bed.

But there was no 'back way', no way to get back into the hospital without attracting attention, and Doug was right, she and her car were a mess.

Sam was taking her home?

He ushered her outside where his Jeep was parked next to her car and she thought…she thought…

This guy was a doctor? A colleague?

He was still only wearing board shorts. Unlike her, though, he didn't look gruesome. He looked like something from the cover of one of the myriad surfing magazines in the local shops.

The Gold Coast was surfing territory, and many surfers here lived for the waves. That's what this guy looked like. He was bronzed, lean, ripped, his brown hair bleached blond by sun and sea, his green eyes crinkled and creased from years of waiting for the perfect wave.

He was a doctor and a surfer.

Where did dog owner come into that?

He grabbed a T-shirt from the back seat of his Jeep and hauled it on. He looked almost normal, she thought, even after what had happened. His dog was fixed and he was ready to move on.

She glanced down at her oversized theatre gown and the bloodied jeans beneath them and something just… cracked.

For hours now she'd been clenching her emotions down while she'd got the job done. She looked at the mess that was her car, her independence, her freedom, she looked down at her disgusting jeans—and control finally broke.

'Let's go,' he said, but she shook her head.

'What were you thinking?' she managed, trying hard to keep her voice low, calm, incisive, clear. 'Leaving her waiting on the beach? Leaving her alone? To be so far out and leave her there... If I hadn't been there she'd be dead. You have a dog like Bonnie and you just desert her. Of all the stupid, crass, negligent, cruel...

'Do you know how lucky you are to have a dog? Of course you don't. You're a doctor, you're a healthy, fit, surfer boy. You can buy any dog you want, so you just buy her and then you don't care that she loves you, so she lies there and waits and waits. I was watching her—and she adores you, and you abandoned her and it nearly killed her. If I hadn't been there it would have! She nearly died because you didn't care!'

So much for calm, incisive and clear. She was yelling at the top of her lungs, and he was standing there watching, just watching, and she wanted to hit him and she thought for one crazy moment that it'd be justifiable homicide and she could hear the judge say, 'He deserved everything that was coming to him.'

Only, of course, she couldn't hit him. Somehow she had to get herself under control. She hiccuped on a sob and that made her angrier still because she didn't cry, she never cried, and she knew she was being irrational, it was just...it was just...

The last few days had been crazy. She'd spent her whole life in one small community, closeted, cared for. The move here from Adelaide might seem small to some, but for Zoe it was the breaking of chains that had been with her since childhood.

It was the right thing to do, to move on, but, still, the

new job, the new workplace, the constant calls from her parents—and from Dean, who still couldn't understand why she'd left—were undermining her determination and making her feel bleak with homesickness.

But she would not give in to Dean. 'You'll come to your senses, Zoe, I know you will. Have your fling but come home soon. All we want to do is look after you.'

Aaagh!

She did not want to go home. She did not want to be looked after.

But neither did she want to yell at this stranger or stand in a theatre gown covering a bra and jeans, looking disgusting and feeling tears well in her eyes and rage overwhelm her, and know that somehow she had to get back into the hospital apartments, past strangers. Plus she'd intended to buy milk on the way home and…and…

And she would do this.

She fumbled under her gown to fetch her car keys. She had to lift the thing but what the heck, this guy had seen her at her worst anyway. She grabbed her car keys from her jeans pocket but Sam lifted them from her hand before she could take a step towards the car.

'We go in my car,' he said in a voice that said he was talking her down, doctor approaching lunatic, and she took a step back at that.

'I'm not crazy. I might have yelled too much but you deserve it.'

'You think I don't know it? I love Bonnie,' he said. 'I deserve everything you throw at me and more, apart from the accusation that I could just buy another dog because I never could. I am deeply, deeply sorry for what happened. The fact that Bonnie has been watching me surf since she was a pup twelve years ago doesn't mean it's okay now. The fact that it's a secluded beach and the guys in the buggy were there illegally doesn't mean it's okay either. Years ago Bonnie would have watched the whole beach. Tonight she just watched me and she paid the price. Zoe, you're upset and you have every right to be but I can't let you go home alone.'

'You can't stop me. It's my car. Get out of the way.'

'Zoe, be sensible. Get in the car, there's a good girl…'

He sounded just like Dean—and she smacked him.

She'd never smacked a man in her life.

She'd never smacked anyone in her life. Or anything. Even in the worst of the bleak days, when the first transplant had failed, when she'd heard the doctors telling her parents to prepare for the worst, she'd hung in there, she'd stayed in control, she hadn't cried, she hadn't kicked the wall, she hadn't lashed out at anything.

Not because she hadn't wanted to but it had always seemed that if she did, if she let go of her relentless control, she'd never get it back. She'd drop into a black and terrifying chasm. She was far better gripping her nails into her palms until they bled and smiling at her parents and pretending she hadn't heard, that things were normal, that life was fine.

And here, now, the first week of her new life, standing in the dusk in a veterinary surgeon's car park, with a doctor from the hospital where she wanted to start her new life…

She'd hit him.

The chasm was there, and she was falling.

She stared at him in horror. The yelling had stopped. There was nothing left in her and she couldn't say a word.

His face stung where her hand had swiped him in an open-palmed slap. The sound of the slap seemed to echo in the still night.

She was staring at him like the hounds of hell were after her.

It didn't take a genius to know this woman didn't normally slap people. Neither did it take a genius to know she was on some sort of precipice. She was teetering on the edge of hysteria. She was hauling herself back, but she was terrified she wasn't going to make it.

What did you do with a woman who'd just slapped you? Walk away, reacting as he'd been taught all his life to react to people who were out of control?

Her eyes were huge in her white face. She was dressed in an oversized theatre gown and blood-splattered jeans and she looked like something out of a war zone.

And he could tell that there were things in this woman's life that lay behind even the appalling events of the last few hours.

She'd hit him and she was looking at him as if she'd shot him. In his private life he avoided emotional contact like the plague. But with this woman... What was it about her?

Walk away? No.

He took her hands in his and he tugged her forward. He folded her into his arms and held her, as he'd not held a woman for years.

She'd slapped him.

He didn't care. He just...held.

* * *

One minute she was out-of-control crazy. The next minute she was being hugged.

She was rigid with shock, but maybe rigid was too mild a word for it. She felt like she was frozen.

If she moved… But there was no if. She *couldn't* move. She didn't know who she would be if she moved. She would be some out-of-control creature who screamed and hit…

She had to apologise. She had to pull away and say she was sorry, but her body wouldn't obey. Tremors were starting, shudders that ran all through her. If she pulled away she'd have nothing to hold her. All she could do was let this man—this stranger—keep her close and stop her crumpling.

She was falling into him and he was holding her as she had to be held. She was moulding to him, feeling the warmth and strength of him, feeling the steadiness of his heartbeat, and it was as if in some way he was giving hers back.

She was delusional. Crazy. She needed to pull herself together, but not yet, not yet. For now she could only stand within his arms while the world somehow righted itself, restored itself to order, until she finally found the strength to pull away and face the consequences of what she'd done.

Sam specialised in paediatric cardiology. He treated children and babies with heart problems. In his working life he faced parents on the edge of control—or who had tipped over into an abyss of grief. He never got used to it. He'd learned techniques to keep control of his emotions. To express quiet sympathy, to offer hope when hope was possible, to listen when listening was all he had to give.

But he'd never felt like he did now.

This made no sense. Yes, his dog was hurt. Yes, it had been an appalling evening but if this woman was a trained nurse... For her to collapse like this...

For him to feel like this...

Why? What was it with this woman that was making his heart twist?

He held her and felt her take strength from him. He felt the rigidity ease, felt her slump against him, and he felt her quietly gather herself.

He should move her away but his rigid protection of personal space wasn't working right now. She was so vulnerable...and yet what she'd done, how she'd acted, had taken pure strength. There was no way he could let her down now, and when finally she found the strength to tug away he was aware of a sharp stab of loss.

She hadn't cried. She was still white-faced, but she was dry-eyed and drained.

She shoved her hands through her curls, tucking stray wisps behind her ears, and he felt an almost irresistible urge to help her. To fix a tiny curl that had escaped.

He wasn't an idiot. He'd been slapped once. It behoved a man to stay still and silent, and wait for her to make the first move.

'I...I'm sorry,' she managed at last.

'It's okay,' he told her, striving hard to lighten what was an unbelievably heavy situation. 'I was feeling guilty about Bonnie. Now I can feel virtuously aggrieved at being assaulted.'

'And I get the guilt instead?'

'Exactly,' he said, and tried a smile.

She didn't smile back. She looked up at him, and he thought, whatever had gone before, this woman wasn't one to crumple. There was strength there. Real strength.

'Hitting's never okay,' she said.

'You were swatting flies,' he said. 'And missed.'

She did smile then. It was the merest glimmer but it was still a smile and it made him feel...

Actually, he didn't know how it made him feel. Holding her, watching her...

Why was this woman touching him? Why did he look at her and want to know more?

It was Bonnie, he told himself. It was the emotions of almost losing his dog. That's all it was.

'Let me take you home,' he said carefully, and took a step back, as if she might swipe him again.

The smile appeared again, rueful but there.

'I'm safe,' she told him. 'Unarmed.' She tucked her arms carefully behind her back and he grinned.

'Excellent. Would you accept my very kind offer of a ride home?'

'I'll stain the Jeep.'

'I'm a surfer. I have a ton of towels.'

'I need milk,' she said.

And he thought excellent—practicalities, minutiae were the way to get back on an even keel.

'Because?'

'Because I've run out,' she said. She took a deep breath, steadying herself as she spoke, and he knew she knew minutiae were important.

She'd been in the abyss, too? There seemed such a core recognition, at a level he didn't recognise, that it was an almost physical link.

But she seemed oblivious to it. 'I'm on duty at six tomorrow morning,' she said. 'I have no milk. How can I have coffee with no milk? And how can I start work with no coffee?'

'I see your need,' he said gravely. 'And I'm trained for triage. Priority one, the lady needs milk. Priority two, the lady needs home, wash, sleep. I can cope with milk and home. Can you take it from there?'

It was the right thing to say. Setting limits. Giving her a plan. He'd used this with parents of his patients hovering at the edges of control, and it worked now.

There were no more arguments. She gave him another smile, albeit a weak one, and he led her to his car.

He climbed in beside her, but still he felt strange. Why?

Forget imagined links, he told himself. This was crazy. He didn't do emotional connection. He would not.

Get this night over with, he told himself. Buy the lady some milk and say goodnight.

He drove a great vehicle for surfing. It was no doctor's car, she thought as he threw a heap of towels on the front seat. The Jeep was battered, coated with sand and salt, and liberally sprinkled with Labrador hair. Any qualms she had about spoiling the beauty of one of the sleek, expensive sets of wheels she was used to seeing in most doctors' car parks went right out the window.

Sam wasn't your normal doctor.

He didn't look your normal doctor either. He was sand- and salt-stained as well, with his sun-bleached hair and crinkled eyes telling her that surfing was something he did all the time, as much a part of him as his medicine must be.

But he was a doctor, and a good one, she suspected. She'd seen his skill at stitching. She'd also heard the transition from personal to professional as he'd coped with her emotional outburst.

Though there'd been personal in there as well. There'd been raw emotion as he'd seen Bonnie—and there'd been something more than professional care as he'd held her.

Well, she'd saved his dog.

She was trying to get a handle on it. She was trying to fit the evening's events into the impersonal. Nurse saves doctor's dog, nurse angry at doctor for leaving dog on beach, nurse hits doctor, doctor hugs nurse.

It didn't quite fit.

'I'm normally quite sane,' she ventured as he pulled up outside a convenience store.

'Me, too.' He grinned. 'Mostly. What sort of milk?'

'White.'

His grin widened. 'What, no unpasteurised, low-fat, high-calcium, no permeate added...'

'Oi,' she said. 'White.'

He chuckled and went to buy it. She watched him go, lean, lithe, tanned, muscled legs, board shorts, T-shirt, salt-stiff hair—everything about him screaming surfer.

He was pin-up material, she thought suddenly. He was the type of guy whose picture she'd have pinned on her wall when she'd been fifteen.

She'd pinned these sorts of pictures all over her wall when she'd been a kid. Her parents had had a board they'd brought in to her various hospital wards to make her feel at home. She'd had pictures of surfing all over it. She would lie and watch the images of lean bodies catching perfect waves and dream...

But then Sam was back with her milk and she had to haul herself back to the here and now.

'My purse is in my car,' she said, suddenly horrified.

'I'll fix it,' he said. 'You'll get it back tonight.'

She knew he would. *I'll fix it.*

She actually didn't like it all that much. Other people fixing stuff for her…

She had to get a grip here. Getting her purse and paying for her milk were not enough to start a war over.

She subsided while he drove the short distance to the hospital apartment car park. The parking space he drove into indicated it belonged to 'Mr Sam Webster. Paediatric Cardiology'.

Mr. That meant he was a surgeon.

Paediatric cardiology. Clever.

She glanced across at him and tried to meld the two images together—the specialist surgeons she'd worked with before and the surfer guy beside her.

'I clean up okay,' he said, and it felt weird that he'd guessed her thoughts. 'I make it a rule never to wear board shorts when consulting. Hey, Callie!'

A woman was pulling in beside them—Dr Callie Richards, neonatal specialist. Zoe had met this woman during the week and was already seriously impressed. Callie was maybe five years older than Zoe but a world apart in medical experience. In life experience, too, Zoe had thought. She'd seemed smart, confident, kind— the sort of colleague you didn't want to meet when you were looking…like she was looking now. She'd also seemed aloof.

But Sam was greeting her warmly, calling her over.

'Callie, could you spare us a few minutes?' he called.

'We've had a bit of a traumatic time. Bonnie was hit by a car.'

'Bonnie!' Callie's face stilled in shock and Zoe realised she knew the dog. Maybe the whole hospital knew Bonnie, she decided, thinking back to those trusting Labrador eyes. Bonnie was the sort of dog who made friends.

'We think she'll be okay,' Sam said hurriedly, responding to the shock on Callie's face, 'but I need to get back to the vet's. This is Zoe...' He looked a query at Zoe. 'Zoe...'

'Payne,' Zoe said. She was on the opposite side of the Jeep from Sam and Callie, and knowing how she looked she was reluctant to move.

'I know Zoe,' Callie said, smiling at her. 'New this week? From Adelaide?'

That was impressive. One brief meeting in the wards, doctor and nurse, and Callie had it.

'Yeah, well, she's had a baptism by fire,' Sam said grimly. 'I was out in the surf when Bonnie was hit, and she saved her life. We've just spent two hours operating and Zoe rocks. But now she's covered in gore and she's got a bit of delayed shock. I don't want to leave her but I need—'

'To get back to Bonnie—of course you do.' And Callie moved into caretaker mode, just like that. 'Go, Sam, I'll take care of Zoe.'

'I don't need—'

'Let Sam go and then we'll discuss it,' Callie said, and Zoe hauled herself together—again—and gave a rueful smile. Sam handed Callie Zoe's milk, as Zoe climbed out of the Jeep. Then, he was gone.

* * *

Callie was brisk, efficient and not about to listen to quibbles. She ushered Zoe into the lift and when it stopped on the first floor to admit a couple of nurses she held up her hand to stop them coming in.

'Closed for cleaning,' she said, and grinned and motioned to Zoe. 'Or it should be. Catch the next lift, ladies.'

The lift closed smoothly and they were alone again.

When they reached the apartment Zoe realised her keys were in her purse. No problem—one phone call and Callie had the caretaker there, and he didn't ask questions either. There was something about Callie that precluded questions.

Or argument. Zoe gave up, let herself be steered into the bathroom, stood for ten minutes under a steaming shower and emerged in her bathrobe, gloriously clean. Two plates of toast and eggs were on her kitchen counter with two steaming mugs of tea, and Callie was sitting over them looking as if this was completely normal, like they were flatmates and it was Callie's turn to cook.

'I hope you don't mind,' she said. 'But I'm starving, and there's nothing in my apartment. I was going to ring for pizza but you have enough to share.'

Zoe smiled and slid into a chair and thought she should protest but she was all protested out.

And the toast smelled great. She hadn't realised she was hungry. They ate in what seemed companionable silence. Zoe cradled her tea, her world righted itself somehow and when finally Callie asked questions she was ready to answer.

'How's Bonnie?' she asked first, and Zoe thought

she was right in her surmise that Bonnie was a beloved presence in this hospital.

'She has a fractured leg, now plated. Lots of lacerations and two broken ribs, but Doug—the vet—seems confident that she'll be okay.'

'Thank God for that,' Callie said. 'Half the hospital would break its collective heart if she died—not to mention our Sam. Those two are inseparable.'

'He left her on the beach,' Zoe said carefully, trying not to sound judgemental, 'while he surfed. She was hit by a dune buggy.'

Callie closed her eyes. 'Damn. But that beach is closed to anything but foot traffic.'

'You know where we were?'

'Sam always surfs at the Spit at the Seaway. The surf's great, dogs are permitted off leash and it's the safest place for Bonnie.'

'He still shouldn't have left her,' Zoe said stubbornly, and Callie shrugged and started making more tea.

'Okay, I'll give you some back story,' she said. 'You need to get used to this hospital, by the way. Everyone knows everything about everybody. If you want things kept private, forget it. I don't normally add to it, but tonight you've earned it. Bonnie was Sam's fiancée's dog. According to reports, Emily was wild, passionate and more than a little foolhardy. She surfed every night— they both did. With Bonnie. When Emily bought her as a pup Sam tried to talk her into exercising her and then leaving her in the car while they surfed, but Bonnie was Emily's dog and Emily simply refused.

'So now Bonnie's in her declining years but what she loves most in the world is lying on the beach at dusk, waiting for Sam to come in. If Sam leaves her at home, or in the Jeep, she'll howl until the world thinks she's being massacred. For months she howled because she missed Emily and Sam decided he couldn't take her beach away from her as well.'

'So...what happened to Emily?' Zoe asked.

'Killed by carelessness,' Callie retorted. 'Not that Sam will admit it, but there it is. They went down to the beach to surf but the waves were dumpers, crashing too close to shore. Sam knew it, they both knew it, but Emily went out anyway. Word is that she simply did what she wanted. She was clever and bright and she twisted the world round her finger.

'That night she and Sam had words. Sam took Bonnie for a walk along the beach to let off steam and Emily took her board out, got dumped and broke her neck. To this day Sam thinks he should have picked her up and carted her off the beach by force, but I guess it's like telling Bonnie she can't stay on the beach on her own. Immoveable object means unimaginable force. One of them has to give.'

'Oh,' Zoe said in a small voice, and Callie gave her a swift, appraising glance.

'Let me guess—you gave Sam a lecture?'

'I...might have.'

'And that red mark on his face? The mark that looks suspiciously like finger marks?'

'Oh...' She felt herself blush from the toes up.

'It'll settle,' Callie said, grinning widely. 'They don't usually bruise with the fingermarks still showing. And I promise I won't tell.'

'How do you know...about the fingermarks?' Zoe managed, and Callie's smile died. There was a moment's awkward pause and then Callie seemed to relent. She shrugged.

'I worked in a women's refuge for a while,' she said curtly in a voice that told Zoe not to go there. 'I was getting over a mistake myself. But I wouldn't worry. You saved Sam's dog, and I suspect even if the world knew you'd hit him he'd consider it a small price. Do you want to sleep in tomorrow? I can alter your shifts.'

She was changing the subject, Zoe thought, steering away from the personal, and she thought there were things behind this woman's competent facade...

As there were things behind Sam's surfer image.

She should think about sleeping in. She tried for a whole two seconds, but the warmth, the food, the effects of the evening's fright suddenly coalesced into one vast fog of weariness. It was like the blinds were coming down whether she willed them or not.

'I'll be fine for tomorrow,' she managed. 'But I do need to sleep.'

'I'll tuck you in,' Callie said cheerfully. 'Bedroom. Come.'

'I don't need tucking in,' she said, affronted.

'Remind me to ask when I want to know what you need,' Callie retorted. 'I'm thinking Sam Webster is going to ring me from the vet's to find out how you are and I'm telling him I've tucked you into bed, whether you wanted it or not.'

By midnight Doug was sufficiently happy with Bonnie to order Sam home.

'I'll be checking on her hourly. I'll sleep when I'm relieved in the morning but I suspect you have work tomorrow. Right? So, home. Bed.'

Bonnie was sleeping soundly, heavily sedated. Sam fondled her soft ears but she didn't respond, too busy sleeping.

Doug was right.

He headed out to the car park. Doug had locked Zoe's car but it still blocked the entrance.

He needed to retrieve her purse, and he might as well move it before handing the keys back to Doug.

It took him three minutes to get it started and Doug came out to help. They shifted it and then stood looking at it in disgust, not only because it was blood-soaked.

'She's driven that thing from Adelaide,' Sam said at last. 'How?'

'Blind faith,' Doug said. 'Some wrecking yard must have paid her to cart it away.'

It was structurally sound, Sam thought, but only just. Once upon a time it had been a little blue sedan, but its original panels had been replaced with whatever anyone could find. Some were painted bright orange with anti-rust. Some looked like they'd been attacked by a sledgehammer.

When running, the car sounded like a wheezing camel. Even the drive from entrance to car park was bumpy.

'There's a roadworthy sticker on the front,' Doug said. 'You reckon that's because she needs to prove it to the cops half a dozen times a day?' He grinned. 'Never mind, it did its job. It got your dog here in time. Girl and car both need a medal.'

'Yeah,' Sam said absently. 'I need to fix this.'

He bade Doug goodnight and headed back to his Jeep. It was a grubby surfer truck but compared to Zoe's it was luxurious.

He should go back to the hospital. Friday was a normal working day. In eight hours he'd be on the wards.

Zoe would be there in six.

Zoe…

His head was doing strange things.

He climbed into his truck and headed where he always headed when he needed to clear his mind.

The beach was deserted. A full moon hung in a cloudless sky. His board lay where he'd dumped it hours ago. Just as well the tide had been going out, he thought, but, then, he'd been granted a miracle and a surfboard would have been a small price to pay for Bonnie's life.

He needed to pay…something.

The hoons in the beach buggy would pay. Zoe had got a clear view of them, the hire-car logo, even part of the number plate. Doug had already made a call to the cops.

But Zoe?

What was it about her that twisted something inside him?

'Maybe the fact that she saved your dog?' he said drily, out loud. 'Maybe that'd make anyone seem special.'

But there was something about her…

A heroic run with a dog far too big for her. An anger that he'd deserved.

But more. What?

Where were his thoughts taking him?

He was trying hard to haul them back on track. Sam Webster was a man who walked alone. He'd had one disastrous relationship. He'd loved Emily, but he hadn't been able to protect her from herself. She'd died because of it, leaving him gutted and guilty and alone.

That night replayed in his head, over and over. Emily had had a stressful day in the wards and had come home to a letter saying she'd missed a promotion. Her mood had been foul as they'd headed to the beach. There'd been a storm and the surf had been unpredictable. He'd suggested a close-to-shore swim instead of their usual surf, but Emily had been coldly determined.

'The surf's fine. Sure, it's dumping but we're experienced enough to know which waves to leave alone. I've had enough people telling me what I can't do today. Surf with me, Sam, or leave me be.'

He let her be. He was fed up. In truth he'd been growing more and more fed up with Emily's erratic mood swings and her insistence that everything be done her way. He watched Emily for a while but she'd gone far out, waiting for the perfect wave, so he and Bonnie headed along the beach to walk out their wait.

They turned just as Emily lost patience and caught a wave she must have known was dangerous.

He remembered yelling. He remembered seeing Emily rise, catching the beginning of the curving swell, and he remembered seeing her look towards the beach, towards him. She waved and her wave was almost triumphant.

And then the wave sucked her high, curled and tossed her onto the sandbank with a force that even today made him shudder.

Enough. Don't think about it. That had been five years ago. Surely the memory should have faded by now. And what was he doing, thinking of it tonight?

Because he'd met Zoe?

This was crazy. Where his thoughts were taking him was just plain weird. She was just another woman and

there were plenty of women in his life. Half his colleagues were female. He had his mother, his sisters, his
workmates, and for years their position in his life had
been carefully compartmentalised.

Zoe…the way he was feeling…it didn't fit.

Maybe it was because he owed her, he decided. He
did owe her, big time, and Sam Webster always paid
his debts.

Her car was a wreck.

Excellent. His mind cleared. He had a way to pay
his debt and move on.

And he needed to move on, because for some reason it felt really important that he stop thinking about
Zoe Payne. He needed to pay the debt and get her out
of his mind.

CHAPTER THREE

ZOE SLEPT FITFULLY, waking during the night to flash-backs—to dune buggies crashing down, to Sam's haunted face, to the thoughts of the mess in her car. She slept enough to function, however. Uniformed and professional, she hit the wards with determined cheer—and found she was a minor celebrity.

She'd been at Gold Coast City for almost a week. Her new colleagues had been friendly enough but she still felt very much an outsider. This morning, though, Ros, the ward clerk, met her with a beaming smile and practically boomed her welcome.

'Here she is, our Zoe the lifesaver. You've saved our Bonnie!'

'*Our* Bonnie?' she said faintly.

'Everyone in the hospital loves Bonnie,' Ros told her. 'When she's not surfing with Sam, she comes in as a companion dog. We use her for the oldies or for distressed kids. If Sam tells her to stay with a needy patient she treats them as her new best friend until Sam comes to pick her up again. I can't tell you how many patients she's calmed and comforted. And the hoons nearly killed her.'

Her face lost its beam and creased in distress. 'Of all

the…well, never mind, we heard the cops have already charged them. The report from the vet half an hour ago said Bonnie's on the mend, and Sam says to tell you he left your purse downstairs in the safe in Admin for you to collect when you go off duty. How lucky was it that you were there? Callie says you saved her.'

'I was glad to help,' Zoe muttered, embarrassed, and headed to changeover fast, only to be met with more congratulations and thanks.

It went on all day. She was tired, she was still feeling fragile, but by the time her shift ended she seemed to be best friends with everyone in the hospital.

At three she was done. Yay, Friday. The weekend stretched before her, and even fatigue didn't stop it seeming endless with possibilities. Her first weekend here. Her first time alone.

It felt fantastic.

She walked down to Admin to collect her purse, and hummed as she hit the lifts. Last night had been horrible, but the outcome looked good. This job seemed great. She'd been rostered onto the paediatric ward for older kids. She'd been run off her feet all day—which she loved—and somehow what had happened last night seemed to have made her accepted as a part of the Gold Coast team faster than she'd thought possible.

She had an almost irresistible urge to ring Dean and gloat.

How childish was that? She grinned, the doors of the lift opened at the administration floor—and Sam Webster was waiting for her.

Sort of.

This was a different Sam Webster.

Last night he'd looked every inch a surfer. Now he looked every inch a cardiologist.

He must have been consulting rather than operating, she thought, dazed. He was wearing the most beautiful suit—Italian, she thought, and then wondered wryly what she would know about Italian suits. But the sleek, blue, pinstriped suit looked like it was moulded to him. His shirt was crisp, white, expensive-looking, and the only hint that he worked with kids was the elephants embroidered on his blue silk tie.

This was an image that would give frantic parents reassurance that they were in the hands of the best.

He looked the best.

Why was she standing here, gawking, when she should be doing, saying…something?

She managed a smile and moved forward, squashing the dumb, irrational wish that she wasn't in her nursing pants and baggy top, that her hair was free and not hauled into a practical work knot, that she had some decent make-up on—and she didn't look like she'd just come off a long, hard shift.

'Hi,' she managed. 'They tell me Bonnie's still good. Actually, everyone tells me Bonnie's still good. I hadn't realised she was a celebrity.'

'She has good friends,' he said, smiling at her in such a way that her heart did a crazy twist. 'She made a new very good friend last night. Callie told me your shift finished at three. I came down to make sure you got your purse.'

'I'm getting it now,' she said, uselessly, and then couldn't think of anything else to say.

He had a faint mark on his cheek. Callie was right,

the fingermarks had faded, but the bruise was still there. It made her want to crawl under the floor and stay there.

'It doesn't hurt,' he said, and grinned, and she flushed. How did he know what she was thinking?

'I'm sorry.'

'Sorry that it doesn't hurt?'

'Of course not.' Her chin tilted a bit and she regained her bearings. If he was going to tease…

'I've fixed your car,' he told her, and his grin faded but the faint, teasing mischief was still behind his eyes. 'Come and see.'

'It's not at the vet's?'

'The least I could do was bring it back here. Grab your purse and I'll show you where.' Then, as she still hesitated—what was it with this man that had her disconcerted?—he smiled at the girl at the desk, who handed over her purse, having obviously been listening to every word of their conversation, and he ushered her out to the car park.

That made her feel even more disconcerted. He was so…*gorgeous*. She was in her nurse's uniform.

People were glancing at them, smiling at Sam, smiling at her as if she was somehow attached to Sam. It felt weird.

'You didn't have to fix my car,' she told him as he led her across the car park. 'How did you get it done so fast?'

'What do you do when you're faced with a laundry basket full of dirty shirts and you need a clean shirt straight away?' he asked.

'I…' Uh-oh. What she suddenly suspected was dumb—wasn't it? Surely.

'You buy a new one,' he told her, confirming her

lunatic thought in five words. 'Or, in your case, a good second-hand one because I thought a brand-new one might be a bit over the top.' And he stopped and motioned to a small white sedan parked right next to where they were standing. It was the same model as hers, only about twenty years younger. It was about a hundred years less battered.

'It's two years old,' he told her, 'but it's a take-a-little-old-lady-to-church-on-Sunday vehicle. The local dealer had a son born with a mitral valve disorder. I'm still running routine checks on Dan's son after successful surgery, but he's doing brilliantly, and Dan's assured me this vehicle is almost as good as his kid's heart.'

'You bought me a car?'

'I need to thank you,' he said gently. 'You saved my dog's life. Doug and I could barely get your car started last night and we thought it'd cost more to clean than you'd get for it if you sold it. I'm a surgeon and a well-qualified one at that. I'm not married. I have no kids. All I have is my dog. Thanks to your actions last night I still have her. I can easily afford to do this, and I hope you'll accept with pleasure.'

She stared at the car. It was little and white and clean. It looked a very nice car. It looked very dependable.

It looked sensible.

She thought back to the bucket of bolts she'd driven from Adelaide. She thought of all the times she'd had to stop.

She'd bought a mechanic's manual in Adelaide before she'd left and she'd studied it with one of her sisters' boyfriends. She'd spent half the time she'd taken to get here sitting on the roadside studying that book or ringing her sister's boyfriend and having him talk her through what she needed to do.

She looked again at the little white car.

I hope you'll accept with pleasure.

Why not? She had no doubt this guy could afford to buy her a car. It'd be years before she could afford one this good—and she *had* saved his dog.

'But it's not my car,' she heard herself say, before the sensible side of her could do any more sensible thinking.

'This is better.' He was eyeing her sideways, like she was a sandwich short of a picnic.

'Yes,' she said. 'It's lovely. I dare say there's some other little old lady who'll love driving it to church on Sundays.' She took a deep breath. 'But not me. It's a great offer, but it's way out of bounds of what's reasonable. I don't want to be indebted—'

'Neither do I,' he said flatly.

'You shouldn't feel indebted. I saved your dog for your dog, not for you. Besides, this is ridiculous. Pay for cleaning, yes, but a new car?'

'It's not a new car.'

'Okay, it's not, but I'm still not accepting it. And, yes, I know you can afford it but I'd still feel indebted.'

She took a deep breath, seeing that he really wanted her to accept it, knowing that, yes, to this man on consultant's wages this car was a small thing, knowing that also for some reason indebtedness was almost as big a deal for him as it was for her. But for him to hand his obligation over to her...

She thought of the indescribable pleasure she'd felt when she'd slipped behind the wheel of her battered little vehicle and she thought that feeling was far too important to let go. There was no way she was giving that feeling up just to make this man feel better.

'I love my little car,' she said.

'That's crazy. It's a bomb.'

She'd slapped him once. She wouldn't slap him again, even though her slapping fingers itched. Besides, she conceded, he was right. It was a bomb—but it was *her* bomb.

He'd gone to a lot of trouble to buy this car for her, she conceded. Anger was inappropriate. He deserved an explanation, even though she didn't much want to give it.

'I haven't had very much money,' she told him. 'Nor...nor have I had much independence. My car is the first big thing I've ever owned. For me. I know it's a wreck but I bought it with my eyes wide-open.

'My sister's dating a mechanic. Susy spent her summer sunbaking on our back lawn while Tony mooned over her, so I persuaded him to teach me about cars while he mooned. I've learned a whole lot about the insides of cars. I have a great car manual. I have excellent tools and it gives me huge pride to keep her running.' Another deep breath. 'You don't know how much pride.'

'Is this because of the kidney transplant?' he asked, and her world stood still.

Kidney transplant.

The words hung.

He knew, she thought, stunned beyond belief. No one here was supposed to know.

A new life. That's what this was supposed to be. From the time she was eight years old, when she'd first come home from school feeling dreadful, Zoe Payne had been categorised as a renal patient. That's how she'd been treated. As an invalid. She'd been cosseted by her parents and her siblings, by her teachers and doctors and nurses and the kids around her.

Her kidneys had finally failed completely. There'd been the agonising wait and then a transplant that had failed as well.

That was when her parents had thought she was going to die.

The wait then had been interminable. She'd held on by a thread while her two sisters and her brother had grown through adolescence into adulthood, while the kids she'd met in the brief times she'd gone to school had lived normal lives, taken risks, got colds that hadn't landed them in hospital, hadn't been cocooned with worry and with care.

And then, finally, miraculously, she'd had a transplant that worked.

'You have your whole life ahead of you now,' her renal surgeon had told her at her last check-up. 'Career, babies, the world's there for you to do what you'd like with. Go for it.'

Only, of course, that wasn't possible. Not when her parents still panicked every time she coughed, while her siblings still treated her as if she was made of glass, while Dean still treated her as something to protect for ever.

All this she thought in one appalling moment as she stared at Sam and thought, *How did he know?*

She'd come all the way to Queensland because no one here would know. She'd be normal.

Even her car… Her parents had mortgaged everything to cover her medical treatment and she'd ask them for nothing more. Adults bought their own cars, and she was an independent adult. This was her life now, to do with what she wanted.

And she wasn't a renal patient.

'I'm sorry,' Sam said, and she knew he was reading her face. 'Doug and I saw the scar last night, so of course I checked out your arms.'

Of course.

She was so careful. She wore long-sleeved shirts to cover the scars from years of dialysis, and she'd never voluntarily show anyone the unmistakeable renal scar that ran from behind her arm to under her breastbone. But she hadn't been careful when faced with a dying dog. She'd taken off her shirt to treat Bonnie, and she was paying the price now.

'I'm fine now,' she managed, and Sam nodded.

'I can see you are, but is this dumb pride thing about the car a matter of declaring your independence to the world?'

'It might be,' she said grudgingly. 'But if it is, I like it. I bought my car with my own money, and after years of being totally dependent on so many people, you have no idea how good that feels. My car's battered and old but it's *my* battered and old. You haven't sent it to the wrecking yard, have you?'

'I wouldn't do that without your permission.'

'You don't have it. I want my car.'

She met his gaze head on. There was a moment's silence, a sort of unspoken battle, and finally he nodded, even conceding a lopsided smile. 'I understand,' he said at last. 'Sort of.'

'Meaning you still think I'm dumb?'

'Meaning you're looking a gift horse in the mouth.'

'You make a pretty sleek gift horse,' she said before she could stop herself. Not the wisest remark.

'Sleek?' he said, sounding bemused.

'It's an impressive suit.'

'Thank you,' he said faintly.

'You're welcome. How do I go about getting my car back?'

'I'll get it for you. But I *will* clean it.'

'I'll let you do that.'

'That's big of you,' he said, and she smiled.

'Sorry. Thank you. It was an amazing gesture. Really generous.'

'I would like to do something more for you than cleaning your car.'

'You can. Don't tell anyone about the renal transplant.'

'I won't, but tell me…how long ago?'

'Three years.'

'You talk as if it was a long-term problem.'

She sighed. She didn't want to talk about it but she'd already snubbed this man. He was a doctor and he was curious, and he'd promised to keep her secret.

'I had an infection when I was eight, and things pretty much went downhill from there,' she told him. 'I had a transplant at fifteen, but it failed. The second one worked. I had it three years ago and it's been a major, unbelievable success.

'The doctors are telling me to get on with my life, I'm cured, so that's exactly what I'm doing. I have my whole life ahead of me and I'm planning to enjoy every minute of it. If you knew the things I've dreamed, things I can now do…'

But he was into practicalities, not dreams. 'Three years...' He frowned. 'When did you train as a nurse?'

He was still thinking of her as a renal patient, she thought, and winced. She really didn't want to go further with this conversation. She hated talking about it, but he wasn't asking from idle curiosity. It was friendliness and a bit of professional interest thrown in.

He was...nice, she thought. Gorgeous, too. A girl would be dumb to snub him.

'I trained for ever,' she said briefly. 'It took me seven years, in and out of illness, but for the last two years I've been a hundred per cent well and working full time. I'm normal, and I want to be treated as normal.' She gave him a wry smile. 'So that's where I'm coming from. Accepting a car isn't normal.'

His smile faded. 'I'd have given you the car even if you hadn't had a transplant,' he told her, seriously. 'This car is about my need, not yours.' He paused, as if searching for the right words. 'There are things in my background that make me a bit of a loner,' he said at last. 'I hate being indebted and I feel indebted now. Let me off the hook. Okay, not a car,' he conceded. 'Maybe a car's over the top, but I need to do something. You've just arrived at the hospital. There must be something you need. Furniture for your apartment. Shopping vouchers. Something.'

She opened her mouth to say *'Nothing'*—and then she paused.

She looked at him. She really looked at him.

This guy was a surfer and a consultant. Standing here now, in the sunshine, in the car park of one of Australia's top hospitals, in his gorgeous suit, looking lean, fit and gorgeous, he looked like a guy who had the world at his feet.

He wasn't. Callie had told her his fiancée was dead.

He'd just said he was a bit of a loner and she knew it was true.

She'd spent a long time in dialysis wards. She'd watched tragedies unfold. She'd seen so many of her renal-patient friends struggle with always being the recipient of help, never being able to give back. Bad things happened, she thought as she watched him, and when bad things happened, good people helped. But it was one of the hardest things in the world to keep on taking.

That was part of what this car was about, she thought. This guy would have done his share of taking, and taking sympathy was especially hard. Sam would have had to take again last night when she'd been the only one there to help. The shock must have hauled him straight back to the time his fiancée had died—and she knew suddenly that he needed to give back in order to right his world. Loner or not, he had to do something for her to repay the balance.

She didn't know how she knew it but she did. This man was hurting.

She glanced again at the car he was offering. If she was really generous she'd accept it, she thought ruefully, and in a weird way the thought made sense to her. It'd leave him as a loner. It'd give her a good car.

Only she wasn't generous enough. She wanted her own little car. It meant too much to her.

There must be something you need...

What? She stood in the warm Queensland sun and watched this man with his sun-bleached hair and his crinkled eyes and thought.

'There is something,' she said slowly. 'Something I would really, really appreciate.'

She saw his face clear and she knew she'd been right. He needed to do this.

So say it, she told herself and she did.

'I'd like you to teach me how to surf.'

Whoa.

Teach her to surf? Was she kidding?

Last night the thought of buying her a car had seemed brilliant. The girl was a needy new arrival to town and she'd saved his dog. He wanted to do something big for her, to show her how much he appreciated her help, and then he wanted to walk away. If she'd taken it, he could have handed her the keys, felt a warm glow every time he saw her car in the car park and think he'd paid for Bonnie's life with a bruised cheek and a small dent in his bank balance.

He wasn't being let off so easily.

He did not want to teach this woman to surf. He didn't want to teach anyone to surf.

Surfing was his personal space. Since Emily had died he'd surfed almost every day. It was a ritual, a space where he could be totally alone, focussed only on the waves. The surf was the place and time where the demons that had haunted him since Emily had died finally let him be.

He didn't know why, but he'd loved surfing before he'd met Emily and he loved it even after her death.

He'd taught Emily to surf.

But Emily's death was nothing to do with this woman, he told himself. That was no reason to knock back her request. Surely he no longer needed to be so isolated, to surf until he was so tired at night that he finally slept, to have time when he could block out the judgement in his head.

She was watching him, waiting for his response. Reading his expression?

'It's okay,' she said quickly, taking a step back. 'It's no big deal. I told you, you don't owe me. Tell Bonnie to visit and give me a big lick when she's better. That's all the thanks I need. Now, where can I find my car?'

'I'll find someone to teach you to surf.'

'Thank you,' she said stiffly.

'I'm not a good teacher.'

'And I'm not a good surfer, but we both know it's not about that,' she said. 'You don't want anyone in your personal space, just like I don't want anyone pushing into my independence.'

'That's not what this is about.'

'I think it is,' she said softly. 'It's okay, Sam. Callie told me about your fiancée. You saw my scars, I guess I'm seeing yours as well. So let's respect them. My dream is to be independent, yours is to crawl into your shell and stay there. So let's just leave it at that. You don't mess with me and I won't mess with you.'

And unbelievably she reached out and touched him lightly on the back of his hand, the faintest of touches, a moment of connection…

'Leave it,' she said softly. 'It was a pleasure to help and that's it.'

And she turned and started walking away.

'Zoe?'

'It's fine.'

'Zoe!' It was practically a yell and she stilled and

turned. One eyebrow rose in a faint, quizzical look that was almost a smile. As if she was teasing.

Teasing... It needed only that.

'Yes,' he said.

'Yes?'

'Yes, I'll teach you to surf.'

His words were too loud. They resonated around the car park, and he thought there was no way he could take them back.

He wanted to, but they were out there.

There was a moment's silence while she watched him. The teasing had faded.

'That sounds more like, yes, you'll teach me to walk on nails and you'll be forced to demonstrate first. It sounds like it'll hurt.'

'It won't hurt.'

'It sounds like it'll hurt.'

'It won't hurt,' he exploded, and she took another step back—and suddenly she grinned.

She thought this was funny?

'I'm pushing your buttons,' she told him. 'It's okay, really. I'm not intending to intrude. I've always thought it'd be cool, but I wasn't even able to swim until two years ago. I've been so conscious of infection. But for the last two years I've swum every day, pushing myself. That's part of the reason I moved here, for the sun and the beach. I do want to learn to surf, but you don't have to teach me. As you said, there are other teachers. You can recommend someone or I'll ask around.' She smiled at him then, and it was a kindly smile. 'Let me know when my car's ready. See you later, Sam, and thank you.'

And she turned again and walked away, definitely, surely, putting distance between them with every step.

He stood and watched her. She was a nurse in a nurse's uniform. From the back she looked like any other nurse.

Just a woman. Nothing special.

But she was special. That's what scared him.

He was being selfish and dumb and emotional and there was no need to be. He could teach this woman to surf. He could give her a few impersonal lessons on the beach, get her to the stage where she could surf in the safe, rookie areas, and then leave her to it. What was the big deal?

She'd almost reached the hospital entrance. She was nothing but a nurse, moving away.

She'd saved his dog. That was all. This was a debt he needed to repay, and he would, whether she wanted it or not.

'Yes,' he called out, and she paused but didn't turn.

'Nails,' she called back, and started walking again.

'It's not nails. It could even be fun.'

She turned again then and looked at him. She was a hundred yards from him. Distant. Impersonal. A medical colleague.

From here he couldn't see the twinkle in those gorgeous, violet-blue eyes. From here he couldn't see if she was still laughing at him.

He suspected she was.

'Fun?' she called.

This was dumb, having a conversation so far apart. People were streaming in and out of the entrance. A couple of colleagues looked at Sam and looked at Zoe and then looked at Sam again, and he could see the questions growing.

Get this over with and get out of here.

'Bonnie will be at the vet's all weekend,' he called. 'First lesson Sunday. Meet me at two o'clock, here.'

'Really?'

'Yes,' he called, goaded. 'And your car will be ready by then, too.'

'Wow!'

Even a hundred yards apart he could see her face split into a grin so wide it was like the sun had come out. A brilliant sun. Cade Coleman, the hospital's new neonatal specialist, a guy Sam was only just getting to know but who had already created sizzle among the hospital's female staff, had just emerged from the entrance. Cade paused and smiled at Zoe's gorgeous grin—well, who wouldn't?—and Sam had an almost irresistible urge to stride forward and claim the grin as his own.

To claim the woman as his own?

How dumb was that? Somehow he forced his feet not to move. He needed to climb into his own car and go find the dealer he'd left Zoe's car with. He also had a long ward round to do before he could spend some time with Bonnie.

'Two o'clock, then,' he forced himself to call to Zoe, and she waved and grinned some more.

'I'll bring snacks,' she called. 'I'm feeling homesick and when I'm homesick I cook. I'll make lamingtons.'

'You can make lamingtons?' Cade demanded, and Sam watched his colleague move in, smoothly smiling, laughing with Zoe. They turned and walked back into the hospital and Sam stood in the car park and thought...he'd just lost something.

That was an even dumber thought. He had nothing to lose.

Except a dog, he reminded himself. He needed to go and see how she was. He needed to haul himself together and remember priorities and put the thought of one beaming smile behind him.

He needed to pay his debt and get the connection with Zoe behind him.

'Sam Webster bought you a car?'

Zoe had walked out of the lift, turned the first bend in the corridor—and run straight into Callie Richards. She stopped dead when she saw Zoe, and Zoe had no choice but to stop, too. Who else knew about the car?

'Yes.'

'And you knocked him back and now he's teaching you to surf?'

'Okay, I give up,' Zoe said, exasperated. 'Do you guys have the parking lot bugged for sound?'

Callie chuckled. 'No need. Don't tell me Adelaide South is any different. Hospital staff have their own specialist spy network, which beams gossip around the hospital before it even happens.'

'I guess.' Zoe gave a rueful grin. 'Adelaide South was small, though. I hoped Gold Coast City might be more impersonal.'

'Fat hope,' Callie said. 'How are you feeling?'

'I'm fine.'

'Be careful of Cade Coleman.'

She frowned. 'What?'

'He's new, from the States, but he comes with a health warning. Breaker of hearts.'

'I talked to him for two minutes,' Zoe said, astounded. 'I'd have thought you might have warned me about Sam.'

'I don't need to warn you about Sam. There's no way anyone's going to break through that impervious barrier.'

There was a moment's loaded silence. Then...

'Is there anyone else I need to watch out for?' Zoe demanded. She'd tried—and failed—not to sound snappy but she couldn't help herself. This woman was a senior physician. Warning nurses about consultants wouldn't be in her job description. On top of that, Callie normally seemed reserved. Zoe was starting to suspect what was going on, and she didn't like it.

'I'm sorry. I know it's none of my business,' Callie said. 'It's just...'

'Just that you've read my personnel records?' Zoe ventured, and Callie looked a bit nonplussed. Then she shrugged.

'You've come to work on my ward, Zoe. I check my staff from the ground up.'

'So you've read about my renal transplant—and you think I need looking out for?'

'Okay, backing off now,' Callie said, and held up her hands in mock surrender. 'Yes, I read your records. I was on the selection committee and it's my job. I knew a transplant wouldn't impede your work and I put it to one side. But of course I didn't forget. Then when you came in last night covered in blood, my mother-hen instincts took over.' Her smile was beguiling, appealing for forgiveness. 'I don't normally do the mother-hen thing,' she confessed. 'It was a momentary weakness and I apologise. If you fancy Cade Coleman—or indeed Sam Webster—then you go, girl.'

It was impossible to be angry in the face of that smile—and the in the face of an apology for what, after all, was only care. 'It's okay,' Zoe said, her anger fading. 'As long as the whole world doesn't know about the transplant. Now Sam knows...'

'Sam knows?'

'He saw my scars yesterday, but he's promised to keep it to himself. If it's possible in this hospital.'

'It's possible. Only the head of each unit has access to records. It won't go past me. Or Sam.'

'Thank you.'

'So are you interested?' Callie said, relaxing a bit.

'In who?'

'Either of 'em.'

'No!' Zoe said. She hesitated but this woman had been good to her. Why not say it like it was? 'I went out with the same boy for more than ten years. He wrapped me up in cotton wool so tight I couldn't breathe. Now I'm breathing just as hard as I can, and I don't want a relationship.'

'Good for you,' Callie said. 'Men!'

And Zoe thought of Callie's comment about working in the women's refuge.

'They're useful, though,' Callie conceded. 'Love 'em and leave 'em. There's a good rule in life. Enjoy your surfing with Sam, and anything else that comes along.'

'Thank you,' Zoe said, and watched Callie head round the bend to the lift.

She thought, Yes, I will.

She shouldn't have said anything.

The last thing Callie Richards thought of herself as

was a mother hen. She had a reputation for staying aloof, and normally she did.

It was just that something last night had touched her. One bloodied, bedraggled girl whose medical history said she'd been to death's door and back.

That, and knowing Cade Coleman was on her patch.

She hadn't even met the guy but his reputation had preceded him. His stepbrother, Alex, had rung her and asked if there was a vacancy.

'He's a fine neonatal physician, Callie. The best. He's looking for a complete break, so he wants to move from the States. Queensland would be prefect. If you have room on your team...'

She had. And Cade's qualifications were impressive, to say the least.

There'd been one caveat. Women.

The man was running, Alex had told her. Personal stuff. Problems. Callie hadn't pushed and Alex hadn't offered more, except to say they were 'worse than mine'. For Alex, that was really saying something. The time between Alex and her...

Yeah, well, block that out. She put it aside deliberately now, and thought of the good stuff. Cade's qualifications outweighed any potential womanising.

But he'd arrived yesterday and already there was a ripple doing the rounds about how good-looking he was.

Forget it, she told herself harshly. On Monday she'd meet him and see just how good a doctor he was. Meanwhile...

Yeah, warning Zoe had seemed over the top, but Ros had seen Cade talking to her and had reported it with excitement.

'Our new nurse has just found our new physician. Ooh, I do love a good bit of intrigue. Bring it on.'

So she'd overreacted. Cade was probably harmless, she conceded, and as for warning Zoe over one chance meeting...

Ridiculous.

She took a deep breath, turned toward the lift—and Cade Coleman was right in front of her.

He was standing by the lifts, his hand on the buttons as if he'd pushed more than once and was getting irritated. As well he might, Callie conceded. The lifts in this building were notoriously slow.

How long had he been standing there?

'Hi,' she managed, and put out a hand in welcome. 'I'm Callie Richards.'

'Yeah, the woman who hired me.' He was tall, over six feet or so, tanned, lean and ripped. He'd just flown halfway round the world but if he was suffering from jet lag he certainly didn't show it.

What he was suffering from, though, was anger. She could feel it coming from him in waves.

'I didn't hire you,' she managed evenly. 'I just recommended you to the powers that be.'

'Because Alex recommended me to you.'

'I know Alex,' she said evenly. 'We've worked together. His word—that you're the best—was good enough for me.'

'So good that you need to put out a warning to the nursing staff?'

He had heard.

'I'm so sorry.' There was no getting out of this one. She felt like turning and running but his anger kept her locked in. 'I thought…shift change is over. There's never anyone around.'

'We all have apartments on this floor, it seems,' he said, icy cold. 'I came up in the lift with Zoe—all the way, without seducing her once. The key Admin gave me for my apartment worked when I first arrived but it doesn't work now. Neither does this elevator.'

As if on cue, the lift arrived. The doors slid open.

Callie wanted to get in, but Cade was blocking her way.

'So why am I so dangerous?' he demanded, tossing his useless key in the air and catching it again. He seemed dangerous, Callie thought. Lean, mean and dangerous to know.

'You're not. It's just…Zoe's been unwell.'

'A renal transplant. I heard. And she doesn't want it known but your carrying voice took it all the way to here.'

'You shouldn't have been listening.'

'You want me to block my ears in my own apartment building?'

'I'm sorry,' she said again.

'Not good enough. Tell me why the warning.' It was almost a growl.

She took a deep breath. Wow, Alex had really landed her in it with this one. She'd greeted his call querying work for his brother with pleasure and she hadn't expected to land in it up to her neck.

This was Alex's call, she decided. Not hers.

'Alex told me you were the best neonatal physician he knew,' she said. 'I respect that. He also said you'd had trouble with women.'

'Did he just?' He practically snarled. 'Generous of

him. Well, you needn't worry. Your sick little nurse is safe from me.'

'Zoe's not sick—and I've said I'm sorry. If you have any argument, take it up with your brother, not me. Now, if you don't mind, I need to get back to the wards. Only I'm taking the stairs.'

And she turned on her heel and stalked to the fire exit, thinking four floors of stairs was a small price to pay.

Sam had two patients to see and then he was free for the day. Or almost. He emerged from his consulting rooms to find Cade Coleman waiting for him. Looking furious.

For a moment Sam thought about his ridiculous re-action as he'd seen Cole in the entrance with Zoe. His response had been almost primeval—wanting to go and claim this woman as his. It had been dumb and irrelevant, and nothing to do with his new colleague. But why was Cole looking at him so angrily?

'Not guilty?' he tried. This guy had only been here since yesterday. The hospital bigwigs had been delighted to hire him, and for good reason. Sam had been the one elected to meet him at the airport and he'd spoken to him a couple of times since. Already they were planning research projects. This guy was seriously smart.

This guy looked like he was about to punch a hole in the wall and then get on a plane back to the States.

'Dr Richards,' he said through gritted teeth.

'Callie?' Sam tried for a smile. 'What's she done to upset you? The lady's one classy doctor.'

'Who's warning the female staff that I eat them for breakfast.'

'What's she doing that for?'

'She saw me talking to your nurse.'

'My nurse?' God, this hospital grapevine. 'You mean Zoe?'

'Apparently it's a wonder I didn't grope her in the elevator.'

'What the hell has got into Callie?'

'She might,' Cade admitted, 'have been warned by my brother.'

'Right,' Sam said, steering for safe ground but not quite knowing in what direction it was. 'So your brother warned Callie that you grope nurses in lifts?'

He met Cade's angry gaze head on, his own expression noncommittal, doctor calmly asking colleague whether he ate nurses for breakfast. Cade's glare faded in the face of calm enquiry, and he shrugged, and in the end even managed a rueful smile.

'I guess you never know with Americans,' he said.

'There was a phrase the Aussie guys used for the Yanks when you lot were out here during the war,' Sam said mildly. 'Overpaid, oversexed and over here. Maybe Callic has a residual phobia.' He sighed. 'Look, Zoe's new here—'

'And I know about the renal transplant.'

'How the hell did that get around the hospital?'

'Your Dr Richards,' Cade said, his anger surfacing again. Then, as he saw Sam's face and maybe saw the anger beginning to surface there as well, he shook his head. 'It's okay. I know your lady wants to keep it private. You'll note I made sure there's no one in earshot now.'

'She's not my lady.'

'She's not mine either,' Cade said. 'I didn't touch her

and I don't intend to touch her, so if you could tell Dr Richards to keep out of my face...'

'I'll talk to her.' This conversation was weird. What was going on with Callie?

'Excellent,' Cade said, calming down. 'See to it. I'm here to do a job. I don't care what bee Dr Richards has in her bonnet, but I'm not a woman-eater. Nurse Zoe is all yours.'

And he turned and stalked away, leaving Sam staring after him.

Nurse Zoe is all yours...

Not in a million years, he thought.

Except he had to teach her to surf.

Why was it worrying him so much? Why did he feel this was a huge mistake?

It was the way she made him feel, he thought, and he had to do something about that. Once upon a time he'd been engaged to be married and if that was where his judgement took him...never again.

Teach the lady to surf and move on.

CHAPTER FOUR

SAM WORKED MOST of Saturday. It was supposed to be his time off, but medical imperatives didn't necessarily fit around weekends. When a baby was admitted with a major heart abnormality early on Saturday morning there was no choice but to abandon his plan to spend the day with Bonnie, and instead concentrate on saving Joshua Bennet's life.

Operating on a baby as frail as Joshua was fraught, the odds seemed stacked against them, but Sam's team was seriously good. Luck played out on their side and by the time he walked out of Theatre at six o'clock he felt like Joshua had every chance of making it to a ripe old age.

He also felt seriously wiped.

Callie found him at the sinks. She was a mate, a real friend, and she walked straight up and gave him a hug.

He wouldn't accept a hug from anyone else, but Callie Richards wasn't one to hold back. She'd known him since training. She'd been there when Emily had died and the armour he'd put up around himself didn't stop her pushing the boundaries.

'That was magnificent, Sam,' she told him. 'I've just

seen Josh's mum. She can't stop crying, and for good reason. She knew the odds.'

'This is a great team,' he said gruffly, extricating himself, fighting back emotion and finding a safe retreat. 'Um...Callie, what's the deal with the new guy? Cade?'

'Yeah, I may have stuffed that up,' Callie said. 'A bit of overreaction. I went into protection mode with your Zoe.'

There it was again. Your Zoe.

'She's not,' he said pleasantly, but with a hint of steel behind the words, 'my Zoe.'

'Of course not,' Callie said, and had the temerity to chuckle. 'But you have to admit she's cute. And you gave her a car and now you're giving her surfing lessons. For lone wolf Sam to get that involved...'

'It's just a thank-you gesture,' he said stiffly. 'A couple of hours' surfing every Sunday and nothing more.'

'Yeah, well, good luck with that. I've known her for all of a week and already I'm seeing she's special. She's brilliant on the wards—skilled but also incredibly empathetic with the kids and their parents. She seems to make people relax, taking the fear out of this place. And if she can make sick kids relax...beware, Sam.'

'Callie...'

'Yeah, it's not my business,' she said, and grinned and backed off. 'Just saying. Two hours' surfing every Sunday? Hmm. This hospital's a fish bowl, Sam Webster. You spend two hours with her and then try and avoid her for the rest of the time...well, there's not far you can go, working here. You'll hit the walls and bounce right back. Zoe's a solid part of our paediatric team. She's already proved she's your friend and from where I'm standing I'd like her to have a chance of being even more than that to one of my favourite colleagues.'

This hospital!

It drove him nuts, Sam thought as he headed for the vet's to see Bonnie. Gossip, matchmaking, innuendo...

He'd moved here from Perth after Emily had died, wanting a clean break, wanting to work in an environment where no one knew his story and he could retire into his seclusion of work and surfing. But, of course, Australia may be geographically big but in terms of population it was a small country, and the medical community was even smaller. He'd walked into the wards on the first day and met Callie, a doctor he'd trained with. The chief theatre nurse had spent time in Perth and knew Emily and her story. The janitor, a kite-surfing nut, had been a volunteer lifeguard on the Perth beach the day Emily had died.

So much for anonymity. But until now he'd kept his distance. Callie had fretted at the edges but he didn't want her concern. He didn't want anyone's concern. He just wanted to get on with life on his terms. Medicine, surfing—and Bonnie.

He felt his pulse rate rise a bit as he pulled into the vet's parking lot. He'd been in touch all day but still it'd be good to see his dog for himself.

She was twelve years old. He had to lose her one day, but not yet. Please, not yet. He should have been here sooner, he told himself harshly, but there'd been no time. He'd organised Zoe's car in brief intervals between work commitments, but his tiny patient Joshua couldn't have been set aside so he could be with his dog.

Still, the thought that she was here, in the recovery

room at the vet's, probably alone, had eaten at him, and his stride became a run as he headed up the steps to the entrance. The receptionist smiled at him and motioned him to go through into the recovery area.

He swung through the door. 'Bonnie's in the end cage,' the receptionist had said, and his eyes went straight to the end of the room—and saw Zoe Payne crouched in front of the floor-level cage. The cage door was open and Bonnie was half in, half out of the cage.

Her great soft head was lying on Zoe's lap.

Girl and dog.

Neither girl nor dog had heard the doors swing open. Bonnie seemed asleep. Zoe was turned away from him. She was simply dressed in jeans and soft cotton shirt, with her hair loosely caught back in a bouncy ponytail. He could just see the profile of her face.

She was talking to Bonnie.

'He's agreed to teach me to surf, and I need you to help. I'm a bit scared of the big boards. It's always seemed magic—you must love it too, watching it night after night. But do you know what I've done? I found a discount store today and they sell all sorts of flags. They're actually Tibetan prayer flags, so I'm thinking they'll give you even more safety—almost a blessing as you watch us surf. They're attached to long poles and I'm going to stick them in the sand right where you lie so people can see for miles that someone very special is snoozing in the sand. That would be you. You get that leg better and we'll make the beach safe so you can live happily ever after.'

What was it with this girl? Sam thought numbly. What was it that made his heart clench?

He didn't want this feeling. He didn't want to feel

like he wanted to walk forward, crouch down and hug the pair of them.

How could he stop wanting?

'How long does it take to learn to surf?' Zoe was asking Bonnie now. 'How long does it take before I'll be brave enough to catch one of those gorgeous, curling waves that loop right over? I want that so much.'

She wanted the big waves—and that was enough to make things right themselves. Any thought of hugging went right out the window. This woman wanted what had killed Emily.

He knew it wasn't the same, yet it was enough for him to haul himself together, remind himself that this was a professional colleague and their only personal connection would be a two-hour surfing lesson each Sunday. He pinned a smile on his face and walked forward, allowing his feet to make a sound on the tiled floor so she heard him and looked up.

She smiled a greeting and that was enough to set him back again.

Professional. Colleagues.

She had his dog's head on her knee.

'Hey,' she said softly. 'I hope you don't mind. I just popped in to check, and Doug said it'd be okay.'

'I don't mind at all,' he said, crouching beside her, and there was another jolt. What was it with this woman—the way she made him feel? He did not want this. 'Thank you for caring.'

'I love dogs,' she said. 'I've always wanted one. My parents said they had germs.'

'Maybe I can buy you a puppy instead of a car.'

'No way,' she said, fondling the sleeping Bonnie's ears in a way that made him feel…odd. Needful? Weird.

'The deal is surfing lessons. I'm living in a hospital apartment, working long shifts. That's no life for a puppy—even if I did get permission to keep a dog. I don't know how you managed it.'

'Deal breaker,' he said. 'Gold Coast offered me a job. I said it's me and Bonnie or neither of us. We come as a package deal and they accepted.'

'I would have thought a little house with a back yard might be better for her.'

'Believe it or not, the apartment's better. I couldn't get a house within five minutes' drive of the hospital so Bonnie would be left alone all day. As it is, I can take her out to the foreshore three or four times a day instead of taking coffee breaks, and she's even found herself a job in the wards.'

'As a companion dog,' Zoe said, her hands still doing that gentle stroking. 'Callie says she's great.'

Bonnie hadn't moved. The painkillers would still have her heavily sedated, but even so...why would she move when she was lying on Zoe's knee? Why would anyone move?

It was strange, sitting on the floor of the vet's recovery room, with this woman and his dog. A cat was snoozing down the far end of the room, and above them a fat snake was lazing in a heated tank. The snake had some type of dressing round its rear end. Weird, Sam thought, and wondered idly how a vet would treat the heart of a snake.

'How would you go about putting an aortic stent into that?' Zoe asked, following his gaze.

How did she do that? It was like she could read his thoughts.

Nonsense—it was coincidence and nothing else.

'I reckon if I had a snake with heart disease I might buy another snake,' he told her.

'Like you'd buy another Labrador?'

'Different thing.'

'Not to the owner of the snake,' she said. 'Love's where you find it.'

'That sounds like something my grandma might say.'

'Does your grandma like snakes?'

'Excluding snakes,' he said, and grinned. 'You can't cuddle a snake.'

'Yeah, love needs cuddles,' she said, and bent and cuddled Bonnie some more, and there was all sorts of stuff happening in his chest and he didn't want any of it. 'Sam...'

'Mmm?' He'd like to back out of here, he thought. He needed to leave and come back when this woman wasn't here. It was bad enough that he'd nearly lost his dog, but the way Bonnie was lying there, it was like...he was losing her a little anyway. Giving part of her to Zoe.

Jealous?

No. It wasn't jealousy, he thought. It was sharing, and he didn't do sharing. Sharing meant...sharing. Since Emily's death he carefully hadn't shared anything at all.

'Doug said she'll need to stay off her leg for weeks,' she said. 'Even though it's plated, he wants the bone fragments to have every chance they can get to fuse. I was thinking...if you wanted to share care, I go onto night duty on Monday. Bonnie could stay with you during the night, but you could pop her into my apartment during the day. You need to sleep at night. I need to sleep during the day. Bonnie needs to sleep all the time but you can't tell me she won't sleep better in a basket right next to a human. I know you're best but for the next few days, would you like me to be second best?'

Whoa.

Say no, he told himself fiercely. He did not want to be further indebted.

The trouble was, she was right. Bonnie wasn't just suffering from a broken leg. The lacerations were deep and nasty, she had fractured ribs and she had massive bruising. Even though the plate would allow her to weight-bear almost immediately, she'd still need to be kept quiet.

For her to sleep by Zoe during the day...

'Just add another surfing lesson to the end of my course,' Zoe said, smiling at him. 'But, honestly, it'll be as much for me as it is for Bonnie. I've never lived away from home before. I wanted to come here, but I am lonely.'

Help.

He wasn't used to this. Emily would never have looked at him frankly and admitted loneliness. Admitting weakness was...weak.

Maybe it wasn't. There wasn't much about Zoe that spelled weakness, he thought. She was direct and honest, and she was waiting for an answer to an offer that made sense.

'Thank you,' he said, because he had no choice, and she gave a businesslike nod that said her offer had no emotional overtones at all, that it was all about sense.

'Excellent. Would you like to slide in here under Bonnie?'

As if on cue, his dog opened her eyes and looked at him. He'd been expecting her to look like she was in pain, shocked, confused. Instead...she almost looked smug, as though to say, 'I have the two of you at my disposal. You want to get this shift change over fast so I can go back to my comfortable snooze?'

He sat beside Zoe, she eased back and handed over her position, but as she did, his body brushed hers, his hands touched hers, and she was so close…

And then she moved away.

'Bye, Bonnie,' Zoe whispered. 'You keep on getting better. Bye, Sam. See you tomorrow.'

And she was gone.

She wasn't imposing, he thought. She'd come to see Bonnie but she had no intention of interfering with his time with her.

It'd be okay. He could share Bonnie's care with her for the next few weeks, and he could teach her to surf, because she'd respect his boundaries. He could tell that about her already.

The problem was…

'The problem is that I don't know where those boundaries are any more,' he told Bonnie, but Bonnie was already asleep again.

Bonnie was happy. Bonnie was safe and settled, and he should feel good.

He did feel good. He just didn't feel…settled.

He approached Sunday with a certain amount of trepidation, but it wasn't justified.

What had he expected? Some needy kid, giggling, treating it as a joke? Or—and subconsciously maybe this was what he'd most feared—a woman treating it as a first date? An excuse to get close, as so many woman had tried to since Emily's death.

He knew he had been seen as fair game by the single female staff since Emily had died, and maybe he'd been expecting the same from Zoe.

But she wasn't the least bit interested. She made that clear from the outset when she ran out to the parking lot to meet him, carting an armload of wetsuit and a box full of lamingtons. She was wearing faded shorts and a rash vest, she'd hauled her hair back into a loose knot to get it out of the way and her face was coated in thick, white zinc.

No woman he knew wore the practical, sensible but thick and obvious white zinc sunscreen. Better a bit of sunburn than sporting a pure white nose, but Zoe appeared oblivious.

'Callie lent me her wetsuit,' she told him. 'I'll buy my own as soon as I'm assured this sport's not going to humiliate me.'

She had no time for niceties, for social chitchat. He'd promised her two hours and she was intent on taking every single moment of those two hours and using them to full effect. They spent the first hour on the beach, practising lying full length on the board then doing the seemingly simple yet vital sweep to standing. He told her what to do, he helped her, he corrected her, he held her while she balanced, and there was no hint she even saw him as a person.

He was the conduit to her surfing, and she ached to surf.

When he finally told her she'd graduated to the shallows her beam was almost house-wide, but it wasn't for him. She was totally inward-focussed, and by the time the two hours were up he knew that she was fulfilling a dream she'd had for years. It was as though she was watching a rainbow and having someone steer the boat while she headed for it. All eyes were on the rainbow.

So there, he told himself ruefully as they hauled the surfboards up the beach at the end of the two hours and hit the box of lamingtons with relish. Zoe had managed to do a wobbly stand in six inches of water, but by her beaming grin you'd have thought she'd conquered twenty-foot boomers.

'It was awesome,' she said, smiling and smiling.

'So are these lamingtons.'

'Thank you.'

'I'll be down on the beach tomorrow night if you want to come,' he heard himself say—and then did a double-take inside. Had he really said that?

But she was shaking her head.

'Night duty tomorrow,' she said. 'I don't want to start tired. Plus I need to decorate my room. I have so many plans, you can't imagine. Besides, this is your time, your surfing. I don't want to interfere with your private space. Two hours on Sunday is all I ask, and it's all I'll take. Thank you, Sam, for a magic two hours.'

And she heaved her surfboard—one she'd hired at his suggestion until they could figure what would suit her—on top of her battered little car before he could help her, tied it down with clinical efficiency, gave him a wave and another of her bright smiles, and left him.

She'd gone, and the beach was emptier for her going.

Well, of course it was, he told himself savagely. What was he, an idiot? Why was he standing looking after her like a teenage kid with a crush?

He had another couple of hours before he needed to get back to the real world. Bonnie would be discharged from the vet's tomorrow. This might be the last chance for weeks to have a really solid surf.

He hauled himself together and headed back to the waves, but the thought of Zoe stayed with him.

He didn't need to worry about boundaries, he thought. *I have so many plans, you can't imagine...* Surfing was simply one of them and any thought that she'd see him as part of those plans was pure ego.

Or pure desire?

There was definitely desire. Sense or not, she'd left him with half a box of lamingtons—and he wanted more.

He didn't see her all Monday. Even if he'd wanted, he had no time to see her. He, Cade and Callie treated Molly Carthardy, aged four, who presented with shortness of breath at kindergarten. The kindergarten teacher had queried asthma but Molly had ended up on the operating table getting a full graft to replace a faulty artery. She'd make it, which made Sam smile, and he was left seriously impressed with Cade's skills. Great colleagues or not, though, he left work exhausted. Then he collected Bonnie and brought her home.

She was sore and sorry for herself but she could walk with a heavy limp, and she was overjoyed to be back with him, back in her own basket.

He spent the night with her, carrying her outside twice so she could sniff the grass in the small entrance garden. At seven in the morning he needed to be back in the wards, and Bonnie whined as he dressed—she knew what his suit and tie meant. Zoe's offer was there. It was sensible and Bonnie came before pride. 'It's only a couple more surfing lessons and you're worth it,' he told her, and he picked up the gear she'd need for the day and went and knocked on Zoe's apartment door.

Zoe answered with the smile that did his head in. It was the beam he was starting to know—and love? It was like the sun had come out, radiating straight from that smile.

'Hey, I hoped you'd take me up on my offer.' But she wasn't beaming at him. She was hugging Bonnie, who gave a little snort of pleasure and shoved her nose into Zoe's armpit.

Zoe had obviously just come off night shift, showered and changed into sleeping gear. Her gorgeous curls were spiralling, damp and wild, down her back. She was wearing a vast, soft, powder-blue dressing gown, which looked like it'd fit two of her in it, and he had an almost irresistible desire to see if two would fit.

Dog-girl greeting over, Zoe looked up at him and he almost had his face under control by the time she did.

'If you meant your offer...'

'Of course I meant my offer. You've brought her stuff—great.'

'I've just taken her outside. She should be right to sleep for hours.'

'I never sleep well anyway,' she confessed. 'I get up and snack, so if I need to get up and take Bonnie outside it won't affect me at all. Do you have a number I can reach you on if I need you?'

'I... Sure.' He waited while she grabbed a pen and then watched in astonishment as she scrawled it on her hand.

'There,' she said. 'May I never need to wash again.' Then she chuckled. 'Okay, I'm a nurse, I need to wash, but one of the hospital techies is fixing my phone. I'll get it back tonight and then you can have your own permanent place in my friends' list.'

And what was there in that statement to make him feel uncomfortable? To feel like he was stepping over boundaries? A colleague, putting his cellphone number in her list of contacts? What was weird about that?

'Hey, don't look like that,' she told him, and this time, thankfully, she hadn't read his thoughts, or if she'd tried, she'd got it wrong. 'I know it must be awful leaving Bonnie but she's in safe hands. I won't let her on my bed—I won't let her risk her leg by jumping. If she gets distressed I might even drag my mattress onto the floor. Bonnie and I intend to have a lovely, cosy time, don't we, Bon? She'll be safe, Sam. I will look after her and I don't take risks.'

And there it was.

I don't take risks.

What was it in that statement that made his world change?

She was a gorgeous, warm, vibrant, clever, kind, resourceful woman, and she was standing in front of him, declaring that she didn't take risks.

A knot inside him seemed to be unravelling.

Something inside him was saying that maybe he could just…take a risk himself?

'Go,' she said, and suddenly, before he knew what she intended, she straightened, stood on tiptoe and kissed him, lightly, on the cheek. 'Off you go to save the world while woman and dog keep the home fires burning. Work well while we sleep well.'

And then she ushered Bonnie into her apartment, she gathered Bonnie's bedding from his seemingly limp

arms, she gave him another of her gorgeous smiles—
and she backed inside and closed the door behind her.

Zoe closed the door, stooped to comfort a worried Bonnie, and then found herself leaning against the door as
if the weight of her body could stop it opening again.
As if she should lean against it and keep Dr Sam Webster on the other side.

There were two Sam Websters, she thought, trying
to catch her breath. One was the guy who surfed. He
was lean, bronzed and ripped, with sun-bleached hair
and eyes the colour of the sea. The other was the chief
paediatric cardiologist of Gold Coast City Hospital, a
skilled, empathetic surgeon at the top of his game. She'd
been here long enough to learn Sam's reputation was
second to none. The package of Cardiologist Sam included sleek Italian suits, the faint scent of masculine
aftershave and gorgeous silk ties. His tie was dotted
with embroidered teddy bears this morning, and had
seemed enough to make her go weak at the knees.

'It's not fair,' she told Bonnie, letting go of the emotions she'd been fiercely repressing from the time she'd
heard the doorbell. She felt herself blush from the toes
up. 'Whoa, this is my teenage years catching up with
me. All those times while my sisters had adolescent
fancies and I was too sick to join in. I guess I had to
have 'em some time. Here we go. Let's get it all out in
one fell swoop with Dr Sam.'

Three deep breaths. Okay, she was over it, she told
herself as she went back to reassuring Bonnie. Or…she
was sort of over it?

'I shouldn't have kissed him,' she told Bonnie, but
then she thought, no, the kiss was okay. It was the sort

of kiss a woman who wasn't being hormonal would give; a kiss of friendship and reassurance that she'd take care of his beloved dog.

She took Bonnie into her bedroom, settled her in her basket beside the bed and slipped between the covers. Getting to sleep after night duty, at a time when the rest of the world was heading to work, was always hard. She'd learned relaxation techniques. She explained them to Bonnie.

'I know you're anxious about being with me and not with Sam, and I know you're sore, but sleep's good. First of all you stretch your toes—or pads. Flex every muscle—only don't flex so far it hurts. Then, tell yourself every single muscle is going to sleep. Focus only on your toes, one after the other. Think of nothing else. Nothing else.'

Silk ties with teddy bears. Aftershave. Sun-creased eyes and a smile to die for.

'See, that's the way to stay awake,' she said crossly to Bonnie, who was showing every sign that the relaxation lecture was working. 'Thinking of Sam. I can think of him and still relax, though. It's sort of like winning Tatts,' she told herself, not very convincingly. 'A girl can dream. As long as you keep those dreams where they belong. Right here on this pillow.'

Bonnie wuffled and stirred and she put her hand down and soothed the soft brown head.

'I know,' she said. 'I'm keeping you awake. I'm stopping now. I can be very sensible when I try.'

She closed her eyes and concentrated on her toes.

Silk ties with teddy bears...

She was going to have to try very hard, she thought.

She finally did drift off to sleep but silk ties with teddy bears—and one sexy smile—were right there with her in her dreams.

CHAPTER FIVE

To say Gold Coast City ran on gossip was an understatement. Staff worked long hours under stressful circumstances. The hospital apartments were right next to the hospital, so medics saw each other off duty as well as on. The huge emergency department meant medics and paramedics saw first hand every day how fragile life was. Staff could crack under the pressure, or they could let off steam in other ways, and one of those ways was gossip. Hot affairs were common, but not as common as rumour had it, so Sam shouldn't have been surprised that within two weeks the grapevine had Zoe and him bedded and almost wedded.

The grapevine had played with him before—at one stage he and Callie had been whispered to be a hot item. It hadn't bothered him then that long-term friendship was construed as something else. Callie had almost seemed to enjoy it— 'I'm rumoured to be a bad girl, Sam, so what's a bit more wickedness on the side?' They'd let it run its course and it had done no harm.

So why was the grapevine disturbing him now?

It was because he couldn't step away from her.

Though actually he could. Zoe was on night duty so their paths rarely crossed on the wards. He met her twice a day when he dropped Bonnie off and picked her up. Handover was brief. Zoe always seemed pleased to see him, but maybe she sensed his need to be impersonal. They exchanged a few brief words, an update on how the rapidly recovering Bonnie was faring, and he left as soon as possible.

They had their surfing lessons each Sunday but even then Zoe was so focussed on learning to surf it was as if she hardly noticed him. He'd never seen someone so intent, so determined, and so joyous at each tiny step along the way.

The first time she managed to wobble to her feet and stay upright for a whole ten seconds, a casual observer would have assumed she'd just won Olympic gold for her country. She whooped and whooped, and he had an almost insatiable desire to take her in his arms and lift her and swing her in triumph—and then crush her to him so her triumph was his.

He didn't. He managed to stay back and watch, smiling a little, instructor pleased with student. She looked at him and laughed out loud and kicked and sent a vast spray of water out over him.

'Look at you. You look like I'm pretending to be Einstein because I've just switched on an electric light. I know I have a million miles to go but I've just taken the first step.'

'More than the first step,' he conceded. 'Balancing's hard.'

'It is, isn't it?' she said, and gave a huge, happy sigh and dragged her board back out a little so she could try again. 'Was I standing too far forward? If I go a bit back will I be more stable?'

There it was—the personal moment was over, and they were back to student-teacher.

Impersonal?

He thought of those mornings when he handed Bonnie over, of this girl snuggled in her bathrobe, about to go to bed, and he thought…he thought…

He thought it was just as well she was treating him as a teacher and Bonnie's master and nothing else, because if she made one tentative suggestion that it could be anything more…

Then he'd stand firm, he told himself. He had no choice. He'd been thrown into the chaos of caring once in his life and he had no intention of going there again.

They were colleagues, he thought, with the added dimension that she'd saved his dog and he was teaching her to surf. There was nothing more to it.

Excellent.

But then, two days later, he met her on the wards and things got a bit more complicated.

Ryan Tobin was ten years old and Sam had been worried about him for months now.

He'd first presented with a worsening of what had, until then, seemed mild asthma. Callie had started him on methylprednisone and albuterol but four days later he was back in Emergency, struggling to breathe.

At that stage Callie had called in Sam. A chest radiograph showed an enlarged heart and pulmonary oedema, and from there things had gone from bad to worse.

The diagnosis was dilated cardiomyopathy with nonspecific inflammation.

Ryan had spent weeks in and out of hospital, needing

oxygen, needing diuretic therapy to ease the oedema. Sam had done everything he could to improve cardiac function, but now...

Sam worked with him for most of the afternoon and into the night, as he finally conceded what he'd worked for months to avoid. The only way for Ryan to live was if he had a transplant.

He'd need to be moved to a hospital where such transplants were performed. They had time; they could get Ryan stable, but Sam couldn't sugar-coat it for his desperate parents. The next few weeks would be touch and go.

At midnight he finally left Ryan's bedside. His parents weren't moving. Ryan's mother was asleep with her head resting on her son's bed, and his father was staring rigidly at the ceiling while he lay on the stretcher bed provided. The hospital encouraged one parent to stay, and while there was no room for two, neither parent intended to leave.

'Tell Mum what's happening. Tell her to take Luke home,' Ryan's father said, and Sam thought of the elderly woman he'd seen day after day in the waiting room, keeping Ryan's eight-year-old brother company.

They'd both seemed stoic. The old lady must be exhausted, Sam thought. If he'd known she was still out there he'd have asked a nurse to see to her hours ago.

But someone was already caring. He walked out of the cardiac care ward, and Ryan's grandma was fast asleep in the waiting room. Someone had hauled out a care chair for her—usually used for patients in terminal care, it was a chair that became a bed and encased its user in a cloud of comfort.

Someone? Zoe. She was sitting beside the chair, and

she had her arm around the little boy Sam recognised as Luke.

Zoe smiled as she saw Sam, and her grip on Luke tightened. Luke's face was bleary with exhaustion and distress, and Sam thought, He's only eight years old, he shouldn't be facing this.

'I tried to get Lorna to take Luke home,' Zoe said softly. 'But she won't. Everyone's so worried about Ryan that maybe…they can't see there's another need. Luckily our ward's quiet so I've had a little time to stay with Luke. He's been telling me all about things to do here. He says Sea World's awesome. I've been thinking I should go.'

Lorna woke up then, and demanded answers. Sam sat and explained things to all of them—that Ryan's heart was failing to such an extent that a transplant was the only option, that Gold Coast City didn't have the facilities to perform transplants, so he'd be moved the next day to start the process of assessment, and his parents would go with him.

'Is he going to die?' Luke whispered, and Sam sent an urgent mental signal to his grandma to reach out and hug him, but Lorna started to cry so it was Zoe who did the hugging.

'Why has Grandma been crying and crying?' Luke asked in a scared whisper.

'Hey,' Zoe said, still hugging. 'No drama. I'm sure your grandma's crying because she's relieved. Ryan might need to wait a while until he gets a donor heart, but once that happens he'll be brilliant. Back to the old Ryan.

'But transplants don't work,' Lorna sobbed. 'Or if they do they only last a few months.'

Luke's face bleached white—and Sam saw the moment when Zoe decided to stop being gentle and tell it like it was.

'That's nonsense,' she snapped. 'I'm sorry, Lorna, but your information's way out of date. Look at me.'

'You?'

'Me,' Zoe said, and lifted the hem of her baggy uniform tunic and the soft T-shirt underneath. She turned side on so they could all see the long, distorted scar that spelled renal transplant.

'I was the same as Ryan,' she told them. 'I had an infection as a kid, only instead of messing with my heart it messed with my kidneys so I needed a transplant. I was given a new kidney three years ago, and it's working fine. My doctors tell me I'm going to live for ever and I'm even learning to surf. I have so many plans now—plans for the rest of my life. Who says transplants always fail?'

And Lorna's sobs stopped, just like that, and she stared at Zoe as if she was some sort of mirage.

Zoe stayed with her shirt pulled up, as if she knew they needed time to examine the scar.

'Wow,' Luke breathed, and put out a finger to touch it. 'Did it hurt?'

'Nah,' Zoe said with insouciance. 'I'm brave. Isn't that right, Mr Webster?'

'She's so brave she surfs in four feet of water, on eighteen inch waves,' Sam said, and the tension was broken. Even Lorna was smiling as Zoe pulled her shirt back down and got to her feet.

'I need to get back to the ward,' she told them, but then she hesitated. 'Lorna, you said Luke's staying with you. Will he keep staying with you while his parents are with Ryan?'

'Yes,' Lorna said, and Sam watched Luke's face tighten. He could guess what sort of strains this small boy was facing—he'd seen those pressures a lot in the siblings of dangerously-ill children. All attention had been on Ryan for months. Luke would be fitted in around the edges, and now he was being asked to stay indefinitely with an elderly grandmother who looked like she wept more than she kept a child entertained.

'Will you take me to Sea World on Sunday, then?' Zoe asked, and he blinked. What?

'Will *I* take you?' the little boy said cautiously, and Zoe looked a question at Lorna.

'If it's okay with your grandma. Luke, you've lived on the Gold Coast all your life, but I've never been here before. I need a guide—someone to tell me what to see and the cool rides to go on. Is there a Ferris wheel? I love Ferris wheels.'

'But you'll miss your surfing lesson,' Sam said before he could help himself, and copped a reproving look from Zoe for his pains.

'Some things are more important than surfing lessons. I'm on night duty this week, which means I need to sleep on Saturday, so Sunday's the only time I have free. I'm dying to go. Will you take me, Luke?'

'Yes,' Luke said. 'There are cool rides. The Ferris wheel's not at Sea World, though, but there's one near it.'

'Excellent,' Zoe said, and beamed.

'That would be lovely,' Lorna said, and Sam looked at Zoe and thought...*lovely?*

He knew how much she loved surfing. He knew how much she was aching for next Sunday to come. He'd only offered two hours every Sunday, and he knew she'd love more, yet here she was, putting it aside to take a child to an amusement park, to give some fun to a kid who was desperate for time out.

She'd pulled up her top and shown her renal scar and he knew how much she hated doing that, and now she was giving up her Sunday...

'Can I come, too?' he asked, before he even realised he was about to offer, and he found everyone looking at him.

'You?' Zoe said in astonishment.

'They have great water slides,' he said weakly. 'Almost as good as surfing. And I like Ferris wheels. Callie will look after Bonnie.'

'Cool,' Luke said cautiously, and Lorna pulled herself together, thanked them, set a time for them to pick Luke up, and the thing was done. Grandma and grandchild left, and Sam was left in the empty waiting room with Zoe.

'Thank you,' she said, and it needed only that. It was Zoe who was generous. He'd grudgingly given her two hours' surfing a week, and she gave so much more.

'For offering to have fun on Sunday?'

'You like your own company. It'll be more than two hours.'

'Yeah, but I don't have to talk to you all the time,' he told her, and she smiled, and then her smile faded.

'What are Ryan's chances?'

'Good, as long as a transplant's found soon. Thank you for showing your scar. You realise Lorna will tell Ryan's parents and you've just reassured everyone in a way no one else could.'

'My pleasure.'

'It's not your pleasure. You don't like telling people.'

'It's different,' she said. 'I choose to no longer be a renal transplant patient. I choose also to use my experience to reassure others that there is life on the other side.'

'So I can use you for show and tell whenever I need you?'

'I say who, I say when,' she retorted, and he grinned. And then he couldn't help himself, he had to reach out and touch her.

He touched her face, just touched. There was no way in the world he should touch this woman, and yet how could he not? She stood there in her plain hospital greens, she looked tired and a little bit worried, she still had hours of her shift to go, and he was a consultant cardiologist and he had no business at all touching a nurse.

But this wasn't just a nurse. This was Zoe.

Her skin was amazing. Soft, clear, almost luminescent. Her gorgeous, clear eyes were looking up at him, asking a question.

He wasn't sure what the question was.

Or actually…

He did know.

Are you going to kiss me? That's what her eyes were asking, and that's exactly what he did.

And the kiss was like quicksilver. Light, hot, fast… As fast as the feeling that burned right through him as his mouth claimed hers.

She was yielding to him. Her lips were parting. She was leaning forward so he could kiss her…as he wanted to kiss her.

He wanted to kiss her. Every sense in his body

wanted to kiss her. She was soft and warm and yielding, and brave and true and gorgeous.

He'd sworn never to touch another woman. He'd sworn never to fall...

That had been before he'd met Zoe, he thought in the tiny section of his brain that was still capable of holding thought. That part was getting smaller by the moment.

He was entirely centred, entirely focussed, on kissing Zoe.

He was holding her, tugging her into him, and she was rising on her toes to come closer. Her arms were around him, and he felt her heat, felt a response from her body that made him tug her closer still.

He was plundering her mouth, tasting her, wanting her, and nothing was more important, nothing could get in the way of here, now, this woman.

Except there was a nurse at the door who was coughing politely, and then coughing a little louder, and trying to hide a grin a mile wide.

'Um, Zoe, we need to do medication rounds,' she said as they broke apart in confusion. 'I'd give 'em myself but hospital protocol says double-check unless it's a Code Blue emergency or State of General Chaos, and I can't quite see what you two are doing as fitting either category.'

And Zoe blushed, adorably, seemingly from the toes up. But then, instead of looking disconcerted or nonplussed or anything he might have expected, she chuckled.

'I was having trouble breathing,' she said. 'Does that count as Code Blue?'

'You want oxygen?' the other nurse said, grinning back, and the situation eased from the potential to be mortifying to something that was...fun? 'Shall I hit the bells? I can have a crash cart here in seconds. Paddles to restart the heart? A bit of defibrillation?'

'I think,' Zoe said serenely, still grinning at Sam, 'that there's quite enough electricity in here already. Thank you, Dr Webster, for what was a very nice kiss. I'm looking forward to going on the roller-coaster with you on Sunday—it should be a wild ride.'

And she swept out with her nursing colleague, and Sam heard them chuckling again as they headed back to the wards and he thought...

He thought maybe he was taking this far too seriously.

He hadn't wanted to kiss her. He hadn't wanted to take this anywhere at all, but Zoe's attitude said it was fine.

Kiss and move on. Have fun.

Fun... The concept was so far from his mindset...

And that was his problem, he thought. Emily's death had darkened his life. He'd been protecting himself ever since.

Zoe was a girl who'd had a transplant, a girl who simply wanted to embrace life.

She'd kissed him, she'd made him feel...like his life could change, and then she'd chuckled and walked away.

And maybe his life had changed.

He looked after her, at the empty corridor, at the echoes of her smile, her chuckle, the remembrance of her kiss, and he thought...

Fun.

Zoe.

He grinned.

Life was okay. He had his Bonnie. He had the best job in the world.

He was taking Zoe to Sea World on Sunday.

He headed back towards his apartment and met two colleagues on the way, both of whom beamed and made it totally clear the whole hospital knew what had just happened in the cardiac care waiting room.

Did he care? No. He was going to Sea World with Zoe.

Zoe had a very interesting week. She was now officially classified as Gold Coast Central's Hottest Gossip Item, and if she was honest with herself, she was enjoying herself very much indeed.

Somewhere Zoe had read that the happiest people were those who had the most *I'm a*. I'm a daughter, I'm a mother, a teacher, a knitter, a rock climber, a surfer. But for years Zoe's *I'm a* had been confined. I'm a daughter, I'm a renal patient, I'm a cosseted girlfriend.

Now…I'm a nurse and I'm a learner-surfer and I'm Bonnie's daytime carer, and I'm half the equation in sizzling gossip that's zooming around the hospital like wildfire, she told herself, and she liked it.

It was such a weird sensation. She was being seen as…sexy? Dean had never seen her as sexy, she thought, and neither had anyone else in her circle of friends back home. How could she be sexy? She'd been poor Zoe, who needed to be treated with care and kindness, but now… Sexy was delicious.

It wouldn't last. She knew enough about hospital gossip to know it'd die down as something else took over. She and Sam would take Luke to Sea World then they'd resume their weekly surfing lessons. She wouldn't need to care for Bonnie—the fast-recovering dog hardly needed company any more anyway—and the universe would right itself.

She wanted to tell Sam to relax, chill, let it die in its own time, but he was avoiding her. They were having very brief exchanges when they met on the ward. She wanted to tell him that that made it worse—the fact that when he came into her ward he was curt with her rather than his normal friendly self. It raised eyebrows even more.

He was…embarrassed? Mortified?

Well, he'd kissed her, she told herself, so it was his problem. She wasn't about to join him in the mortification department.

It had been a gorgeous kiss. It had made her feel like she'd never felt like in her life and it had added a fabulous *I'm a* to her repertoire.

I'm a hottie.

Sunday.

They were collecting Luke from his grandmother's at ten.

Sam was awake at six, staring at the ceiling.

For once he had no patients in the wards—a situation that happened only a couple of times a year. He had no rounds to do. He could sleep in—or not.

Bonnie was sleeping soundly in her basket beside his bed. She'd taken to being an invalid with aplomb, even seeming to enjoy the extra fuss made of her. He'd had no fewer than three offers to look after her today while he and Zoe went to Sea World.

At ten.

He had four hours before ten.

He had time to go surfing, he decided. He had time to clear his head, to get back to being a loner for a while.

He tossed back the covers and Bonnie opened one eye and looked at him almost indulgently. Two weeks ago she'd have been hammering on the door to go with him, but she was a sensible dog and there were compensations to having a broken leg.

Compensations like spending time with Zoe?

See, that's why he needed to surf. He needed to get his head in order before he spent the day with her.

He took Bonnie out for a quick dose of grass then settled her back to bed. He grabbed a muesli bar and a drink and headed to his car.

And stopped. His conscience was like an elastic band, stretched tight, and it wouldn't let him get to the car.

Zoe was missing her surfing lesson today.

Zoe had volunteered to miss her surfing lesson, he told himself. It had been her decision to forgo her lesson to take Luke to Sea World.

She was giving up her surfing lesson to make a desolate kid happy.

Consciences should be abolished, he told himself savagely, but his feet turned all by themselves and the next minute he was knocking on Zoe's door.

He knocked softly, so as not to wake her if she was asleep, but no such luck. She answered, wearing a gorgeous, pink silk nightie, her curls tumbled, her eyes still drowsy with sleep, but when she saw him she lit up and her smile did things to him...

Things that said back off, run—but it was too late. He'd knocked and she was smiling at him, bright with expectation, and he had no choice but to follow through where his inconvenient conscience had led him.

'You're missing your surfing lesson today,' he said, a bit too gruffly. 'I thought…I'm going surfing now. If you'd like to come…'

'Could I?' Her smile lit up her face. 'Oh, Sam, that's so kind. Can you wait two minutes? I have toast in the toaster. Do you like home-made marmalade? My mum's just sent me some.'

So thirty seconds later he was sitting at her kitchen table, scoffing toast and marmalade, while Zoe dressed and chatted and scooted back and forth to eat her own toast while she got ready, and he felt so domestic, so enveloped in something he could hardly describe…

'So where's Bonnie?' she demanded. She finished off the last piece of toast and licked a trace of butter from her fingers and he thought…he thought…

Where's Bonnie?

'Still asleep,' he managed. 'I took her outside for a few moments so she's comfortable. She'll sleep until we get back, then Callie will look after her while we're at Sea World.'

'She has so many friends,' Zoe said, satisfied. 'Do you want to see the beach gear I've organised for when she's well enough for the beach again?' Without waiting for an answer, she hauled open a cupboard and produced a foldable trampoline-type pet bed, and six slender prayer flags. They were multicoloured, light and easy to set up and they'd be visible for miles.

'I know it's more stuff to carry down the beach,' Zoe said happily, 'but Bonnie and I have been practising. She already likes the bed and she knows to stay when you tell her. And see these little hooks? I've made a canopy—it doesn't work when it's windy but on hot, still days it makes the prayer flags into a shade tent. How cool's that?'

'Really cool,' he said faintly.

'I'm not interfering, am I?' she asked anxiously. 'You don't have to use them, but I thought…it'll keep her safe and let you keep doing what you both love.'

It would.

And then he thought…

It'll keep her safe and let you keep doing what you love…

And with that thought came a blast of longing so powerful he had to close his eyes.

To be able to love this woman…and keep her safe…

'Right,' she said. 'Unless you want more toast, are you ready to go?'

'I'm ready,' he said, but he thought, *Am I?*

The beach was amazing. There were half a dozen serious surfers far out, but no one else was on the beach and the surf was magic. The waves were low, even rolls that started way out but somehow kept their momentum so they were still rideable almost to the shore.

'I'll practise in the shallows. You go out with the big boys,' Zoe said, and normally Sam would, paddling out to where the surf promised to be magic.

This morning it promised to be magic right in close.

Zoe was improving by the minute. He'd never seen such intensity in a novice surfer. She was wobbling to her feet consistently now, managing to balance for a few short seconds, managing to ride the wave a few feet, feeling its power, and every time she did she whooped with joy. Then as the wave finally shook her free she tumbled in freefall, went under and surfaced spluttering, laughing and desperate for more.

She was starting to shake him off now, trying to cope alone.

'I can do it. I'm sure I can. Don't push the board, I can get it. Ohhhh…'

And down she went again, and under, and he reached down and gripped her hands and pulled her up. She surfaced half choking, half convulsed with laughter, and it was all he could do to let go of her hands and obey orders.

To give her space.

He started riding the small waves as well, and a couple of times she caught the same wave and they rose together. Her whoop when they managed it could be heard from one end of the beach to the other. One of the surfers from far out rode a wave all the way in, obviously intending to pack up and leave, but he stopped to watch Zoe for a while and the look he cast Sam left Sam in no doubt as to the guy's jealousy.

'She almost makes me want to turn teacher,' the guy shouted to him as he headed past. 'If nippers were all like this, I'd have stayed in the baby class.'

He gave Sam a good-natured grin, watched a bit more as Zoe wobbled gamely to the shore and then left them.

Sam felt pretty much unbearably smug.

'I must be doing well,' Zoe declared, dragging her board out to the next wave. 'Even my instructor's grinning.'

'You have a long way to go,' Sam said, and Zoe's grin matched his.

'I know I have, and you have no idea how good that feels.'

He thought of the kidney transplant.

He watched her some more and he thought this woman had lived in the shadow of an early death since childhood. Now she had a future and she was embracing it with everything she had.

And Sam...the future...

For some reason, here, now, the loneliness and desolation and self-blame he'd felt since Emily had died were somehow slipping away.

Zoe had had her life restored to her and was making use of it. She was giving him a lesson in living.

As a cardiologist he saw patients on the cusp of death every day, he thought, but he'd never learned this lesson from them.

Zoe was...different.

Zoe was Zoe.

They showered and dressed in the amenity block above the beach and then had a very satisfactory second breakfast—egg and bacon burgers from the burger cart above the beach, eaten while fending off a hundred odd seagulls waiting for every crumb.

The sun was warm on their faces. The day was still ahead of them. Zoe was breaking bits off her hamburger bun, trying to aim crumbs directly at a gull with a missing leg. She worked at it, worked at it, worked at it—and finally her crust landed exactly where she wanted. Her one-legged gull grabbed it and flew off—and lowered its 'missing leg' as it flew.

'What a con.' Zoe burst out laughing. 'Of all the actors...'

He looked at her and he wanted…

He wanted.

'So what do you want to do next?' Zoe asked.

'Go and collect Luke?' he said cautiously, and she grinned.

'That's not what I mean. I mean…' She gestured to the sea, to the gulls, to the surfers way out. 'This is one of my dreams. I have so many I doubt I'll cram them all in.'

'Like what?'

'Like going to Nepal. Like learning how to make mango ice cream. Like learning how to jive. I spent so many years not permitted to do anything that my list's a mile long. Even mango ice cream… My mother was paranoid about tropical fruit after I copped an infection from eating paw paw. My restrictions were weird, so my list's enormous. What's number one on yours?'

Sitting here, he thought. Eating hamburgers with you.

What else? When he thought about it there wasn't much else. Since Emily's death he'd pretty much concentrated on taking one step after the next.

He'd had lists, he thought. It was as if he was the opposite of Zoe. After Emily's death, his dreams had pretty much ended.

'Save a few more kids,' he said, and she nodded.

'I'll drink to that,' she said, and raised her juice. 'But there must be more. Would you like to…I don't know… learn to propagate man-eating plants? Did you know the *Nepthenthes rajah* can already trap small mammals? I reckon if you tried hard enough you could grow one big enough to trap a tax inspector. I can't fit that into my life plan right now but you could fit it into yours. You might want to be careful of Bonnie, though.'

'Why would I breed carnivorous plants?' he asked.

'Because you've never done it before. Isn't that a good enough reason? Or you could learn to knit hot-water-bottle covers. That'd sit well as an alternate hobby when the surf's lousy.'

'When the surf's lousy I do more work.'

'Because you can't forget Emily's death unless you're either surfing or working?' she ventured.

He stilled. No one had ever been so blunt—but Zoe wasn't even looking repentant.

'Sorry,' she said, still sounding upbeat. 'It's just… I've learned the hard way to say it like it is. I've spent half my life with people tiptoeing round the fact that I might die, so I guess I'm over the niceties. I still might die,' she said, looking surfwards again with satisfaction. 'But I plan to go down doing something on my list.'

'You're planning on dying surfing?' He could hardly say it.

'Are you kidding?' She was scornful. 'Surfing's right at the top of my list. I'm talking about getting way down the bottom. The way I see it, I have years of following dreams. Seventy years if I'm lucky. But you…how can you only have two things?'

'It's the way I like it.'

'Is it?' She rose and tossed the last of her hamburger crumbs to the frenzied mob. 'It seems to me…' She stopped then and seemed to collect herself. 'No. Sorry. It's none of my business. It's just, I've shaken off all my shackles right now and I'm so happy I'd like to see the rest of the world shake theirs off, too.'

'I don't have shackles.'

'Don't you?' she asked, suddenly gentling. 'I think you do but, as I said, it's none of my business. Now, let's go and get Luke.'

They headed back to the Jeep, and as he drove Zoe fell silent. Sam was free to think.

Did he have shackles, self-imposed or not?

If he did then he liked them, he thought. He'd imposed them himself. They weren't shackles so much as a set of rules to keep his world steady.

He wasn't a man to follow his dreams. He'd achieved what he wanted to achieve and nothing else mattered.

Nothing else was permitted to matter.

Bonnie mattered. That moment when he'd thought she'd died... It hadn't been as bad as seeing the wave hurl Emily to the sandbank but it was still bad.

He didn't want to go there again, and if shackles stopped it happening then that was the way he liked it.

He cast a sideways glance at the girl sitting beside him.

Shackles. He needed them, he thought, to keep himself isolated. Isolation was his plan for the future and he didn't intend to deviate.

Shackles?

How strong could he make them?

They collected a very excited Luke and from there there was little time for introspection, or if there was, Zoe and Luke weren't interested.

Sea World. Fishes, dolphins, manta rays and penguins. Rides, rides and more rides. Luke turned into a little boy again, whooping, being loud as Sam suspected he hadn't been loud for a long time, pleading with them to go on the wildest, splashiest ride and crowing in delight when his grown-ups got satisfactorily wet.

Luke and Zoe fed the manta rays, boggled that such huge flappy creatures could have faces that they decreed were almost adorable. They checked out the penguins and practised their waddles and giggled. They stood waist deep in the dolphin pool, and Luke patted the belly of a dolphin called Nudge, who'd been stranded as a baby at sea and had figured by now that humans were trusted friends.

Luke stroked and stroked and maybe the dolphin—or Nudge's handler, who was empathetic and kind—realised this was what Luke needed most in the world, for there was no hurry. Luke was allowed to be a child again for as long as he wanted to be. Zoe stroked too, but mostly she watched Luke, her eyes suspiciously misty.

And despite the vows he'd just reaffirmed for himself, Sam watched Zoe putting herself out there to make sure Luke had the time of his life. He watched her taking every ounce of enjoyment she could wring from the day as well.

He thought…

He had to stop thinking.

'But we still need a Ferris-wheel ride,' Zoe decreed, as Sam checked his watch and finally decided it was almost time to get Luke back to his grandma.

'Do you know where a Ferris wheel is?' A middle-aged woman and her husband had been standing beside them, dolphin watching. Sam had noticed this pair throughout the day and had become a bit concerned. The woman was determined to go on every ride, but her husband had been wheezing along behind her, looking exhausted.

'We've both got flu,' the woman had said when Sam had helped the guy from the last ride, and she'd coughed to prove it. 'But we're from Perth and this our last day here. I want to do everything. But like you, young lady,' she said now, 'I want a Ferris wheel.'

'There's one on the beach,' Luke volunteered. 'There's one really big one but it's ages away and the carriages are all closed in. This one's part of a circus and it's open and looks awesome.'

He must have seen it as his parents drove back and forth to the hospital, Sam thought. A Ferris wheel would seem magic for a kid whose family was solely concerned with keeping his big brother alive.

'Let's go, then,' Zoe declared. 'And then our day has to end.'

'Rats,' Luke said, and Sam thought that was his sentiment exactly.

CHAPTER SIX

THEY DROVE TO the Ferris wheel, and Reg and Marjory, their new friends from Perth, came along as well.

'It'll be a lovely way to finish our holiday,' Marjory said, still coughing. 'Riding up and down, looking out over the mountains and the sea. Won't it, Reg?'

'I guess,' Reg said, but Sam looked at him, looked at his colour and stepped in.

'I reckon you'd be better sitting it out, mate,' he told him. 'You look exhausted.'

'He's not exhausted,' Marjory said, indignant. 'It's our last excitement. Your little boy looks tired, too, and he's not giving up.'

Luke did look tired. He'd pushed himself past his limit. Sam and Zoe had had to split up, doing every second ride to keep up with him, but the difference between Luke and Reg was that Luke looked gloriously happy. Reg just looked spent.

But then Sam got distracted. 'Luke's not our little boy,' Zoe was telling Marjory, and Sam heard an unmistakeable note of regret in her voice.

Whoa. Regret?

Family. Was that on her list?

He looked down at Luke and saw he'd tucked his

hand into Zoe's. He was a tired kid at the end of a very long day. He'd go home to his grandma and be faced with all the tensions he'd been facing for months, but for now he was one happy little boy. Zoe was holding him and it felt…it felt…

Okay, it felt like family.

And the faint, insidious questioning became louder.

'Tickets,' Zoe said, and he blinked and realised he was staring at nothing. Reg and Marjory were already lining up to get into their gondola and he hadn't even bought tickets yet.

'Earth to Sam,' Zoe said, and he hauled himself together and they went and bought tickets for one last ride.

It was the end of a glorious day and it was surely okay for a girl to dream.

Zoe had come to the Gold Coast to escape caring. She loved her family to bits, she'd even loved Dean, but they were like the wetsuits Sam wore, keeping the cold at bay but too tight for comfort. She'd been in a cocoon of protection ever since she'd become ill and it was time now to shake it off. In the end she'd had no qualms telling Dean it was over, because she'd realised that all Dean saw in her was someone he could protect. Surely he could use some excitement too, she'd thought, for that was what she wanted. Sizzle.

Sizzle was here, now. The way she was feeling…

She had no business sizzling, she told herself. She had no business sitting on the opposite side of the gondola, looking at Sam Webster, thinking he made her toes curl. Thinking she might even be making his toes curl.

Or was she? Was it her imagination? Wishful thinking?

It wasn't. The way he'd been looking at her all day... the way he'd reacted when her body had touched his...

She needed to take a cold shower, she told herself. Surely it was her imagination. She needed to calm down.

But she didn't want to calm down. She'd left Adelaide looking for sizzle, and sizzle was right in front of her. And if he was interested...

She'd be really interested right back, she decided. She felt a warm, zippy tingle from her toes to her ears and back again, and she wiggled in her safety harness and hugged Luke because a girl had to hug someone and it was far safer to hug Luke than it was to launch herself across the gondola at the man looking at her with hunger...

She was sure it was hunger.

Life was pretty exciting, she decided. This was a truly excellent place to be. The sea and the mountains looked almost dreamlike, the man on the opposite seat looked even more dreamlike—and Zoe Payne thought she might, she just might let herself think about falling in love.

It was a terrifying prospect, but Sam Webster, paediatric cardiologist, surfer, all-round loner, might just not be able to keep those shackles in place.

It was lust, he decided as the Ferris wheel gondola rose ponderously up to the peak, hovered for them to enjoy the view and then started its descent again. It was a mighty fine view, he conceded, but the view in front of him was better.

Somehow Zoe Payne had wriggled under his defences.

Somehow Zoe Payne made him doubt his own plan for isolation.

She was saying something to Luke, something that made the little boy giggle. She glanced up and caught his gaze...and blushed.

She was adorable.

'Do I have fairy floss on my nose?' she demanded, a little bit breathlessly. 'Luke, Sam's staring at me. Do I have fairy floss on my nose?'

'Just freckles,' Luke said. 'He's staring at you 'cos you're pretty.'

'Really?' Zoe demanded, looking immeasurably pleased. 'You think I'm pretty? Wow.' She grinned and hugged him. 'Do you have a girlfriend?'

'No,' Luke said. 'That's silly. You can be Dr Webster's girlfriend, though.'

'He already has Bonnie. Have you met our Bonnie?'

'She visited Ryan when he came into hospital the first time,' Luke told her. 'She's nice, but she's not as nice as you.'

And that was a hard call, Sam thought as the Ferris wheel started to rise again. Who was nicest? His dog or Zoe?

The heart expands to fit all comers. He'd read that somewhere and he hadn't believed it, but now...

Now, though, a tiny niggle was building to a huge doubt. How could he resist?

And then a scream ripped apart the peace of the late afternoon and he needed to turn his thoughts in another direction entirely.

* * *

'Sit down, madam, sit down *now*.'

The voice through the megaphone boomed out as the Ferris wheel came to an abrupt, shuddering halt.

Sit down?

They were all sitting. They were harnessed, belted in by the operator with instructions not to undo the harness under any circumstances.

Then came another scream, from a gondola above them.

'He's dead. He's not breathing. Do something. Reg... Reg... Get us down!'

Marjory.

It was the end of a glorious beach day. People were packing up and going home. The Ferris wheel was therefore almost empty. Reg and Marjory were right up the top, two gondolas away from theirs.

Marjory had undone her harness. She was leaning right out of the gondola, screaming hysterically to anyone below.

'Get us down. He's not breathing. Get us down.'

Any minute now she'd fall out, Sam thought incredulously. If the operator started the wheel again she could hit a strut and be knocked out.

'Sit down and do up your harness,' the voice boomed. 'The wheel can't move until you're sitting.'

But Marjory wasn't listening. She was lurching from one side of the gondola to the other, leaning right out as if she could grab someone from below to help her.

'Marjory, sit down,' Sam roared upwards at her, putting every ounce of command he could muster into his voice. 'We can't help you until you sit.'

'He's dying. He's dead.' It was an agonised wail of terror, and Sam realised she wasn't hearing a thing.

'A heart attack?' Zoe whispered, holding Luke close, and Sam looked at both of them and then looked up at the hysterical woman, his mind racing.

Reg had looked to be in his mid-fifties. He was a bit overweight. He'd had flu.

He'd looked...he'd looked like Sam should have intervened, only he'd been distracted by Zoe.

The wheel had come to a dead stop now. Nothing was happening.

'Nothing's moving until you're in your harness,' the voice boomed through the loudspeaker, and Sam looked up at the hysterical Marjory and thought there was no chance of any harness going on.

He unclipped his own.

'Take care of Luke,' he said, tight and hard, and he swung himself up, out and on top of his gondola before Zoe could react.

'Sam!' She didn't scream. She stayed still, she stayed holding Luke, but her face lost its colour.

'I was a monkey in another life,' he said, smiling down at her. 'The light cables make it safe. Luke, hold onto Zoe. She's a bit scared, but you know that this is just like climbing the jungle gym at school. See you soon.'

And he reached up, looped the light cable around his wrist and grabbed the next strut, then swung himself high, grabbed the gondola above, swung, steadied, and heaved himself higher.

Dear God...

He made it look almost easy, Zoe thought as Sam

swung himself up through the next gondola and reached for the strut to swing himself to the next one.

It wasn't easy. She couldn't have done it even if it had been at ground level. As it was... How high were they? She wasn't looking down.

She clutched Luke and Luke clutched back.

'Sit down!' The voice below was a continuous roar of instructions but the voice below was as helpless as she was.

Above, Marjory was sobbing, out of control, but Sam was steadily growing nearer. From the other gondolas people watched with horror.

'He's clever,' Luke said, in a far steadier voice than Zoe was capable of. 'My dad said he saved Ryan's life that first night he got sick. He's saving people again.'

He'd reached Marjory. He hauled himself up, swung himself into the gondola and for one appalling moment Zoe thought Marjory would launch herself at him and hug him so hard she'd propel them both out.

But it was Sam who propelled Marjory. He grabbed both her shoulders forced her to sit, and forced her to stay sitting.

'You sit down and you don't move or I won't look at Reg,' he growled, and it was a measure of the terror all around them that silence let Zoe hear every word. 'Sit. Stay.'

And finally, amazingly, Marjory subsided.

So did Sam. He dropped to his knees, obviously to treat Reg, and was lost to sight.

There was a long moment, or more than a moment—who could tell how long?—while Zoe forgot to breathe. She was clutching Luke's hand so hard he yelped and she had to give him a shamefaced smile and release the tension. Just a little bit.

Then...

'We're secure. Bring it down,' Sam yelled, still unseen, but there was no mistaking he was yelling to the operator below and there was no mistaking the authority in his voice.

'Are you in harness?' the guy below yelled, and Sam told him where he could put his harness.

'Move it. Now. I take full responsibility. Just do it,' he yelled back, and finally the gondolas jerked and the wheel came to life and they headed towards the ground.

'Luke, I'll need to help Sam when we get to the ground,' Zoe told the little boy by her side. She still couldn't see what was happening—Sam was still working on the gondola floor—but she was making the same assumption that had made Sam risk his life by clambering up through the struts fifty feet above the ground. Cardiac arrest.

'I know that,' Luke said. 'You're a nurse and Sam's a doctor. I'll be good.'

'You're always good,' Zoe said to him. 'One day soon I reckon we need to organise you to be very, very bad. How about going to dodgem cars next Sunday and seeing how many cars we can crash?'

'Really?'

'Being good pays off,' Zoe said, and thought Sam hadn't fallen during his crazy climb so someone must have been good.

And if Reg was to live...

Yeah, well, that was to come.

The fairground's ground crew proved extremely competent. Zoe would have thought the obvious thing to do when there was drama in a high gondola was to get it to the ground as fast as possible, but the protocol was obviously geared to make people secure first. While someone was screaming, waving in and out of the gondola, the wheel didn't move, but once Sam had Marjory secure, the wheel rolled straight down, not stopping until Reg and Marjory's gondola was on the loading platform.

Someone else had come running to assist the guy operating the wheel. He helped Sam lift Reg out then helped Marjory out as Sam started work on the seemingly lifeless Reg.

Finally Zoe and Luke's gondola was brought in to ground level as well. The attendant opened the gondola on the far side, away from Sam, but Zoe shook him off.

'I'm a nurse, he's a doctor, we're a team,' she said briefly, and she and Luke were ushered out to the right side.

Marjory was crumpled on the ground, keening.

Luke was clutching Zoe's hand, but he had it figured.

'I'll stay still and be good,' Luke said bravely, and he let her go. Zoe thought, Wow, what a kid, and hugged him. She left him standing by Marjorie and went to see how she could help.

'Has someone called an ambulance?' she demanded.

'Yep,' the attendant told her. 'And Joe's gone to get the first-aid pack.'

She nodded, focussing now on Reg. And on Sam.

Sam had him on his back. Cardiopulmonary resuscitation. Heart massage. He had his hands linked, pushing down with fierce, dogged strength. Fifteen beats, then breathe.

She stooped and knelt beside him. 'I'll breathe,' she said.

'There's no mask.' He was out of breath. He'd climbed, he'd have had to roll Reg, clearing his airway, getting him into position, then getting him out of the gondola, all while trying to breathe and pound.

'Tell that to someone who cares,' Zoe said, and bent and breathed, long, strong breaths that'd make Reg's lungs expand, while Sam pounded with all the strength he had.

She heard a rib crack.

'Breathe, damn you, breathe,' Sam was saying over and over, but he was talking to Reg and it was now Zoe who was breathing.

He'd seemed nice, Zoe thought. Marjory had been voluble and gushing, but Reg had spoken to them a few times during the day. He'd been kind to Luke, and Zoe thought there were probably kids and maybe even grandkids somewhere. People who wanted this man to live.

Come on, Reg...

'You want a defibrillator?' It was the attendant, standing over them, sounding almost apologetic at interrupting, and Sam kept pounding but glanced up and saw what he was offering.

Yes! A decent, comprehensive first-aid pack complete with the portable defibrillators that were increasingly common at large venues.

And masks.

He handed Zoe the mask, she slid it into place and kept right on breathing while Sam shoved the defibrillator into position.

'Three, two, one...' he said, and she pulled back as the defibrillator did its work, then went back to breathing.

Nothing.

'Three, two, one...'

And this time...

Reg's chest heaved, all by itself. He took a ragged, weak breath but it was definitely a breath, air drawn in all by itself.

'Come on...' Sam muttered. 'Live, damn you.'

Zoe breathed a couple more times, then Sam put his hand on her shoulder and she paused.

'Let him take over.'

Would he?

She'd almost forgotten to breathe herself.

CPR hardly ever worked. She knew that. It was supposedly the medical wonder: get to a heart-attack victim in time, administer CPR and, lo, the victim lived. In reality cardiac arrest was almost always fatal and part of medical training incorporated coping with low expectations—coping with the reality that death wasn't caused by lack of expertise.

They'd done all they could. They needed luck now.

They'd already had it in that one shaky breath. They needed more.

Please...

And they had it. Another breath. Another. Another.

Reg's pallid, grey face received a wash of tepid colour.

Please...

And then, blessedly, here came the cavalry. Ambulance, paramedics, oxygen, adrenalin—all the things to make a slight chance a good one. All the things to make Zoe suddenly redundant.

Sam was still working, in charge, taking total control, but Zoe could back off, slipping out of the medical cluster and backing to where Marjory and Luke huddled, together but not together, seemingly both as terrified as each other.

'He's breathing,' Zoe said to both of them. 'Reg is breathing. Marjory, he's still in danger, but he has a good chance.'

And then, because there was nothing else to do and woman and child were white-faced and shocked and seemingly without speech, she did the only thing left to her.

She took them both into a group hug and held them hard.

Sam had to go with the ambulance. There was no choice. Reg was drifting back to consciousness. His breathing was almost regular but Sam was under no illusions. The most dangerous time after cardiac arrest was the next minute, and the next minute after that. The block that had caused the arrest would still be there. There was no relaxing until Sam got him into the cardiac care unit with blood thinners on board and he could see what he was dealing with.

'Go,' Zoe said, snagging his car keys. 'I'll take Luke home.'

'But—'

'You're thinking I can't drive it?'

'If you can drive your car, you can drive anything,' he said, and then on impulse he tugged her into his arms and, for no good reason, astonishingly, seemingly to him as well as to her, he gave her a swift, hard kiss, then he lifted Luke and hugged him, too, and that was all he had time for.

Two ambulances had arrived, a standard van and the

MICA van, Mobile Intensive Care, so there was room for Sam in Mica, with Marjory following in the standard van. Marjory was still weeping.

'I'll catch up with you at the hospital,' Zoe told her, and suddenly Luke tugged Marjory's cardigan, forcing her to look down at him.

'Dr Webster will make him better,' he said. 'He fixes people. He's ace.'

And Marjory sniffed and sniffed again and managed a watery smile and went to join her husband.

'Sam's really good,' Luke said as Zoe ushered him into Sam's car. 'Isn't he?'

'I... Yes.'

'He says I can call him Sam but I like calling him Dr Webster.' Zoe had thought Luke would be upset, but he was recovering fast, and his thoughts were heading off at a tangent. 'Do you think I could be a doctor when I grow up?'

'I'm sure of it.'

'He climbed the Ferris wheel really fast.'

'I don't think all doctors climb Ferris wheels.'

'No,' Luke said. 'But I will and Dr Webster does, too. He's cool, isn't he?

And Zoe thought back to that hard, fast kiss—she could still feel it—she could still taste it—and she thought, yes.

Yes, he was cool.

Or hot, and getting hotter by the minute.

Reg had a blockage in the coronary artery. He'd need a stent to open the artery permanently and he was on the next morning's surgical list. Even though Sam's specialty was paediatric cardiology, Sam worked steadily, making sure the guy was stable, easing the fear, which was enough almost to cause another attack in and of itself. The jury was still out on the damage stress could do to the heart but Sam had his own opinions and he wasn't about to let any of his heart patients face the night in terror.

Then he needed to cope with Marjory—and four younger Marjories, just landed on the express flight from Perth. Reg had four daughters, aged from twenty-six down. Every one of them was a younger version of their mother and every one of them seemed to need their own personal reassurance that their dad would be okay.

They were terrified, and Sam thought back to Marjory's behaviour at Sea World. Reg was the quiet one in this family, the guy who put himself in the back seat as his wife and daughters took the limelight with their extravagant personalities, he thought—and suddenly they'd realised their quiet mainstay wasn't as rocklike as they'd believed.

Sam allayed their very real terror and he thought as long as he got the stent right, Reg might just get a bit of the attention he deserved from now on. Would he like it?

Love was a weird thing, he mused as he finally left them, and as soon as the lift hit his floor he found his feet turning left instead of right, to Zoe's apartment instead of his.

He knocked and she opened the door and she was in her gorgeous bathrobe again, and he thought...

Actually, he didn't think anything. He couldn't, for Zoe reached up, twined her arms around his neck, tugged him down so his face was right by her face—and there was nothing in the world for a man to do but take her face between his hands and kiss her.

He kissed her as a man coming home.

She was warm and soft and yielding. Her kiss was generous, open, welcoming, and he held her and he felt his world shift.

Shackles falling away?

That's what this felt like. He felt rigid control dropping away, the years of discipline, the years of solitude. This was a release that had seemed impossible but which now seemed totally, inevitably right.

This was two becoming one.

He'd heard that line at a friend's wedding. He'd always been cynical. Even when he and Emily had decided to marry he could hardly remember asking—it had seemed like the sensible, practical thing to do. They had been friends, colleagues and lovers, but there'd been no real connection.

But he hadn't known there'd been no connection because he hadn't felt what that was until now.

So now he held Zoe and he kissed her and he felt like he'd come home. So much for shackles. So much for isolation. They stood in the corridor and nothing mattered except that they hold each other, that he had this woman in his arms and she seemed like she wanted to stay there for ever.

Oh, this kiss… It was something he'd never felt before. The heat from her body…the sweet, aching desire…the need he could feel reciprocated straight back to him.

This woman.

His heart.

How corny was that? He was a cardiologist. The heart was a mass of tissues, muscles, blood vessels. It could even be transplanted. But he wasn't being a cardiologist right now, he thought. He was a man claiming a woman.

Or letting a woman claim him.

'You...you want to come in?' she managed when finally, finally she could get a word out, and he set her back at arm's length and looked at her, really looked at her. He knew what she was asking. He knew what she was offering, and it twisted his heart.

Yeah, that dumb bunch of tissue, muscle, blood vessels was being twisted and it made not the tiniest bit of clinical sense but, dammit, it was twisting anyway and he wasn't asking questions.

'Yes,' he said. 'If you'll have me.'

'Bonnie's on my bed.'

'Bonnie's been an invalid for long enough,' he told her, tugging her close and kissing her hair. 'Medical protocols says urgent cases get the most suitable beds. Are we an urgent case?'

She chuckled, a lovely, low chuckle that made that mass of internal tissue twist all over again.

'Why yes, Dr Webster,' she said demurely. 'Why, yes, I believe we are.'

He woke and there was a woman cocooned against his body. She was curved against him, spooned against his chest. He'd gone to sleep holding her and it seemed that during the night they'd only grown closer.

He'd never felt like this.

Lovemaking with Emily had been good, excellent even, but afterwards she'd always shifted firmly to her side of the bed, setting boundaries. He'd never been able to cross those boundaries. She'd resented the least interference with her independence, and she'd died because of it.

If he hadn't said the waves were too dangerous, would she have gone out? The question haunted him, because he knew there was a strong possibility that the answer was no.

He hadn't been able to protect her. She'd reacted with fury every time he'd tried to restrain the craziest of her impulses, and tragedy had been the result.

Yet here magically was her antithesis. Here was a woman who invited him into her bed, who gave herself to him with joyful, laughing abandon, and who in her sleep was giving still.

Zoe.

He held her close, he felt her breath, her chest rising and falling, he felt her warmth and her loveliness, and he felt as if here was a gift without price.

A woman to love.

A woman he could protect and cherish for ever.

She didn't want to wake up.

From the time Zoe had first been diagnosed with kidney disease she'd schooled herself not to want. Not to want the health that other kids took for granted. Not to want their freedom. Not to want their futures.

But now…

Now she had health and freedom and future, and somehow, in the space of a few short weeks, they'd become totally centred on one gorgeous man.

Sam.

He had ghosts, she thought as she lay cocooned against him, savouring the spine-tingling sensation of skin against skin, of the warmth of passion spent, of love.

For it was love. She knew it. Every fibre of her body knew it, but she saw it with clear eyes.

Sam was hero material. He was a gorgeous, sun-bronzed surfer. He was a cardiologist at the top of his game. He was a guy most women would die to get close to—and she'd heard from the hospital gossip that there were many women in this hospital who'd tried.

But he'd lost his Emily, and in a weird way it made him the same as her. Human.

Most medics faced life and death every day but it still didn't teach them what she'd learned the hard way—that there was no personal promise of life. That your own life could be snatched away. That life was for living, here, now.

Losing your fiancée would do that to you, too, she thought, and maybe it explained this instant connection.

Or maybe nothing explained it. Maybe it was magic, and if it was…she was content to take it.

Just for now?

Maybe not. Lying here in the soft dawn light, with Sam's arms around her, feeling his naked body holding her, she let herself dream.

What if his dreams became her dreams?

This was just the start. All those dreams she'd had while she'd waited for a transplant, while she'd watched from the other side while her friends and family had got on with their lives…

She wanted to do stuff. The first step had been to escape the cloying care of her family, not in a way that would hurt them but in a way that would make it clear she was well and independent and free.

The next step was to earn enough money to travel.

She wanted to climb a Himalaya.

Not a very big one, she conceded. She didn't plan on making climbing her life's work, but already she was researching Nepal and looking at the easier treks and making plans.

She also had other things on her wish list. When she'd talked to Sam about them she'd been deadly serious.

She was learning to surf. She wanted to learn to scuba dive.

She wanted to learn to tango as well as jive.

She felt Sam stir and she wriggled deliciously against him and thought...and thought...

'Can you tango?' she asked.

'Um...right now?' He tugged her close and she smiled and wriggled round so she was facing him.

'I forgot the rose to put between my teeth,' she said. 'But hypothetically...'

'No,' he said.

'Would you be brave enough to learn?'

'I might,' he said, cautious, and she smiled a cat-got-the-cream smile and snuggled closer.

Sam Webster...

He had no ties, she thought. Unlike Dean, who'd wanted to stay in their home town for the rest of their days, paying off their mortgage, tending their garden and raising their two point five children—or actually, no, because he wasn't sure she should have children, there was an increased risk because of the transplant, and she wasn't supposed to dig in the garden because of germs, but if she wore gloves and was very careful...

'Zoe, there's a wedding on this Saturday,' Sam said,

and she stilled because her thoughts had been flying ahead, to climbing mountains, ignoring germs, taking risks, all the things she'd dreamed of since her transplant had worked, but now there was this delicious extra dimension, a dimension called Sam...

A wedding this Saturday. Surely it was a bit soon for Sam's thoughts to be going in that direction.

'A wedding,' she said, in the same cautious tone that he'd used when they'd discussed *the tango*. Only possibly more cautious.

'Our nurse manager of Cardiac Care, Alice, is getting married. I'm invited.'

And he said that in the same voice he might have said, 'There's a loaded gun pointed at my head.'

She giggled. She was totally, gloriously happy. Her body was wide awake now and so was his. His hands were starting to do delicious things to her. She felt... sated, she thought, and yet not sated. She wanted more.

'So I need to go,' he said. 'Would you like to come with me?'

'Will there be tango?'

'I wouldn't be surprised.' He was still using the loaded-gun voice.

'Excellent.' There was a couple of minutes' silence after that, a necessary silence because his fingers were doing something to her that took her entire concentration. A girl could explode at the feel of those fingers, she thought. She felt like she could explode. Maybe she already had.

'Wedding?' he said.

'Y-you're catching me at a weak moment.'

'I'm feeling pretty weak myself.'

'You could have fooled me.' She took a couple of deep breaths and forced herself to think. 'Sam, if we go to this wedding…the hospital will—'

'Talk,' he said. 'But do you think every single person from neurologist to ward clerk doesn't already know we're in bed together right this minute? The walls in this hospital have ears, and not only do they have ears, they have great gossipy mouths.' He gathered her further into his arms then rolled and pushed himself up so he was smiling down at her with that gorgeous, wicked grin that made her melt…

But how could she melt? She had already melted.

'Do you mind that they'll talk?' he asked, and she struggled to find the strength to speak.

'How could I mind?' she managed. 'Unless you don't intend to make love to me again, right this minute, and then I mind very much indeed… Oh…'

And then she stopped speaking. She stopped minding. There was nothing in the world but this man. He was the centre of her universe, and Zoe Elizabeth Payne didn't mind anything else at all.

'That was fast.'

He'd taken Bonnie for a brief walk downstairs. Zoe was in the shower. He'd have liked to shower with her—he'd have liked that more than just about anything—but it was Monday morning. Zoe started day shift today, he had patients booked, a ward round to do, things he had to organise for Reg—that stent needed to go in this morning…

How soon before he could take a holiday and spend a couple of weeks making love to Zoe?

'Hey,' Callie said, hauling him back to earth with a jolt as he carried Bonnie down the front steps from the apartment building. Bonnie could walk but stairs were still forbidden. Callie was heading home from the beach. She looked like she'd just been on a beach walk—clean and fresh and windblown. 'I said something,' she retorted.

So she had. He'd been thinking about…other things. He replayed Callie's words in his head, this time focussing. *That was fast.*

'Bonnie's recovery?' he tried, and Callie grinned.

'Nice try, wise guy, but you know very well what I'm talking about. Our Zoe.'

How fast had she become *our Zoe*?

Callie was eyeing him with interest as he set Bonnie onto the grass—but also with a certain degree of scepticism. She was moving into mother-hen mode? With Zoe?

'I'm not messing with your new best nurse,' he growled.

'You'd better not be.'

'So you warned Cade, and now you're warning me?'

'You got it.'

'I'm not messing,' he said, and her eyes widened.

'Really?'

'Really.'

There was a moment's silence and then she reached out and hugged him. 'Oh, Sam, that's awesome. Though…' She hesitated. 'It is pretty fast.'

'Emily and I were together for eight years and we didn't get it right. Maybe fast's the way to go,' Bonnie was sniffing round the grass, taking time to find the perfect spot. Usually Callie greeted Sam with curt friendliness and moved on, but she'd stopped. They were both watching Bonnie, but there were undercurrents.

'So what about you and Cade?' Sam asked, and he was right—there were definitely undercurrents. Callie bristled like a cat who'd just spotted an intruder in her garden.

'What about me and Cade?'

'The grapevine says you're sparking off each other like lightning rods.'

'He's pretty much insufferable.'

'He's a fine doctor.'

'And he's insufferable.' She sighed. 'You realise Alice has invited him to her wedding—and he's accepted. If you take your Zoe...'

His Zoe. Two weeks ago those words would have made him run a mile. Now they had him thinking of what Zoe was doing right now, standing naked in the shower while he stood out here and...

'You are taking her, right?'

'Um...yes.'

'I had you and me as a nice handy pair,' she said, and sighed. 'Now it's you and Zoe, and me and—'

'Cade. Are you going to toss sparks all through the wedding?'

'I'll be good,' Callie said. 'But he really is insufferable. At least you're not any more,' she said as Bonnie finished what she needed to do and limped back to join them. 'Aloof and alone... How insufferable was that? But now our Zoe has made you rejoin the human race, and speaking for the whole hospital we couldn't be more delighted.'

* * *

He went surfing that evening and Zoe was there. Zoe and Luke. They were building the world's biggest sand-castle.

Why hadn't she taken Luke to the beach near the hospital? he wondered. But then he thought, no, the Spit was closer to where Luke's grandma lived. Then he thought maybe Zoe had guessed he'd be surfing here to-night. That was a good thought, and then Luke beamed and bounced up to him and there were no regrets at all.

He put his board down as Luke ran to meet him. He picked him up and swung him round and round until the little boy squealed his delight and then demanded to have a turn on the board as well.

'Where's Bonnie?' Zoe asked, standing and brushing sand from her shorts. He looked at her gorgeous, sandy legs. He looked at the huge sandcastle she and Luke had built, and how happy and relaxed Luke was, and the feeling grew in his heart that this was right, the cards had fallen and he had a stack of aces, or maybe just one ace, but if that ace was Zoe then it was fine by him.

'She's in the Jeep.'

'Bring her down on the sand,' she suggested. 'I'll take care of her while you teach Luke to surf.'

He hadn't intended to teach Luke. Three weeks ago he hadn't intended to teach anyone. But Luke and Zoe were both bright-eyed and expectant and he felt more of his armour shift. What armour? he thought hope-lessly. It was all gone.

'Don't you want to swim yourself?' he asked, and she shook her head.

'I've done a full day on the wards, we had drama after drama and I'm tired. It'll suit me to lie on the sand with Bonnie and watch my…watch *the* men do manly stuff on surfboards.'

He smiled but instead of picking up her slip of the tongue he was suddenly worried. She did look tired.

'It's not too much for you?' he asked.

'No.'

But his concern was still there. 'Zoe, should you be working full time? If it makes you tired…you might be better doing half-shifts.'

She froze. Something on her face said he'd made a major mistake.

'I've had a big day,' she said, carefully and slowly. 'That's all. Every nurse on our ward was tired today.'

'But—'

'There are no buts.'

'Zoe, it's natural to—'

But her irritation was growing. 'Worry? No, it's not,' she snapped. 'One hint that I'm tired and you're worrying whether I should be working full time?' She took a deep breath. 'This is because of the transplant, isn't it? Don't do that to me, Sam.'

'I didn't.'

'You did. If you hadn't known…'

And she was right, he conceded. Gold Coast City was an acute-care hospital catering for a massive population. There were times when they were run off their feet. He was accustomed to colleagues looking tired.

But Zoe was different.

Because of the transplant?

'Will Ryan still get sick after he gets a transplant?' Luke asked in a small voice, and he hauled himself together, but Zoe got there faster.

'Of course he will,' she said, glaring at Sam like

he'd committed murder. 'Just like you get sick. You get colds, you stub your toes on rocks and you fall over and hurt yourself playing footy. Ryan will do those things, too. Right now everyone's being very careful of him, and they'll need to do that until he gets a transplant and for a little while afterwards until he's fully recovered.

'But then he'll be like you and me and all of us. He won't need to be wrapped in cotton wool and he won't have to resign from a full-time job because one day he gets tired. What nonsense. Off you go, the pair of you. Go play in the surf while Bonnie and I have a wee nap because we choose to. Not because we must. Invalids—huh! Off you go, shoo, and don't you dare do that to me again, Sam Webster, ever.'

She lay on the sun-warmed sand with Bonnie and watched Sam teach an eight-year-old to surf.

Luke was a faster learner than she was, but she wasn't envious. She loved watching them. Sam had Luke waist deep in the waves, lying on the board, pushing it into every likely wave and then whooping with Luke as the little boy managed to wobble to his feet and waver the few feet to the shore.

She'd kind of like to be with them but it was nice to lie here and watch them, too, and hug Bonnie and let herself dream. As she'd been dreaming ever since she'd met Sam.

Only now there was a tiny niggle imposing itself on her dream.

'Zoe, should you be working full time?'

The question had slammed her straight back to Adelaide, straight back to Dean.

Zoe, let me carry that. Zoe, it's too cold for you.

Zoe, I don't want you staying up late. This job is far too demanding—remember you have to protect yourself.

Only she hadn't been allowed to protect herself. Dean had done it for her.

If Sam started that nonsense…

He wouldn't.

He might. The way he'd said it…

'If I want to climb Everest, he might try and stop me,' she told Bonnie, and Bonnie looked at her, puzzled.

'Yeah, okay, you have a broken leg and the last thing you want to think about is climbing Everest,' she told Bonnie. 'But how about when your leg is healed and you want to run again, really run, and all your dog friends say, no, don't run because you might hurt your leg again. What's the point of a beautifully-healed leg if you're never allowed to be normal again?'

Bonnie put her big head on her lap and looked dolefully up at her, as if seeing the problem in all its horror. A life without running…

'It won't happen,' Zoe told her, trying to sound sure. Trying to feel sure. 'Sam has too much sense to let it happen. He made one mistake and I've explained and now he won't make it again. He's smart, our Sam. He knows there are invalids and invalids, and we don't fit the job description. We're over it and we want to live.'

He'd overreacted, Sam thought as he held Luke on the board, but so had Zoe. It was okay to worry. It was almost reasonable, especially…the way he was feeling.

If he cared, he'd have to worry. Hell, he'd lost Emily—and he was a cardiologist. He knew bad things happened; he knew how life could turn to death so quickly.

But Zoe wouldn't want that hanging over her for the rest of her life. He could see that.

So...no overt worry. But to ask him not to worry at all...

Care brought worry. He hadn't wanted to care, but caring had been thrust upon him, whether he wanted it or not.

He glanced up the beach to where Zoe was chatting to Bonnie. She *was* tired, he thought, but justifiably. This was still a relatively new job. The kids' ward was hard and he knew today had been frantic, yet she'd contacted Luke's grandma and brought Luke to the beach tonight, pushing herself to make one small boy happy.

And now... She could be lying in the shallows but instead she was intent on making a dog happy.

She was totally, absolutely gorgeous. She was everything he wanted in a woman, and how was a man not to care?

He'd try not to do it overtly, but some things Zoe would need to accept.

She must.

At this time of evening, on a weeknight, this beach was practically deserted, but as Zoe decided maybe she'd best stop watching Sam for a while, stop thinking how drop-dead gorgeous he was and how sexy, she turned her attention to the rest of the beach and realised they weren't the only ones here. A couple of hundred yards along, two kids were digging a hole in the sandy cliff chewed out by the tide. Winter storms had eroded the cliff to form a perilous overhang. There seemed to be some sort of cave behind, and the kids were digging their way in.

Uh-oh. Soft sand. Digging. Even from where she was sitting they made her feel nervous.

Finally she asked Bonnie whether she thought she could manage a short walk. Bonnie thought she could, and they ambled along to see what the kids were doing. They were two almost-grown boys with a project.

A dangerous project.

She edged a bit closer, growing more and more concerned as she realised the level of risk.

'Hi,' she said at last, trying to figure a way to approach this. She'd nursed in paediatrics long enough to known thirteen- or fourteen-year-old kids didn't take kindly to young women telling them what to do, and what authority did she have anyway?

The boys had dug so far in that they were now inside their sandy cave. One stuck his head out and looked at her defiantly.

'Woderyawant?'

Uh-oh. His belligerence was a warning sign all by itself.

'It's a great cave,' she said cautiously. 'But it looks a bit risky. Have you thought about shoring timbers?'

'Wot?'

'Timber supports,' she said. 'All miners use them. Without shoring timbers, these sorts of tunnels cave in all the time. It's a horrible way to die, choking slowly on sand. Yours looks a bit scary. I'd hate you to be buried.'

'This won't fall in,' the kid said scornfully, and Zoe looked at the soft sand and thought maybe diplomacy wasn't the way to go.

'Yes, it will,' she said. 'Soft sand always does.'

'There's tree roots holding it up,' he said belligerently. 'And it goes right in behind the sand. Piss off.'

'The lady's right.'

Zoe had been so intent on the kids and the danger that she hadn't heard Sam come up behind her, but here he was, holding Luke's hand. Both of them were dripping wet. Luke looked excited and interested. Sam looked grim. Had Sam seen where she was going and noticed the risk as well?

Obviously he had.

'Get out,' he said, in a tone that said it was non-negotiable. 'Get out now, or I'll get in there and haul you both out by the scruffs of your dumb necks. This whole thing's about to collapse. Do you want to be buried alive? Out. Now.'

What was it with this guy? If she'd said it they'd have ignored her—she knew it—but there was no way Sam could be ignored. The boys emerged, but they looked sulky and defiant, and she thought, They'll be back. As soon as we're off the beach they'll dig again.

But Sam hadn't finished. He waited until they were clear of the entrance then he bent and checked inside, then leaped lightly up the scarp. There was a dead salt bush right above the boy's cave. That had the roots the boys had been depending on for stability. He grabbed the dead bush by the trunk, hauled and leaned back. The roots came free—and the entire piece of escarpment slid down across the cave entrance.

The *whumph* from the collapsing sand was enough to send a tremor under their feet—and for Zoe to realise how appalling the risk had been.

'Sand goes right into your lungs,' Sam said conversationally. 'You can't stop it. If I catch either of you doing anything so stupid again, I'll get the lifeguards to ban you from the beach all summer.'

'You can't,' one of the boys muttered.

'Try me.'

'It was just a bit of fun,' the other boy said, and Sam relented.

'Yeah, I know, but it was still dumb. I work at the hospital and we see too many kids come in dead. It's not great being dead. I suspect it could be really, really boring. Pack it in, guys.'

They packed it in. The skulked off over the sand hills and Sam and Zoe and Luke were left staring at the collapsed scarp, thinking what could have happened.

Luke bent down to examine the bits of tree trunk in the sand, tugging at a branch that was almost entirely buried.

'They would have died,' the little boy said, horrified, and Sam stooped and lifted him and hugged him.

'Probably not,' he said. 'Probably they would have been buried up to their armpits in sand and they'd have had to stand here all night feeling sillier and sillier. So I scared them a bit too much. I'm sorry I scared you, too.'

'You scared them to stop them being dead.'

'Yes,' he said.

'It must be awful, being dead,' Luke said in a small voice, and Sam hugged a bit harder, and Zoe knew this had suddenly switched from boys and sandhills to one big brother with a failing heart. 'Is it awful?'

'I don't think it is,' Sam said honestly. 'I know I said it might be boring but that was just to scare them. All I know, Luke, mate, is that I'm a doctor and it's my job to stop people being dead. I try everything I possibly can. To watch these kids take risks...'

'They were having fun,' Luke said.

'Dumb fun.'

'Isn't it okay to have fun?'

'Not if it involves risks,' Sam said flatly, and there was something about the way he said it...there was something there that suddenly made Zoe feel uneasy. The qualms of half an hour ago resurfaced.

She didn't want to take risks, she thought—or not many. Not serious risks. But she did want to have fun.

Twelve months ago, when she'd passed her final nursing exam, she'd sent off for some brochures on climbing in Nepal. She'd shown them to Dean.

'We can do this now,' she'd told him excitedly. 'If we save...there's nothing stopping us.'

'Are you kidding? The risks...'

'There can't be all that much risk. I'm not suggesting Everest. An escorted trek below the snow line...'

'And if you get sick?'

'Then I'll die happy,' she'd retorted, which had been a dumb thing to say because he really did think she was risking all. The conversation had stopped there and she'd known, right from that moment, that she wouldn't be marrying Dean.

Like she knew, right now, that there could be no future for her with Sam.

He might change, she told herself, but it felt like a forlorn little hope. There was that look on his face that said some things were non-negotiable. A dead fiancée. No risks.

'Zoe? Are you okay?' he asked. Maybe she looked paler than usual. Yeah, okay, the cave incident had scared her but for him to ask that question...the question that had been hanging over her for years...

Zoe? Are you okay?

'I'm fine,' she snapped, and then fought for and

found a recovery. 'Sorry, yeah, it must have frightened me a bit, too. They were dopes, Luke.'

'I'll ring the council,' Sam told them. 'The over-hang is too large—the storms have really undercut it. They'll get a bobcat along here and knock the top off. Problem solved.'

'Great,' Zoe said, but her 'great' came out flat.

'You didn't really think I should have let them keep digging?' he demanded, incredulous as he heard her intonation, and she shook her head.

'Of course not. Of course you're right, and thank you for sorting it. I just…I just can't help it if I hanker for a tiny bit of risk myself.'

'Not being buried in sand.'

'No, but there are some risks worth taking,' she mut-tered. 'Not dumb ones, but fabulous ones, and I have my whole life to find out what they are.'

CHAPTER SEVEN

SAM DIDN'T UNDERSTAND and she let it go. Maybe she was wrong, she decided. Maybe she was overreacting. Sam was gorgeous and maybe she was stupid for having any qualms at all.

She took Luke home, returned to the hospital and Sam was waiting. He cooked her steak and chips, and they made toe-curling love and she slept in his arms.

He held her tight, possessively, and the niggle of doubt refused to go away.

She was being dumb, she thought. She was being over-sensitive. What Sam had done with the sand cave had been entirely rational, and his talk about risk had simply been reaction.

Relax, she told herself. You're falling for the most gorgeous guy in the universe, so why not let yourself fall?

It was easy to fall when she was in his arms. She could lie here for ever, she thought... And not take risks?

Bonnie whuffled in her basket at the end of the bed and she thought how domestic this was. How wonderful. Life was so good.

Put the doubts aside and soak in wonderful.

Soak in Sam.

* * *

The hospital had no doubts. Sam and Zoe were now an established item. She copped good-natured teasing from all sides, and she was accepted as an even more deeply ingrained member of the Gold Coast team. She worked through the week in a daze of happiness, with Sam popping in and out of her ward—he did have two kids on the ward as patients so there was no reason at all why every kid in the ward seemed primed to make lovey-dovey teasing noises every time he walked in.

Her colleagues sniggered and Zoe blushed—and tried to put away the tiny niggles that had surfaced and were refusing to be suppressed.

Luckily—or maybe unluckily—she was busy. The weather was vacillating from gorgeous to perfect. This was the middle of the northern-hemisphere summer holidays and the Gold Coast was swarming with tourists who did stupid things.

Things like drowning.

Liam Brennan was eleven years old, here with his family from Ireland. His parents had seen the vast, wide expanse of open beach and had elected to swim not in the patrolled part of the main beach but in a secluded area half a mile from the lifesavers' flags.

His parents couldn't swim. Liam could, a little, but not enough to fight the rip that grabbed him and took him out to sea. A local surfer had come to his aid but not fast enough. He was brought into hospital unconscious, and even though Zoe wasn't one of the medics involved in his treatment, she felt the hush through the department and she knew what the outcome would be.

Resuscitating drowning kids was a miracle but more

miracles were needed to stop brain damage caused by interrupted blood supply.

Liam hadn't had that second miracle.

He was on life support, and grief and anger at such needless loss washed through the hospital.

The day after he was brought in, Sam came to find her on the wards.

'I need to speak to you,' he said, and his face was grim. Uh-oh. One look at him and she knew something serious had happened.

'Bonnie?' she said, feeling ill.

'Bonnie's fine,' he said. 'Zoe, I've organised a fill-in for you for a while. Please, we need to talk.'

Bemused, she followed him. She'd thought they'd go into the nurses' station, deserted at the moment, but instead he led her into the lift, down and out to the small garden where he walked Bonnie.

By which time she was starting to feel seriously freaked. What? Images of her parents and siblings flooded into her mind. They'd have contacted her directly if anything dire had happened. Surely?

Or maybe they'd rung the hospital and asked someone close to tell her...

Sam stopped and turned and faced her—and saw her face and swore and grabbed her hands.

'Zoe, no, I didn't mean to scare you. Hell. I didn't think... It's just... I've just come from Liam's bedside— the kid brought in from the near drowning.'

She might have known. He looked sick. Relief on her own account was replaced by sadness for others. *Any man's death diminishes me*... She thought of John Donne's words and she thought how much worse they were when that death was that of a child.

This man spent his life fighting for children's lives. To lose one because of ignorance was particularly gut wrenching. There were signs up all over the Gold Coast, including in the airport itself. *Swim Between the Flags.* Nearly every drowning here was that of a tourist who thought the gorgeous surf looked harmless. The locals knew the safe places. Tourists had no idea.

'We're about to turn off life support,' Sam said, and he gripped her hands harder.

She held him just as hard and then tugged him close so she was pressed against him.

'I'm so sorry.'

'Aren't we all?' He held her for a long moment, his chin resting on her hair. 'But, Zoe, this isn't about that. I mean…I'm not here for comfort. I've faced kids' deaths before.'

'But not got used to them,' she said, still holding him.

'No.'

She held him for a long, long moment. This was a man who walked alone, she thought, but alone wasn't working. He tried to be dispassionate but it didn't work. A child's death defeated him.

'What?' she said at last. 'Sam, what made you come and organise me to be taken off the ward?'

'I need you.'

'Yeah, of course you do.' She pulled away a little and tried a smile. 'I'm a very useful person. I can see that. But why now?'

'I need you to talk to Liam's parents about organ donation.'

She stilled.

'It's a huge thing to ask,' he said softly into her hair. 'And it's your choice. No one knows I'm asking you to do it. You're free to say no, and there'll be no mention of it ever again. No thought of it. It's just...'

'Just what?' she said in a scared little voice she couldn't control, a voice that had him pulling away, holding her at arm's length.

'Hell, Zoe, I can't... I'm sorry. Forget I said—'

'Say it,' she said, and she had herself under control again. Sort of.

'Liam's parents are facing withdrawal of life support. I've been with them. They've been approached by the donor organ team. Our counsellor, Sarah, is good. She's incredibly sensitive, no pressure, and she'll back right off if they don't want to go ahead. But Liam's dad wants to donate, very badly. He keeps saying something good has to come out of this mess, and I know, from past experience, that it'll help long term if it does. Only Liam's mum is wavering. Mary keeps saying it'll only drag out other parents' misery. She says transplants fail eventually. She's been watching her son die for two days and all she sees is that transplants make that waiting longer.'

'So you want me...'

'If you could bear it, you could give them a gift,' he said gently. 'The gift of hope, that their son's death could mean the gift of life for someone like you.'

And he said *someone like you* in such a way...

He loved her. She found herself blinking back tears in a sudden rush of emotion that had nothing to do with the death of one little boy but everything to do with the vulnerability of this man before her, and the knowledge that he'd lost and closed himself to the world but now was opening up again.

He was needing her?

It was a heady emotion, and she shouldn't be crying, but there was Liam's death as well, and Emily's death, and suddenly she found herself thinking of the twenty-year-old kid who'd crashed his car the night before her transplant. She shouldn't know the identity of her donor but it was pretty hard not to know.

He'd given her the gift of life. Could she share back?

Life was so precious. Life was standing in the morning sun, with the sea in the background, with this man asking her to share her story.

He was asking her to share more.

There were still doubts—she knew there were—but at this moment there were no doubts at all.

Liam's parents wished for reassurance she could give them. If she could, she'd give them their son's life back, but some things were impossible.

Instead she'd give them what this man asked of her. Faith in hope.

She was perfect.

Sam stood in the background while Zoe talked softly to Liam's parents, showed them her scar, talked them through what had happened to her, talked them through where she was now, her hopes for the future—she even showed them a corny picture she'd made him take with her phone, of her first wobbling stand-up on his surfboard.

'I can do anything I like now,' she told them. 'I have my whole life in front of me but, you know, there's not a day I don't think of the boy who gave me my kidney. The boy whose parents' loss meant my parents didn't have to face that loss. The boy I'll love for ever, because he's part of me.'

'Do you have to be…careful?' Liam's mother whispered, holding Zoe's phone and looking at the blurry photo.

'No,' she said, and suddenly she was almost fierce. 'At least, not any more than I ought to be even if I hadn't had a transplant. Do you have a clear image of Liam on that last day, on the beach?'

'I… Yes,' his mother whispered. 'Of course.'

'And he was happy?'

'Yes,' his dad said, with a fierceness that matched Zoe's. 'He was in heaven. He had the whole beach, sand, sea, sun on his face. He used my phone to send pictures to his mates, boasting of how he was in Australia in the surf. We were mucking round in the waves; he was standing on my shoulders, diving. It was the best…'

'That's what I want,' Zoe said as the big man's face crumpled and as his wife moved to hold him and Sam moved to hold her. 'I want the best. Liam and I…we're going to go out happy.'

'We shouldn't have…' the man said, and Zoe shrugged Sam off and reached and grabbed the guy's shoulders.

'Never say that,' she said. 'It was a freak wave. It could have happened between the flags; it could have happened anywhere. Liam died having the best holiday of his life, and if you decide on organ donation then others will have the best holidays of their lives, too. But right now others don't matter. This is all about Liam, all about you. You talk about it and you make the right decision for you and for Liam.' She hugged them both.

'Sam and I are leaving you now,' she told them. 'This decision is yours, but know that we'll be thinking of you every step of the way, as almost everyone in this hospital is. No blame,' she said again, even more fiercely. 'You do what you need to do for the future. You do what you need to for Liam. You'll know what that is because you love Liam, he's your son, and whatever you decide, whatever the future holds, that love lasts for ever.'

Sam guided her out into the corridor. He closed the door on the grieving parents and then he took her into his arms and kissed her.

It was a long, loving kiss, a kiss of affirmation, of strength, of healing, and when he finally drew away Zoe knew that Sam wanted her as no man had ever wanted her.

He loved her.

And she let herself be loved. The emotion of the last few moments had been heart-wrenching. She let herself lean on his chest, taking strength from him, feeling his heartbeat, feeling…him.

It couldn't last. They were in a main hospital corridor. He was in his gorgeous suit, consulting cardiologist, and she was in her nurse's scrubs.

She needed to blow her nose. Somehow she managed to tug away, to find a tissue and blow, hard.

When she finished he was grinning at her, and a couple of orderlies walked past and grinned, too, and she thought she may as well stand on the rooftop and declare they were engaged.

Engaged? There was a strong word.

Scary? Definitely scary, but the way he was looking at her… Engaged? Definitely possible.

If he asked, would she say yes?

Not yet, she thought, suddenly panicked. There were still doubts. There was still…life.

She thought of Liam's mum's words.

'Do you have to be careful?'

No.

So should she fling herself into Sam's arms and stay there? Surely that wasn't being careful?

He was gorgeous. He was kind and clever and capable. If she took him home, her mum and dad would almost swoon with delight.

They'd think he was safe.

'Dr Webster?' It was Callie; of course it was Callie. The lady was almost a part of the walls in this hospital—or maybe it was just that she was a friend and Zoe was aware that she cared for her and was watching with interest to see what would happen.

'Sarah's reporting that Liam's parents want to go ahead with organ donation,' she said. 'Sam, they'd like you with them when they turn off life support.'

'I'll come,' Sam said.

'And they said to tell you thank you,' Callie said, eyeing Zoe warmly. 'Zoe, only Sam and I know what you just did, but we thank you, too. I guess…Sam has just been thanking you personally?'

'I… Yes.'

'Are you okay to go back to the wards? I'll make your excuses if you need time out.'

'I'm fine,' Zoe said, and managed a bright smile. 'Just a bit…'

'Discombobulated,' Callie said. 'Gutted about Liam's death, like we all are—but with a few layers of emotional confusion on top. Sam, let the lady go. Give her some space.'

'Thank you,' Zoe said, with real gratitude, and gave Sam a quick, hard hug because what he was about to do was one of the hardest things a doctor would ever need to do.

She turned and headed back to her sick kids.

A girl had to do something. Discombobulation didn't begin to describe it.

Alice's wedding was truly lovely. It took place in a tiny chapel in the grounds of one of the Gold Coast's most spectacular beachside hotels. Alice and her brand-new husband were spectacularly in love. The reception was in the hotel grounds overlooking the beach. The weather was balmy, the band was fantastic, and Sam took Zoe in his arms and danced with her, and she thought heaven was right here, right now.

But she felt funny. She'd woken feeling a bit off. She'd shrugged it off as unimportant—there was no way she was missing this wedding—but the more the night wore on the more she felt like she was floating in some sort of fuzzy, hazy dream. It was like she'd been drinking, she thought, trying to keep a handle on what was happening, but she'd had half a glass of champagne early and had switched to mineral water because of the way she was feeling.

Could hormones do this to you?

'Are you okay?' Sam asked at one stage as the number the band was playing came to an end more suddenly than she'd expected and she found herself stumbling. He had to catch her and hold her up.

'I'm fine.' She smiled up at him. 'More than fine.'

'You look more than fine,' he said, and stooped to kiss her. 'You think we should go for a quick walk down to the beach?'

'How about a slow walk down to the beach?' she

said, because the way she was feeling there was no way fast was coming into it.

'If you guys are escaping, can I come with you?'

Callie. Of course it was Callie. She was looking fabulous, in glorious scarlet, in a dress that made Zoe's home-made effort look…well, home-made, but Zoe didn't begrudge her. In the few short weeks Zoe had been at the hospital this woman had become a real friend. She was a solid friend of Sam's as well, so not at all a third wheel.

Even though Zoe suspected Sam might feel she was right now. The way he was holding her…

Too bad, Zoe thought, and realised she was grateful for Callie's presence. She was feeling strange. The way Sam was looking at her was making her feel even more weird. She felt weak at the knees and if Sam took her into his arms in the moonlight and asked her to marry him—as Dean had done on just such a moonlit night— she might even say yes.

'Of course you can come,' Zoe said, before Sam could say a word. 'Are you up for a paddle? I'm so hot.'

'It's not hot,' Sam said.

'It is so,' Callie retorted. 'And if you're not hot now, you go and stand next to Dr Hotshot Cade Coleman. That man is an arrogant bottom-feeder.' Her anger seemed almost palpable.

'You mean he knocked you back?' Sam asked, and Callie glared at Sam and Zoe stared at Sam in shock.

'Sam!'

'Callie's a mate,' Sam said, holding Zoe but smiling at Callie. 'Mates don't take offence.'

'No,' Callie said. 'They don't. And it's true he might have just told me where to get off.' She giggled suddenly, her anger fading. 'Okay, I might have just had one champagne too many, and there might just have been a dare from the theatre girls involved. Whoops,' she said. 'Now I've shocked your country mouse, Sam.'

'I'm not his country mouse,' Zoe said with an attempt at dignity, and wondered just how many champagnes she'd had. She was sure it had only been half a glass. If she hadn't been among friends she'd suspect something had been put in her drink.

'Are you okay?' Callie asked sharply. Of all the questions Zoe hated, that was the worst.

'I'm fine. I want a paddle.'

'I'm not interrupting anything?' Callie asked, and Zoe figured Callie knew very well that she was but she was interrupting anyway. And Zoe was grateful.

'Of course not,' she said, and linked one arm into Callie's and one arm into Sam's and they headed for the beach.

Cade watched them go.

Zoe was almost as new at this hospital as he was, he thought grimly, but she was one of the team already. He, however, was an outsider. He was always an outsider.

Once he'd used women as an escape from himself, but that had been one woman and one baby ago. No more.

And tonight...Callie Richards had come on to him. First she'd insulted him, telling him within days of his arrival at Gold Coast City to steer clear of Zoe Payne. Now, tonight, she'd apologised, asked him to dance and had then made it very clear that if he wanted more...

He didn't want more. He was here to do a job, steer

clear of gossip and scandal, retrieve a reputation, block out the past and get on with life.

He shouldn't have come tonight.

He stared after the group of three, Zoe in the middle with Callie and Sam on either side of her, weaving down to the beach, and he suddenly felt an almost overwhelming surge of longing for…something.

The ability to be just a friend?

It wasn't going to happen. Not back in the States. Not here.

He watched them disappear into the darkness and he headed off to find the bride's parents and make his excuses. There was an emergency back at the hospital—he was sure of it.

He wanted an emergency right now.

The water felt delicious on Zoe's toes. She kicked off her sandals, lifted her long skirt to knee length and let the waves wash over and over.

Cool was good. Cool was glorious.

If only the fuzz would disappear.

Callie and Sam were talking behind her, talking to her, but she wasn't sure what they were saying. The night was getting blurrier and blurrier.

'It's time for the speeches,' Sam decreed at last, stepping in between waves to tug her out. He and Callie had left their shoes on and she couldn't figure it out. It was so hot. 'Come on back, love.' Then, as she didn't move fast enough and there was a wave coming he wanted to avoid, he tugged her and she staggered and would have fallen.

She didn't. He swept her into his arms and up to dry sand while she tried to get her bearings.

'I'm okay,' she muttered, before he even asked, but even as she said it, she knew she wasn't.

'Zoe?' It was Callie, reacting to the strange way her words had come out, maybe reacting to Sam's snapped concern. Sam was holding her in his arms. Callie reached for her hand and winced. 'Sam, she's burning.'

'I'm fine,' she said, but the night was spinning. 'I'm really, really fine.'

'You're ill,' Sam snapped. 'Zoe, what the...? Why didn't you tell us?'

'I'm fine,' she repeated, like a stubborn mantra. How could she not be fine? Sam was holding her. She was in Sam's arms and the night was drifting away   and she wasn't fine at all.

CHAPTER EIGHT

SHE WAS SUFFERING from influenza, courtesy of one bout of mouth-to-mouth resuscitation on a guy who had been suffering from flu before he'd had his heart attack.

Infection was an occupational hazard for medics. It was an occupational hazard for Zoe now that she was a healthy member of the workforce.

But she wasn't healthy now. She spent twenty-four hours in bed in her apartment. Sam and Callie and nearly every other medic Zoe worked with popped in and out, and Bonnie slept on the end of her bed. Zoe felt not quite as ghastly when Bonnie was with her, but she still felt ghastly and bed rest didn't work.

After twenty-four hours, Sam listened to her breathing and demanded chest X-rays. Pneumonia. She then found herself in the third-floor general medical ward. That wasn't very different because the same faces were around her and the same dog was on the end of her bed, but there were intravenous drips and injections and fuss.

She hated fuss.

'Don't tell my parents.' She must have said it a dozen times to Sam and finally he made a poster-sized sign and hung it in the place reserved over her bed for the

'Nil by mouth' sign used for surgical patients—only Zoe's sign said: 'Don't Tell Mum and Dad.'

It was a joke, but she couldn't bear it if her parents knew—for Sam was fussing enough for both of them.

'Why didn't you tell me you felt foul?'

'I don't tell people,' she retorted. 'I don't want fuss. I just want to be normal.'

'It's normal to tell people you're ill.'

'It's not normal to be ill. Sam, leave it. This is not a big deal.'

'This is a big deal,' he said stubbornly. 'I should never have let you—'

'What? Breathe for the guy?' Three days on, she was recovered enough to argue. She'd had it out with herself. She'd known the guy had had flu. She'd had the choice—to wait for a mask and risk him dying, or breathe when he'd needed breath.

What else could she have done? Cardiac compressions while Sam breathed? That made no sense, because Sam was so much stronger than she was.

'I could have done both,' Sam said, for what must be the tenth time, and she was fed up.

To tell the truth, she was fed up with more than Sam's self-blame. She didn't like being back in hospital as a patient—she didn't like it one bit, and she didn't like the way Sam was treating her. It was flu, for heaven's sake, not plague.

'We need to put you on the surgical roster when you're recovered,' Sam said. 'You need to stay out of medical wards. You don't need to be exposed to any more viruses.'

'I'm a nurse,' she said. 'Exposure to viruses is part of my job.'

'You could have died.'

'And so could you if you'd caught pneumonia.'

'I wouldn't.'

'You know very well you could,' she snapped. 'I caught flu and it turned to pneumonia. I've been unlucky. And if you think that this has anything to do with me having a renal transplant—and I know that's what you're thinking, Sam Webster, you have it written all over your face—you can think again. Poor frail little Zoe. I've been there, Sam, and I'm never going there again.'

'I understand that,' he said carefully, 'but you need to be careful.'

'There's care and there's stupid. My mum and dad refused to let me use public transport so I couldn't visit my friends. The mango thing was only part of the stupid restrictions they placed on my life. And Dean…Dean even started carrying antibiotic wipes and recleaning my cutlery at restaurants before I ate. When I told him to stop, he did it by stealth. The last straw was when he rang them and asked them to do it before I got there. The waiter came racing out just before I ate with a *mea culpa* because he'd forgotten. If Dean knew how close he came to wearing my soup…'

He smiled but it was a worried smile. 'I understand how worried he must have been.'

'Do you?' she said dangerously. 'You're justifying bug-kill wipes?'

'No,' he said. 'But I can see why he was worried.'

'I want to go to Nepal,' she said, and he looked at her like she'd announced she was heading for a Mars landing.

'Sorry?'

'Nepal,' she said, watching his face for his reaction and not liking what she was seeing. 'I told you—it's on my list. You can walk all the way to the Annapurna base camp without needing specialist training. Not now,' she said as she saw his face. 'I may need a couple of years to save, but I will get there.'

'Good for you.'

'There's a nice patronising statement. That's what Mum used to say when I was sick and I'd say as soon as I feel better I'm taking the train to Melbourne to see the new Kylie show. Good for you, she'd say, and then when I was feeling better she'd give me the latest Kylie DVD and organise three nice girls to come over and watch it with me. Only not a fourth girl who was my best friend because Robin kept getting colds and Mum wouldn't let her near. Robin got so fed up that we stopped being friends.'

'I'm sorry.'

'I don't want you to be sorry.' It was practically a yell and the sound of her own voice brought her up short.

What was she doing? What was she saying? She was risking everything. But she felt like she was on a runaway train. The doubts had built to the point where she had to have this out with him, and there seemed to be no going back.

'You do think I got this flu because I had a renal transplant,' she said, feeling ill as she said it. 'You don't want me to work with kids who might be infectious. What sort of nurse does that make me?'

'It doesn't make you any sort of a nurse,' he said, and raked his hand through his hair. 'Zoe, I know it's unreasonable but how can I stop worrying?'

'You can just…stop.'

'Worrying's about caring. I didn't want to care but I don't seem to have a choice.'

'You don't have to.'

'Like that's possible.' Once again those long, strong fingers raked his hair and she could see his distress. 'Zoe, I lost Emily because I didn't care enough. I should have walked into the surf, picked her up bodily and dragged her out of there. She was being unbelievably stupid. She was crazy that night and I was angry and turned away and made the decision not to care.'

'But you did care,' she said quietly. 'You cared and you cared, but it was Emily's life, Emily's decision, and she had the right to do what she did. Like I have the right to nurse a kid with a cold. Only I'm not stupid, Sam. I know the added risks I have because of my transplant and catching flu isn't one of them.'

'So flu turns into pneumonia…'

'Pneumonia is a known complication for healthy people, too.'

'You collapsed.'

'So I made a mistake. I suspected I was ill,' she admitted. 'I wanted to go to the wedding. I wanted to dance with you.'

'Would you have pushed so hard if you hadn't had the transplant?' It was a harsh question—an accusation.

She lay back on her pillows and glared. She was still weak. She still wanted to have the occasional weep. What she needed right now was to let him hold her, curl up in his arms, let him nurture her, love her…care for her?

She did not want to be cared for.

'Possibly not,' she conceded at last. 'I've spent half my life not feeling well. My friends and family have spent half my life telling me not to do things and I've spent my life aching to do things regardless. So, yes, I was feeling foul but there was no way I was missing dancing with you.'

He managed a smile at that, and then he touched her cheek, a feather-light touch that did crazy things to her insides. He'd come to see her between visiting his own patients. He looked gorgeous. He smiled at her and she thought he was melt material and she so wanted to melt.

'You know, I think I've fallen in love with you, Zoe,' he said softly. 'I never thought I'd say that again—I'd never thought I could. But you're lovely and cute and brave and funny, and Bonnie loves you and I love what you're doing with your life...'

But there was that one word that made her doubts grow even stronger.

Brave.

'You love that I'm being brave?' She shouldn't say it. She'd said enough. Enough, enough, enough. She was risking so much.

But there were ghosts in her past and one of her ghosts was Dean. Dean had gone to primary school with her, he'd been her friend, he'd been her constant companion.

Dean had loved the sick kid.

It had become his identity, Zoe realised. He'd been boyfriend to the sick kid. He'd loved caring for her, he'd loved it when she'd been in hospital and he could spend hours choosing movies for them to watch, hours worrying about her, fielding her friends, telling them to limit their time with her.

Dean the protector... She'd loved him back, she'd thought, though she'd had to push back the occasional feelings that he was cloying; that he was a barrier to the outside world rather than a conduit. It had only been after the final transplant that she'd realised it was Invalid Zoe who Dean loved. Healthy Zoe wasn't an option.

And here was another guy telling her he loved her—because she was brave.

'I'm not brave,' she muttered. 'I'm normal.'

'You're not normal. You're Zoe.'

'I am normal,' she said, and suddenly she was yelling, which was really inappropriate because she was in a hospital ward and there were people going past in the corridor and the door was open, but all of a sudden she didn't care. 'I'm completely normal. I'm cured. I'm one hundred per cent normal and if you want to fall in love then you fall in love with the normal Zoe and you stop caring!'

'And let you plunge into the surf like Emily did?'

'No. Not like Emily. How can you compare us?' And then she thought about it. 'Or maybe yes. Maybe, yes, like Emily. I'm an adult. I should be able to make my own decisions, stupid or not.'

'You don't think the person who donated your kidney deserves better?'

She stilled at that. Suddenly it seemed the whole world stilled.

That was such a question…

It was a question she asked herself almost every day. She had the answer—sort of. But how to say it to Sam?

'I'm sorry,' he said, before she could find a reply. He was sorry, too. She saw the flash of regret in his eyes, the wish that he could take the question back, but it was out there in the open, demanding an answer.

He deserved an answer, she thought, as Dean had deserved an answer. She'd tried so hard to explain it to him and he hadn't got it. She'd left him hurt, and even her mum's recent phone call to tell her that he was now going out with Monica, who'd come off her motorbike and broken her leg, hadn't alleviated the knowledge that he'd been there for her and in the end she'd had to hurt him to set herself free.

And now she was looking at another man—and the feeling in her stomach was sick and cold.

'You don't think the person who donated your kidney deserves better?'

Dean had flung that at her, too, after the transplant when she'd wanted to go dancing. Slightly differently but in the same form.

'Someone died for you, Zoe. You have a duty to take care of yourself.'

Put the anger away, she told herself fiercely. Just say it. Say what needs to be said.

'If the boy who died—or his parents who made the decision to donate his organs—had wanted his kidney to be kept in perpetuity, they'd have donated it to the museum,' she managed, trying desperately to keep a lid on emotions that were threatening to overwhelm her. 'They'd have put it in formaldehyde and kept it safe.

'Instead, they elected to use it to let me live. Live, Sam, not wrap myself in cotton wool. I don't want to sit in a jar of formaldehyde for the rest of my life. I want to do every single thing that normal people do. There are things I need to be careful of—I know that. I'm following every single one of my doctor's orders but the last thing he said to me before I left Adelaide was to get out there and have fun. Live life to the full, he said, and that's exactly what I'm doing, except I know my limitations, which is why I'm saying now that I'm recovering from pneumonia and I'm tired and I need to go to sleep. So if you could leave, please...'

'You want me to leave?' He sounded incredulous.

'Yes.'

'Zoe...'

'Sam, I can't do this,' she said miserably. 'I will not be smothered with care. I walked away from Adelaide because I wanted to be free. You're the most gorgeous guy I've ever met—and, okay, I'll admit it, I'm as near to falling in love with you as makes no difference. I also happen to be besotted with your dog, but I won't commit to being smothered. I made the decision that I want to be free and that decision still stands. Back off, Sam, and leave me be.'

'You really mean that?'

'Yes.'

He stood and stared down at her, his face tight and strained. For a long moment there was nothing but silence—a silence that held all the hopes of what might have been but also the knowledge of what had to happen.

Sam was a man who couldn't keep fear at bay, she thought bleakly. He was a man who'd loved once and lost. He was a man who, if he let himself care at all, couldn't help caring too much.

She was a woman who'd had enough of care.

'You'd throw away what we have,' he said at last, and he couldn't disguise his anger, 'because I care.'

'If I must.'

'That's crazy.'

'So I'm crazy, but it's taken me all my life to get this

crazy and I'm not going back now.' She took a deep breath, fighting for control. Fighting to get this right. One part of her was sure she was right. The other was screaming that she was nuts.

But she needed to ignore the part of her that was screaming in anguished protest, the part that was looking at Sam's confusion and wanting to say it didn't matter, she'd love him care and all. For she was not going back to being the Zoe who'd been cared for until she'd felt suffocated.

Why had she come all this way if she was going to sink back into that same sweet trap now? She would not.

So say it and get it over with, she thought, and say it fast, before the anger and confusion she saw on his face broke her resolve.

'Sam, you're awesome,' she said. 'But I don't want this.'

'Because I care.'

'I know it's dumb but yes. There it is. I'm sorry, but enough.'

'Fine,' he said, and his face was rigid with tension—anger? 'Maybe you're right and this is the sensible option. I'm not rational when it comes to relationships any more. I can't do it without fear so it's best if I stand back. I'll wish you luck with your trek in Nepal. I'll expect emails at every summit.'

And he stepped away and it almost killed her. He was back to being consultant cardiologist and colleague. He was backing to the door, backing away to return to his patients, backing out of her life.

But that was what she wanted—right?

No! But it was too late to back down now.

'You're wise for the two of us,' he said, and his

voice had changed. The shield had come up again, she thought. He was under control. 'There's no surfing for you this Sunday—even you need to admit you need time to get over this—but as of next Sunday we'll start again. But that's it, Zoe. Lessons and nothing else. You're right—it's the wisest call for both of us.'

'Are you out of your mind?'

Callie was sitting on the end of Zoe's bed—actually, she was practically bouncing with incredulous indignation. 'You have the sexiest doctor in this hospital making a beeline for your bed and you tell him you want to go and climb mountains?'

'He's kind,' Zoe said, knowing as an argument it made no sense, and Callie practically gibbered.

'Yes,' she said. Or was that yelled? 'He's kind. He's toe-curlingly lovely and he's one of the best doctors we have and he's kind to his socks.'

'Then why aren't you interested in him yourself?' Zoe asked, momentarily distracted.

'A, because I'm not interested in relationships, I'm only interested in sex,' Callie said bluntly. 'I've had all the intimate relationships I'm ever going to have. But, even if I wasn't jaded, B, Sam has never looked at me that way. He's never looked at any woman that way since Emily died. And, C, Sam's my friend and I'm not messing with that for the world. But kind? Zoe, you have no idea how important that is. To knock back a man because he's kind…'

'I'm done with kindness.'

How bad did that sound? Zoe thought. She sounded like a sulky child who didn't like her chosen-with-love Christmas gift. She was being totally unreasonable. She also knew she could well regret what she was doing for the rest of her life, but still she had to do it.

'You know, getting over a kidney transplant takes all sorts of courage,' Callie said gently, changing track, and she winced.

'This isn't about a kidney transplant.'

'I think it is.' Callie went on, inexorably. 'Like Sam's worry is more because he lost Emily. You two have ghosts, but if you worked on it, maybe your ghosts could indulge in mutual trauma therapy while the real Sam and the real Zoe went at it like rabbits.'

'Callie!'

'Just saying,' Callie said, and hauled herself off the bed. 'But ghosts are everywhere and they need to be catered for. I have a few of my own that mess with my life. Meanwhile, I need to go—I have patients to see. Uncomplicated kids with their ghosts just forming. But think about it, Zoe. Are you going to let ghosts stand in the way of grabbing Sam and holding on?'

'I suspect you know very well that ghosts can't be put aside at will,' Zoe said, watching the shadows on her friend's face. 'You don't hold on to anyone. And coming on to Cade like you did…is that your ghosts?'

'Yeah, now we're getting personal,' Callie said, and managed a wry smile. 'I suspect all our ghosts could have a field day together. Mine and yours and Sam's.'

'And Cade's?' This was better, Zoe thought. Talking about other ghosts than hers.

'Cade's?'

'You know he's carrying baggage, and that baggage is striking off yours. The sparks at the wedding—'

'Were the result of champagne and a dare and nothing else,' Callie said soundly. 'Cade Coleman is an ar-

rogant low-life and I want nothing more to do with him.
Unlike Sam…'

'They're both just guys,' Zoe said, gloom descending again. 'But you're right, maybe the ghosts are too strong for all of us.'

Callie left and she was alone with her ghosts.

She lay and let them drift.

Her ghosts had made her set rules, she thought.
Those rules were important. But had those rules messed with the most important thing that had ever happened to her? Sam?

'I can't help it,' she whispered. 'I can't be smothered.
We'd both be unhappy. It's best this way.'

Sure it was. So why did she cover her face with her pillow and close her eyes to try and stop the ghosts from shouting?

'Why the long face? You're better out of it and you know it.'

Sam and Cade had just spent a fraught two hours with a neonate with a heart defect. Rebecca Louise Hayden was six hours old, and for a while it had looked as if she'd get no older. But finally they'd had her stabilised enough for Sam to speak to her distraught parents and tell them that this was a long road, Rebecca had more surgery in front of her, more challenges, but that he and Cade were cautiously optimistic.

Now the two men stood over the incubator in the preemie ward, looked down at the scrap of life that was Rebecca—such a big name for a tiny thread of life—and Cade unexpectedly brought up Sam's love life. Or lack of it.

How the hell did he know that Zoe had ditched him?

Sam thought morosely. But, then, how did anyone in this hospital know anything? Osmosis? Someone should write a thesis.

'Yeah, relationships only cause problems,' he agreed, and turned to look out the ward window. From the third floor you could see the sea. It was glittering in the afternoon sun and he had an almost irresistible urge to walk out of the hospital and go ride a wave.

He couldn't walk away from Rebecca. He couldn't walk away from his work.

He had to walk away from Zoe.

'You're better without them, mate,' Cade said, and Sam glanced at the guy on the other side of the cot. He thought how hard Cade had worked with him to get this tiny baby to the other side of the survival odds and he thought there was stuff in this guy's past as well.

'So you've had three wives, six kids and five mistresses?'

'Not quite,' Cade said, and smiled, only the smile was a bit grim. 'Enough, though.'

'You want to try surfing. It helps.'

'Nothing helps.'

'Sheesh,' Sam said. 'Eight wives?'

He got a grin. He was starting to like this guy. Cade held the rest of the staff at arm's length—he seemed prickly and arrogant—but Sam saw the care that went into Cade's interaction with his little patients and he sensed the arrogance was a shield.

So many shields.

'You still teaching Zoe?' Cade asked.

'Um…yeah.'

'You want me to join your surfing lessons?'

'No,' he said, before his mind could talk sense.

Cade's grin grew wider. 'So you still hold some hope.'

'Not much.'

'You give up and you're dead,' Cade said, and his gaze went back to tiny Rebecca. 'You fight and fight and fight until you can't fight any longer.'

'And then you come to Australia?'

Cade's smile faded.

'Not your business,' he muttered. 'Okay, here's the deal. You stay out of my private concerns and I'll stay out of yours.'

'I will teach you to surf,' Sam said. 'But not with Zoe.'

'I'll buy myself a board and teach myself to surf.' Cade put a gloved hand through the incubator port and touched the tiny girl's cheek—a feather touch—one large finger against a face that was smaller than his palm. 'Independence...you fight for yourself right from the start. It never stops and the sooner you accept it the better for everyone.'

'Rebecca needed us.'

'So she did,' Cade said. 'And we helped and now we back off.'

Zoe's convalescence lasted more than a week. She had a couple of bad days when she realised she wasn't eligible for sick leave yet due to still being on her probation period at the hospital. She thought she'd not be paid and she'd end up eating home-brand pasta for a month, but come payday her bank account was healthy. It appeared that because she'd caught flu from giving CPR to a Gold Coast City patient her time off was covered by the hospital. The paperwork had been organised by Sam.

He was still in the background. He was still dropping Bonnie off at her apartment every morning, but he wasn't staying. In, out, gone.

She tried not to mind. She and Bonnie recovered together. They slept. They took gentle walks along the beach. They sat in the morning sun and shared ice cream, and they treated themselves with care.

They'd both rather that Sam was with them. Zoe only had to look at Bonnie when she heard footsteps approaching—how fast her big head swivelled and the way she sort of drooped when it wasn't Sam—to know how much Bonnie loved him, and she tried not to, but she felt exactly the same.

The ghosts were yelling she was crazy, crazy, crazy.

'You're never satisfied,' she told them. 'What do you want me to do? Be cosseted for the rest of my life? Is that what you want?'

They didn't answer. Ghosts made lousy communicators. They were all accusation and nothing else.

Sunday was the hardest. She wasn't fit enough for a surfing lesson; she knew she wasn't, but Sam was going anyway, taking Bonnie with him. He dropped in to pick up Bonnie's flags and trampoline bed.

She watched them go and she felt...desolate.

He surfed and he thought of Zoe.

How could he stop caring?

He couldn't. He just...couldn't. Emily's death had hit him too hard for him to stand back and take risks.

Everyone took risks. He knew that. For him to say Zoe shouldn't work with kids who might be infectious had been over the top. He knew that, too. He should say it to her, but it wouldn't make a difference. It nearly killed him that she'd caught pneumonia and he knew that the next time she was in harm's way he'd react exactly the same.

How to stand back and let the woman he loved take risks?

He'd crowded her, he'd scared her, but it was Zoe's problem as well as his, he thought. He cared too much and she didn't want care.

Catch 22. There was no solution but to surf.

He didn't go far out. He was too aware of Bonnie lying on her trampoline bed, surrounded by Zoe's crazy flags.

The flags made him smile.

Zoe cared.

The perfect wave swept up behind him and he missed it.

He swore and rolled one eighty degrees so he was lying under his board rather than on top of it. He stayed underwater until it was necessary to surface if he was to breathe. He surfaced spluttering, hoping he'd vented enough spleen, but his spleen wasn't vented.

He missed another wave.

'How can I love her and not care?' he demanded of the universe, but the universe didn't answer. In his experience it rarely did.

Impasse. There was no solution at all.

CHAPTER NINE

WORK WAS A welcome relief. It was great to be back on the wards, Zoe thought, even if ward work came with sympathy that the promising affair between Zoe Payne and Sam Webster seemed to have fizzled out.

She met him occasionally on the ward. They greeted each other as warmly as both could manage, aware that every eye was on them, but it was strained and by Wednesday Zoe was starting to wonder if she should request a transfer to one of the adult wards. Somewhere a paediatric cardiologist was unlikely to visit.

But then she wouldn't see him at all—and that hurt. Everything hurt.

'What's happening with Bonnie?' she asked as he finished examining a little boy who'd been admitted with rheumatic fever, who'd recovered but was showing signs of heart strain.

'She's back on the wards, too,' he told her.

'Back?'

'Her day job while I work is spending time with patients who need her. There's an old lady in the trauma unit. She and her husband were in a car accident three weeks ago and her husband died. Bonnie's asleep on her bed. Hospital rules say basket on the floor even for companion animals but no one's shifting Bonnie.'

'That's lovely,' Zoe whispered. 'Bonnie's awesome.'

'She's not the only lady who's awesome,' Sam said and left, with her staring after him.

How could she not want him to care? Was she out of her mind?

But the memories of the smothering were too strong, too real for her to put them aside. She could cast herself on his chest right now, she thought, and the webs of care would go round her again and she'd wake up feeling strangled. She knew she would.

And yet she felt terrible. Her family may have smothered her during her years of illness but at least they'd been there. They were still there, she told herself, but it didn't help. Why did she feel so gut-wrenchingly, desolately alone?

'Katie Foster's wet her bed,' her colleague Hannah told her, cutting across her chain of bleak thoughts. 'And she's mortified. Strain does bad things to kids. You want to read her a story while I change the sheets?'

'Of course,' Zoe said, and went to read to a mortified Katie, but while she did she thought...

Strain did bad things to kids.

Strain was doing bad things to her.

Wednesday night and she was going nuts. After work she walked on the beach near the hospital but it wasn't enough. There were too many tourists, too many people, not enough space for her thoughts.

On impulse she took her car—it only took three attempts to start—bought fish and chips and headed out to the Seaway to eat them.

It'd be lovely out there. This late midweek there'd only be the odd surfer.

That surfer might be Sam, but she carefully put that thought aside. If it was Sam she could sit in the sand hills and watch from a distance. He didn't have to know she was there.

He wasn't there. She seemed to have the beach to herself, except for a couple of kids far along the beach. She settled on a sand hill and ate her fish and chips and thought how Dean would have told her off for eating fatty food, and she ate a few more chips in his honour. And then she thought of Sam and she defiantly ate a few more.

'I don't want anyone caring,' she said out loud, and it sounded stupid. It was stupid. And bleak.

She wouldn't mind compromising.

But Sam wasn't interested in compromising, she told herself. It was all or nothing. He wouldn't even want her nursing kids who might have a cold. Huh!

Kids.

She glanced along the beach to where the kids were playing, and she thought...hang on. Where were they?

They'd been just there.

Just...just...

She stared a bit longer and saw sand sliding down. Masses of sand.

Dear God.

A car was pulling into the car park just above her. She glanced wildly round and it was Sam, lifting Bonnie out of the passenger seat.

'Sam!' Her scream was so loud it was like it cut the beach. 'Sam...the kids have dug into the cliff again and it looks like it's come down on them.'

* * *

Sam was heading to his evening surf but he'd been having trouble looking forward to it. Bonnie's great head was on his knee and the Labrador seemed to pick up his moods—when he was sad, so was she. He had the radio up loud, trying to gear himself up with a corny Elvis song, but Bonnie wasn't fooled. She was heaving sighs as if she was thinking exactly what he was thinking.

Where's Zoe?

He was being dumb. All he had to do was back off in the care department and they could have fun. But…

'Come on, Sam, don't be a wuss, the surf's fine.' They were the last words he'd heard from Emily and they echoed through his head every night of his life.

Don't be a wuss, the surf's fine.

Risk.

He couldn't bear it, he thought savagely. He couldn't bear watching Zoe, knowing that something could happen, knowing she could be snatched away. And to watch her and pretend not to care…it was enough to make a guy go nuts.

He needed to surf. He needed to do anything rather than think of Zoe.

He climbed out of the car, reached in to lift Bonnie down—and a scream came from the beach below.

'Sam… The kids have dug into the cave again and it looks like it's come down on them.'

Zoe!

He put Bonnie back into the Jeep and slammed the door.

He ran.

The council had bulldozed the overhang, making it safe—unless you were a kid who knew there was a cave hidden behind the bulldozed sand and you'd decided to dig back in and find it. And now…it looked like a whole slab of the foreshore had caved in, on top of whoever was inside.

Zoe had started running even as she'd screamed. She reached the collapsed section before Sam, and by the time he got there she was already hurling herself at the sand, scraping great swathes of it away using her looped arms as a scoop.

'They're in there,' she gasped as Sam reached her. 'I saw them. I think it was the same boys we saw…'

'You're sure?'

'They were just here. I was throwing chips for the seagulls and then…and then they weren't here any more.'

'H-help.' It was a faint, muffled cry, really muffled, but it had them pausing, staring at the mound of collapsed cliff, trying to figure where…where…

'Stay absolutely still,' Sam yelled. 'Tug your shirts over your mouths and noses and don't move. Not one muscle. We're coming but it will take time. Do not move!' He was scooping at the sand, using Zoe's method but with ten times more strength. Sand was being shoved aside with a force Zoe hadn't thought possible.

'We need a spade,' Sam threw at her. 'Zoe, stop. We need help, and it's up to you to get it. See the lifesaver station? It's empty and locked apart from weekends. It's up on stilts so you need to swing yourself up. The windows are barred, the whole place is locked, but the base is made of plywood. Kick it in and get spades, and masks and oxygen. Go. You have a phone? Use it while you run. Ask for fire services—they have the heavy moving equipment—but ask for ambulance back-up. The Seaway Spit, south of the car park. Got it? Go?'

He was digging deeper as he clipped orders, deeper, deeper, and Zoe looked at the mass of slippery sand around and above him and gave a sob of fear.

'Go,' he snapped, and she went.

She screamed into the phone for emergency services, and somehow she made herself coherent enough to be understood. 'Two kids buried by cliff collapse at South Seaway Beach. Bring digging equipment, men, medics.'

How far did they have to come? Oh, God... She ran with the image of partly collapsed cliff hanging over Sam's head. Why wasn't she with him?

She was following orders.

The deserted lifeguard tower was a high yellow cube on stilts, with steel grates over the windows. The door was eight feet from the ground. A ladder hung underneath, firmly locked so no one could tug it down.

She wasn't great at breaking locks and she didn't even consider it. Instead, she jumped and clung, monkeylike, to the first strut. She thought, *You can do this, Zoe*, and before her sensible side told her no way, she swung herself harder, up to the next strut, then up and onto the platform so she was somehow balanced on the thin, unwelcoming doorstep.

Inside there'd be spades and masks and oxygen. Sam had said there would be. There had to be. Sand collapse must be something these guys would be equipped for.

The door was padlocked. The grilles were immovable. Kick in the plywood, Sam had said, so that's exactly what she did, and she kicked harder than she'd ever kicked in her life. She heard—and felt—her toe give an ominous crack but she was through. The plywood splintered and she could haul pieces clear, enough to wiggle inside to find what she wanted.

God bless lifesavers. There seemed a place for everything and everything in its place. It took her a whole twenty seconds to grab what she needed from the carefully labelled cupboards.

She shoved everything out through the hole and let it fall—she could hardly climb with shovels and oxygen cylinders and masks. She worried fleetingly about tossing oxygen but she hardly had a choice. Equipment hit the sand and she hit the sand seconds after it.

Her toe told her it was broken. She told it not to whinge. She grabbed her booty into one huge armful and ran again.

All the while thinking Sam...

And two kids. She *was* thinking two kids, it was just that Sam was there, too, and this was Sam and she was feeling...

Sick, empty, terrified.

So she ran and searched the beach in front of her—and he was gone.

Gone?

There was only a swathe of freshly collapsed sand. The last of the cliff above had come down.

Oh, God...

But as she neared the collapse...a hand surfaced above the sand, and then...then a head, coated by a shirt. He hauled the shirt away and coughed and shoved sand from his face.

Sam! It was all she could do not to scream. He was waving to her to hurry and she couldn't run any further, her lungs were about to explode.

'Masks?' he yelled, before she reached him. 'Oxygen?'

She was there, staring hopelessly at what was before her. There was so much sand above Sam. It could still slip.

'They're in here and they're alive,' he snapped, as she reached the foot of the mound. 'There's a scooped-out spot that's letting them breathe but I can't haul them out without bringing the whole mass down. Hand me the masks and canister.'

'Sam, come out.'

'Start digging from the edge and don't put any pressure on the top,' he said abruptly, and reached out, sand coated, buried to his shoulders, grabbing what he needed. 'Is help coming?'

'I... Yes.'

'We need manpower and care and luck. Dig from the left, Zoe, and make them take care. It's up to you to make sure they don't stuff it.'

He shoved a mask across his mouth, swiped his eyes, checked the oxygen canister—and then, unbelievably, he ducked down again. The sand seemed to ooze over his head and he disappeared from sight.

'Sam!'

'Dig,' came the muffled response, and then nothing.

She dug from the side like a woman possessed, but the amount of sand was massive. She'd made no headway at all before the emergency services arrived—fire, police, ambulance. She gave them stark facts, she was put aside and the big guns went to work.

It wasn't brute force—it couldn't be. They still had to use care but there were men here much better with spades than she was. Even though they could no longer hear anyone, the assumption was that there was a cave somewhere inside that mass of sand, that three people were alive in that cave, and there was no way they were going to bring the whole thing down. A guy arrived from the council, an engineer with a truckload of shoring timber. That stopped the sand slipping back down where they'd dug.

'They'll be using every ounce of energy to breathe,' the fire chief told her. 'If they have masks and oxygen and they're not crushed, they have a chance. If they have sense—and if Dr Webster's with them he'll give them sense—they'll lie stock-still and not touch their masks. To shift a mask to yell could mean catastrophe. So don't give up hope, girl. We'll reach them but we need to do it with care.'

She had to leave them to it. It was the hardest thing she'd ever done but there was only room for about six men to dig and they wanted the strongest, the burliest, and Zoe didn't fit the job description.

She backed off. She went and let Bonnie out of the car then sat on the sand and hugged Bonnie and watched until her eyes ached.

Bonnie stared, too. It was as if she knew.

People were coming from everywhere now as the news spread. Callie came rushing down from the car park, still in her white coat with her stethoscope swinging. She stopped short when she saw Zoe. She stared at the mass of caved-in sand and she, too, slumped to the sand and hugged Bonnie.

Zoe hardly noticed. She had eyes only for the diggers.

The cops were putting up a line of yellow plastic

tape, keeping onlookers out. The search was getting methodical.

The boys' parents arrived, distraught and hysterical. The cops had to restrain them from throwing themselves at the cliff.

Oh, God, how long had it been? Twenty minutes? More?

'They must have gone right into the cliff,' the fire chief said grimly. He was overseeing operations right by where Zoe knelt with Bonnie and Callie. By rights he should ask them to go to the other side of the tape but they weren't moving and he wasn't asking. 'We're reaching the end of the soft sand—they must have burrowed right in behind. That's good but it also makes our job harder. There's so much stuff that can still come down.'

Zoe gave a sob of fear and clung harder to Bonnie. Bonnie shoved her big head into her armpit and seemed to hug back.

Callie hugged them both.

Waiting. It was the hardest, hardest thing.

She thought suddenly of her parents, of all those years in waiting rooms, waiting for the news of their daughter's health.

Worrying. Frantic with fear.

She'd known at a superficial level but not like this. Dear God, to love someone and have to wait…

She loved him. She loved Sam. She loved him with every ounce of energy she had within her.

He'd said he was falling in love with her.

She'd pushed him away because he cared.

She cared so much now she was going crazy. She was dying inside, every minute killing her as the spades dug in, as the timbers were put up so they could dig in a few more inches, as the moments ticked by...

And then...

A shout.

'They're in here. All still. More timbers...'

The crowd behind the tape hushed. The whole world hushed. No one breathed.

More timbers went sliding in. The fire chief barked instructions. There was a change of the order at the site, someone ducked low into the timber-lined chasm, and there was more silence.

And then...

One of the diggers, hard hatted and masked, backed out, tugging...

A boy...

There was a sob of fear from behind her, a woman lurched forward and was restrained...

Arms lifted the boy, sand-coated, masked. Someone tugged the mask free and the child looked around and saw his mother...

'M-Mum.'

There was a collective gasp as the paramedics moved in to do their job. Callie rose to help but Zoe was no longer watching. Her attention was back with the diggers.

Please...

Another shout. Another child was pulled free. They were using shoring timbers to hold him flat and someone yelled for Callie.

Spinal injuries?

But he, too, quavered a whisper as his parents reached him.

Please...

And then, emerging behind the board...looking like

the abominable sandman, coated from head to foot, letting men pull him, blinking in the light, wiping his face, accepting a towel and brushing sand away, hauling the mask off and shaking his head as paramedics moved in...

Sam.

She couldn't move. She could only stare. Sam.

Alive.

He was searching the crowd. Men were gripping his shoulders, one of the paramedics was offering mask and oxygen, but he was searching...

He found her.

His gaze met hers.

And right there, right then Bonnie realised that this sand-coated apparition was the guy she loved with all her heart. Unequivocally. No conditions. The big Labrador bounded forward with as much bounce as her splinted leg allowed, and Sam was covered in Labrador, he had his dog in his arms but he was striding forward as he hugged, and somehow she was standing and moving as well.

And then he reached her. 'D-down,' Sam said in a voice that was none too steady. 'Sit.'

And Bonnie subsided and sat and Sam Webster looked at Zoe Payne and there was something in that look that was a marriage vow all by itself.

'You got help,' he said, and she blinked back tears and reached for his hands and held and held and held.

'You got out.'

'I had to get out for you.'

'I don't suppose it's any use for me to say never, ever, ever do anything so terrifying ever in your life again,' she whispered. 'Sam, I thought you were going to die.'

'I thought I might,' he said. They were almost formal. They were standing holding hands while the rest of the world watched, while people grinned their approval, while the world came to terms with this rescue and while Zoe and Sam came to terms with something new. With the rest of their lives.

'I couldn't bear it,' she whispered. 'To lose you.'

'I guess we'll have to bear it one day,' he said. 'But not today. I'm giving us sixty years.'

'Not if you keep taking risks like today.'

'I couldn't not,' he said soberly, looking back at the collapsed sand. 'I couldn't not go in there. Like you can't stop nursing kids with sniffles. Or climbing mountains. It's who we are.'

'But I love you, Sam,' she said, and it was a vow. 'If you ever scare me like that again I'll...'

'You'll?'

'I'll love you more,' she whispered, and at last she fell forward and he tugged her into his arms. He was a mass of sand, it felt like hugging a crumbed rissole, but he was her Sam, he was here, he was alive, and he was...

Sam.

'I'll let you worry,' she whispered.

'That's big of you,' he said into her hair.

'But I need to worry back.'

'Granted,' he said, and tugged back and tilted her chin so he could look into her eyes. 'Zoe, I might get paranoid...'

'And I'll tell you you're paranoid. I might get dumb and try to climb mountains too big for me.'

'Then I'll tell you you're dumb.'

'I foresee fights.'

'I like a decent fight. Will you let me win?'

'Half the time,' she said. 'We'll put a chart on the refrigerator. Fifty per cent me, fifty per cent you. Sam…'

'Mmm?'

'When Dean cared…he loved me because he could care. He loved me because he loved worrying. It took me years to figure it out and it scared me.'

'And when Emily took risks she took them because she loved taking risks,' Sam said, just as gravely. 'I can't tell you how much that scared me. You reckon, though, if we know what we're fighting, we can work through it?'

'We can try,' she said shakily.

'Zoe?'

'Mmm?'

'I think that's enough negotiation for one afternoon,' he said, and suddenly there was no hint of shakiness in his voice. This was Dr Sam Webster who'd just saved two lives. This was Dr Sam Webster who was standing in the late afternoon sun holding the woman he loved. This was Dr Sam Webster about to kiss the woman he loved with all his heart.

There was no more prevarication. The time was right to kiss his Zoe—and he did.

Callie was helping to load the two kids into the ambulance when Cade arrived. Word must have gone around the hospital like wildfire—every off-duty medic from Gold Coast City seemed to be on the beach now. These kids couldn't possibly get better attention.

Cade saw Callie and headed straight for her.

'Status?' he said in the clipped, unemotional tone of an emergency physician working out triage.

'No deaths,' Callie said, responding to his tone and

trying to keep her voice unemotional. 'Two teenagers, one with a smashed shoulder, the other with suspected fractured hip, possible ribs, query spine, but there's movement so we're not looking at paraplegia.'

'And Sam?'

Sam was Cade's colleague, Callie thought. They'd only worked together for a few weeks but Callie knew there was already respect and friendship between the two men.

'He managed to get himself through falling sand into the cave they were buried in,' she said. 'He took in masks and oxygen and kept them alive until help arrived.'

'He's okay?'

She gestured down to the beach where one man and one woman were totally entwined, kissing as if there was no tomorrow, even though there was a crowd around them and one chocolate-coloured Labrador was nudging between them with increasing impatience.

'What do you think?'

Cade stared down the beach for a long moment, and his mouth twisted into a wry grimace.

'Love conquers all,' he said, and he couldn't disguise the sarcasm.

'So it seems,' Callie said steadily.

'You're going to advise her to cut and run?'

'I'm not advising anyone,' Callie said. 'I know nothing and understand less. I love it that they're happy. I hope it lasts.'

'Me, too,' Cade said unexpectedly. 'Other people can be happy. Just not us, right?'

'You've got it in one,' she said, and turned back to help load two battered kids into the ambulance.

* * *

Sunday.

It was surfing lesson number twenty-nine and she did it.

She hit the green room.

The green room was a special, magic place, known only to surfers who've been surfing for years. Zoe wasn't ready. The great, curling wave came from nowhere. If Sam had had time he'd have yelled to Zoe to let it go, it was too big, she wasn't expert enough.

She caught it with ease.

He'd been lying on his board two hundred yards away. The great wave curled towards him.

He could watch over it and wait with fear until Zoe came out the other end—*if* Zoe came out the other end—or he could catch it himself.

The board lifted him and he pushed forward and felt the magic force as wave and board came together.

It curled high, high, higher…and over.

He was totally enclosed, a ring of green water, a tunnel pushing him forward. Sunlight glinting through the green walls. Force was all around him. Breathtaking beauty.

Somewhere in the same wave was Zoe.

He could hold his breath in terror or ride his wave, and somehow there was no room for terror.

The green room enclosed him in its magic and somehow he knew that the magic was closing around Zoe as well.

His surfing girl. His Zoe.

The wave was an endless curve, a once-in-a-lifetime ride, curling more and more for almost the full length of the beach. He rode its length until it fell away as the beach became shallow, as the green room became a simple breaking wave washing to the shore. He emerged to sunlight and to a whoop of pure joy from twenty yards away.

He turned and she was there, laughing, crying, joyous, his beautiful surfer girl. His Zoe.

He'd meant to wait. He'd had it planned, a three-week holiday to Nepal, a trek to the base of Annapurna Two, a candlelit dinner organised by sherpas, a ring, a question.

Instead, he paddled the few feet between them, he tugged her from the board, he lifted her into his arms and he kissed her so deeply he knew that no time would be more perfect.

No woman would be more perfect.

Somehow he unfastened their leg ropes, letting the tide carry their boards to the shore. She smiled and smiled, as if she knew what was coming, as if she, too, knew the perfection of this moment.

He put her down, he sank to one knee—and a wave knocked him sideways.

He surfaced spluttering, to find her choked with laughter and sinking to her knees to join him.

'You drown, we drown together,' she told him.

'Does that mean you'll marry me?''

There was a long, long silence while four more waves washed over them, while more curling waves broke and ran for shore, while the world settled on its axis to what was right, what was perfect, what was now.

'Why, yes,' Zoe whispered at last as he drew her close. 'Why, yes, Sam Webster, I believe it does.'

He whooped with joy. He kissed her long and deep and with all the love in his heart.

And then one brown Labrador bounded into the water to join them, a kiss became a sandwich hug and Sam Webster and Zoe Payne became a family.

* * * * *

GOLD COAST ANGELS:
TWO TINY HEARTBEATS

BY
FIONA McARTHUR

MILLS
BOON

Dedicated to my cousin John, who is toughing it out,
so proud of you, and to Aunty Yvonne, Lee, who is also awesome,
Gay and Eveline.

First published in Great Britain 2013
by Mills & Boon, an imprint of Harlequin (UK) Limited.
Harlequin (UK) Limited, Eton House, 18-24 Paradise Road,
Richmond, Surrey TW9 1SR

© Harlequin Books S.A. 2013

Special thanks and acknowledgement are given to Fiona McArthur
for her contribution to the *Gold Coast Angels* series

ISBN: 978 0 263 89916 0

Harlequin (UK) policy is to use papers that are natural, renewable
and recyclable products and made from wood grown in sustainable
forests. The logging and manufacturing process conform to the
legal environmental regulations of the country of origin.

Printed and bound in Spain
by Blackprint CPI, Barcelona

Dear Reader

I've loved being a part of the *Gold Coast Angels* series, and can't wait to catch up with all the amazing people who work there.

My heroine, Lucy, is ready to take on the world. She's a dedicated midwife, of course, and loves her job—until she finds out she is going to be a single mother with twins.

Without support of family, Lucy would be finding it even tougher without the warmth and caring of her work friends—and that's where Gold Coast City Hospital comes into its own.

But it's gorgeous Dr Nikolai Kefes who really takes her under his gorgeous wing (those shoulders…!), and Lucy discovers that she's not the only person who has someone special missing in her life. Can she heal Nikolai's past hurts and make this wonderfully caring doctor love again?

I hope you have as much fun as I did with Nick and Lucy's love life—enjoy the *Gold Coast Angels* series.

Warmest wishes

Fiona McArthur

GOLD COAST ANGELS

The hottest docs, the warmest hearts, the highest drama

This month, sexy lone wolf Sam is given a second chance
at life by bubbly nurse Zoe in
A DOCTOR'S REDEMPTION by Marion Lennox

And midwife Lucy's first day at work
takes an unexpected turn when gorgeous new colleague Nick
suggests she takes a pregnancy test in
TWO TINY HEARTBEATS by Fiona McArthur

Then, in November, nurse Chloe falls for brooding surgeon
and single dad Luke in
BUNDLE OF TROUBLE by Fiona Lowe

While Cade and Callie can't get that steamy one-night stand
out of their minds in
HOW TO RESIST TEMPTATION by Amy Andrews

Don't miss this fabulous four-book series full of breathtaking
drama, heartwrenching emotion and sizzling passion!

**These books are also available in eBook format
from www.millsandboon.co.uk**

CHAPTER ONE

LUCY PALMER WAS so excited even the ride up in the lift made her feel queasy. She'd thought she'd grown out of that.

Today, officially, she could say she was a part of the state-of-the-art Gold Coast City Hospital and she'd done it all herself. Her excitement had been building since graduation fourteen weeks ago.

This wasn't just three years of hard study and unpaid practical placements, this was the start of a mission she'd lived and breathed for ever.

Lucy couldn't wait to be allocated her first birth suite caseload because she was going to be the best midwifery grad they'd ever seen.

The midwifery floor manager, Flora May, ex-air force medic with a gruff voice and, Lucy suspected, a well-camouflaged heart of gold, had met Lucy in one of her placements during her training. Flora's assessment of Lucy's aptitude for the profession had helped very much in her successful interview and Lucy couldn't have asked for a better role model than Flora.

As the orientation tour ended Flora snapped her heels together and waved to the busy floor. Unexpectedly her angular face changed and she smiled with genuine warmth.

'And welcome, Palmer. I've given you Monday to Friday shifts for the first month, so I'll be here if you need advice.'

A friendly face while she settled in. Lucy decided that sounded blissful. 'Thank you.'

'Hmph.' Sentiment should be set aside, obviously, Lucy thought with an internal smile as Flora went on. 'Take Sally Smith, she's a teen mum admitted for threatened premature labour at thirty-three weeks. She needs someone she can relate to.'

This was accompanied by a dry look. 'Night staff will give you Sally's handover in birth suite one.' Flora raised an eyebrow. 'You'll be fine. Let me know if you need help and I'll be your wing man. Any questions, find me.'

The boss would be her wing man? Lucy grinned at the funny wordage and resisted the urge to salute.

Flora marched off and Lucy felt for the first time that someone other than her fellow ex-students was willing to believe she had the makings of a good midwife.

It would have been nice if her mother had been supportive instead of bitter and twisted, but she wasn't going there because nothing was going to spoil this day. Or her confidence, because Flora believed she could do this well.

Her stomach fluttered uncomfortably again and she sucked in a breath. Forget nerves, this was what she'd been born for.

When she knocked and entered the first birth suite and the night midwife didn't look up from writing her notes, Lucy faltered, felt tempted to cough or go back and knock again, but she didn't.

The pale young woman lying curled on her side blinked so Lucy stepped just inside the door and smiled, but the girl on the bed rolled her eyes, and then looked away before shutting them. Tough room, Lucy thought ruefully before, with another deep breath, she crossed to the bed.

The night midwife still didn't look up, so Lucy passed her by and smiled at her patient as she tried to imagine what it would be like to be seventeen, pregnant, and now scared her baby would be born prematurely, in a place where she knew no one.

'Hello, Sally, I'm Lucy. I'll be looking after you today when your night midwife goes home.' Lucy glanced around the otherwise empty room, and no boyfriend or mother was tucked into any corner she could see. Maybe Sally's mother had trained in the same school as hers, Lucy thought, and she knew how that felt. Lack of family support was not fun at all.

The young mum-to-be opened her eyes briefly, nodded, and then rolled carefully over onto her other side, stretching the leads that held the monitor on her stomach.

Really tough room, Lucy thought with a gulp.

Finally the night midwife put down her pen and looked across. 'I'm Cass. I've just done my fifth night shift and can't wait to get out of here.'

Lucy blinked and glanced at Sally's rigid back. Not a very nice intro, she thought, or what Lucy expected from a hospital she'd only ever heard praise about.

To make it worse, Cass didn't look at anything except her notes or, occasionally, the graph of contractions on the machine. 'So this is Sally, seventeen, thirty-three weeks, first baby, and has had intermittent back pain since three this morning. No loss on the pad she's wearing and the CTG is picking up the contractions as five-minutely.'

The lack of emotion sat strangely in a room where emotion was usually a big factor and Lucy began to suspect why Flora May had sent her in here. Lucy wanted to care for Sally, not treat her like an insect in a jar.

Cass sighed as if the story would never end and Lucy wished the midwife would just go home and let her read the notes herself. But of course she couldn't say that, especially on her first day. But she was feeling less timid by the second. Something she'd discovered inside herself when she'd discovered midwifery.

Then Cass went one worse. 'The foetal fibrinectin test for prem labour couldn't be done because she's had sex in the last twenty-four hours.'

Brutal. Lucy saw Sally's shoulder stiffen and winced in sympathy for the callousness of a clinical handover that lacked sensitivity. Lucy vowed she'd never be like this. And now she seriously wished the other midwife gone.

Cass certainly didn't notice and went on in the same bored tone as she read from her notes. 'No urinary symptoms or discharge but we've sent swabs and urine away for microscopy.'

Okay, Lucy understood that she needed to know it had been done, because infection was the most common reason for early labour and miscarriage.

Cass went on. 'She's had three doses of oral tocolytic, which has slowed the contractions, been started on antibiotics four-hourly, and the foetal heart trace…'

She glanced at the long strip of paper cascading from the monitor that evaluated baby heart rate and uterine contractions without looking at the patient. Lucy hated impersonal technology. It was too easy for staff to look more at machines than the patient.

Cass shrugged. 'I think she's more stable than when she arrived. First dose of steroids was given at three-thirty a.m., so she's due another that time tomorrow morning, if she's still here.'

Cass looked up. 'Any questions?'

No way did she want to prolong Cass's stay. Where did you *not* learn your people skills? Lucy thought, but instead she asked, 'What time did the doctor last see Sally?'

'It's all in the notes.' Cass glanced down. 'The registrar at four a.m., but her obstetrician, Dr Kefes…' For the first time some emotion heightened the colour on Cass's face and she looked almost feline. 'Nikolai's delicious.' She sighed as if he was there in front of her and Lucy cringed.

'Nikolai will see her at rounds this morning. He's always punctual at eight so be ready. I'm off.' She snapped shut the folder and uncoiled herself from the chair. 'Bye, Sally.' She handed the folder to Lucy and left without waiting for her patient's reply.

Lucy frowned at the door as it shut, decided even the mention of the doctor as delicious was unprofessional, glanced around for inspiration on winning Sally's confidence after the nurse from hell had departed, and set about changing the dynamics of the room.

She spotted a little black four-wheeled stool and pulled it around to the other side of the bed to see her patient's face before sitting down.

The stool brought her not too close but just under the level of Sally's eyes so she wasn't crowding or looking down at her. After a few moments Sally opened her eyes. 'So how are you feeling, Sally?'

'Crap.'

Lucy smiled. Succinct. 'Fair enough. Can you be more specific? Your back?' Sally nodded and Lucy continued, 'Worse or better than when you came in?'

'A lot worse.' Sally blinked suspiciously shiny eyes and Lucy wanted to hug her. Instead, she considered their options.

'Okay, that's not good. Let's sort that first. I'll take the monitor off for a few minutes while I check your observations, and have a little feel of your tummy before we put the belts back on more comfortably. Then we'll see if we can relieve some of the discomfort.'

Lucy glanced at the little watch that her friends had all pitched in for her on graduation. Pretty and practical, like her, they'd said, and she still winced because they'd known her mother wouldn't show for the event and she'd be disappointed.

That might even have been why she'd made that dumb choice with Mark after one too many unfamiliar mojitos, but it had been nice to bask in appreciation for a change.

She shook off regrets because they were a waste of time. She'd learnt that one the hard way by watching her mother.

Seven-thirty a.m., so she had half an hour before the obstetrician arrived to assess her patient's condition. Lucy wanted an overall picture of Sally's general health and mental state before then. But mostly she wanted Sally to feel comfortable with her so she could best represent her concerns when more new caregivers arrived. She'd better get started.

Nikolai Kefes, Senior Obstetrician at Gold Coast City Hospital, discreetly named Adonis by his female colleagues, had a strong work ethic. Seventy per cent of his life centred on work, twenty per cent went to his sister, Chloe, and the other ten per cent was divided equally between sport and brief affairs with sophisticated women.

Nick hated being late for ward rounds but there was no way he could have ignored the distress call from his sister, and by the time he'd parked his car at the hospital it was half an hour after he'd expected to start.

Chloe worried him. She had worried him since she was sixteen and in more trouble than he could have imagined, so much so that she'd changed both their lives. But he could never regret giving her the support she needed when she needed it.

Not that she'd always appreciated his attempts to shield her from the hardships that arose when two young people were suddenly cast out in the world without a penny. He still cringed to think how she would have survived if he hadn't followed her.

It was a shame their parents hadn't felt the same, but he'd given up trying to fathom them years ago.

But this morning Chloe had been adamant she would do things her way, despite this last disastrous relationship, and he wished she'd just swim to the surface and avoid becoming involved for a while.

He could only be glad he was in control of his own brief affairs. Short and sweet was not just a concept, more like a mantra for his life, because emotion was best left out of it. That way nobody got hurt.

The lift doors opened and he stepped out on the maternity floor. His eyes narrowed as he noted the arrival of his registrar at the nurses' station just ahead of him. If he wasn't mistaken, Simon had got dressed in a hurry, because his shirt showed the inside seams and the shadow of a pocket.

He guessed he should be thankful the majority of his own nights were left undisturbed at this stage of his career, so he smiled, and cleared his mind of everything but his work. The familiar focus settled over him and his shoulders relaxed as he zeroed in on his junior.

'So, Simon. Tell me what's happening this morning.' He paused, looked him up and down and smiled. 'Then perhaps you could retire into the staffroom and turn your shirt the other way?'

Eight thirty-five a.m. In the past fifteen minutes Lucy had decided Sophie would definitely have her baby today. Around eight-fifteen the contractions had become strong and regular and Lucy had slipped out and rung the registrar because the eight a.m. arrival of the consultant hadn't occurred.

Neither had the arrival of the registrar, Lucy fumed, and twenty minutes' time lag wasn't good enough. She wasn't happy as she looked for Flora May again to let her know her patient still hadn't been seen.

Instead, she saw a tall, very athletic-looking man arrive at the desk, his immaculate suit dark like his short wavy hair, but it was his air of command that convinced Lucy he could be the person she expected. She diligently ignored the fact he was probably the most handsome man she'd ever seen and that maybe the horrible night midwife hadn't been far off.

'Dr Kefes?'

Both men turned to face her but she went straight for the one who obviously held the power.

'Yes?' His voice was low with a husky trace of an accent that was delightfully melodious, Mediterranean most likely, but she'd think about that later when she had a chance.

'I'm sorry to interrupt. I'm the midwife looking after Sally Hill. She's seventeen years old and thirty-three weeks gestation in prem labour. I believe she's establishing active labour as we speak and you need to see her now.' She handed him the notes and said over her shoulder, 'This way, please.'

As he opened the notes and followed, Nikolai wondered briefly why he had allowed himself to be steered so determinedly when he usually had handover by his registrar and then did his rounds.

Of course, the young midwife seemed concerned, so that was a good reason, and she had made it difficult for him to refuse, he thought with an internal smile as he watched her reddish-brown ponytail swing in front of him.

He was more used to deference and suggestion than downright direction, but this day had started unusually, and it seemed it was going to proceed that way.

Ten minutes later Lucy stood beside the bed as she watched Dr Kefes and the respectful way he talked to Sally, and she could feel the ease of the tension in her own shoulders.

Thankfully, he was totally opposite from the way the night midwife had been. This tall man with the accent seemed genuinely empathetic with the young mum's concerns and symptoms. Even the tricky business of the physical examination was conducted with delicacy and tact.

Afterwards Nikolai removed his gloves and washed his hands then came back to the bed, where Lucy had helped Sally to sit up more comfortably. The two young women watched his face anxiously.

Dr Kefes smiled. 'It seems your baby has decided to have a birthday today. You are more than half-dilated and we will let the special care nursery know to expect a new arrival.'

Sally's face whitened and the first real fear showed in her eyes. He sat down on Lucy's stool and smiled gently at the young mum. 'This is a shock to you?'

Sally nodded but didn't speak. Lucy could see her lip trembling and she reached across and put her hand out. To her relief Sally grabbed her fingers and clung on while the doctor addressed her fears.

'You are in a safe place. Your baby is in a safe place. If you are worried, listen to your midwife.' He gestured at Lucy. 'This one, who was so determined I would see you first she practically dragged me in here before my round began.'

He smiled at Lucy and she could feel her cheeks warm with embarrassment, and something else, like pleasure that this gorgeous man had complimented her on her advocacy. But the best result was that Sally smiled as well.

He went on. 'We will all work towards this being a very special day for you and your baby.' He stood up. 'Okay?'

Sally nodded, and Lucy could tell she wasn't the only

person in the room who had decided Nikolai Kefes was a man to put your faith in.

And Sally's birthing was special. Her baby was born three hours later. Dr Kefes was gentle and patient, and Sally was focused and determined to remain in control.

Lucy had borrowed the ward camera and captured some beautifully touching shots soon after the birth, because the neonatal staff were there for the baby, Dr Kefes managed the actual delivery, Flora May unobtrusively supervised, and she didn't have much to do herself.

The stylish bob of the neonatal specialist, Dr Callie Richards, swung as she paused and spoke to Sally while her staff wheeled tiny Zac out the door on the open crib towards the NICU. 'I think he'll be promoted to the special care nursery very quickly, but we'll check him out first in the NICU.'

Her eyes softened. 'You come and visit him as soon as you're up to it or I'll come to see you if he misbehaves before then.' Her gentle voice was warm and compassionate and Sally nodded mutely. Her eyes met Lucy's as her baby was wheeled away.

'He'll be fine,' Lucy whispered. 'He looks little but very strong.'

Sally sniffed and nodded and Lucy squeezed her hand. 'Let's get you sorted so you can go and see what he's up to.'

Afterwards, when Sally had showered and the two young women had had a chance to look at the photos, Lucy was very glad she'd taken them.

The luminous joy on Sally's face as she gazed at her tiny son—a close-up of a starfish hand, a tiny foot lying on his mother's fingers, and one of him snuggled against his mother's breasts before he'd been whisked away to the neonatal nursery, were all a comfort to a new mother whose baby had been taken for care somewhere else.

Even on the poor-quality prints in black and white that Lucy printed out on the ward computer Sally looked a beautiful mum.

As she waited in the wheelchair, Sally's finger traced the distinguishing features of her tiny son's face and body on the images.

'I'm glad I had you looking after me.'

Lucy squeezed Sally's shoulder. 'I'm glad I was here. Thank you for letting me share your birth.'

Her first birth as a proper midwife had been as empowering for Sally as she could make it. And she could tell that the young mum was pretty chuffed at how she'd managed everything that had been asked of her.

Lucy had never felt so proud of anyone as she was of Sally. She glanced around to see that they had collected everything from the room and pushed the chair forward. 'We'll drop this stuff in your room and then we'll go and see this gorgeous son of yours.'

Five hours later, at the end of the shift, a shift that had held her first prem birth, a quick catch of another impatient baby keen to arrive before the rest of the staff were ready, and a smile from a very senior obstetrician for a job well done, Lucy picked up her bag from the staffroom.

She should be feeling ecstatic as she walked past the sluice room on the way out but, in fact, she felt dreadful.

The nausea that had been building all day suddenly rushed up her throat in an imminent threat—so much so that she had to launch herself at the sluice-room sink in desperation.

Nikolai, too, was on his way out the door when he saw the sudden acceleration of the new midwife who'd been so diligent today.

He frowned as he realised the nature of her distress, and glanced hopefully left and right for someone else in scrubs, but saw nobody he could call on to assist her. He sighed, shrugged, and approached the doorway.

'Are you okay?' By the time he reached her it seemed it was over.

Her forehead rested on the tips of the fingers of one hand as she rinsed the sink. The fragility of her pale neck made him reach for his handkerchief and he leaned past her and dampened it under the cold running water. He wrung it out before handing it to her to wipe her face.

To his amusement she was so intent on patting her hot cheeks that she muttered thanks without turning. Later, perhaps it would be different, but at the moment it seemed she was just glad she'd made it to somewhere manageable.

Then she glanced back and he saw her glance hesitantly past him and he wondered if she expected the whole staff to be lined outside, watching her.

'Nobody else saw.'

Her shoulders sank with relief and he bit back a smile. So transparent.

'Thank goodness. It's crazy.' He could just catch the words because she seemed to be talking to his tie. 'I've been feeling nauseated all day and it just caught up with me.'

'Not pregnant, are you?' He smiled, in no way expecting the startled look of shock that spread over her face as she glanced up at him. Oh, dear me, Nikolai thought, and couldn't help flashing back to his sister all those years ago.

No doubt it was that connection that caused his sudden surge of protective feeling towards this wilting poppy in front of him, but the sudden urge to hug her disconcerted him. He hadn't wanted to drop a bombshell like that, neither had he had any intention of ruining her day, but it was far too late now. He resigned himself to waiting for her to gather herself.

'I can't be.' But even in that tiny whisper Nick heard the thread of perhaps. Perhaps. Perhaps?

She lifted her gaze to his again and he could see the intriguing green flecks in the hugeness of her horrified hazel eyes.

He'd put his foot in it, obviously. 'So you haven't tested for pregnancy?'

'Hadn't given it a thought,' she mumbled, and blushed. 'I didn't consider that precautions might let me down during my first and only ever one-night stand. And that was ages ago.' Her bitterness was unmistakable. She leant back over the sink to cover her face.

Nick winced at the vagaries of fate. Here was a woman anything but pleased by her fertility, while his sister would give anything to be able to fall pregnant again.

He didn't know how he could help, or even why he wanted to, but he couldn't just leave.

Maybe he was wrong. He knew nothing about her. 'Perhaps you're not pregnant. Could be gastro. Lack of food. You could try a pregnancy test. I have some in my rooms. Might even be negative.'

She looked at him, he saw the brief flare of hope, and she nodded. 'That seems sensible. Of course I'm not...' She blushed, no doubt at the blurting out of the indiscreet information she'd given him. He'd have liked to have been able to reassure her he could forget her indiscretion—no problem—but he wasn't sure how.

She didn't meet his eyes. 'It could just be the excitement of the day. Would you mind?'

'It's the least I can do after scaring you like that.' He smiled encouragingly and after a brief glance she smiled back tentatively. 'Follow me.'

He glanced sideways and realised she'd had to skip a little to keep up. He guessed he did take big steps compared to hers, and slowed his pace. 'Sorry.' He smiled down at her. 'It's been a busy day and I'm still hyped.'

Lucy slowed with relief. She'd been hyped, too, until his random suggestion had blown her day out of the water.

Neither of them commented as she followed him to the lift, luckily deserted, an ascent of two floors and then along the corridor to the consultant's rooms. Lucy's lips moved silently as she repeated over and over in her head, *I am not pregnant, I am not pregnant!*

CHAPTER TWO

TEN MINUTES LATER that theory crashed and burned.

Lucy sank into the leather chair in Nikolai's office with the glass of water he'd given her in hand and tried to think.

She shook her head and closed her eyes for a moment. 'I'm my mother all over again.'

When she opened her eyes he was smiling gently. 'All mothers are their mothers.'

She sat up with a sigh. 'Well, I really am mine. On the brink of a career I've worked so hard for and I've ruined my life.' She could not believe this.

'It's been a shock. Can you remember when…?' He paused delicately and Lucy felt her cheeks warm again. This just got worse and worse. 'The night of our graduation.' Her hand crept over her stomach. This could not be happening, but the tiny bulge of her belly, something she'd been lamenting over the last week and blamed on the huge box of rocky road chocolate she'd been given, suddenly took on an ominous relevance to her queasiness.

How could she have been so stupid not to notice? She was a midwife, for pity's sake! But she'd been so excited about her job, and the house-sitting opportunity that would allow her to save money. She'd always been someone who got car sick, plane sick, excitement sick, thanks to an anxiety to please she'd thought she'd beaten.

It was a wonder she hadn't been throwing up every morning if she was pregnant, the way her stomach usually reacted to change. 'I can't be pregnant. It must be something else.'

He had such calm, sympathetic eyes. But she could tell he thought the test was valid. She guessed he had experience of this situation. Well, she didn't.

'Would you like me to run a quick ultrasound to confirm the test?'

She wanted to say, no, that would be too real. She knew a little about ultrasounds in early pregnancy. She had seen obstetricians during her practical placements using the machines on the ward when women were bleeding.

Find the sac. Foetal poles. Heartbeat if far enough along. She didn't want to know how far she had to be along. Somewhere around fourteen weeks, seeing as that had been the only time she'd ever had sex. Did she want more proof?

Maybe it was something else. Yeah, right. Fat chance. And she may as well face the reality until she decided what she was going to do and how she was going to manage this.

He was asking again, 'Would you like me to ask a nurse to come in? My receptionist has gone home. Just while we do this?'

God, no. 'No, thank you, if that's okay. Please. I don't want anyone to know.' She covered her eyes. *She* didn't want to know, but she couldn't say that.

'I understand.' His voice was low, that trace of accent rough with sympathy, and she had the sense he really did understand a little how she was feeling.

Maybe she was even glad he was there to be a stabiliser while she came to grips with this, except for the fact she'd have to see him almost every day at work, and he'd know her secret.

'Just do it.' Lucy climbed up onto the examination couch in his rooms, feeling ridiculous, scared and thoroughly embarrassed. Lucy closed her eyes and the mantra kept running through her head. This could not be happening.

Nikolai switched on the little portable ultrasound machine he kept in the corner of his rooms. This must have been how his sister had felt when she'd found out the worst thing a sixteen-year-old Greek Orthodox girl could find out. He just hoped there was someone here for this young woman.

He tried not to notice the unobtrusively crossed fingers she'd hidden down her sides as he tucked the towel across her upper abdomen to protect her purple scrubs from the gel. He didn't like her chances of the test strip being disputed by ultrasound.

He tucked another disposable sheet low in her abdomen, definitely in professional mode, and squirted the cool jelly across the not so tiny mound of her belly. She had silky, luminous skin and he tried not to notice.

When he felt her wince under his fingers, he paused until he checked she was okay, and she nodded before he recommenced the slide of the ultrasound transducer sideways. He couldn't help but admire the control she had under the circumstances. He wondered if Chloe had been this composed.

He glanced from her to the screen and then everything else was excluded as he concentrated on the fascinating parallel universe of pelvic ultrasound.

An eerie black-and-white zone of depth and shadings. Uterus. Zoom in. Foetal spine. So the foetus was mature enough for morphology. Foetal skull. Measure circumference. Crown-rump length. Placenta. Cord. Another cord?

He blinked. 'Just shutting the blinds so I can see better.' He reached across to the wall behind her head and the remote-control curtains dulled the brightness of the Queensland sun. Zoomed in closer. Uh-oh.

The room dimmed behind Lucy's closed eyelids and then she heard it. The galloping hoofbeats of a tiny foetal heart. No other reason to have a galloping horse inside her belly except the cloppety-clop of a baby's heartbeat.

She was pregnant.

It was true. She couldn't open her eyes. Was terrified to confirm it with sight but her ears wouldn't lie.

She couldn't cope with this. Give up her hard-won career just when it was starting. Throw away the last three years of intense study, all the after-hours work to pay for it, all her dreams of being the best midwife GCG had ever seen.

Cloppety-clop, cloppety-clop. The heartbeat of her baby, growing inside her. Her child. Something shifted inside her.

She had to look. She opened her eyes just as Dr Kefes sucked in his breath and she glanced at his face. She saw the frown as he swirled the transducer around and raised his eyebrows.

What? 'Has it got two heads?' A flippant comment

when she was feeling anything but flippant. Was her baby deformed? Funny how the last thing she wanted was to be pregnant but the barest hint of a problem with her tiny peanut and she was feeling…maternal?

'Sort of.' He clicked a snapshot with the machine and shifted the transducer. Clicked again.

Her stomach dropped like a stone. There was something wrong with her baby?

'What?'

'Sorry. Not what I meant.' He was looking at her with a mixture of concern and…it couldn't be wonderment surely. 'Congratulations, Lucy.'

That didn't make sense. Neither did a second heart-beat, this one slower than the other but still a clopping sound that both of them recognised. 'The measurements say you have two healthy fourteen-week foetuses.'

'I'm sorry?' He had not just said that. 'Two?'

'Twins.' He nodded to confirm his words. Held up two fingers in case she still didn't get it.

Lucy opened and shut her mouth before the words came out. 'Twins? Fourteen weeks?' Lucy squeaked, and then the world dimmed, only to return a little brighter and a whole lot louder than before—like a crash of cymbals beside her ear. She wasn't just pregnant. She was seriously, seriously pregnant.

She watched the screen zoom in and out in a haze of disbelief. Followed his finger as he pointed out legs and arms. And legs and arms. Two babies!

'I don't want twins. I don't want one,' she whispered, but even to her own ears there might be a question mark at the end of the sentence. She couldn't really be considering what she thought she was considering.

She thought briefly of Mark, her midwifery colleague already settled in Boston at his new job, a good-time guy with big plans. Their actions had been a silly impulse, regrettable but with no bad feelings, more a connection between two euphoric graduates than any kind of meeting of souls.

They'd both been sheepish after the event. The whole 'do you want coffee, can I use your bathroom', morning-after conversation that had made it very clear neither had felt the earth move—friends who should never have been lovers.

Dr Kefes broke into her thoughts and she blinked. 'If you are going to think about your options you don't have much time. In fact, you may not have any.'

Think about what? Terminating her babies that she'd heard? Seen? Was now totally aware of? She didn't know what she was going to do but she couldn't do that.

'Do they look healthy? Are they identical?' From what she'd learned about twin pregnancies there'd be more risk with identical twins than fraternal and already that was a worry.

'Looks to be one placenta but it's hard to tell. Early days, to be sure. They look fine.' His accent elongated the word *fine* and her attention zoned in on something non-traumatic—almost soothing—but he was forging on and she needed to pay attention. 'Both babies are equal size. Nothing out of the ordinary I can see.' He smiled and she was distracted for a second again from the whole tragedy. He was a serious darling, this guy. Then his words sank in.

Relief flooded over her. Her babies were fine. Relief?

She didn't know how she would manage. Certainly with no help from her own mother—how on earth would she tell her?—but she would manage. And no way was she going to blame her babies like her mother had always blamed her for ruining her life.

But that was for home. For quiet, intense thought. And she'd held this kind man up enough with her sudden drama that had blown out of all proportion into a life-changing event. Events.

She was having twins.

Holy cow.

On the first day of her new job.

She had no idea where to start with planning her life but she'd better get on with it. 'Thank you.'

Nikolai removed the transducer and nodded. As he wiped her belly he watched in awe as this slip of a girl digested her news with fierce concentration.

She was thanking him?

Well, he guessed she knew a lot more than she had half an hour ago because of him. And she seemed to be holding together pretty well. He thought of his sister again and his protective instincts kicked in. He didn't stop to think why he felt more involved than usual. But it was all a bit out of left field. 'Will you be all right?'

He wasn't sure what he'd do if she said no, and as he caught her eye, her delightful mouth curved into a smile and he saw her acknowledge that.

'Not a lot we can do if I'm not, is there?' She sat up and he helped her climb down. 'But, yes, I'll be fine. Eventually.'

He thought of his sister and the disastrous decisions she'd made in the heat of her terrifying moment all those years ago. And the ramifications now.

He thought of this woman under the care of a less-than-proficient practitioner like his sister had been, and his mind rebelled with startling force. 'I realise it's early, but if you'd like me to care for you through your pregnancy, I'd be happy to. There'd be no additional cost, of course.'

'Thank you, Dr Kefes. I think I'd like that when I get used to the idea of being pregnant. That would be most reassuring.'

She straightened her scrubs and he gestured for her to sit in the office chair.

'Wait one moment and I'll print out a list of pathology tests I'd like you to have. The results will come to me and we'll discuss them when they come back.'

The little unexpected catches of his accent made him seem less formidable and Lucy could feel the relief that at least she wouldn't be cast adrift with the bombshell all alone.

She watched his long fingers fly across the keyboard as he opened a file on his desk computer. He made her feel safe, which was dumb because she was just a silly little girl who'd got herself pregnant, and she almost missed it when he asked for her full name, date of birth and residential address.

Luckily her mouth seemed to be working even if her brain wasn't and she managed the answers without stumbling.

He stood up. Darn, that man was tall. 'The rest we will sort out at your next visit.'

Lucy nodded, took the form, and jammed it in her bag. 'Thank you. It's been a huge day.'

'Enormous for you, of course.' Nikolai decided she still looked dazed and he resisted the urge to give her a quick hug. He would have given Chloe one but he wasn't in the habit of hugging patients or staff.

'And…' he hesitated '…may I offer you congratulations?'

'I guess congratulations are in order.' She shook her head and he didn't doubt she was only barely comprehending what her news would entail.

There was an awkward pause and he searched around for something normal to say. 'Sister May tells me it was your first day of work. You did well and I look forward to working with you.'

He sounded patronising but had only intended to try to ease her discomfort about seeing him on the ward tomorrow.

He tried again. 'Of course your news will remain confidential until you decide to say otherwise.'

She nodded and he saw her draw a deep breath as she faced the door. She lifted her chin and he leaned in front of her to open the door. 'Allow me.'

He actually felt reassured. She would be fine. He now had some idea how strong this young woman really was. He would see that she and her babies remained as healthy as possible, he vowed as he watched her walk away.

But she did look heartbreakingly alone.

Lucy had always been alone.

Half an hour later she pushed open the door to her tiny cabana flat and the really bizarre thing was that it looked the same as when she'd left that morning.

It was she who'd changed. Drastically. And she was alone to face it. But then again when hadn't she been alone to face things? Luckily she had practice at it. The upside was that in about six months' time she'd never be alone again.

Upside? There was an upside? Where was the anxiety she should be feeling? She'd lived her whole life with that. Trying to do the right thing. She searched her feelings for anger and blame for the life-changing event that had just been confirmed, but she didn't find any.

Why aren't I angry with my babies? Didn't my mother get this feeling I'm feeling now? Almost—no, not almost, definitely—a real connection with her babies. Maybe this was what she was meant to be. A mother.

But twins. Fourteen weeks pregnant was ridiculous. Her first pregnancy was going to be over in twenty-six weeks' time, because she'd already gone through more than a third of it.

She'd better get her head around it pretty darned quick. Let alone the known fact that twins often came earlier than expected.

She guessed she'd had her official first antenatal visit with the delicious Dr Nick.

She had to snap any of those thoughts out of her brain. Not only had he been there to see her throw up but to hear her whole sordid story of a one-night stand resulting in an unwanted pregnancy. Times two.

She frowned, and her hand crept to her tiny bulge. 'It's okay, babies, I do want you now that I know about you, but you could have waited for a more opportune time.'

Lucy rolled her eyes. 'Like in about ten years, when I'd found a man who wanted to be your father. Preferably after the wedding.' Someone like Dr Kefes?

She straightened her shoulders and patted her belly. 'But don't worry. I'll give you all the love I never had and there will be no string of uncles staying over. If I don't meet a one hundred per cent perfect daddy for you, we'll do this ourselves.'

Her voice died away and she glanced around the empty room. She was going mad already. She'd bet Dr Kefes thought she was mad.

Twenty-two, single and taking on twins instead of the career she'd worked so hard to achieve.

She had almost been able to feel his soothing persona. He'd been very kind. Incredibly supportive considering he didn't know her. She could understand why women fell a little in love with their obstetricians if they were all like him.

Though she didn't think there could be a lot of tall, dark and dreamy docs out there with such a delicious hint of a foreign accent.

But at the end of everything, she would be the one holding the babies, and she'd better stop thinking that some demi-god was going to swoop in and lend her a hand.

This was her responsibility and hers alone.

She glanced at the tiny cabana she'd been lucky enough to score in exchange for house-sitting the mansion out front, and she was thankful. *Be thankful.* She needed to remember that. If the owners decided to sell, something else would turn up. She had to believe that.

And she would find a way to support her babies. She'd just have to save every penny she could until she finished work.

At least she'd get maternity leave—or would she if she was fourteen weeks pregnant on her first day? More things to find out.

But they did have a crèche at the hospital so eventually she'd be able to go back. If Flora May would have her after she told her the news. She put her head in her hands.

And how would she tell her mother?

A kilometre away, Nikolai threw his keys on the hall table inside the door of his flat and pulled off his tie. What a day. And not just with work.

He wasn't sure why he was so rattled by his encounter with Lucy the midwife, and her news, but he guessed it had to do with the day starting with his sister's phone call. He'd obviously associated the two women in his mind.

That explained his bizarre feeling of connection with young Lucy. And that was what she was. Young. Barely over twenty, and he was a good ten years older so it had to be an avuncular or older-brother protectiveness. He'd just have to watch it in case she got any ideas.

Because he certainly didn't have any.

Maybe it hadn't been so clever to offer to look after her during her pregnancy, but it had seemed right at the time. And he genuinely wanted her to have the best care.

But when the next day at work he only saw Lucy in the distance, she waved once discreetly because both of them were busy with their own workload, and by the end of the day his concerns had seemed foolish.

He wasn't piqued she hadn't made any effort to speak to him. Of course not. His concerns were ridiculous. But it seemed he had no worries that she might take liberties with his offer.

Then the day suddenly got busier and Lucy and her problems disappeared into the back of his mind.

The busyness of the ward continued for almost a fortnight, so much so that the staff were counting back in the calendars to see what had happened around this time ten months ago. Solar eclipse? Power blackout?

There was an unofficial competition to see who could come up with the most likely reason for the surge in births.

It was Lucy's fifth shift in a row and she was finding it harder to get out of bed at six in the morning.

'Come on, lazybones,' she grumbled to herself as she sat up on the side of the bed. 'You've got no stamina. You think it's going to be easier when you've got to get two little bodkins organised every three hours for feeds?'

She stood up and rubbed her back. 'They all say it's going to get quieter at work again soon. You can do this.' And she still hadn't told her mother. She'd told Mark and he'd offered money. And no strings. That was a good thing because she knew in her heart an unwilling Mark wasn't the answer for either of them. The last thing she wanted was her babies to see her in an unhappy relationship.

When Nikolai saw Lucy he could tell she was starting to feel the frenetic pace. Her usual determined little walk had slowed and he didn't notice her smile as often.

The next time he saw her he decided she looked far too pale and he couldn't remember any results from the blood tests he'd ordered a fortnight ago.

He added 'Follow up with Lucy' to his list of tasks for the day and tracked her down towards the end of the shift.

'One moment, Lucy.'

She stopped and smiled tiredly up at him. 'Yes, Doctor?'

He felt like offering her a chair. Wasn't anyone looking after this girl? It had been hard enough for him to look after Chloe and he'd been the same age as Lucy was now. And a man, not a slip of a girl.

It was tough making ends meet when you were trying to get through uni and feed yourself. He wondered if she was eating properly before he realised she was waiting for him to finish his sentence.

'Sorry.' He glanced around but no one was near them. 'I wondered why I haven't seen those results yet.'

Lucy racked her brain. An hour of the shift to go and she was finding it hard not to yawn. Now he wanted results and she had no idea whose he was talking about. For which patient? She frowned. 'Was I supposed to give you some results?'

'Yours. Antenatal screening.' He looked so hard at her she felt like he'd put her under the microscope.

'You look pale.'

She felt pale, if that was possible. She'd forgotten the tests. She ran back over that momentous day, back to his rooms. Yes, he'd given her forms, and the form was still scrunched in the bottom of her bag. Maybe there was something Freudian about that.

She sighed. 'I keep meaning to get them done. Maybe I'm not ready to tell the world.'

She saw him glance at her stomach and raise his eyebrows. She looked down, too. And didn't think it showed much yet.

He was frowning and he rarely frowned. That was one of the things she liked about this guy. One of the many things.

'I'd like you to do them today, if you could, please. Outside the hospital if you want to. But if you have them done internally there will be no charge for the pathology.'

And pathology tests could be expensive. Expenses she needed to cut back on. 'Big incentive.' She nodded. Just so he knew she meant it. 'I'll go after work.'

He stayed where he was. Looking so calm and collected and immaculate. She felt like a dishrag. Her back hurt. What else did he want?

'And could you make an appointment to come and see me in two days? I'll let my secretary know.'

Lucy laughed for the first time that day. It actually felt good. She could even feel the tension drop from her shoulders and reminded herself she needed to shed a few chuckles more often. She didn't want to forget that. Her mother had rarely laughed while she had been growing up.

But two days? It seemed she wasn't the only one who was tired. 'Two days is a Sunday. I don't think your secretary will be take an appointment on that one. But I will make it for Monday.'

Nick smiled back at her and she felt her cheeks warm. She frowned at herself and him. He shouldn't smile at emotional, hormonal women like that. Especially ones who were planning to be single mothers of twins.

She was never going to feel second best again and he made her feel like she wanted to be better than she was. The guy was just too perfect. For her anyway.

'Thanks for the reminder. Have to go.' She turned and walked back to the desk and she could hear his footsteps walking away. She could imagine the sight. The long strides. The commanding tilt of his head. Not fair.

'You okay there, Palmer?' Flora May was staring at

her under her grizzled brows. She glanced at the receding back of Dr Kefes. 'Is he giving you a hard time?'

'No. Of course not. He's been very kind.' Though she smiled at her fierce protector. 'I'm just tired.' Flora May did not look convinced. Lucy tried again. 'Not sure if I'm not coming down with something.'

Flora and Lucy were very similar in the way they viewed their vocation, and Lucy appreciated having Flora on her side. Never warm and fuzzy, Flora's no-nonsense advice was always valid, and usually made Lucy smile.

'You do look peaky. Pale and limp probably describes you.'

Lucy had to smile at the unflattering description. 'Thank you, Sister.'

'If you're unwell, go to the staff clinic at Emergency. Nobody else wants to catch anything. Either way, you can leave early. I'll do your handover. You get here fifteen minutes early every day and you're the last to leave. You've earned some time in lieu.'

The idea was very attractive.

Flora's lips twitched. 'But don't expect it every week.'

'I certainly won't.' Lucy looked at her mentor. Maybe now was a good time. She'd hate Flora to find out from someone else or, worse, through a rumour. 'Can I see you for a moment, Sister? In private.'

'Of course.' Flora gestured to her office.

Lucy drew a deep breath and Flora frowned at her obvious trepidation. 'Spit it out, Palmer.'

'I'm pregnant.' Lucy searched Flora's face for extreme disappointment. Anger. Disgust. She'd suspected Flora had plans for her training and knew she had been instrumental in choosing Lucy over other applicants. But Flora's expression didn't change. Except to soften.

She stepped forward and put her arm around Lucy's shoulders and gave her a brief, awkward hug before she snapped back into her professional self.

'That explains a lot,' she said gruffly. Cleared her throat. 'You've been a little more preoccupied than I expected.' To Lucy's stunned relief she even smiled. 'When, in fact, you've been a lot more focused than you could be expected to be.' Flora gazed past Lucy's shoulder while she thought about it.

Then she concentrated on Lucy again. 'And Dr Kefes is looking after you? He knows?'

Lucy blinked and nodded. How did Flora know this stuff? 'I forgot to have some tests and he was reminding me.'

'He's a good man.' Then she said something strange. 'Don't go falling for him. Easy people to fall for, obstetricians.'

Didn't she know it! A mental picture of Dr Kefes, five minutes ago, smiling down at her and her own visceral response highlighted that dilemma. No way was she going down that demoralising path. 'I won't. I'm not that stupid.'

Flora sniffed. Her piercing gaze stayed glued on Lucy's face. 'Is there a man on the scene? Some help coming?'

Lucy shook her head. She wasn't anxious to go into it but, judging by the sigh, it seemed Flora had expected that. 'Your family?'

Lucy shook her head again. She could dream her mother would turn into a supportive, caring, helpful shoulder to lean on but it was highly unlikely. She so dreaded that conversation but after surviving telling Flora today, maybe she could even hope a little that it would be as bad as she dreaded.

'I've got your back, Palmer. Go home now. Rest. You still look peaky. And if you want help or advice—ask!'

Lucy nodded past the lump in her throat. How had she been so lucky to end up with Flora as a boss?

Flora smiled at her. 'Look after yourself, Palmer. I still have big plans for you.'

Now she felt like crying, and if she didn't get out of here quickly she'd disgrace herself by throwing her sobbing self onto the starched front of her boss.

Lucy almost ran from the ward, past Cass who was on day shifts for a few weeks, and in her hasty departure she didn't see the speculative look that followed her.

She also forgot all about the blood tests she was supposed to get as she pressed the button for the lift and escape.

The doors opened. When she stepped in Nikolai was standing at the back of the lift like her nemesis. 'Are you going to Pathology now?'

Lucy blinked. She felt like smacking her forehead but instead refused to be goaded into saying she'd forgotten again. 'Are you following me?'

Thick, dark, eyebrows lifted. 'I imagine that would be difficult from the inside of a lift. Not being able to see through the walls.'

She played the words back in her head and winced. Impolite and ungrateful. It wasn't Dr Kefes's fault she felt physically and emotionally exhausted. 'Sorry. And, yes.' She sighed. 'I'll go to Pathology now.'

The lift stopped on another floor and two intense,

white-coated doctors entered, and the conversation died a natural death.

Lucy recognised one of the newcomers, Callie Richards, the paediatrician who was looking after Sally's baby. They both nodded at Nick but the tension between them was palpable to the other two in the lift and, fancifully, Lucy decided the air was actually shimmering.

It seemed other people had dramas, too. The man raised his eyebrows at Nick, who didn't change his expression, and Callie offered a forced smile to Lucy, who smiled back awkwardly.

One floor down the late arrivals stepped out and as the doors shut Lucy let out the breath she hadn't realised she'd been holding in a little whistle. She looked at Nikolai. 'Who's the guy?'

Nick smiled. 'Cade Coleman, prenatal surgeon from Boston. And you've met Callie Richards, the neonatal specialist. She's in charge of the NICU here and is looking after Sally's baby.'

'Yep. I remember her. She seems nice. It was just him I didn't know. I guess I'll recognise everyone soon.'

They reached the ground floor and the lift light changed to indicate 'up'. Lucy realised she hadn't directed the lift to take her further down to the laboratory.

Nikolai shook his head and pressed the lower-ground button for Pathology to override the person above. He put his hand across the doors to hold them open. 'Are you working on Monday?'

'One in the afternoon.'

'Perhaps you'd like to see me to get your results before you start. My rooms. Twelve-thirty? In case you forget to make the appointment.'

Ooh. It was her turn to give him the look. 'Fine.

Thank you.' As he took his arm away from the doors she said, 'Are you this helpful to all your pregnant ladies?'

He shrugged and she couldn't read the expression on his face. 'Only the really vague ones who forget to have their bloods done.'

'Touché,' she said cheekily, and he smiled. She watched him walk away until the doors shut and the lift sailed downwards. Well, she had been vague to forget again but she needed to sleep. As soon as she got home she was going to bed and sleeping the clock round.

Nick's hand tightened on his briefcase as he strode to the doctors' car park. She had a point. But the memories of Chloe, gaunt and drawn, haunted him and when he'd seen Lucy was looking so tired it had brought it all back. He needed to stop worrying about her. She wasn't Chloe, neither was she his responsibility. Although even Chloe would have a fit if she thought he still felt the need to keep her under his wing.

His phone rang. His registrar. Thoughts of Lucy shifted to the back of his mind again as he turned back to the hospital.

CHAPTER THREE

THAT NIGHT, AFTER a nap and crossing her fingers after her less-than-traumatic disclosure to Flora May, Lucy decided to talk to her mother. She glanced at the clock. It was too early for the dinner date her mother always had before clubbing with her friends on Friday nights but hopefully late enough to be after the ritual bath and nail preparation that took place prior to departure.

'Mum? It's Lucy.' There was a vague affirmative and Lucy bit back a sigh. One day she was going to stop hoping for a shriek of pleasure from her mother that she'd rung.

'I know you're going out. Can I talk for a minute?'

The conversation went downhill from there. If being told she had always known she would let her mother down, done the exact thing her mother had told her not to do, been called an immoral, stupid little girl, being told that no way was she ever minding her brats or even admitting to being a grandmother counted as a conversation going downhill.

Lucy was pretty sure it was, because she could feel herself curling into a protective ball as the tirade continued. She just got more numb and wasn't even aware of the tears as they rolled down her cheeks.

When her mother paused for breath, Lucy finished by whispering, 'And by the way, I'm having twins.' There was a further stunned silence and Lucy decided to put the phone down gently. Enough.

Yep. It had been as bad as she'd feared. Probably worse. She sucked in a breath and forced her shoulders to loosen from the deathlike squeeze she had them in.

Her hand crept to her belly. She wasn't having brats. She was having gorgeous babies and maybe they would be better off without a vitriolic grandmother. Maybe she would finally be able to separate her mother's idea of who she was from her own version. It might take a bit of practice but she had six months to do it before her babies were born.

Surprisingly, or perhaps not surprisingly given her exhaustion and mental distress, Lucy slept most of the night for the first time in ages.

On Saturday she did the bare minimum of housework and lazed and snoozed all day, recharging her batteries for next week's onslaught.

She started a journal, wrote down her thoughts and all the things she had to be grateful for, and began to talk to her babies. It was amazing what a difference a small change like that made.

By Sunday morning she was rested and felt more like her old self. In fact, she felt better than better. Maybe it was knowing that the dreaded call, despite being as horrific as she'd dreaded, was over. Done.

Some time in the night she'd felt the first real joy of what was to come. So this was her path. What she couldn't change, she would just do better.

Her midwifery would be put on hold, but at least it might have prepared her a bit for what was ahead.

Pregnancy, birth, maybe not twins but, hey, twice the joy. She'd been chosen for that double blessing for a reason, she just hadn't figured out what that reason was.

So, it was a beautiful day, her stomach growled with hunger for the first time in weeks, and she lived in a fabulous part of the world with the ocean right outside her landlord's front door. What wasn't to celebrate?

Filled with new vigour, Lucy tidied her cabana and afterwards scooted around the big house, plucked dead leaves off ornamental ferns, cleaned the aquarium filter and steam-mopped the outside terrace because the salt was crusty underfoot from the storm a few days ago.

Besides, she loved the front terrace, where she could look out over the white sand just behind the boundary fence, watch the paddle-boarders and hope to catch a glimpse of a whale or a dolphin.

As she hummed a country ballad the gate screeched as she took the garbage out, so she hunted out the lubricant spray, sang a few words and patted her stomach as she wandered back to fix it. 'We'll be okay, kiddos.'

Nick's Sunday morning wasn't going as planned. He'd knocked on Chloe's door to see if she was interested in them having breakfast together. It was handy having a sister in the flat next to his. He was starving and maybe they could catch up.

But after the third knock nobody came to the door, so she was either out or not answering. He'd go for a jog and see if she was there when he came back. He tried to check the impulse to find out where she was or who she was with. Just check she was okay, he reminded himself.

Nick was sick of his own company—which was

almost unheard of—and just a little bored. As he set off he reminded himself that exercise often worked to shut the voices down.

The beach felt great under the soles of his runners but while the long jog along the sand had helped his restlessness it had also stoked up his appetite for that iconic Sunday breakfast—one of his favourite times on the Gold Coast. With so many great places showing off the ocean, choice was a problem but the idea of eating alone, again, was less than appealing.

Not that there wasn't activity and people everywhere. Kids were learning to be lifesavers on the beach with their little tied-on caps and colourful swimmers. Paddle-boarders skimmed the backs of waves and made him wish he'd bought one. Apparently it was a useful and not sexually orientated exercise diversion—as his sister had wryly commented.

He didn't know why Chloe had a thing about his carefree love life. He wasn't promiscuous, he just didn't feel the need to belong to anybody.

He was happy to concentrate on his work and have fun with like-minded women. He wasn't out to break anybody's heart, and relationships were for dalliance, not drama.

Still, a diversion would be nice, he thought as his shoes slapped the footpath and he finally spied a shapely little surfer girl in a tiny bright skirt and floaty top ahead, kneeling beside the driveway of one of the mansions. She was doing something to a gate. He couldn't help his appreciative smile as he jogged closer.

The sunlight danced in a deep auburn cascade of hair that hid her face and the way she was leaning over promised the sort of shapely curves men liked and women didn't.

So it was a shock when she looked up to see hazel eyes and a rosebud mouth he already knew. Not a babe. It was Lucy. Pregnant-with-twins Lucy.

His social skills dropped with his confusion. 'Hey, stranger.'

She grinned at him. Looked him up and down and shook her head. 'Ha. I'm not the strange one. I'm not wearing shorts and joggers with black socks.'

'Ouch.' He looked down at his trunks and runners, and decided to throw away the socks, even though they barely showed above his shoes. He'd thought he looked okay. 'I'll have you know this is the latest in trendy jog wear.'

'My bad, then.' She didn't look sorry. She sat back and wiped her hair out of her eyes and the thick mane flashed like fire in the sunlight. Funny he hadn't noticed her hair that much at work. 'So, where do trendy joggers run to?'

He blinked. 'Mostly to and from the beach. And back to the hospital apartment building where a lot of the trendy staff stay.' He sounded like an idiot, so he glanced away and pointed to a tall building a block back from the ocean.

'Wondered where that was.'

He looked back at her and the slight breeze rippled her hair as she turned her head to look. He'd never had a thing for redheads before—but now he could see the attraction. He'd heard they had a tendency for fire and passion and he could just imagine young Lucy letting fly. The thought made him smile even more.

'I didn't know it was so close to the hospital,' she said. 'Been there long?'

His mind was five per cent on the conversation and ninety-five on admiring the view. 'Not that long. I live next door to my sister, Chloe. Two years now. Very convenient.'

'Someone said you had a sister who was a nurse at the hospital.' She nodded, and everything on the top half of her body wobbled a bit. He tried not to stare at her cleavage.

Things were getting foggy. 'Bless the grapevine. Yep.' Why was he brain dead? 'We used to share but she wanted her own place and couldn't see any reason to shift.' He was rambling. 'It's close enough to the hospital that I can walk if I want to. Or run in an emergency. Most times I drive because usually I'm going somewhere later.'

She nodded again and this time he made sure he didn't look south.

His mouth was dry. From the jogging, of course. He could seriously do with a drink. 'Is this your house?' He couldn't keep the surprise out of his voice but when she laughed he acknowledged relief. The last thing he wanted to do was offend her. She was having things tough enough.

Her lips curved. 'Yeah, right. I'm a closet millionaire.' She raised her eyebrows haughtily and grinned. 'I'm the house-sitter. These people are friends of an older couple who used to put up with me visiting a lot when I was a kid. They were the first people I told about the babies. Nearly time to go public.'

He thought about that. About the hospital and the rumours, and he consoled himself it would blow over in a week. He'd try to make sure he checked she was okay when it all blew up. 'Seems a very nice place to stay. You living in the house?'

'No.' When she shook her head it was better than nodding because everything really jiggled.

He should go but he enjoyed the way she talked. Bubbly and relaxed. Not like the women he usually hung out with, who were always on their best behaviour. He knew that Lucy wasn't trying to attract him. Which was a good thing because she needed a fling like she needed a hole in the head. And he didn't do relationships, and you couldn't have much else with a woman who was pregnant by someone else.

'I have the cabana out back, which suits me fine. I just open the house up every couple of days, let the breeze blow through, water the indoor plants. Feed the fish. That kind of stuff.'

She was sort of restful, too. He could picture her pottering around. Maybe humming off key. 'Spray the rusty gate kinda stuff?'

She waved the can. 'That's me. Handy Lucy.'

'Nice.' He refused to think about where he wanted to put his hands. Instead, he said, 'Would you like to go for breakfast?'

Where the heck had that come from? Nick couldn't believe he'd just said that. Hell, and he'd told himself he was going to be careful to keep it professional.

But apparently that thought couldn't stop him from embellishing the offer. 'Maybe bacon and eggs down at the surf club near Elephant Rock? My shout. We could try and get a table on the veranda and soak in some Vitamin D.'

He didn't even recognise what he was saying. Some

devil inside was using his mouth. Didn't it know she was going to be a patient of his as well as a work colleague? This was an invitation with disaster written all over it.

Lucy's face lit up with the happiest smile he'd seen all week. Too late to back out, then. So maybe having a devil using his mouth was worth it if she got that much of a kick out of company.

Her chin jutted as if she expected an argument. 'I'll pay my own way, thanks, but I love that place.'

Independent, then. He'd already guessed that. But he'd bet she was lonely, too.

'And I understand sunlight is very important for pregnant women.' She grinned. 'Gee. Breakfast on the beach and my appetite's back.'

A glow expanded in his chest, because he could have a cooked breakfast and not have to eat it alone, and he'd made a girl happy. Three good things from one action. 'I'll grab my car and meet you back here, in...' he glanced at his watch '...say, fifteen minutes?'

'Perfect.'

Nick lifted one hand as he jogged off towards the tall building Lucy could see further up the road. She recognised the bulk of the hospital behind and how it could be useful to have the consultants' units so close.

So it seemed Dr Kefes jogged by her door regularly. This morning she'd had her headphones in and hadn't heard him approach so it had been a shock when he'd stopped. She'd thought him just a well-built jogger and had been happy to admire the fitness machine, until she'd recognised him, then she'd been bowled over by the sheer physical presence of him.

That must have been where the black-sock comment

had come from. She'd felt like smacking her forehead when that had popped out.

'Just trying to make him human,' she muttered, and bit back a giggle. She should be aghast at herself for teasing him—but she wasn't, and he hadn't seemed to mind. He probably had women sucking up to him everywhere. She'd never been a toady—except to her mother, but she was going to train herself out of that—and wasn't going to start now.

Lucy gave the gate a final generous spray of lubricant and stood up.

And she darned well refused to feel nervous about going for breakfast with him. Dr Kefes. Nikolai. He hadn't actually said she could call him Nick but she'd worry about that later. She hadn't felt this good for weeks so she may as well enjoy it, and now there was a bit of unexpected excitement in her day.

Who knew when the next pregnancy ailment would strike? And she was in for double dose when it did come.

As for having breakfast with a consultant at her work who'd also offered to be her obstetrician, well, she wasn't going to get out of line, and there was no way he would. No reason they couldn't be friends.

By the time Nick arrived to pick her up Lucy was standing at the gate in a yellow sundress, complete, he couldn't help noticing, with bra. He saw the straps and stifled his disappointment. Stop it.

He leaned across and opened the passenger door for her because he could see she wasn't going to wait for him to get out and do the job properly.

She slid in, accompanied by a drift of some light and spicy perfume that smelt like the spring flowers Chloe kept around her flat, and she must have felt comfortable because she slid her sandals off.

Suddenly his car took on a new life. There was something earthy and incredibly sexy about bare brown toes rubbing over each other as she settled back in the leather seat.

She sighed blissfully and his day got better. 'Always fancied a convertible.'

He laughed. She made him laugh. 'Me, too.'

'This car would go with my house.'

He nodded sagely. 'Hell with a stroller, though.'

'Especially a twin stroller.' Their eyes met and he was pleased and surprised to see the serenity in hers. He admired her more each time they talked.

He'd have to watch that. 'I see you're at peace with your decision.'

'Yes. Thank you, Dr Kefes.'

'Nick.' He pulled over into a parking space right outside the restaurant that someone had just pulled out from, parallel to the beach. 'You must be very lucky to have around. I usually park twenty minutes away from this place.'

Her head was back against the headrest and her eyes were shut as the sun bathed her in bright yellow light. 'Lucky Lucy. That's me.'

He soaked the sight in for a few seconds, shook his head at her ability to just enjoy the moment and then leaned forward and removed his keys from the ignition. 'Handy and lucky? Worth cultivating.'

She opened her eyes. 'Hopefully someone will think so one day.' There was no self-pity in the statement. Just truth. 'I'm starving.'

He laughed again. 'So am I.' Typically, she was out of the car before he could get to her door.

They scored a table right on the corner of the big verandah overlooking the beach. 'More luck,' Nick murmured, and Lucy just smiled.

The salt-laden breeze blew their big umbrella backwards and forwards a little so that most of the time they were in the shade but every few seconds a brief wash of sunlight dusted her shoulders with golden light. Nick decided the view was great in every direction.

'So, have you thought about what you'll do when the babies are born?'

She rested her cute chin on her fingers. She made him feel so relaxed. 'My next-door neighbour used to say, "Planning to make a plan is not a plan", so, yes. I have a plan.'

He was intrigued. 'And that is?'

She straightened. 'I'll work as long as I can then hopefully I'll get maternity leave from work. It won't be paid but from what Flora May said I think I get to keep my job. The hospital has a crèche, so I'll go back to work one day a week part-time as soon as possible, and that's only eight hours away from them. That's not unreasonable.'

She shrugged. 'When we all get used to that I'll do two days and so on. Not quite sure how I'll survive financially with that but that's a few months ahead. And I've saved a little money.' She grinned at him. 'Luckily, I'm not a material girl.'

It sounded pretty shaky for a plan but she hadn't had much time. 'What about your parents?'

Her face changed and he wondered if she really was shrinking into the chair or if he was just imagining it.

She looked away out over the waves and he seriously regretted having asked the question, judging by her response.

'Parent.' She shrugged and still didn't meet his eyes. 'Only ever had Mum, though she's a two-edged sword. She always said I ruined her life.'

'Your mother?' He tried to imagine an older Lucy with a nasty mouth.

She shrugged and he decided she had the best shoulders in the restaurant.

'Imagine one of those anxious-to-please, quiet little girls who could never get anything right?' She forced a smile and Nick decided it actually hurt to watch. Maybe she wasn't so together after all.

He couldn't quite put this girl together with the one who had dragged him in to see her patient on her first day.

'Anyway. That little girl was me. The only time I ever felt like a winner was when I accepted my midwifery degree. And Mum didn't make it to see that.'

But, still, her mother? Nick thought. 'So she won't help you?'

'Mum?' Lucy laughed but it wasn't the sound he'd heard before. Surprisingly there was no bitterness in the sound, just the scrape of raw nerves. 'She taught me to rely on myself. That's a pretty helpful trait.'

He guessed his own parents had done that to Chloe and him as well. 'And you're not bitter?' He certainly was. Not for himself now but for the young teen his sister had been when they'd cast her off, and him for supporting her.

He guessed his parents had hurt him the way he could see Lucy's mother had hurt her, but he hadn't really had time to worry about it. He'd been more worried about getting food on the table and pushing Chloe to study.

Lucy was staring over the waves and fancifully he wondered why the sun wasn't playing with her any more.

'Mum managed as well as she could with her own disappointments. Now she is a material girl.'

She straightened and he saw a little more of the midwife advocate he'd seen on the ward. 'If there's one thing I know, it's that my children won't feel a burden. I'm ambitious for my midwifery, but I'll be there for them no matter what.' It seemed she could fight for others but not for herself. He'd think about that later.

'My mother told me she'd left it too late to get rid of me, and I'm so pleased I can say I made the choice to keep my children.'

Hell. Her mother had told her that? Nick had thought his parents were insensitive but he couldn't imagine what being told that would do to the psyche of a young woman.

But she'd moved on. At least in this conversation. 'I'd hoped that by the time I had kids my husband would have a warm and fuzzy mother who would tuck me under her wing and do girl things with me. Looks like that's not going to happen.'

He didn't usually mention it, in fact, he couldn't re-member ever mentioning it, but maybe it would help if she knew other people had failures as parents. 'Or you could end up with a mother like ours who just wiped Chloe and me out of her life and broke off all contact.'

'What do you mean?'

They'd behaved as though their two children hadn't

existed. My word, he remembered that, the way he'd pleaded with them to soften towards his sixteen-year-old sister, when all he'd wanted to do had been to tear strips off them for their unforgiveable behaviour.

He'd taken too many bitter rebuffs for Chloe to ever forgive them.

It had been a defining moment in his life to learn that people could choose to exclude others regardless of how much pain they'd caused. It was also the perfect reason not to become emotionally involved, and that mantra had worked for him very well.

And Chloe was suffering because she still couldn't do the same. 'Refused to communicate. Didn't answer calls when I tried to get them to talk to Chloe.'

'That sucks. I'm sorry.' Then she looked away and he almost missed her further words. 'But you have your sister. I had no one.'

She lifted her chin. 'Sorry. I'm spoiling your breakfast with my complaining. I didn't mean to. And I'll have my babies soon.' She lifted her chin higher. 'I'm tough. I'll give up whatever I need to for my babies to have a good life and I will always be there for them. Money and possessions aren't important. Love is.'

This had got pretty deep pretty fast, but he'd asked for it. He shifted in his seat. Contrarily, now he wanted out of this discussion. He tried for a lighter note. 'Money buys you sports cars.'

She raised those haughty brows. 'Yeah, but you can't fit twin strollers in them.'

The waitress arrived to take their orders, the conversation bounced back to impersonal, and thankfully the sun came back and danced on her. He didn't know if he'd directed it that way or if she had, but seagulls wheeled overhead, and the breeze made him want to push the hair out of Lucy's eyes.

They talked about the hospital, the great facilities the birth suites had, their young mum's baby's progress and how the young mum had been so diligent in the special care nursery after her own discharge. They were both careful not to mention anyone's names, and it made it more intimate that only the two of them knew who they were talking about.

To his disappointment, the meals were on the table in no time.

For the first time he wished the usually 'snowed under with orders' staff were not so efficient because by the way Lucy was tucking into her meal they'd be out of there in half an hour.

They ate silently until Lucy sat back with an embarrassed smile. 'Wow. I even beat you.'

He admired her empty plate. 'I can see you were hungry.'

She shrugged. 'Rather feed me for a week than a fortnight, eh? But up until today I haven't been eating well.'

She was too cute. 'I think you're cured.'

She patted her round stomach. 'Not too cured, I hope. I don't want to look like a balloon by the time these babies are born.'

His eyes slid over her appreciatively. 'I don't think you have to worry. But I'll mention to your obstetrician to keep an eye on your weight.'

She wagged a finger at him. 'You do that.' Then she began to fiddle with her teaspoon and he wondered what was coming. You never knew with this woman. 'I need to thank you.'

He shifted uncomfortably. 'What for.'

Hazel eyes caught his. 'For looking after me on the day the bomb dropped.'

He glanced at the children playing in the surf. 'My pleasure.'

She laughed and he looked back at her. Couldn't avoid the urge at the sound. 'I'm sure it wasn't. I fell to pieces.'

Her eyes crinkled and her white teeth were just a little crooked. That tiny unevenness made her seem more real than other women he'd dated. Seriously delightful. 'I didn't see any pieces. I though you held up remarkably well.'

She threw back her head and laughed and he saw a man at another table look their way with an appreciative smile. Nick stared and the guy looked away.

Lucy was oblivious to anyone else. 'Come on. I threw up in front of you.'

That made him smile. 'But very tidily.'

He shrugged. 'I didn't actually see anything...' He shook his head mournfully. 'And have tried not to think about it.'

She laughed again and he enjoyed that he'd made it happen this time. 'I had no idea you were mad.'

'I hide it.' He shrugged.

She pretended to clap her hands. 'Very well, if I may say so. Anyway. Thank you. If it wasn't for you I would have been alone.'

She shouldn't have been. It made him wonder just where this one-night stand was now. It took two to tango. 'What about the father?'

She brushed the unknown man away and, contrarily, now Nick winced in sympathy for the mystery sperm donor. 'I don't expect anything more from him. My mother managed when my own father walked out.'

'But does he know?' Nick still had issues with that. He'd certainly want to know if a woman he'd helped make a baby with hadn't told him.

Almost as if she'd read his thoughts, she said, 'I've told him. He had a right to that information. He suggested termination.'

'Did that offend you?' He'd sort of put it out there, too, not that he was an advocate, especially after Chloe's disaster. Did she hold that against him?

'It clarified his level of commitment. Although he sent a generous amount of money for a termination and said to use it as emergency fund if I didn't use it for that. I won't be putting him on the birth certificate, or expect financial assistance again, unless the babies want that sometime in the future.'

Some conversation that must have been. 'Is that wise?' She was so clinical. 'Won't you need more financial help?' Judging by her 'plan', he thought she might.

'He's a friend. You don't ask friends for money. Even ones you accidentally sleep with. He has his own life and these are my children.'

In this sense she was so tough. So focused. And if he admitted it, just a little scary in the way she seemed to have taken this momentous news in her stride.

It was in his culture to expect women to need help. Greek heritage was all about family. Except for his own toxic parents.

Chloe had allowed him to be there when she'd needed him, but she was his sister. And she was less amenable now. This woman was nothing to him and he was nothing to her. He should be glad she could stand on her own feet.

Lucy heard the brave words leave her mouth and almost believed them. She pushed away the tiny ache for someone else to share some of the responsibility at least. It certainly wasn't this lovely doctor's problem. A shame, that.

She needed to man up. The thought made her smile. Like one of those insects that changed sex once they were pregnant, except she was going the other way. Actually, quite a disquieting thought. 'Thank you for bringing me with you for breakfast.'

Ouch, Lucy thought, she sounded like a little girl after a party. But he was too sweet. Too darned handsome and masculine and eminently capable of carrying responsibility. She rummaged in her purse and brought out the correct change for her meal and slipped it discreetly under her napkin.

Thankfully he didn't say anything. Just picked it up and put it in his pocket. 'I gather you're ready to go?'

'Yes, please.' She picked up her bag and stood before he could come round to her chair. She had the idea she was frustrating his attempts to treat her like a lady but she wasn't his date and she wanted to make that clear.

Judging by his face, he got it. 'I'll fix this up and meet you outside, then.'

Good. She'd have time to go to the ladies' room. She smiled to herself. Being pregnant certainly affected her bladder capacity.

Nick tried not to watch her scurry off and he remembered she was pregnant. How could he have forgotten that? There was no reason they couldn't be friends but

the sooner he dropped her home the better. Afterwards
he might go and buy himself a paddleboard and take
some of that frustration out on the waves.

CHAPTER FOUR

Before lunch on Monday Nick had a strange conversation with Callie Richards, ostensibly a neonatologist discussing a case with attending obstetrician.

Nick wasn't sure how Sally's baby in NICU had somehow ended up with Cade Coleman, the prenatal surgeon, who was apparently giving Callie a hard time. Which was a bit of a joke because Callie loved to straight-talk, too, and the whole hospital was buzzing with the sparks those two were striking off each other.

Callie was a good friend, but there was no chemistry between them, despite their pretty similar outlooks on relationships and no-strings sex.

He thought to himself with amusement, as Callie raved, that any chance of that was out there amongst the waves, with Cade now on the scene.

He put up his hand to stem the flow. 'You fancy him.'

Callie stopped. Shocked. 'I do not.'

Nick raised his eyebrows. 'So this is you being oblivious is it?'

She glared at him. 'I'm just sick of being growled at.'

'I've seen him work in prenatal surgery.' Nick shrugged. 'The guy's intense, he cares, and he's even great with the parents. He's allowed a little growling.'

'I'm whining, aren't I?' Callie drooped.

'A little.' Nick couldn't help but smile.

Callie lifted her head and drew in an audible breath. 'I needed that.' She picked up her briefcase. 'You're right. Thanks.' And she sailed out.

Nick shook his head and glanced at his watch.

Lucy should be here in a minute. He'd given her the time slot he usually reserved for completing the paperwork from the morning and he guessed he could start it now.

He sat down at the desk and tried to concentrate to stop himself opening the door to see if she'd arrived yet. Obviously she hadn't because his secretary would have rung. He picked up his pen again and his eyes strayed to his watch.

Lucy turned up for her first real antenatal appointment at the hospital and despite the fact she was going straight to work from there, she'd tried to be inconspicuous by dressing in loose civilian clothes.

It didn't work. The first person she saw as she opened Nick's office door was the Callie Richards, who was just leaving.

'Hello, there, Lucy isn't it? You're the midwife who looked after Sally, aren't you?'

'Yes, how is little Zac?' Lucy could feel the heat in her cheeks as she smiled and nodded, pretending it was wonderful that the senior paediatrician had recognised her entering an obstetrician's office. On one level it was, but on the other, not so great.

Callie must have picked up her discomfort because her expression changed. 'Great.' And then, cryptically, she said, 'No problem, by the way.' She smiled reassuringly. 'Have a good day.'

This was silly, feeling embarrassed. It was all going to come out pretty soon anyway. 'You, too.'

Callie left and as Lucy crossed to the reception desk, her cheeks only got pinker. This was terrible.

Nick opened his door. 'Lucy?'

The receptionist looked up and waved her through and as she walked past him into his rooms she started to feel better.

Nick seemed so broad and tall and she realised she really liked that about him. It was reassuring for some reason. He was a man to have beside you in a dark alley. Or a single-parent pregnancy.

At five feet seven she wasn't short, but he made her feel tiny as he shut the door behind her. She crossed the room, sat in the seat she remembered from nearly three weeks ago and tried to relax.

So much had changed in that time. She looked up at him, fighting the urge to stare, and wasn't so sure it was going to work, having Nick as her obstetrician. She remembered Flora's words and promised herself she wouldn't fall for her obstetrician.

Having lunch with Nick yesterday, he with his flash convertible and trendy clothes, and she a single-parent house-sitter with no assets, had shown her how big the distance was between them. It had also shown just how easily he could get under her skin.

She did not have the head space for that.

'Thank you for seeing me so quickly.' Being friends might prove a little dangerous but she owed him at least that for being so kind to her.

He settled behind his desk and opened her file.

'You're welcome. I know you're on your way to work.'
He glanced at her clothes. 'And need to get changed
as well.'

Yeah, well, that had been a non-starter. 'I was trying to be discreet but that failed dismally when I ran
into Dr Richards.'

His face softened and she knew he got that. 'If you're
worried about people finding out, Callie won't say anything. But it's going to happen soon. Just remember it
will all blow over.'

Yeah well. 'It's fine. I was being silly. I'm not
ashamed, I just don't want to answer a lot of questions
and talk about stuff I haven't had much time to think
about. I've told Sister May, anyway. She was the only
one I'd worry about finding out from someone else other
than me.'

'What about your mother? I meant to ask yesterday.
Have you told her about your pregnancy?'

He saw the look that crossed her face, and the intensity of it shocked him. He hadn't picked that up yesterday. He had thought she was safer behind the wall she'd
built than she really was.

He wanted to find Lucy's mother and shake her. But
as he watched, the look faded and Lucy lifted her chin.

Lucy did not want to think about her mother. It had
swamped her for a moment when Nick had asked. She
hated sympathy, it always made her want to weep, and
she wasn't doing that here.

It was nice he cared but what was her mother to him?
'Yes. But I haven't spoken to her since. I'm not in the
mood for a lecture and it's not like listening to her rage
is going to change my life.'

He sat back and studied her. She tried not to squirm. 'So how are you feeling in yourself?'

'Still great.' She nodded and glanced at her watch. 'So, did the blood tests all come back okay?'

Nick pushed his less-than-professional questions away. What was he doing anyway? He should be going through the motions. A normal antenatal visit. Not thinking about yesterday. Not thinking about it really hard.

And she was impatient to be gone. So typically Lucy. He should have guessed from the first morning she'd herded him into Sally's birth unit. No beating around the bush. She was a bit driven, like Callie Richards, and he'd always admired Callie.

The difference was that Lucy refreshed him and he didn't know why. 'The tests were, on the whole, fine. You're a little low with your haemoglobin, so taking iron tablets won't go amiss. Your white cells are a little elevated, so I just wanted to check you're not feeling the effects of any symptoms of infection.'

Her ponytail flipped from side to side. 'Nope. Since yesterday morning I've never felt better.'

Nick smiled and he remembered her appetite from the restaurant. He smiled. 'The second trimester of pregnancy is often the most enjoyable healthwise.'

Lucy reminded herself that she was going to be thankful for everything. 'I'm determined to enjoy it.'

'Good on you. Hold that plan.' He stood up and glided the BP machine over to her chair. 'That sounded patronising but I was sincere. I see a lot of women who expect to be really ill, for some reason, like their mother was, and not surprisingly they are.'

When Nick leaned towards her she could smell that

aftershave he'd worn yesterday and she was transported back to sitting with him in his car.

The aftershave had been part of that lovely drive to the beach with him. The whole lovely morning.

But this was now. She watched his big hands wrap the blood-pressure cuff around her arm and pump it up, and she tried not to think about his fingers on her skin.

Before he put the stethoscope into his ears he murmured, 'I just wonder if some women subconsciously programme their bodies to suffer more than they need to.'

She concentrated on his words. Intensely, so she didn't think about his hands. 'Interesting idea and guaranteed to stir up a hornet's nest of debate. My mother hadn't even noticed she was pregnant until too late.'

Déjà vu, then, she thought, and closed her mouth.

That will teach you to stop rabbiting on when he was trying to listen. She kept forgetting he was the senior consultant and she was a new grad midwife—but he was so easy to talk to.

'It's not silly.' He let the blood-pressure cuff all the way down and entered the result on the computer, as well as writing it on the yellow antenatal card he'd started. 'Blood pressure's normal.'

She looked at the card. Something she'd seen so many times held by pregnant women in antenatal clinics everywhere. Funny how something simple like that could bring it all home to her. She was going to have her own babies. 'I'm going to get my own yellow card with my whole pregnancy documented. I never thought I'd have one of those so soon.'

'Yep.' He smiled. 'Don't lose it.'

As if she would. 'Do many women lose their pregnancy records?'

He shook his head. 'No. It's funny really. They lose
scripts, ultrasound requests forms, consult letters, but
even the dottiest of my patients knows where her card
is. I think of it as the first maternal instinct.'

Lucy grinned. 'That's pretty cool, actually.'

'I think so.' He gestured towards the couch with a
smile and she knew he was remembering the first sight
of her babies up there with his portable ultrasound. Not
something she would forget either.

When she'd climbed up onto the couch she pulled up
her shirt and they both looked at her belly. It seemed a
lot bigger already.

She chewed her lip as she lay down. 'Lucky I wear
scrubs at work to hide this.'

He smiled. 'Soon it won't matter what you wear because these little people are going to pop out in front
for everyone to see.'

Nick felt above her belly button and gradually moved
the heel of his hand down until he felt the firm edge
of her uterus. 'You're already above the level of eighteen weeks.'

'Is that good?'

'Expected to be a little over dates.' He slid the little
ultrasound Doppler across her belly and they heard one
of the baby's heartbeats and then to the left the other
one for a brief few seconds. They both smiled. 'We're
very lucky to have found them both. It's hit and miss
this early to find a single pregnancy heartbeat unless
you're using the full ultrasound machine.'

It was incredible how warm and excited just hearing
her babies made her feel. Like Christmas was coming.

Along with the most expensive credit-card bill yet when she finished work.

He helped her climb down and she could feel the leashed strength under his fingers. There was a funny little knot in her stomach as their hands parted. Uh-oh. She stood on the scales so he could write down her weight and surreptitiously wiped her palm down her jeans.

She looked down at the digital readout. 'I've put on a kilo!'

'I'll mention that to your obstetrician.' They smiled at each other, both remembering Sunday's conversation about ballooning in pregnancy.

She stepped off the scale and sat down again in the chair, and he entered the weight in his computer. 'Everything looks fine.'

'Good.' She glanced at her watch. She had plenty of time to get changed.

'Excellent. Then I'll just send you for a formal ultrasound towards twenty weeks and I'll see you after that. If you have any problems or concerns, you can contact me on this number or just ask if you see me.'

She took his card and glanced at where he'd written his mobile phone number in bold numbers across the back.

'Thank you.' Did he do that for all his women? Not like she could ask. She slipped it into the back of her purse. So it was over. She was back to being just a little new midwife on the ward. Well, that was a good thing.

Nick felt he'd let her down in some way but he couldn't think how so he went back to impersonal mode. Lucy was the same as any other pregnant patient of his.

'You're welcome. Just ask my secretary for an appointment in four weeks.'

He imagined the changes that would happen between now and then. She would be over halfway. She'd be able to feel her babies move. He'd always been fascinated by that.

He watched her jump up. No gentle, ladylike rising for Lucy. Always in a hurry and usually with a smile. He admired her coping ability very much.

'I'll do that.'

'Have a good shift, Lucy.'

The next two weeks passed and Lucy went to her ultrasound appointment when she was just under twenty weeks pregnant with the surprise support person of Flora May.

Flora's enthusiasm was such a pleasure. They smiled with mutual excitement as the ultrasonographer pointed out legs and arms and movements. The babies jiggled about with every move of the ultrasound wand, and Flora laughed and said, 'They'll be a handful.'

Once she'd found out about Lucy's predicament Flora had proved to be her greatest champion, without mollycoddling her.

Unlike Lucy's mother, who'd had only negative comments to offer when Lucy had steeled herself to call, Flora had useful tips and hints on some of the common and less comfortable aspects of pregnancy.

Uncharacteristically, Flora had also quizzed her on how she liked Nick as her doctor, and Lucy had been a bit flustered about that under Flora's knowing gaze.

Coincidentally or not, she'd found herself looking after patients who weren't under the care of Dr Kefes and it actually became easier not having to see Nick all the time because the last thing she needed on top of everything else was a crush on a man who was just being kind.

Nick saw very little of Lucy despite a small unobtrusive effort to keep an eye on her. He found himself thinking often about how Lucy's mother had hurt her.

He could see the shame and hurt of abandonment—it was exactly how Chloe had looked all those years ago when he'd had to tell her their parents hadn't asked about her. Chloe was still affected by the things she'd done because she'd thought she'd had to for their parents' approval. What a disaster that had been.

Initially he'd thought Lucy a confident and independent young woman. She'd certainly made a strong stand on her first shift, but, in fact, he suspected she was vulnerable, and that underneath that bravado she was insecure. That had changed the way he looked at her. Pregnant and fragile, she needed someone to keep an eye on her.

So when he did his morning rounds he tried to check on her, but lately she seemed to melt into the background, and at the end of the day, when he'd taken to visiting the ward one more time before his afternoon appointments, he only caught glimpses of her in the distance.

He was starting to wish he'd made that next antenatal appointment a bit closer, but the latest guidelines were leaning heavily towards fewer visits, not more, for pregnant women, and he didn't want to draw attention to her.

She still hadn't told anyone else except Flora and he was surprised the gossip mill hadn't found out and run with the news. When it did he hoped he was around to make sure she was okay.

In fact, Nick was there when it broke. He rounded the corner just as the night-shift midwife passed the news to the oncoming staff.

'Did you know Flora May's little pet is pregnant? No boyfriend. And twins! What sort of mother will she be?' The words hung in the air as Nick approached and both young women shut their mouths as Nick descended on them.

He actually needed to count to ten before he said something because what he wanted to say would have caused a much bigger furore than just the announcement. 'Gossiping again, Cass?' He shook his head. 'You'll get a name for it.'

The blonde flushed with embarrassment but Nick was still trying to control his protective reaction. 'By the way, I'm not happy with the observations in birth room one either. Can you do them again before you go off? I'll drop by and check them in the chart later.' He glanced over both women without smiling. 'Thank you.'

He walked away, still fuming, and didn't see Flora May step out of her office into his path.

'Excuse me, Dr Kefes?'

Nick stopped. He refocused, not sure why he was so upset. Focused on Flora. 'Yes?'

Flora watched his face and he tried to lose any expression that would give away his thoughts. 'Do you have a problem with my staff?'

Did he? He was calming down now. He blinked and let his breath out. 'No. Of course not.'

Flora nodded. 'I didn't think so.'

Nick nodded and prepared to move on. Maybe head

back to his office to think about what he'd just over-reacted about.

'And, Dr Kefes?'

'Yes?'

'Most people are supportive.'

'Good.'

On the Sunday morning, four weeks after her last appointment, the sun was beating down and Lucy was using the leaf blower to clear the path down to the fence that backed onto the beach.

The blower seemed heavier than last week and her back ached a little and she wished the palm trees gave her a little more shade. She knew she had to be careful because her body was designed to stretch but there was increased risk of pulling a muscle or over-stretching a ligament thanks to the pregnancy hormones.

She could imagine Flora May saying, 'When you have twins there is even more pregnancy hormone and you have to be careful.'

So she stopped, leaned on the gate in front of the beach, looked over the fence towards the waves and just breathed in the salt-laden air. Her backache eased and the breeze helped. As she began to feel better, she tried to ignore the little skip to her breathing when she thought about seeing Nick tomorrow.

Tried to bring down her silly euphoria by reminding herself her days off were nearly over and the new week ready to begin. Could she do this for another three months?

At least everyone knew she was pregnant now. It was too hard to hide even with the baggy scrub uniform, and Maternity was the best place to work when you were having a baby yourself because it was the place with the least germs.

There'd been a few snide comments, mostly originating from Cass, but a lot of unexpected support from others. Especially Flora May.

She'd be okay. Nick would make sure of that, her inner voice said with a shimmy.

A tall paddleboard rider lifted his hand and waved and instinctively she waved back. Now even the board riders looked like Nick. She needed to settle before tomorrow.

She glanced back at the rider and gulped when the unknown man turned the board towards her and rode the next wave to the beach opposite her fence.

Good grief, she thought as she watched him pull his board onto the sand, and was about to beat a hasty retreat when she realised that it really *was* Nick.

Nick couldn't believe his luck. He'd known it would be a good idea to buy this board. He trod through the hot sand up to her gate. 'Morning, Lucy.'

Lucy leant on the fence. 'Morning, Nick. I thought I'd accidentally given the come-on to a stray surfer for a minute there.'

He was surprisingly glad she hadn't waved at a stray surfer. He'd known exactly whom he was waving at.

She was dressed in red and green, vibrant like one of the lorikeets feeding off the bottlebrush, but her face was strangely pale. 'Sorry if I scared you.' He wondered if she'd guessed he'd been looking out for her.

'All good. So, what made you paddle by?'

He glanced down at the board under his arm. 'To show off my new toy, and see how you are.'

She gave his board a thorough inspection. 'Your board is very sleek and...dark.'

It had been the best one he could buy. 'I've got a thing for black.'

'I noticed.' She glanced pointedly at his bare feet and raised her brows as if to say, 'Where are your socks?' 'And as for how I am, won't you see me tomorrow?'

He ignored the tomorrow comment and looked a bit closer. 'You look a little tired.'

Her brows shot up. 'You should know women hate being told that!'

'You still look good.' She did, but she wasn't her usual robust self.

'I got hot. Probably need a drink, actually. The owners are coming down tonight and I'm sprucing up the house. Don't want to get kicked out. Especially now.'

He frowned. She did too much. Days off were for her to rest. 'Want a hand? You don't need to work every day.'

Lucy looked at Nick, semi-naked, barefoot, with an extremely cumbersome board hooked under his arm like it was a matchstick, and thought about having him follow her around while she tidied.

It would be much, much easier on her own. And she still felt that little thrill his comment had left her with about looking good. That had been unexpected.

So it wasn't sensible to invite him in, and she was practising sensible. 'Thanks, but, no, thanks.'

She could see Nick hadn't expected the knock-back. She watched him try his special, come-on smile—she'd bet that usually got him the response he wanted. 'I may look like a distinguished obstetrician, but I can mow, trim and clean gutters.'

She could feel a smile inside growing with his determination to get her to change her mind. He was like a stubborn little boy who wanted to play.

'Luckily, I'm not responsible for any of those things, but thanks for the offer.'

She could see that had not been the response he wanted. In fact, he'd crashed and burned, and she watched him assimilate that.

Safety sucked but she needed to stick to her guns.

'The last thing I want is to be a nuisance.'

'As if you could.'

He shrugged easily. 'No problem. I'll see you tomorrow.' He picked up his board and turned back to the sea.

She couldn't believe she'd given the most gorgeous guy she knew the brush-off. But it had been the right thing to do. Depressed, she picked up the blower and her back reminded her it was heavy.

Maybe she should have taken up his offer. She flicked a wistful glance his way but she could see his strong thighs as he strode towards the water and the bulge in his biceps as he carried the board back towards the waves. It was too late. It was actually hard, watching him walk away.

Unexpectedly she felt a strange cramp low at the front of her abdomen and her annoying backache took on a more sinister significance. What if it wasn't just the heaviness of the leaf blower?

Then she realised her babies hadn't moved much that morning, and a deep unease expanded in her chest.

When the cramp came back, this time intensified into a painful drag in her belly, she had to drop the blower and clutch at the fence.

'Nick,' she said in a small scared little voice. Not

surprisingly, he couldn't hear because he was almost into the waves. She edged towards the gate and opened it as if her voice would carry further. She just needed the pain to stop so she could call out.

To Lucy's intense relief, before he climbed onto his board, Nick looked back and waved. She waved, signalled him back, a little frantically, and he stopped.

Stared at her.

She saw him tilt his head as if wondering if he'd misunderstood. The pain came again and she put both hands on the fence.

When she looked up Nick was through the gate and beside her. His board was halfway up the sand where he'd dropped it. All she could think was how good it was he'd come back.

The concern in his voice made her eyes sting. 'You okay?'

'I'm not sure.' Her voice cracked.

Nick saw the tears at the corners of her eyes. What was this all about? Somewhere inside a voice mocked him, told him to watch out, and he panicked that she was getting needy for him. He did not do needy.

Then she said the unexpected. 'I've had a few cramps in my back this morning and thought it was because I was carrying the blower. But now they've moved to the front.' Big worry-flecked eyes searched his face for reassurance.

What?

All thoughts of himself disappeared.

She chewed her lip. 'I'm scared it's the babies.'

His mind went blank except for the big words, 'miscarriage', 'prem labour', and they were suddenly unpalatable thoughts. She'd be twenty-two weeks.

That was too early for the babies to have a fighting chance. He didn't ask himself how it was he knew exactly how far along she was. But instinctively he stepped in, gathered her against him and his arms went around her.

Surprisingly she fitted into his body like a jigsaw piece he'd always been missing and he soaked in the warmth of her as if he'd been chilled.

'It's okay,' he murmured into her hair as he breathed in the scent of herbs and spring and Lucy.

He squeezed her gently. His hand came up and smoothed her hair and he suddenly connected with what he was doing and his relationship force field snapped back into place. He did not do emotional.

He loosened his arms. Stepped back.

Steered her to the wrought-iron seat while his mind beat him up with reminders not to get involved.

'Sit. Take it easy. It might be nothing.' He hoped it was nothing.

He hadn't picked the amount of investment he had in these babies already. He needed to snap out of that and get back to the person with the medical degree. 'Have you had any bleeding?'

'Not that I know of.' She'd wrapped her arms around her lower belly, protecting her children, and it did strange things to his chest to see her so panicked.

Distress vibrated off her in bigger waves than those in the nearby ocean.

She sat as directed, as if it would all be all right if she did everything she was told, as if he held her fate in his hands. No pressure. Not.

'Okay. No bleeding. That's good. It might have just

been a warning sign for you to take it a little easier. Have you any pain now?'

She shook her head and her hair fell into her eyes. He resisted the urge to brush it back.

'Just a tiny ache in my back.'

Her back. Still suspicious. 'Is it coming and going or there all the time?'

'There all the time.'

Best of the bad. 'Again, that's good. Maybe you have a low-grade kidney infection. Very common with pregnant women and a big player in causing premature labour.'

He saw her wince when he said it but she needed to know he wasn't joking. Maybe he should have tested her again for infections, even though she'd said she was fine.

There was that raised white cell count. He didn't stop to ask why he was beating himself up about something he would have done for anyone else. But this was Lucy.

Lucy was in shock. From two things—the stark terror of risk to her babies and the absolute comfort she'd gained from being wrapped up in Nick's arms. All that salty skin and muscle around her had felt like a shield from the world.

As if nothing in the universe could go wrong as long as she was snuggled into his arms. So it had been a nasty reality when he'd disentangled himself and sat her away from him.

Now he expected her to take in what he was saying when her mind felt like she was inside a big ball of cotton wool and danger was waiting if she peeked out.

'Sorry?' She concentrated and the cotton wool thinned a little. 'Kidney infection?'

Yep, maybe. She had been dashing for the ladies more often this week. She should have picked that up. They could fix that. Everything would be okay if she took it easy until antibiotics sorted that irritation.

Maybe she'd take Monday off. Thank goodness she'd told Flora May about the pregnancy. And Nick could take her aside and explain as well. Or was that presuming too much?

He glanced up towards the house. 'You go to bed. I'll write you a script. In fact, I'll get the antibiotics from the chemist for you. We'll get a sample from you before you take your first dose so we can make sure we've targeted the right bug.'

Lucy listened to him laying out the strategy and she couldn't help thanking whatever lucky stars had directed Nick to paddle past her door today. She had no idea what she would have done if he hadn't been around. And she'd sent him away.

'I'll get my sister to bring a sterile container from work for the specimen. She's at work this morning and she won't mind dropping in.'

Lucy's stomach sank. She hadn't met Nick's sister. What would she think about a pregnant junior midwife latching onto her brother and asking for family favours?

Cringe factor of ten. 'It's okay. I can get one of the girls from work to do that.'

Nick shook his head decisively. Not the easygoing Nick, this was the consultant—Dr Kefes, Nick. 'Too much organising when you're going to bed to rest. I'll sort this.' He looked past her. 'Where's your place?'

'Down behind the pool.'

'Do you want me to carry you?'

Oh, my word, she could picture it. Feel his arms. 'No. I'll be fine.'

'You sure?'

Sob. 'Yep, sure.' She stood up and the pain was there at the back but the front was okay at the moment.

Nick followed her closely along the narrow path, as if she was going to faint or something.

Halfway down the path the contraction pain came again and this time she really got scared. She stopped and swayed and then his arms came around her gently and he pulled her back against his chest.

'I've got you.'

Then he lifted her—like she wasn't a tall girl with two passengers, but a tiny wisp of nothing—and cradled her against his chest, but sadly she was too focused on the grinding ache low in her belly to enjoy the ride.

CHAPTER FIVE

NICK PUSHED OPEN the screen with his shoulder and angled Lucy through the door still in his arms. She pointed to her little room that had come furnished, all designer white cane furniture with hibiscus quilt and pillow covers and Hawaiian surf photos, and he carried her through.

When he put her down, tears threatened and stung her eyes but she was darned if she was going to let them fall—while he was here anyway. 'I'm fine.'

'Mmm-hmm.' He glanced around. 'Much more of this and I'll admit you to the hospital.'

Too real and scary. 'Seriously. It's gone now.'

He narrowed his eyes at her. 'So that pain was in the front?'

'Yep.' She looked at him, dwarfing her little room, so out of place amongst the white doilies and spindly cane. 'But I'll rest.'

'I'll go to the chemist.' He glanced at his watch. Calculating which chemist would be open probably. 'But I'll have to go home first. Is it okay if I go out the road entrance?' He was so full of purpose. She wasn't used to people taking control. Being a back-up for her. It felt dangerously good, and she needed to snap out of it.

'Sure. The gate will lock behind you.' She reached onto her bedside table and gave him her keys. 'Use these to get back in. The blue key is for the gate.' She consoled herself that he wouldn't listen anyway if she said she'd be fine on her own.

He glanced back into the other room—lounge, kitchen, dining all in one—and focused on the fridge. 'You look like the kind of girl who keeps bottles of water in the fridge.'

He crossed the room in a few steps and peered into the refrigerator. 'Knew it.' She had to smile as he grabbed a pink plastic drink bottle, picked up her mobile phone from the table, and put them beside her bed.

He pointed his finger at her. 'Stay!'

She sank back on the pillows and to be honest it felt good not to be standing up. 'Yes, sir.' Yes, sir?

He raised his brows. 'Now she gets cheeky. Ring me if you need me.'

'Thanks, Nick.' He was such a hero. But not her hero. The tears got closer.

His face softened and she needed him to go. Now. 'Thank me later,' he said, and left.

Nick frowned at himself as he trod back to the beach entrance, hopped down onto the sand and picked up his paddleboard and paddle. As he locked the gate and retraced his steps past her little bungalow he berated himself. Thank me later? What was that? Asking for a what? A kiss? Get a grip.

The driveway gate clanged shut behind him as he set off along the road for his flat. The board and paddle were bulky and a nuisance under his arm. The path was hot under his bare feet and her keys felt strange in his other hand.

He was getting way too involved here. If he wasn't careful there'd be emotion involved and he didn't want to go there. He knew where that led. To people being able to stamp on you when you were at your weakest. No way was he going there. But what could he do? She didn't seem to have a friend in the world. He was here. What else could he do? He'd ring Chloe when he got home.

Chloe wasn't as supportive as he'd hoped she'd be. His sister didn't take it lightly. 'So she's a patient?'

What was with the suspicion? 'Yeah. But she's a friend. A colleague.'

There was a definite worried tinge in her voice. What was with that? 'She's your patient, though. You're caring for her during her pregnancy?'

He'd already answered that. 'Yes. She's a midwife on the ward.'

He could hear the frown in her voice. 'It's not like you to become involved. Be careful, Nick.'

Nick lifted the phone away from his ear. He did not want to hear this. He put it back. 'Hell, Chloe. Just get me the container and drop it off here when you come home.'

There was a pause. Then, 'I finish work in twenty minutes.'

'Thank you.' He disconnected and threw the phone on the bed. Stripped off his board shorts and trod across to the shower.

Sisters. When had he ever tried to tell her what to do? He paused with his hand on the tap.

Maybe a couple of times, or more if he was being

honest, but that didn't give her the right to go jumping to conclusions about him and Lucy.

He turned the cold tap on with controlled force and stepped underneath the spray. Sucked his breath in and forced himself to stand there.

Not that he needed to have a cold shower because he was thinking about Lucy, but it was hot outside. And he wanted to get back to her as soon as he could. He hoped she wasn't going to miscarry her babies.

He'd been going to wait for Chloe to come first before heading out to the chemist's but if he got a wriggle on he reckoned he could get there and back before she finished work. Then he could go straight to Lucy's.

He hoped to hell she didn't get stronger contractions. As long as she didn't bleed it looked okay. Antibiotics should take care of the irritation and with a little rest she'd be fine. Her babies would be fine.

He'd see if he could do something practical in the yard for her or she'd be lying there worrying that the house wasn't perfect for the owners. No. She didn't want help. She was too independent.

He turned the water off and grabbed the towel. Dried himself quickly and dragged on underwear, some shorts and a shirt.

Lucy's crisis had taken over his day and he didn't stop to think why this threatened miscarriage was any different from the dozens he'd dealt with in the past.

During his time when he'd mostly concentrated on IVF, dealing with bereaved parents had been a part of almost every day, and his own sadness had been one of the reasons he didn't do as much of that these days. But this was different.

He grabbed his wallet and keys and a script pad and pen. It would be fine. He could deal with this.

Back at her house Lucy told herself she was starting to feel better.

What more could she ask for? If she'd gone into the emergency department there was nothing they could do for her except what Nick was doing. And that would be after a long wait in the waiting room.

She was only just pregnant enough for it to be noticeable in the obstetric ward. They probably wouldn't even have done an ultrasound unless she bled.

That had been the first thing she'd done when Nick had left. She'd jumped up and checked she wasn't bleeding. The relief that she wasn't had been immeasurable.

So if she'd gone to the hospital all anyone could have done would have been to check for an infection that could be irritating her body into contractions, treat any infection that was there, and send her home to rest. She didn't want to think about what would happen if she progressed into full premature labour.

It would be termed a tragic loss of an unviable twin pregnancy. They'd tell her to hang on for another week. As if she wouldn't do anything to hang on.

Her abdomen tightened ominously and she sucked in her breath and forced herself to breathe out. Be loose. Be relaxed. Don't get stressed.

She tried to swallow the lump lodged in her throat. Even the wonders of medical science couldn't help her babies if they were born. Dreadful odds for a healthy outcome.

In the last few weeks she hadn't even contemplated losing them. 'Very premature birth' were three terrifying words. Why would she have thought this could happen?

She stroked her tight little mound gently and sniffed back the tears. 'Come on, babies. Stop frightening your mummy.'

She had the top obstetrician in the hospital looking after her, at her home, sending off samples, procuring her antibiotics, all without her having to leave the comfort of her bed. And without the whole hospital rampant with curiosity.

Maybe Nick was right, and she just needed to be more careful. Had she been doing too much in the garden? Or maybe she shouldn't have reached up for those overhanging fronds?

Guilt swamped her and it didn't help that she knew, rationally, she hadn't done anything wrong. 'I'm so sorry, babies,' she whispered.

As if in answer a tiny knee or elbow rose in her stomach and poked her as if to reassure her. She smiled mistily. It was incredible, the bond she felt to these tiny pods of humanity who had slipped into her heart so unexpectedly. Her whole life was affected by their now planned-for arrival in around four months' time and she realised, far too belatedly, that she'd be devastated if she lost them.

She looked imploringly at the ceiling. 'I promise I'll be more careful, God. Honest.' A tear trickled down her cheek.

'If I can just keep my babies.' She glanced around the room, feeling slightly guilty with the fact that she only thought of praying when she wanted something. And she hadn't realised how much she really wanted these babies.

A knock on the door had her reach for a tissue and she blew her nose just as Nick poked his head in. 'How are you doing?'

As he approached the bed Nick saw the traces of tears on her cheeks and her eyes were suspiciously bright. But her voice was normal so he hoped nothing too catastrophic had happened while he'd been away. He put down the backpack he'd brought stuff in.

'You okay?' She looked damp but tragically beautiful. It was the first time he'd thought of her as beautiful, didn't know why he hadn't seen it before. But it wasn't helpful in this situation.

'I'm fine.' She sniffed and sat up straighter. Squared her shoulders and smiled bravely. 'And no bleeding.'

'Good.' Relief warmed his belly. 'Let's keep it that way.' He lifted out the paper bag his sister had given him and the packet of antibiotics he'd picked up. 'Start the antibiotics as soon as you visit the bathroom.'

He saw her blush and he knew that she felt embarrassed about all this. But it all needed to be done and done properly.

'I brought you a mini-quiche and a yoghurt, in case you were hungry.' He took them from the bag, too. It had seemed a good idea at the time but now he felt a bit dumb about it. She was in her own home and of course she'd have food in the refrigerator.

She didn't look like she thought it was dumb. 'Thank you. That's very kind. And I just ran out of yoghurt.'

He handed her the yoghurt. 'It's acidophilus. Always a good idea if you're on antibiotics.'

She frowned and then her face cleared as he guessed she got the homeopathic connection of antibiotics and

yeast infections and the natural fighting abilities of acidophilus. Because she laughed.

He wasn't sure if it was a good thing to be laughed
at for thinking about things like that but he was a gyn-
aecologist, too. He actually saw the tension fall from
her face and decided it was a good thing even if it was
at his expense.

She grinned at him. 'Not a lot of girls get that kind
of service.'

'Well, you're special.' And she was. But just because
she didn't have anybody else and she did still remind
him of the sort of support Chloe should have had when
she'd had her teen pregnancy. Not that Lucy was a teen.
Far from it, but it explained the affinity he felt with
her. And the fact that he knew she was more vulnerable than she let on.

'Thank you, kind sir.' She looked past him to the
kitchen. 'Did you want a cup of tea or anything?'

'Nope.' He paused. 'Look. I know I've already asked
but things are a little different now. If you rest up here,
is there anything you really need me to do outside before the owners come?'

He thought she was going to refuse again, but saw
the tiny hesitation. 'Come on. Spit it out.'

Her cheeks were pink and he could see she hated
to ask. It seemed he needn't have worried she'd abuse
his help. Not that he'd really thought she would, but
Chloe had mentioned it again, and he mentally poked
his tongue out at his suspicious sister.

'I left the blower down by the beach gate. Could I ask
you to put it back in the garden shed for me, please?'
She chewed her lip and he wanted to ask her not to do
that. It made him feel uncomfortable.

He nodded. 'I'll do that and poke around to see if there's anything obvious to tidy up then I'll be back. Don't stress if I take a while. Do you have a computer here?'

'No, unfortunately. It's getting fixed.'

'I brought my tablet computer if you want to go on-line and search the web.' He reached into the backpack and withdrew it.

'Wow.' She peered over the edge of the bed and pointed to his pack. 'Mary Poppins, eat your heart out. What else have you got in there? Maybe a lampshade and an umbrella?'

He didn't get it. A lampshade? Why would he want an umbrella? 'Who's Mary Poppins?'

She grinned and he had to smile back. She had a great smile. 'Didn't you watch Disney movies when you were a kid?' She smiled. 'My mother was always going out and I was left with a big pile of Disney movies to keep me company.'

He really wasn't liking the sound of her childhood. But, then, his had been the opposite. Too strict. 'Disney must have been too commercial. Not on our Orthodox parents' video list.' He glanced at the almost empty bag. 'Nothing much left in there.'

He didn't want to tell her he had a Doppler for listening to foetal heartbeats because he didn't really want to go there. He wasn't quite sure why he'd brought it. Maybe just for his own peace of mind in case she asked.

'I'll just slip out and sort the blower. Take the antibiotics as soon as you can, won't you?'

She blushed again. It was kind of cute the way she did that. 'Yep. Will do.'

Nick blinked and stepped back. Whoa. Stop that

thought. 'Right. I'll sort outside, then.' He spun and headed for the door like the hounds of hell were after him. Maybe Chloe wasn't so dumb after all and he did need to be careful.

By the time he'd used the blower around the pool, fished out some palm fronds and cleaned the filter box, he decided he'd devoted enough of his Sunday to Lucy. But when he went back to say goodbye she was asleep.

And he couldn't leave until he made sure she and her babies were okay.

So he sat down beside her bed on the spindly cane chair and watched her sleep.

Once she mumbled, as if talking to someone, and her hand drifted to her belly as she smiled the softest, gentlest smile, and it tore unexpectedly at the wall he'd built so successfully around his heart so many years ago.

When she rested her hand over the babies inside her he had to stifle the urge to reach across, lay his hand over hers and feel what she was feeling, assure himself these tiny beings who had somehow pierced his armour were healthy and happy.

Instead, he reminded himself that this family was not his family—and they needed someone with a heart to give, not someone moulded by callous parents who could cast off their children without a backward glance.

Nikolai forced his eyes away and checked his email. Browsed the web. Closed his eyes.

When Lucy woke up, Nick was asleep in the chair beside her bed.

Was this guy for real? She'd never had anyone care about her like he had. Except maybe Lil and Clem next door, when she'd been a kid and had got lonely while her mother had been out.

Which reminded her, she needed to let the kind older couple know how she was doing. They were thrilled she had twins coming. Had promised her all manner of equipment they'd finished with. They'd had their own IVF twins the year before she'd moved out and started her training. They'd understand about twins. But that was for after all this worry went away.

She felt her belly and it seemed softer than before. There were no pains in her back or low in her belly. Maybe it was all going to be okay anyway. She hoped so. When she looked back at Nick he had woken up and was watching her. He smiled and she smiled back.

'Hey, sleepyhead,' she said.

'Hey, sleepyhead, yourself. I was on my way out and your snoring was so loud I thought I'd better wait till you woke up.'

As if. 'I do not snore.'

'So I've found out.' He smiled at her. 'And you look better. Less tense.'

She gently touched her belly. 'And no pain that I know of.'

He stood up and the chair creaked a little. She had to smile. 'That's great. I still think you should have tomorrow off.'

She'd been thinking that, too. 'It scared me. I'll do whatever you recommend, Nick.'

'I'll talk to Sister May. You've still got my number?'

She nodded and he picked up his backpack and the paper bag she'd left there for him. He raised his brows as he picked it up, checking she'd done the deed, and she nodded.

Her ears felt hot. 'I tightened the lid as tight as I could get it.'

He grinned. 'Good.' He slid his tablet in after the paper bag and zipped up the rucksack. 'Ring me any time and I'll drop in if you need me. Or even if you just have a question. It's okay, Lucy. You can ring me and if it's not a good time I'll have my phone on silent and will ring you back. Okay?'

She nodded. 'Otherwise I'll see you for our appointment tomorrow.'

That was good. They could do another check. 'Why don't I arrange for you to have another scan beforehand? We can compare it to the one you had two weeks ago. That way you can be sure everything is fine.'

She'd been going to ask him for that. Her shoulders dropped with relief. 'Thanks. That would be good.'

'I'll ring you with a time when I find out tomorrow. See you then,' he said, and she could tell he wanted to get going.

Of course he did. The poor guy had had his whole Sunday hijacked by her and she felt terrible. And special. He'd said she was special but she'd better not get any ideas.

Because she didn't want to get all gooey and mushy over a certain obstetrician, one who probably thought of her as the biggest nuisance out, because no man would want to hook up with a pregnant, single mother of twins.

But seriously! What wasn't there to love about Nikolai Kefes?

The guy had created calm out of her sudden plunge into uncertainty, had tidied up the outside of her house-sitting mansion so she wouldn't feel like she'd let the owners down, and had even run to the chemist's and now the pathology department for her.

But in reality the last thing she needed was a broken

heart to carry along with two babies, because even a twin stroller wouldn't be big enough to carry all that.

So she definitely wasn't going there.

CHAPTER SIX

NICK HAD RUNG to say Lucy's new ultrasound appointment was at twelve o'clock and as she dressed, she wondered who was missing out on their lunch to do the favour for Nick.

When she was shown into the little room and directed to climb up on the couch in her patient gown, the bombshell blonde ultrasonographer, a different technician from last time, wasn't behind in letting her know. 'Dr Kefes wouldn't take no for an answer so let's see why these babies of yours are causing him such concern.'

As she dimmed the lights there was a knock on the door and BB opened it to Nick. 'Hello, there, Nikolai.' She laughed and signalled for him to come in. 'I wondered if you'd show up for this.'

Lucy blinked at the familiarity in her tone and couldn't help wondering if these two had been more than just professional colleagues. Not that it was any of her business.

'Hi, Jacqui. Thanks for this. I owe you one.' Nick followed the woman into the small room, which suddenly became much smaller, and Lucy didn't like the way he smiled back at the technician. Not that she even had the right to notice who Nick looked at.

Jacqui seemed pretty happy. 'Oh, goody. Dinner.'

He grinned and nodded at Lucy. 'How are you, Lucy? No more pain?'

'I'm fine, thanks.' Except for this ridiculous feeling of exclusion she should not be feeling. An exclusion she had no right to complain about when Nick and Jacqui were both going out of their way to help her. She was an ungrateful wretch.

And they were going out to dinner.

'So let's see what these kids are up to.' Jacqui tilted the screen so Lucy, and now Nick, could see the pictures, and thankfully Lucy could concentrate on the still unfamiliar excitement of actually outlining the shapes of her babies. Thankfully, everything else disappeared from her mind.

With the extra power of the large machine, Lucy could even see their little faces. Could hear and watch the chambers of their hearts all moving as they should. Gaze with wonder as a tiny hand clenched and unclenched. Then a tiny leg kicked.

They were so tiny, and fragile, and vulnerable. She could have gone into proper labour yesterday, and with lungs too small to breathe for long they would have been gone today.

An explosion of fear ballooned in her chest and she drew a breath. They were her family. Her babies, who would always love her, and she would always love them. What if she'd lost them?

Nick must have sensed her distress because he drew closer and rested his hand on her shoulder. Pressed down. With his fingers sending reassuring vibes, she could feel her panic subside a little. 'It's okay, Lucy. They look great.'

She tore her eyes from the screen to search his face. His eyes met hers, intense, reassuring. He nodded. Wordlessly he told her he was telling the truth and she breathed out.

Suddenly exhausted by the fear that had come from nowhere and was so slow to ebb away, she sank back into the pillow. Okay. It was okay. Nick said everything would be fine.

'Good two-week growth from last time. Do you want to know the sex?' Jacqui was intent on the screen and had missed the byplay. Probably a good thing, Lucy thought with a tinge of guilt, judging by the way this hospital picked up scandal.

Nick's hand lifted away but it was okay. Lucy dragged her mind back to what Jacqui had said. Sex? Not sexes? 'Are they identical?'

'It looks like it to me.'

Lucy grinned at that. Identical twins. Awesome, and how cute! And her babies would never be alone because they would have each other. Lucky babies. Did she want to know what sex? 'No. I don't think so. I like the idea of a surprise.'

Jacqui was very good at her job. In no time she'd done all the measurements, estimated both babies' weights and checked all around the edge of the big placenta to see if there was any sign of bleeding or separation.

'Nope. All looks good. Nice amount of fluid around the babies. Good blood flow through both umbilical cords. Nothing out of the ordinary except there's two of them. Measure at twenty-two weeks.' She put the ultrasound handpiece back on its stand and handed Lucy a towel to dry her belly while she concentrated on Nick. 'Satisfied, Dr Kefes?'

'Very. Thank you, Jacqui.' Lucy swiped the jelly off her belly and tried not to look at the way Jacqui leant towards Nick. It was none of her business.

She swung her legs over the edge of the couch but before she could jump down, Nick was there with his hand to help her. 'Can you follow me to my office, Lucy, and I'll chase up the results of those tests?'

She kept her voice upbeat with an effort. 'Great. That saves me waiting till the later appointment.'

'That's fine.' He opened the door for her. 'I'll meet you there in a minute.'

Lucy went past him into the ultrasound waiting room and he shut the door. She wondered with just a tinge of acid just how he was thanking Jacqui until she smacked herself. None of her business.

Whatever appreciation he'd offered, it didn't take long because Nick caught up with her outside the lifts.

Meanwhile, above Nick and Lucy and inside the lift that sailed towards them, Callie Richards ground her teeth, silently but no less effectively as she stewed. Cade Coleman! Grrr.

She could see him in her mind's eye without turning her head. She didn't want to look at him. Dark brown, wavy hair. Those light brown eyes assessing her. Always assessing. Coldly. As if she came up short every time. Well, she wasn't short, she was five feet ten, for heaven's sake, and she was damn good at her job.

This last case had been gruelling. Nick had called them in at three a.m. and it hadn't finished until an hour ago, but by the time she'd spent eight hours trying to ignore Cade Coleman in a room full of people she'd had enough.

Her nerves had been shredded and the worst part was she didn't know why she couldn't just rise above him. Build a bridge. Get over him. All the things that grown-up, footloose women did.

She jumped when he spoke. 'How come you didn't stay long in the recovery room? Those parents will have more questions.'

'Don't tell me my job. I'll go back again later.' She shook her head. 'Soon.'

I just need a few minutes to calm down first, she thought despairingly. If this stupid lift could get its act together and get her to the ground floor before she burst into tears.

She seriously needed sleep. There'd been a long session in the NICU the previous evening and her eyes felt grainy. That was the only reason she was feeling fragile.

'Really?'

She turned her head in time to see him look her up and down and her blood pressure escalated again.

There was censure in his tone. 'I heard you were the real heart of this hospital. Hearts don't leave.'

Oh, yeah? Not that she thought about it much, but her heart had left years ago. And so apparently had his. Even his brother had warned her when he'd suggested Cade for the job.

He'd been the one who'd said that happily ever after wasn't for people like them.

Those words haunted her. If he wasn't interested, why didn't he just leave her alone and stop pushing her buttons?

But he didn't. 'Is this to do with me knocking you back for a dance at the wedding? When you were tipsy?'

Callie winced. Now, that had been a dumb dare from the girls. 'Don't be stupid.' She certainly regretted draping herself all over him but that was why she hadn't had a glass of wine since.

He looked her up and down. 'Because we could make a date. Dance the night away and more. No strings, no expectations. Get it out of our systems.'

After being an absolute horror to her all night. Was he joking? 'Strangely, I decline.'

He shrugged and she wondered if he was as laid back about it as he looked. 'Have to find someone else, then.'

The doors opened and Cade and Callie moved back against the wall. Callie forced a smile and nodded at the little midwife, Lucy. With Nick again?

She frowned slightly. These two seemed to end up in the same space a fair bit. She glanced at Nick and he barely looked tired, despite the long night.

He grinned at them both. Where did he get his energy? 'Thanks for the big night, guys. You were incredible. The parents are still coming to grips with things and I said you'd see them again later. That right, Callie?'

'Half an hour. Just have to sort something first.'

'Great. That's what I told them.' He glanced at Cade. 'Amazing job, Cade.'

'But tense. I think I need some heavy exercise to get the kinks out of my neck.' He glanced sardonically at Callie and then at Nick. 'You up for a game of squash later, Nick?'

'What time?'

'Six-thirty and I'm going to flog you.' What a poseur,

Callie thought as she listened, but Nick didn't seem fazed. She hoped he wiped the floor with Cade.

Nick just smiled. 'Make it seven, and meet your match.'

She gave Lucy a look that said *Men!* and Lucy grinned as the lift stopped and she and Nick got out. 'I need to catch up with you later, too, Nick.' Callie saw Nick pause and he turned back, saluted her, and the lift doors shut.

Cade looked thoughtfully at the closed door. 'You think Nick is having an affair with that girl?'

'No.' She hoped not because she'd heard the girl was pregnant. 'There's enough gossip in this place already, without making up more.'

'Makes me wonder if they sail up and down the lift together all day.'

The lift finally made it to ground level and the doors opened. 'As long as they don't think we are, it's all good,' Callie muttered, and hurried off.

She could feel his eyes drilling into her back and she picked up more speed.

Back on the level of the consultants' rooms, Nick ushered Lucy through the door into his office and Lucy passed the empty secretary's desk. She'd forgotten it was lunchtime for everyone else because she'd arranged this before she'd known she'd be off sick.

Lucy took her usual seat while he opened up the screen for the results and she thought about the conversation in the lift.

They must have all been in Theatre together. He didn't look tired. 'Were you up all night, operating?'

'Half the night. Complicated triplet pregnancy.'

He clicked the mouse. 'Ah, here they are. Yep. Right antibiotics for the bug and a probable cause for your irritable uterus.'

Lucy was still thinking about the three babies. Gulp. 'So there's people out there who are more complicated than me.'

'Always. And lots that are simpler. People forget that twins are tricky. With IVF we get a lot more twins and triplets than normal and it's a serious pregnancy we need to keep a close eye on.'

They did the blood-pressure and weight check and skipped the abdominal palpation because the ultrasound had shown them both the babies were growing well. Nick handed back the card he'd filled out. 'Don't hesitate to call me if you have any concerns.'

He was in doctor mode and she needed to remember that's who he was. He was her doctor, not her friend.

She stood up. 'Yes. Thank you. I'd better get home and put my feet up or I'll be feeling guilty I didn't go to work.'

CHAPTER SEVEN

AT THREE-THIRTY that afternoon Flora May dropped by at Lucy's house to check that she was okay. The company was appreciated because Lucy felt strangely flat.

Flora glanced around at the secluded alcove with palm trees overhead and birds flying in and out. 'It's like being on a little tropical island. No wonder you like it here.'

Lucy watched a lorikeet dart past and tried to lift her mood. Yes. She was lucky. It was a great place to live. 'Plus it's rent-free for very little maintenance of the big house. And nice and close to the hospital.'

Actually, Lucy wanted to throw herself on Flora's motherly chest but she'd been stifling those urges since she'd been a little girl. She'd thought she was pretty good at it but lately her reserves seemed to be running low.

She felt Flora's scrutiny. 'How are you, Lucy?'

'I'm fine. Nick arranged for another ultrasound. The babies are fine. We're just being careful.'

Flora's eyes it up. 'So how was the ultrasound? Did they move much? And that was very sensible.' She'd brought a cake and they set up the little table outside Lucy's door.

Lucy remembered that moment when she'd thought about losing them, and how Nick had reassured her. 'They looked good. Kicking well.' She didn't know what she'd have done without him the last few days but she didn't want to get used to relying on him. It was nice having Flora visit, too. Almost like a family, but who was she kidding? She needed to get better at going it alone, not worse.

Flora poured the tea. 'So when do you think you'll be back at work?'

'Tomorrow.'

'Good.' Flora sat back. 'Dr Kefes is looking after you well?'

Lucy smiled at the question in Flora's voice. As if she would have words with him if he wasn't doing his job well. 'I wouldn't be going tomorrow if he thought it was dangerous.' She could just imagine Flora taking Nick to task for being negligent. 'In fact, he's been great.'

She couldn't tell Flora how great or the rumour mill would go into overdrive. Not that Flora gossiped. That wouldn't be in her psyche, but it could be awkward if Flora thought she and Nick had something going on when, of course, they didn't. 'I'd like you to try and come with me to the next ultrasound if you're not busy?'

Flora's face softened and she smiled. 'I'd like that.'

Flora stayed another hour and then left, but not before Lucy promised to phone in sick if she felt unwell.

She was so glad she'd told Flora, who'd suggested she allow the news to spread so people would understand and be a little more thoughtful in what they asked Lucy to do.

* * *

The next day at work Lucy felt as good as new. Maybe it was because she had slept in that morning, and starting work after lunch instead of before breakfast seemed to suit her better.

The ward was busy, and after checking Lucy was okay Flora glanced at the clock.

'Right, then.' Back to business. 'I'll get you to care for Bonny Shore. Her husband can't be here because they have no one to mind their two toddler daughters.'

'Oh, poor thing.'

'Yes. Meg's in there and I don't think she'll go home before the birth so the two of you will be there. The exciting thing is that Bonny's having twins, too.' Flora smiled and Lucy wanted to give Flora a hug because this was just what she needed—an insight into the happy ending of a twin pregnancy.

'The neonatal nursery is aware we're close but ready to come when we think they'll be needed. Dr Richards and Dr Coleman have been to see Bonny and explain that two neonatal teams will be there just in case either baby decides to be naughty.'

Lucy had to smile at that but inwardly she quailed at the thought of so many consultants in the room. Especially the terrifying Dr Coleman.

But she'd have to get used to it. This was her world and she vowed she would become a valuable part of the network at Gold Coast City Hospital.

Flora went on. 'Of course, Dr Kefes and his registrar will be there also, so the room will become very busy when the time comes.

'Until then...' she looked at Lucy from under her stern brows '...try and give Bonny some reassurance that despite the cast of thousands she does have some control over her birth and that she is still doing what she is designed to do.'

Lucy grinned. 'Absolutely.' She looked up at her mentor. How she wished she'd had someone like this kind woman as her mother or even her aunt. Her dream had been that one day she'd get a warm and fuzzy mother-in-law who would be the kind of mother she'd never had but that dream had slipped further away. He'd have to be some man to want a wife who already had twins.

Maybe that would never happen but Flora was becoming her friend.

'And thank you.' She looked away because her silly hormones were filling her eyes with tears again. 'For caring.'

For a moment Flora's eyes softened and then she looked towards the birthing suites. 'Away you go.'

As Lucy knocked and entered, her patient, Bonny, was shaking her head and pushing the straps off her belly. 'I need to go into the shower.' Her voice cracked. 'I can't sit on this bed any more.'

Bonny Shore was thirty years old, this was her third pregnancy, and she'd had normal births with her two little girls who were waiting at home. By the strained look on Bonny's face, this was all very different.

Lucy suspected her patient was stressed by the extra observations needed for twins, plus she was heading into late active labour.

Lucy had seen that this could be the most challenging time, transition between the first and second stages of labour, before the pushing became compulsive, a time that often left a woman agitated, fearful and sometime quite cross.

As she learnt more each day, Lucy was starting to realise that mums needed extra-calm support right about
now. She could remember Flora telling her in her training that this was the usual time for women to abuse
their husbands, if they weren't at home minding the
other children.

Lucy wondered briefly if she would have anyone to
be cross at when she had her babies then scolded herself for being self-absorbed and crossed over the room
to Meg. The other young graduate midwife looked up
from the foetal monitor as Lucy appeared.

They smiled at each other, acknowledging silently
the excitement of the impending birth. They both
glanced at the two resuscitation cots set up together at
the side of the room.

'Well, here's Lucy come to help you into the shower,
too,' Meg, said reassuringly. 'This is the midwife I told
you about who's expecting twins as well.'

Bonny looked across and rolled her eyes at Lucy.
'Hi, there. And poor you.' She glanced down at her
large rounded belly and then suddenly smiled softly.
'And lucky you.'

As they helped Bonny down from the bed, Meg quietly went through her patient's progress. 'Bonny began
her contractions this morning at home about six a.m.
She came to us at ten, once she had her girls sorted, and
was four centimetres dilated already by then.'

'Wow.' Lucy was impressed. 'That was great progress at home.'

'My husband was a mess by the time he dropped me
off and I got into trouble from Dr Kefes for not coming earlier.' Bonny grinned as she shuffled across the

room towards the bathroom, her hands under the swell of her huge abdomen to support it.

Lucy could tell she was not at all abashed at the scolding. Then the next contraction took hold and they all stopped as Bonny leant against Lucy and breathed through the contraction.

As they stood quietly and gently breathed together, Lucy realised there was no tension in the room, just a feeling of solidarity, and she thought again how lucky she was to have found her niche in life.

The contraction eased and Bonny went on as if she hadn't stopped. 'He listened when I said I didn't want an epidural. Though he did get an intravenous pin in when I didn't want one.'

Bonny looked up under her hair at Lucy. 'Though it's coming to that point in this labour when you tell yourself you'd forgotten how strong it gets.' She pushed forward grimly and held onto the doorpost as the next contraction rolled through, then she sighed again and forced herself to relax.

'Getting to the business end,' Lucy said gently.

'Precisely.' Bonny's eyes were fixed on the shower nozzle as if it was calling her. 'Which is a good thing.'

They settled Bonny into the shower and Meg completed her handover quietly as Bonny closed her eyes with relief as the warm water cascaded over her stomach. 'Bonny had progressed to eight centimetres dilated when Dr Kefes came in half an hour ago.' Meg stopped as the next contraction hit.

'We've negotiated a short time off the monitoring from Dr Kefes just so she can move around a bit before the birth, but we have to head back to bed as soon as she feels any urge to push.'

Lucy had to agree. 'With twins that's understandable.' The two midwives grinned at each other. It could be tricky balancing two babies and eight people in the bathroom.

Twenty minutes later Bonny looked up with a startled expression on her face. 'It's time.' She turned to face Lucy. 'But I don't think I can move.'

Meg blinked and her face paled but Lucy had a little more experience of this and knew what to do. She leant in and turned off the shower. 'I know. But it's safer for your babies if you do, so we're going to move anyway. Okay?'

She put her hand on Bonny's arm and motioned to Meg to do the same on the other side. 'And I'll buzz so that someone will come and start ringing the troops while we get you back to bed.' She leant across Bonny's body to the wall and pushed the call button. 'Let's go.'

Meg's eyes widened in relief as Bonny stood up and suddenly took off nearly at a run for the other room so that the midwives were almost left behind. She climbed up onto the bed as if she was being chased and by the time Flora arrived they were drying her off and slipping on her open-backed gown.

By the time Nick arrived and Bonny was giving her first push, the foetal monitor was back in place and two baby hearts were making clopping noises.

Nick saw Lucy as soon as he entered the room and forced himself to ignore her.

For some reason, today she distracted him and he wondered if it was because he didn't want to think of Lucy as the patient in a few months' time. The twin thing. He focused on where he should be. 'How are you doing, Bonny?'

'Business end.' Brief and to the point, Bonny wasn't wasting energy on small talk.

Nick nodded and headed over to the basin with a small smile and washed his hands. While he pulled on his gloves, he looked across at Meg and raised his eyebrows in a silent request for an update. Meg was fiddling with the foetal monitor and Lucy stepped in and filled in the blanks, so he couldn't ignore her.

'Bonny went to the shower and about five minutes ago felt the first urge to push. She's had three pushes since then and both foetal hearts have been reassuring.'

Good. Another woman brief and to the point. He liked that. He nodded and snapped his second glove into place.

Bonny groaned as the next powerful urge took over and when they lifted the sheet a tiny dark head of hair slowly appeared like magic between her legs. He stepped in next to the bed. 'You're doing an amazing job, Bonny. Nice and gentle.'

Nick glanced at Lucy. 'Get the paeds, thank you.'

Lucy nodded, sped over to the phone and passed the message to the neonatal staff. A few seconds later she put down the receiver. 'They're on their way.'

At that moment Cade and Callie and two experienced neonatal nurses slipped unobtrusively into the room and he nodded. Not that he expected trouble but he wanted to be prepared for it.

Bonny groaned again, and he looked back at his patient.

Women never failed to amaze him with their strength in these situations. He couldn't help just one quick glance at Lucy, who was holding Bonny's hand as they all waited for the birth. In the not-too-distant future he'd be here to see Lucy give birth.

Lucy watched Nick's large capable hands as they supported the first baby's head as it lifted and turned. She didn't think she would ever forget this moment.

The room calmed as a tiny shoulder appeared, Nick murmuring praise as Bonny silently and unhurriedly eased her baby out. The first of the twins had arrived safely to a sigh of relief from in the room.

Cade stepped up next to Lucy, not saying anything, but she could feel the concentration he was directing her way as Nick passed baby one up to his mother. Lucy rubbed the little body dry until the baby grimaced and then made no bones about complaining loudly.

Bonny's firstborn son screwed up his little face until he was bright red and roared his disapproval and he kicked his legs, exposing his impressive scrotum and penis to everyone except his mother.

Lucy felt Dr Coleman step back and she had to admire his unobtrusive readiness. Maybe he wasn't so bad after all, because he'd certainly achieved what he needed with very little impact on Bonny's birth experience.

Lucy liked that. A lot.

One of the neonatal nurses replaced him and helped Lucy settle the baby between his mother's breasts, mouth and neck nicely positioned for ease of breathing, skin to skin, with a warm bunny rug over them both.

'So what have you got?' Nick smiled at Bonny, because everyone else in the room knew but hadn't said the words.

Lucy lifted the blanket and then the baby's rear end

to show his mother, who lifted her head to glance down, and then Bonny laughed. 'A boy. We have our William.'

As they all waited for the next contraction the relief in the room gave way to the tiniest rise in tension. It was always tricky to see how the second twin settled in its mother's uterus after the first had made more room.

Hopefully the baby would turn head first towards the big wide world, but Lucy knew that often second twins would settle into breach position, which was less straightforward for the birth.

What they didn't want was the baby not making a firm decision between the two and lying across the mother's uterus to block the cervix with a shoulder or arm. Such a position became incompatible with a normal birth and Caesarean of the second twin would have to be considered.

'Start the syntocinon, please, Lucy. We want a few more contractions.' Lucy uncapped Bonny's IV cannula and connected the infusion.

Nick's big hands gently palpated Bonny's stomach until he found the hard, circular head of the second twin, who was apparently still undecided on the direction of the exit. Nick kneaded gently downwards along the baby's back through the mother's soft abdomen until the next contraction halted his progress.

After several contractions and Nick's gentle persistence Bonny began to push again.

This time the baby wasn't in so much of a hurry to be born, and the tension crept up until Lucy found herself holding her breath and Nick quietly urged Bonny on.

'Come on, baby,' Bonny muttered. 'If it's a boy, he's called Benjamin.'

Finally the baby's hair and then rest of the head was

born, and during what seemed an eternity, but which after Lucy's third glance at the clock she knew was only ninety seconds, the flaccid little body of a slightly smaller twin boy was born in a flurry of floppy arms and legs.

'It's Benjamin,' Nick said. 'We'll take this little one over to Dr Richards for a few minutes, Bonny.' Nick cut and clamped the cord and Callie swooped in, dried the limp baby with the warmed towel and then gathered up the tiny scrap in her confident hands to carry him across to the heated resuscitaire.

'He's a bit stunned so he hasn't taken his deeper breaths to start off,' Lucy said quietly in Bonny's ear. 'Needle,' she warned as she gave the injection to help separate the placenta and reduce the risk of bleeding after birth.

She glanced across to where the two neonatologists were working quietly on Bonny's second twin.

The neonatal nurse who'd stayed to observe William began to explain to Bonny what was happening and Lucy's attention was drawn that way, too.

Within thirty seconds the tiny oxygen saturation probe had been taped to Benjamin's tiny hand and they were puffing little bursts of air into his lungs.

From where she stood she could see his heart rate was reading eighty and that wasn't too bad if it crept up over a hundred with the inflation of his lungs.

But that didn't happen. In fact, the heart rate slowed agonisingly and dropped to fifty.

She heard Dr Coleman's comment to Dr Richards. 'So, secondary apnoea. Change from air to oxygen. I'll do the cardiac massage.'

Smoothly Dr Coleman changed position, circled the

baby's chest with his big hands and began to compress the little rib cage three times to every breath from the face mask Callie held over the nose and mouth.

They began inflating baby's lungs with more oxygen and immediately his blueness seemed to wash away.

'He needs a little oxygen until he gets the idea of this new breathing business,' Nick said in answer to Bonny's worried look. 'Pinking up now.' He glanced back at the sudden gush of blood that was forming a ruby puddle in the bed.

The placenta came away and Nick passed it swiftly to Meg in a dish. 'Check it's all there because we've got some bleeding.'

'Fundal massage, Lucy.' Lucy leant over and rubbed Bonny's soft belly firmly until the underlying uterus contracted under her hand to slow the bleeding.

Swiftly Nick checked for any trauma that could be contributing to the blood loss while Meg carried the placenta over to the bench and made sure none of the lobes of tissue were missing from the circle. Lucy knew that sometimes lobes or even membranes from the bag of waters left behind could cause bleeding after a birth.

Nick pulled the spare drape from the trolley and tossed it up onto Bonny's belly. 'I'll do the massage now, Lucy, if you draw me up another five units of syntocinon and get two fifty micrograms of ergometerine ready just in case.'

His big hand came in over Lucy's with the drape between them and Lucy stepped back to assemble the drugs. Nick went on, 'I'm afraid your uterus has gone on strike, Bonny. I have to rub it until it contracts and stops the bleeding. Sorry if it's uncomfortable.'

Lucy held up the first drug to check with Nick and

he read the name, dose and expiry date out loud. 'Fine. Give it slowly intravenously. Then start the forty units in a new flask of saline in the line.'

Meg was back. 'Placenta looks complete.'

'Good.' He looked over his shoulder at his registrar. 'Simon, put another cannula in, please, and draw some bloods as you do. Repeat coags and full blood count. We already have blood cross-matched if we need it. You can run normal saline through that as a replacement fluid. I think this bleeding is settling now.'

Lucy leaned towards her patient and took her wrist. Amazingly, Bonny's pulse was only slightly raised. 'You okay, Bonny?' she asked as she strapped the blood-pressure cuff to the woman's arm.

Bonny nodded. 'I'm more worried about my baby.' At that moment a little wail came from the second re-suscitaire. 'But I think he's getting the hang of it.'

Lucy watched the unhurried way Nick moved through the mini-crisis. She tried to estimate the blood loss and decided it would have been around a litre or two pints. 'Blood pressure one ten on sixty, pulse eighty-eight.'

'Thank you,' Nick said to acknowledge he'd heard, he looked at Bonny. 'You lost an amount of blood that would certainly have caused problems for most adults but thankfully you pregnant ladies have mechanisms in place to cope with extra blood loss at birth.'

He smiled reassuringly a Bonny. 'You still look the pink-cheeked and bright-eyed mum we started with, though tomorrow might be a different story.'

He went on quietly, 'Tummies that have carried twins are notorious for being tired after birth, Bonny, but it's all settling now.'

He gestured to the two IV lines now hanging above her. 'Sorry about the two drips but one can come down when we've replaced a little of the fluid you've lost. We'll run this new flask over four hours and see how you're doing then. Might be able to just put a cap over your IV lines after that.'

Bonny nodded. 'I'll forgive you,' she said, and stroked the little body that still lay across her chest. 'I just want Benjamin.'

Nick glanced across at the team, who only needed to observe her baby now. 'I know. He'll be across here as soon as we can.'

By sixty minutes after birth everything had settled. Benjamin, the second twin, spent a little time with oxygen near his face while he lay on his mother, but soon he was sucking as robustly as his brother from his mother's breast. He'd go to the nursery as soon as he'd finished so he could be watched for another hour.

Nick had gone. Meg had gone home. One of the neonatal nurses had stayed to help Lucy with the babies and they'd been weighed—both had come in at just under seven pounds—and the neonatal nurse was in the process of dressing them.

Lucy took Bonny into the shower and helped her freshen up and climb into her pyjamas, all the time alert in case Bonny began to feel faint, but to her relief the new mum just kept going.

It was incredible how reassuring the whole experience had been for her on a personal level, Lucy thought.

Ten minutes later she finally helped Bonny into bed with her two little guys beside her in the twin cot.

The room was peaceful for five minutes until Bonny's

husband arrived with their two little girls, and excited pandemonium broke out.

There were squeals, bed-jumping and excited tears as Bonny's husband squeezed his wife tightly in relief that she and the babies were well.

Lucy was still smiling as she walked away with a promise to return in fifteen minutes to make sure the bleeding remained settled and to check that Bonny had survived the onslaught.

Three hours later, after another emergency trip to Theatre, Nick walked down the corridor to his rooms and deliberately loosened his shoulders.

He was mentally tired but there really wasn't any reason for him to be this drained.

Last night had been torrid in Theatre but ultimately successful.

Today, there had been another good outcome, and he was glad everything had worked out fairly smoothly for Bonny because they'd had many long talks during her pregnancy about her preference for as little intervention if possible. In the end they'd achieved most of that.

But mentally he was distracted, and he didn't do distraction, so where the heck had that come from?

Lucy's worried face at the ultrasound yesterday slipped into his mind. It wasn't a certain little midwife causing all this, he hoped.

He ran his hand through his hair. He guessed he hadn't slept well on Sunday night after Lucy's scare and then they'd been up most of the night after that.

And he'd spent a bit of mind space hoping the scan would come back normal, to the point that he'd made sure he had been there for the appointment yesterday, which, when he thought about it, hadn't really been necessary.

Because Lucy was only a colleague. And a once-only pleasant breakfast companion. And a patient of his. Nothing else.

Not a sister he could put up in his flat until her world righted itself. Not someone he had to go in to bat for when other people let her down. But she was vulnerable and she didn't have anyone else.

Was that why he'd wanted to take her aside after Bonny's birth and make sure she was okay? Maybe give her a hug and reassure her that her own birth would be fine? Her babies would be fine.

This was getting out of hand.

The only ironically amusing part about this was how horrified his parents would have been at his involvement, and how fortunate for Lucy that he didn't speak to them.

He was developing an interest in a non-Greek, pregnant nurse with twins by another man! Well, he knew she was a midwife and not a nurse, but it would be the same to them. Anyone less than a specialist would be a failure to them.

He could hear his mother now. 'This woman, she is after your money. You are a doctor. You are too good for her.'

In fact, he had a sneaking suspicion that Lucy was too good for him. But for some reason she just had to look his way, smile in that cheeky, sexy way of hers, and he was hot. What was that about?

Lust, his inner demon suggested sardonically. He laughed out loud and then glanced around. A hospital orderly dragging a garbage bin looked at him strangely and he pulled himself back under control.

But it was darkly humorous and the joke was on him.

Because lust wasn't going anywhere with a woman pregnant with twins.

Not like he could drag her off to bed for goodness knew how many months so he'd be better casting his gaze elsewhere and scratch that itch with a woman who understood that he was footloose and fancy-free and staying that way. Plenty of those around.

Somehow it just wasn't an attractive thought. But what was most important was that he keep everything under control.

'Would Dr Kefes please phone Emergency. Dr Kefes, please phone Emergency.'

The page boomed overhead and Nick ducked into the nearest nurses' station to pick up the phone, actually a little relieved to be called to an emergency. Looked like he was going to miss the squash game with Cade as well.

At eleven that night Lucy pushed open the night exit at the front of the hospital and stepped out into the balmy evening.

She was limp with exhaustion but exhilarated by the way Bonny was managing with her babies, and how well both little boys were.

She'd felt so reassured about how Nick had agreed to less intervention, how calm and wonderful he'd been with Bonny, and if everything went well she was going to have babies like that. With Nick as her carer.

She wanted to ask Flora to be her support person because her senior was certainly taking an interest in her well-being and Lucy didn't really have any other friends she could ask to be with her.

It was all months away but she guessed in another couple of months she'd have to start looking for ante-natal classes. And going to those alone, too. She lifted her chin.

A car stirred the warm air as it flew past with its headlights on and she stepped up onto the path towards home.

The bonus of living close to the hospital was that it was quick to walk to and fro, but the disadvantage was that at night it could be a little creepy, heading along a street that comprised of mainly driveways and garages behind big walls.

Another car started up and she waited for the accel-eration of sound but unexpectedly this one rolled up beside her and Lucy's heart rate soared.

She stared doggedly ahead and refused to look at the driver. It was even harder not to glance round when the passenger window was wound down, and her heart rate bumped up another notch.

'You're not walking alone at night, are you?'

Nick. She blew out the breath she'd been holding in a long stream. Grrr. 'Hell, Nick! You frightened me half to death.'

'Sorry.' He didn't sound it and her irritation went up another notch. 'Would you like to hop in and I'll run you the rest of the way?'

She could guess what had happened. He'd obviously seen her and decided to go all interfering on her. But now her nerves were shot it would be a horrible walk until she was safely inside her own yard.

So she'd look pretty silly if she said no. Especially

when her feet were killing her. But there was no use getting used to it.

He wouldn't be waiting every night so what was so special about tonight? The last thing she needed was to feel let down after every shift because Nick wasn't there to pick her up.

Lucy sighed and opened the door but after she'd climbed in she frowned at him. 'Aren't you going the wrong way?'

The seat felt fabulous as she rested back and took the weight off her feet, and that only made her feel more cross. 'Do you have any idea how bossy you sound?'

'Sorry again.' He didn't sound it and she was glad someone was amused. Not. 'It's the Greek in me,' he said mildly. 'I don't like to see a woman walking alone at night.'

Bully for him. 'It's not my preference, but the Australian in me says get over it and get home.'

'I'm Australian,' he said mildly. 'But I'm also second-generation Greek.'

'Hmm.' As in not my problem, Lucy thought, still grouchy from her fright. 'And this is my house. Thank you for the lift.'

He pulled on the handbrake. 'I'll walk you in.'

'No, thank you.'

Nick tamped down his frustration. He was sorry he'd startled her but he hadn't been able to believe it when he'd seen her head off in the dark. He didn't know why he hadn't thought of it before. He guessed he'd assumed she caught a taxi home or something.

But she was so darned independent he should have known she'd put him on the back foot. He forced him-

self to relax and smile at her as he leant across to open
the door. 'Our first fight.'

She didn't smile back. 'It was fun. Goodnight.' She
pushed the door wider and climbed out and he watched
her walk to the gate, and hated it that nobody would be
there to greet her when she got home.

He thought for a moment she was going to just
march away but when she took out her key she looked
back. Shook her head and sent him one of those ray-o-
sunshine smiles he could live off if he had to.

'Sorry. You scared me.' She shrugged. 'I was cross
with myself for being nervy and you copped it. Thank
you for the lift.'

He let out his breath. At least she didn't hold grudges,
though he'd done nothing wrong by wanting to see she
was safe. 'In penance you should have breakfast with
me on Sunday.'

She grinned at him. 'Now, that would be a hardship.
Love to. But I'm—'

He finished the sentence for her. 'Paying for yourself. Excellent. I'm broke.'

She looked startled for a moment and he patted himself on the back. It had made her smile again. Keep 'em
guessing, good motto. 'I'll pick you up at eight?'

'Eight's perfect. See you then.'

Lucy closed the gate behind her as the automatic
lights came on then she heard Nick's car accelerate
away.

The night noises surrounded her. The owners had
only stayed for two nights and now she was back to
being home alone.

CHAPTER EIGHT

ONE OF THE fronds from the palm trees crashed down somewhere along the path near the pool and Lucy jumped at the noise and spun around before her brain recognised the familiar sound.

Her babies wriggled and fluttered and she patted her stomach. 'Sorry, guys.' Leftover nerves from the fright Nick had given her.

For the first two weeks she'd house-sat she'd been sure someone had been outside the house when that had happened, but she could have done without it tonight.

She glanced up at the big house and then frowned at the flicker of unexpected light she could see in the lounge room.

There was a small tinkle of glass and this time she knew it wasn't normal. Her hand edged into her bag and she felt around for her phone as she backed towards the gate.

As soon as she was out of sight of the house she pressed the button for contacts and Nick's name lit up. Without hesitation she pressed his number and he answered it on the second ring.

'Lucy? You okay?'

'I'm coming back out,' she whispered. 'Someone's in the house.'

'I'm on my way and I'll ring the police as I come. Get out into the street and under a streetlight.'

By the time Lucy had crossed the street and hurried away from the driveway Nick's car was roaring up the road towards her, and she'd never been so glad to see anybody.

Nick saw her a hundred yards down the street under a lamppost, her arms wrapped around her belly and shaking.

He screeched to a halt and was out of the car in seconds with his arms wrapped around her and her face buried in his shirt. 'You were quick,' she mumbled into his shirt, and he stroked her hair. Poor Lucy.

'I should have walked you into your house.' His arms tightened. 'I'm so sorry.'

'I said no. And I'm not your responsibility.' She eased back as she looked up at him, chin thrust forward and her eyes showing she was bravely determined not to crack. All the conversations, concern, downright worry and now this scare twisted in his gut.

Maybe that was why he tilted her chin with his finger and murmured against her lips, 'It's sure starting to feel that you should be.' And then he kissed her.

It was intended as a gentle salute, a comfort peck, sympathy even, but that wasn't what it turned into.

As soon as she melted against him he lost it, lost where, why, everything except how much he'd wanted to taste this woman, feel her against him.

Her instant response, to open under him and hotly welcome him in, lit a desire that flicked along his arms, tightened his hold and fanned a deep need he hadn't realised he had. He wanted more. He wanted Lucy. He wanted it all.

Lucy was lost. Nick's mouth against hers was intoxicating, hot, hungry and totally in charge. And she wanted more. Wanted to push the boundaries into the world she'd always wondered about. It wasn't safety she wanted at this moment, it was danger.

Apparently 'lost in a kiss' was the way it went with Nick. Swirling sensation, swirling red colours against her closed eyelids.

It wasn't until he was gently pulling away that she caught on to how lost they'd been.

Nick's arm slid over her shoulder and pulled her against him as he faced the uniformed patrolman that had answered Nick's call.

Lucy came slowly back to the real world.

And Nick's voice. 'I'm sorry, officer.'

Officer? Someone else was here? Real red lights were flashing.

Nick's voice again. 'Yes, it was me who called.'

So they'd been sprung in mid-kiss by the patrol car. Embarrassing. Lucy bit back a giggle, still drunk with the sensation of Nick making no bones about the fact that he desired her. Or maybe he'd just been kissing her for comfort and it had been her hormones that had screamed sex. Either way she was a wanton, bad woman and bad mother—so why was she still smiling?

Nick turned her to face the young man in blue, who didn't meet her eyes. She blushed. 'I'm Lucy Palmer, the house-sitter. Yes. I heard glass breaking and there was a strange light moving in the lounge room.'

The young patrol man nodded. 'So you exited through the rear gate and rang Dr Kefes. Who rang us?'

'That's right. We...' She blushed again. 'We haven't seen anyone leave this way.'

The policeman glanced at her this time with a slight smile. He raised his eyebrows but refrained from comment.

Nick stepped forward and pointed to the gate.

'This path also leads to the beach. It goes past the house, behind the pool and onto the beach.'

Still stunned by her response, Lucy let Nick take control because she was still a foot or two off the ground. At this moment he could run the show for all she cared. They'd stopped talking and it seemed like they were waiting for her to do something. Both of them looked at her hand holding the keys.

'Do you want me to open the gate?'

'If you give me the keys, we'll deal with this. I'm pretty sure they'll be gone now.'

Lucy handed over the bunch. 'The blue is for the gate, the red for the house, and the green for the gate to the beach,' she told the policeman.

'Would you both wait here for us?'

'We'll be here.' Nick pointed to his vehicle and the policeman nodded and motioned to his men to accompany him onto the property.

Nick and Lucy watched them go and the moment stretched to awkwardness as both tried to think of something, anything, that was not embarrassing to say.

Lucy was the first to give up on that unlikely occurrence. 'I thought I was seeing red lights because you were kissing me.'

Nick blinked and then smiled and soon they were grinning at each other. 'And I heard roaring in my ears, which was probably the patrol car trying to run us down.'

Lucy chewed her lip. 'At least no one from the hospital saw us.'

And then Nick said something she hadn't foreseen. 'Much more of that and we have the reality of finding you a new obstetrician.'

Lucy's stomach dropped and she thought, *No-o-o!* with an internal wail of distress. Nobody would be like Nick. She wanted Nick to look after her. Felt so safe under his care. Maybe it wasn't too late. They could pretend it had never happened. 'It was just the stress of the moment. What about if I promise never to kiss you again?'

Nick winced. She could promise that, could she? Maybe she hadn't felt what he'd felt. 'Actually, I kissed you.' *And I'm not promising anything of the sort.* He didn't know what had happened, but he didn't say it out loud.

So it seemed Lucy wasn't ready to hear anything like that and he wasn't going to rush her, or himself, but things had certainly changed.

Or had the possibility of change. And professionally his judgment could be clouded.

He wasn't ready to say just what it was between them but the chemistry was blatant. He wanted to enjoy more of her company, even if it had to be platonic, and he could not believe he was thinking this. That had to be a first.

But he could see she was upset. How to explain? 'It's becoming a little hard to manage your care with the dispassion that is required.' He winced. That sounded sensible but stuck up.

He took her shoulders and tried not to think about what he was feeling beneath his fingers. 'I'm already second-guessing myself, questioning decisions I don't question with other patients. That's not fair to you or to me.' And that was the truth. Apart from the fact his Hippocratic oath forbade him to have a relationship with a patient and he'd just kissed her. And wanted to do it again.

He dropped his hands. Definitely time to bail out.

Why did she have to look so crushed? But as he should have expected, she lifted her chin and accepted reality. It just took a few seconds, and he was reminded of the way she'd coped the first time he'd seen her in his rooms. No hysteria, no tantrums.

He heard her sigh. 'I think I understand, but I wish you didn't have to.'

He wanted to hug her again. More proof he was doing the right thing. 'I'm doing this because I still want to be here for you, Lucy. You're not losing me. You're just gaining an impartial second person.'

She nodded but he didn't think she was convinced. 'If you were impartial, you could keep looking after me.'

'Sorry. Not impartial.'

She smiled shyly and then chewed her lip. 'Do you want me to find the other doctor?'

No! Definitely not. What if she picked someone useless? Someone like Chloe had had? He'd be a mess. How could he say that diplomatically? 'Not unless you want me to. I have a very good friend, just moved back to Gold Coast City after his wife died, David Donaldson, whose care I think is excellent.'

He'd been Nick's mentor. David was old enough to

be Lucy's father, and his own too, for that matter, but he was the best with twins, Nick reassured himself. 'I worked with him in IVF at another hospital and he's very experienced with twin pregnancies.'

'He sounds fine. Thank you.'

The conversation died when the police reappeared. They were carrying a plastic bag with a heavy metal bar in it. 'Seems they jimmied open the back door. You must have disturbed them because they left this behind.' He frowned at Lucy. 'Not sure you should stay the night here, miss, it's a bit of a mess in there, and you being pregnant and all.'

But where would she go? 'I'll be fine. I'll lock up and they wouldn't come back tonight.' She swallowed and stuck her chin out. 'Surely.'

She felt Nick bristle beside her and the officer sighed. 'It's up to you, miss.' But he looked at Nick. What was with that? It had nothing to do with Nick.

It was the other Nick who answered. The one from the hospital. Consultant Kefes. 'You're absolutely right, officer.' She could hear it in his voice. 'We'll arrange somewhere Lucy can stay tonight and sort it out in the morning.'

Lucy's mouth opened but Nick went on, 'Has there been a series of these break-ins?'

The officer nodded. 'Half a dozen over the last week, and some injuries to people who have disturbed them.'

Oh. Lucy's heart plunged. Okay. Not sensible to stay if she wanted to keep her babies safe. But a hotel room was going to hurt her budget severely. A wave of tiredness broke over her and she just wanted to go to bed. Somewhere safe.

Nick was shaking hands with the officers and distractedly Lucy thanked them as well.

The policeman shook his head. 'You did the right thing. Pregnant lady like yourself. You hear noises you don't understand and there's someone in the house, you get out, and ring us—any time.' He glanced at Nick. 'We'll respond as quickly as we can.'

'Thank you, officer. We appreciate that.'

Lucy was still trying to decide which hotel would be the best at this time of night. That was one thing about the Gold Coast. Plenty of hotels. Or maybe she could find a free empty bed in the ward? The man nodded. 'Have a good night.'

They watched the police drive away but all Lucy could think about was how she wanted to sink into the ground. In fact, she wished Nick would go. She had a lot to think about.

Like where to sleep and…that kiss. And how she'd shown him just how much she was attracted to him and the fact that now he just wanted to get her off his books faster than a speeding bullet.

Cringe. Nick's voice broke into her swirling thoughts. 'Come to my flat.'

What? 'I can't do that.' As if.

He opened the passenger-side door of his car. 'Of course you can. It's just sleep. I've got a spare room.'

She couldn't go there. Maybe he could sleep at her place. But she knew he couldn't. Like he could sleep on her two-seater here or in her single bed.

But she couldn't go to his place. 'I can just imagine the gossip.'

'To hell with the gossip. I'm sure a single mother with twins created more gossip last week. And you survived. You can't stay here. It's crazy to pay two hundred dollars for a hotel when you're only going to use it for a few hours. Plus you shouldn't be alone after a scare like that.

'It's for one night.' He glanced at his watch. 'Actually, for about six hours. Are you working the morning shift or the evening?'

'Evening.' So she'd have to come home tomorrow night after work and do the whole thing again. Not an attractive thought.

'Again, problematic.' Nick looked at Lucy wilting under the streetlight. 'It's okay. Just be a little less independent for one night and get in the car.' He gestured to the open car door. 'We'll worry about it in the morning.'

He'd said 'independent' but by his tone he'd meant 'stubborn'. She wasn't being stubborn. Just realistic. It wasn't going to change anything for tomorrow, because this was still her home, but she had to admit it would be horrible to try to sleep at the flat tonight with the trashed house a few feet away.

But she needed to learn to cope with crises as they came along—because she was going to be doing this alone. Nick wouldn't always be there to rescue her.

Nick watched her struggle with the concept of accepting his offer. He wasn't sure either if this was the right thing to do or not, but she couldn't stay here.

She must have been too tired to argue because to his relief she moved past him and slid into the car.

He couldn't stop himself shutting the door quickly in case she changed her mind. He didn't have control issues but the idea of driving away from Lucy while he couldn't be sure she was safe just wasn't happening. He could hear his sister's voice, complaining, the word 'over-protective' ringing in his ears. But this was different.

Tomorrow he'd figure something out. He was good at that. He could fix this. Protect Lucy. Now that she was finally letting him do the work.

CHAPTER NINE

'WHAT FLOOR ARE you on?' Ten minutes later they were standing in the basement car park of Nick's units, waiting for the lift to arrive.

'Nine. It's got a great view.' Nick looked disgustedly relaxed about bringing back a strange woman to his flat after midnight. He probably did it all the time, Lucy thought tiredly.

It was like he hadn't even noticed the tension between them in the car, or the fact that she'd been almost glued against the door on her side, as if she could wipe away any thoughts he might have that she was attracted to him. Too late for that, though.

Lucy had her fingers crossed behind her back. Please don't let them meet anybody in the lift.

The place would be crawling with hospital staff on call for emergencies at all hours of the night and she did not need the stress of smiling and pretending everything was normal when her whole world had been rocked on its axis.

Or was she being a little prude to worry about taking just one night's shelter at a friend's house because her own had been compromised?

A friend she'd kissed, though.

She sighed and forced herself to relax a little. She really couldn't help it.

At that moment the lift doors opened and of all the people she didn't want to see was the glammed-up version of the night-duty midwife, Cass. Even more surprising, she was hanging on the arm of Dr Cade Coleman, and they were obviously on their way out somewhere for very late drinks.

Dr Coleman's eyebrows shot up but he didn't say anything except, 'Evening.'

Nick's sardonic 'Evening' back made Lucy wonder bitterly if this passing of ships in the night was a common occurrence in this building. Neither of the girls said anything, and Lucy's embarrassed smile was met by a disbelieving frown as she and Cass passed.

The lift doors shut and Lucy felt like stamping her foot in frustration. Of all people! Grrr. She looked at Nick, thinking *this was his fault*, and was even more incensed to see he had a slight smile on his lips. 'Well, I'm glad someone is amused.'

'Sarcasm, Lucy?' Nick said mildly, and then he draped his arm around her shoulder and hugged her once before he let her go. 'You're having a night from hell, aren't you?'

She was going to say yes, categorically, but then her sense of fair play, the reasonable side that allowed her to get over the disappointments she'd grown up with, remembered how Nick had come to her aid immediately, had worried about her safety and even provided an answer to her immediate dilemma.

She sighed out her frustration, tried another sigh, and felt better for it. Get over what you can't change. What did she care what Cass thought? But she'd tell the world, her inner caution wailed. Not a lot she could do about it now, though.

So it wasn't the worst night ever. Not quite. 'Not the best.' Though one particular part had been incredible, she wasn't going to think about that until she was safely back in her own house. 'But the night could have been a whole lot unhealthier if I hadn't had you to call on.'

The lift stopped and Nick waited for her to leave the lift in front of him. He lowered his voice. 'Number six. And you're welcome.'

Lucy followed the direction of the numbers until she came to the corner flat. Number six. Nick leant in front of her and opened the door with his key then held it to allow her through first.

Down a small hallway and across the huge living room, floor-to-ceiling windows held the eye, with sheer curtains and a narrow balcony that ran round the whole corner of the building and the view beyond. 'Wow.'

'Yep. It's nice. And there're two bedrooms, so you can have the guest room. You've got your own bathroom and there's towels and a robe hanging on the door if you feel like a shower before bed.'

Bed! It sounded divine. Night attire was a minor problem, but he'd said there was a robe. She looked down at her scrubs. She didn't want to sleep in them or she'd look a hundred times worse tomorrow morning when she met the next nemesis in the lift on her way out.

'I should have grabbed some clothes.'

He shrugged. 'I've got a heap of T-shirts. I'll try and find one that's not black.' He grinned at her. 'We'll sort all that out tomorrow'.

He went to his refrigerator and brought her an unopened bottle of spring water. 'Take that. You're dead on your feet.'

He scooped a folded T-shirt out of a laundry basket of clean clothes that was sitting on a chair, handed it to her and kissed the top of her head like she was a five-year-old he'd picked up from school. 'And I'll see you in the morning.' And then he left her.

Just walked into his room and shut the door.

Lucy blinked. Well, that had been easy. And bizarrely disappointing, which was ridiculous. But he was right about one thing. She *was* dead on her feet and she could worry about everything else in the morning.

Nick had to get out of the room. Or he would have drawn her into his arms again and who knew where that could have ended? Scary stuff.

He heard her bedroom door shut and a few minutes later the sound of the shower. He tried really hard not to think of Lucy naked, round and glistening, with the water running over the places he wanted to run his hands.

He decided a shower was a great idea because he was damn sure there wasn't much chance of sleep just yet.

The cold water helped and as he dried himself he knew he did need to hit the sack. He had a late start tomorrow but the day would be a long one. Especially if he hung around until Lucy finished work. There was plenty he could do in his office.

They had to sort somewhere safe for her to go. Or she could stay here.

He was getting way too involved in her life but she was like a freight train heading for disaster. Not that she'd see it that way.

* * *

After a brief, glorious shower, where she rinsed out her underwear, wrung them dry in a towel and hung them up for the morning, Lucy pulled the T-shirt over her head and tried to ignore the fact she was naked under something that had been against Nick's skin.

A slow heat started in her belly and she couldn't help thinking about Nick's arrival under the lamppost, and the kiss.

She was pretty sure he'd just meant to comfort her but she'd melted against him like a candle under a blow-torch. She would have been a puddle if he hadn't held her up.

She'd never been kissed like that. Nowhere near it. Had never lost herself until all she could feel was a need for more. Her face heated at the thought. And wanted more.

Maybe she'd just been scared? She'd been so glad to see him, and to be wrapped in his arms and protected by him had seemed the most natural thing in the world. Her babies shifted and wriggled and she patted them gently as her head hit the pillow. 'He's not your daddy. And he's not going to be. So get used to it.'

Suddenly there were tears on her pillow and her throat felt raw. She sniffed. 'Stop it.' She rolled over and after many determined breaths and tight closing of her eyes she did eventually fall asleep.

But her dreams were not so easily controlled. Someone was following her. Every time she stopped, they stopped.

When she turned round she couldn't see who they were but she knew they were there and she couldn't find the gate to get out of the house courtyard. Every path seemed to lead to a bare piece of fence with no opening and they were getting closer.

Suddenly she started to cry. She never cried. But the tears just fell more heavily.

A sob caught in her throat and she tried to hold back the flood because the stalker would hear her. Unconsciously she pulled her pillow over her face to muffle the sounds and cried as if her heart would break.

Across the lounge room Nick thought he heard something. Was that Lucy, talking to someone? He slipped from his bed and opened his door.

Nothing. No sounds. Then it came again. Very soft but audible out here. It was Lucy. Sobbing, and nothing could have stopped him knocking briefly and crossing the room to her.

'Shh.' He brushed the hair from her face but she just turned away. 'Lucy, wake up.' He shook her gently but she just became more agitated.

He couldn't stand it. He didn't know what to do except slip in beside her and pull her against his chest and cradle her in his arms. Nick wrapped himself around her until she buried her nose in his chest. He'd never let anything happen to Lucy.

Her hair was in his face. Her forehead in his chest. Babies up against his belly. Now, that was a new experience and he couldn't help a tiny smile.

'It's okay.' He stroked her back. 'My poor brave girl. Life just keeps throwing stuff at you.' He smoothed her hair. She mumbled something he couldn't make out. 'You're fine. You're safe.'

Slowly her breathing settled, and when Nick kissed

the top of her head and then her cheek, still with her eyes shut she turned her damp face towards him.

He kissed her mouth gently and she smiled sleepily. 'Go to sleep. I've got you.'

She murmured something and rolled in his arms so she was facing the other way, spooned into him. Nick swallowed uncomfortably. Exquisite agony to lie there with her so trusting against him.

His hand rested as if it belonged in the gorgeous hollow between her breasts and the other splayed on top of her rounded tummy. She snuggled in even closer and he stifled a groan. If it had been anyone else but Lucy he'd have said they were deliberately teasing him.

He felt the first roll of her belly and then a clear kick from one of the little people inside, and he couldn't help but grin.

'Hello, there,' he whispered barely audibly, and the little foot or hand poked at him again.

Warm feelings expanded in his chest. Affection for these little scamps. These wriggling little babies who would have their mother's characteristics.

And their father's! They weren't his babies.

The thought crashed in on him and for the first time he felt the loss of not being a father. Not having the right to cradle a woman's belly and know that he had created a life—or two—within her. The loss stung unexpectedly. Especially with Lucy in his arms. And yet the man responsible wasn't here, and he was.

Nick wondered what sort of father he would have been. Would he have found it easy or hard to relate to his children? Maybe he would be no better than his own intolerant father, but even at this moment he knew that wasn't true. Especially if he had someone like Lucy to guide him.

The babies kicked again and Lucy murmured something. He smoothed the T-shirt-covered belly under his hand. 'Hey, don't wake your mother up.' And he knew he cared far too much about these tiny little girls or boys and had already invested in their future.

Was he just indulging the over-protective nurturing tendencies he'd carried since Chloe had been sixteen?

Tendencies that had been amplified by his profession? He'd always thought he had an inbuilt reservation about commitment. So where had that gone?

He was a fool. Had he invested his heart in Lucy?

Sure, she wanted him to look after her, but she also had no problem saying she'd never kiss him back again if he didn't pass her on to David. Not exactly the relationship he was looking for.

Unconsciously he tightened his hold and she murmured in protest. He loosened his hands and backed away. He needed to get a grip—and not on her. She seemed settled now and maybe it was time to go.

He slipped slowly backwards out of the bed and apart from a small disappointed noise she let him leave. An omen? He pushed his pillow into her back and tucked her in.

Definitely the most sensible thing to do anyway.

Lucy had the best dream.

When she woke up she was smiling despite the shaft of sunlight on her cheek and a baby playing trampoline on her bladder. And the smell of coffee.

Lucy stretched and admitted grudgingly to herself

that it had been the best sleep she'd had for months. She slid out of bed and padded across to her bathroom.

After she'd indulged herself with another quick shower and climbed awkwardly into her now dry underwear, she looked at the scrubs and screwed up her nose.

Soon she would change back into a purple Teletubby but not yet. She lifted the thick white towelling robe from the hook on the door and slid her arms into the sleeves. She'd always wanted to walk around in one of these.

She grinned at herself in the mirror, surprised how light her spirits were considering everything that had happened the night before, but maybe that was because she couldn't do anything about all the disasters now anyway.

She tied the belt over her definitely growing belly, and opened the door.

Nick was in the kitchen, breaking eggs into a pan. He was wearing board shorts and a black singlet top.

She swallowed the 'Wow' that hovered in her throat and coughed. 'Morning.' Tore her gaze away and admired the way he added four little rashers of bacon to the pan.

He pointed to the coffee plunger on the bench. 'Good morning. Decaf, my lady?'

The heavenly scent. Oh, yes, please. She looked at him. There was something different about him this morning but she couldn't put her finger on what it was.

She poured herself a coffee and sipped the aromatic brew before she put the cup down and pointed her finger at him. 'You, Dr Kefes, are a prince.' She could squirm and beat herself up over being here or she could just enjoy this and to hell with the ramifications. No choice really.

'And I can even cook.' He smiled a long, slow smile that fitted right into the particularly gorgeous day outside and the incredible aromas inside. Life could not get any better at this moment.

'You look rested. And back to your incredibly serene self.'

She felt great. 'I am. This is a very nice hotel. Your bed is divine and comes with delicious dreams.' She could feel herself blush and went on hurriedly, 'Your shower is glorious.' She twirled and showed off her robe. 'And this is very trendy.'

He took his time admiring her robe. Or he might have been avoiding her eyes. She wasn't sure which.

'Sadly, they don't come in black, apparently.'

'Well, I'm not sad about that.' She picked up her cup and wandered over to the window with maybe a tiny hint of extra wiggle.

Nick must have pulled back the curtains when he'd got up because the unobstructed view of the ocean was breathtaking and there was even a cruise liner out on the horizon.

To the left the balcony looked over the Gold Coast city skyline. 'Wow.' She glanced back at him. 'It must be hard to leave this and go to work in the mornings.'

'Nope. Love my work.' He concentrated on turning the eggs without breaking them. 'Love my life.' The toast popped up and he tossed the slices onto the waiting plates with a whistle.

And let that be a warning to you, Lucy, she told herself sternly. He wasn't looking for a relationship any more than she was, let alone one that came with twin babies and commitments. And she had a very busy life to plan and some serious juggling to make ends meet. Hence the reason she was not moving out of the cabana.

But she wasn't going to let it spoil the short time she had before she dived back into reality.

'Good on you. I love my job, too.' She moved towards the long table set with two places. 'And where do I sit?'

He gestured vaguely. 'Either or. I don't eat here enough to have a favourite chair.'

'But you had bacon and eggs in the fridge in case?' Lucy raised her brows.

He shrugged. 'Mrs Jones does my shopping and laundry as well the flat. She keeps me stocked.'

Cleaning lady. Bliss. This was a five-star resort. 'Fine. I'll take the chair facing the view.'

So will I, Nick thought, and could barely take his eyes off her. Obviously she didn't remember the nightmare or the fact that he'd gone in to lie with her until she settled. In the harsh light of day that was a good thing.

He sat down at the table opposite Lucy and watched her tuck into her food, like she had that time they'd eaten together at the surf club, and it was surprising how much he'd enjoyed cooking for her. He enjoyed having her in his home.

And he wanted her in his bed. He'd lain awake for hours last night. Of course she'd had nightmares. It had been a shock and she could have easily been attacked. He'd spent a fair while beating himself up for not taking her all the way to her door or he would have been there when she'd been first frightened.

Which brought them to the next dilemma, but he let her finish her breakfast in peace before he brought that up. If he knew Lucy, it wouldn't take long for her to polish her food off.

Or disagree with his suggestion.

He could feel a smile tug at the corners of his mouth as she put her fork and knife together in the middle of her empty plate. 'Wow. That was good. Thank you.' Typically she followed that with, 'And I'm washing up.'

She just couldn't let him do anything for her without paying for it. Stubborn woman. He didn't know why that pushed his buttons but he almost ground his teeth in frustration. Maybe that was the reason he was less than diplomatic with his next wording.

'It's not safe to go back there after work tonight. You know that, don't you?'

He frowned at himself. But she was so darned independent she infuriated him. That wasn't to say after it came out of his mouth he didn't regret his bluntness.

She put her cup down and met his gaze steadily. Surprisingly even-tempered as she gently turned him down. Why did he feel like she was the grown-up here?

'I appreciate your concern, Nick, but I have to go back. It's my home. And my job to house-sit the big house.' She held his gaze. 'I need to save money for when I can't work, and it's rent-free.'

He would not lose this battle. 'And what if the burglars come back?' It seriously worried him and he couldn't believe it didn't worry her either.

Lucy sighed. 'The thought of getting home late at night and opening my door isn't a comfortable one, I admit, but I'll have a chat to Flora at work today and see if she can swap me to day shifts for a few weeks.'

He opened his mouth but she held up her hand. Bossy little thing. It had been years since someone had held up their hand to tell him to be quiet. He subsided reluctantly but stewed about it.

'I'll phone the owners this morning when I go home and see what the damage is. I'm sure they'll be happy to beef up the security and maybe even hire a firm to keep the place under surveillance. It's in their interests, too.'

He could see she was determined. But so was he. 'If you work this evening, before you can change to the day shift, I think you should spend one more night here.'

She opened her mouth and sardonically he held up his own hand.

She narrowed her eyes at him but he just smiled. 'My turn. Another day or two will give the security firm time to make their adjustments as well.'

It was a sensible idea—and, though Lucy hated to admit it, it was an attractive one as well. And that was without the eye candy of a dreamy Greek doc cooking her breakfast. And in reality there was plenty of room here for the two of them.

It would only be for one more night. And the idea of not having to go back until the place was made more secure was very attractive. Maybe he'd let her pay...

'And if you offer to pay board I will stomp on your scrubs so that when you leave, everyone will think you slept in them.'

She widened her eyes at him. 'Ooh. Nasty.'

He wasn't fazed. 'I assure you. I can be.'

'Okay. Okay.' She had a sudden vision of Nick jumping up and down on her purple scrubs and bit her lip to stop an unseemly snort. But it seemed there was no stopping the eruption of giggles that escaped. She gave up and threw back her head and laughed at him.

'You crack me up.'

'Obviously.' He grinned at her. 'Now, that has to be good for you.' Nick was thinking that it was good for him, too. He loved the way she laughed. Loved a lot of things about Lucy because she continued to amaze him with her resilience.

'So you'll stay tonight?'

She nodded. 'Yes, please.'

'I'll walk you home. I've got a backlog of work so I'll meet you in the doctors' car park after eleven.'

'No.' She shook her head. 'It's two hundred yards across a road. Doesn't your sister walk home after an evening shift?'

Yes, she did, but this was a bit different. Or was it? Was he going too far the other way? What was wrong with him?

Hmm. 'You're right.' He held up his hands. 'My brain's gone AWOL.' He stood up, walked over to an empty vase and tipped it up to retrieve a spare set of keys.

'The big one opens the door on the street to the foyer. The smaller one the front door to the flat.'

She looked at the keys in his hand and reluctance shone out of her worried eyes. 'I'll try and be quiet when I come in.'

'I sleep through anything,' he said to make her feel better, but he knew he wouldn't.

CHAPTER TEN

LUCY FELT THE change as soon as she walked into work. The morning staff, normally chatty and warm, suddenly stopped their conversations when she entered the tea room, and even the friendliest midwives, while they still smiled a greeting, didn't meet her eyes.

Lucy took one guess at what had happened. Cass.

She put her bag away and went back out to the ward to wait for the clinical handover to start.

She'd thought she'd got over that insecurity thing left over from her mother, that not-good-enough-to-be-included cloud that had hung over her whole childhood.

So what if these people she'd hoped were her friends thought that, because she was pregnant, she'd shacked up with the nearest available rich guy and had just made it easy for herself?

Now she wished she'd actually tried to seduce Nick so at least she would have had the memory. And what a memory that would have been…or would she have been just like her mother? Looking for a quick fix to her life's bigger problems?

Then they'd have the right to say she'd be a terrible mother, too, but she knew in her heart that wasn't true. She would love her babies with all her heart. Though there would always be a part of her that belonged to Nick in her dreams.

Lucy lifted her chin. She'd always been a bit of a loner when the going got tough. Other people didn't need to know how she was feeling so she pinned a smile on her face and put her bag away.

But the unfairness burned a hole in her euphoric feeling of belonging here. How would they have liked a break-in? At eleven at night? When they were on their own?

All they saw was the pregnant little midwife who might be sleeping with the ward consultant. A man who wasn't even the father of her baby. Or maybe they thought Nick was.

Poor Nick. His only fault was that he'd helped her out. Well, blow the lot of them.

Flora appeared at her side. 'A moment, Palmer?'

Lucy felt her stomach plummet. She'd thought Flora would have given her the benefit of the doubt. 'Certainly, Sister.'

Flora steered her into her office and shut the door. Then, to Lucy's complete surprise, offered one of her jerky and uncomfortable hugs before she pulled back and stared into Lucy's face with concern. Not censure. 'Are you all right?'

Dear, dear, Flora May. Lucy stamped fiercely on the urge to cry. 'My landlord's house was broken into last night and I disturbed the robbers when I went home.'

Flora gasped.

It all tumbled out. 'Nick came and phoned the police and waited with me. He thought it wasn't safe to stay alone in the flat.'

'He's right.' Flora looked away and glared into the

distance. 'Stupid rumours. Stupid people.' Flora looked back at her.

Now seemed a good time to mention the roster change, Lucy thought. 'I was going to ask if you could change me to day shifts for a few weeks. I spoke to the owners today. A security firm has put the house under surveillance but I'd like to avoid going home at night for a little while.'

Flora nodded vehemently. 'Absolutely. Consider it done. You could have night shift if you wanted. Then you'd only be there in the daytime.'

But then she'd have to work with Cass and they just might come to blows if she still treated her birthing women like she'd treated young Sally. Or Lucy herself. 'Can I think about that?'

Flora nodded. 'No problem. Why don't you have split days off this week? Have tomorrow off and come in Friday and Saturday morning because I have a space on the roster then.'

Flora stepped back to the desk and checked her print-out. 'Yes. Then have Sunday off then do a week of mornings starting Monday?'

Sounded perfect. Lucy wondered if Nick still wanted to have breakfast together on Sunday—he might be sick of her by then after having her in his house for two days in a row—but either way she still wasn't working. Flora was a champion.

She did have friends. 'That sounds wonderful. Thank you.'

Flora glanced at her watch. 'Let me know if you want nights next week.' Then she looked back at Lucy's face. 'And where are you going tonight after work?'

'Um, Dr Kefes has offered his spare room for one

more night.' Flora didn't look happy and Lucy went on, 'The new locks and cameras at my place will be installed tomorrow. So tomorrow night I'll go back there.'

'Fine. I'll have a word with a certain midwife.'

Lucy shrugged. 'It really doesn't matter. I should be used to it.'

Flora lifted her chin. 'You shouldn't have to be. But I will fix her little red wagon.' Goodness knew what that meant, Lucy thought, but she wouldn't like to be on the end of Flora's displeasure.

'Oh. And Dr Kefes said because it could be misconstrued, he's moved me on to a Dr David Donaldson. Do you know him?'

Lucy hadn't known that Flora could actually blush, though there was a definite heightened colour to her face.

The older woman seemed fixated on the ward clock now. 'Yes. I heard he was coming back.'

Lucy wasn't sure what the problem was, but she hoped it wasn't because Flora didn't agree he was the right doctor for her. 'Apparently his wife died.'

'Hmm.' Flora wasn't buying into the conversation. 'You don't see your mother much, do you? Did you ask her to come and stay with you?'

Lucy shrugged. Would her mother offer her help if she needed it? She really didn't want to find that out the hard way. 'She's got her own life. I respect that. And my flat's too small for two people.'

Flora nodded noncommittally. 'I have my own life, too, but I'd like to think that if you need a friend I am there for you, Lucy.' It seemed a strange thing to say and not related to anything.

Lucy mumbled, 'Thank you,' and the subject closed on that.

'Take birthing unit two,' Flora said. 'Judy is in there and will give you handover.'

Eight hours later, as the shift drew to a close, Lucy couldn't help the little release of excitement that had bubbled quietly all day because she'd be going back to Nick's flat again tonight. And everyone already thought they were having an affair.

But this was the last time she'd stay there. It had to be.

Tomorrow, a Thursday off for a change, she'd have all day to sort things out and be ready to sleep in her own bed tomorrow night. She needed to get back to running her own life.

A shame it had felt so safe at Nick's flat last night. As if the weight of the world had been lifted off her shoulders and this morning had been the perfect way to start the day. The picture of Nick, with his muscles, in the kitchen, cooking her breakfast, would be hard to beat.

As Lucy turned towards the consultants' flats she hoped she wouldn't meet anyone in Nick's lift this time but it probably didn't matter now. She was already the scarlet woman of the hospital, just like her mother, heading to sleep over at a man's flat.

Not such a good example to her children, and something she'd sworn when they were peanuts she wouldn't do, but this was different. How far she'd fallen since that first exciting day when she was going to be the best grad midwife GCCH had ever seen.

Lucy's hope that tonight's stay at Nick's would remain unnoticed shrivelled and died as the nurse walking ahead turned into the front entrance to Nick's lobby door.

Not much she could do about it unless she wanted to walk around the block in the dark, and that defeated the purpose of being safe, she thought grumpily. She rubbed the tender ache in her side where one of the babies had been poking her with an elbow or foot on and off throughout the day.

As she opened the foyer door a few seconds later with Nick's key she could see the other nurse was still waiting by the lifts so she'd even have to say hello.

She sighed and admired the thick loose twist of dark hair on the woman's head and even the escaping brown curls looked more artful than untidy. She'd always wanted to be able to do a bun.

Lucy brushed back the hair from her own eyes and felt hot and bothered and frumpy and fat. Where had all that excitement of five minutes ago gone?

Quite a few years older than Lucy, the other girl offered a friendly smile. 'Evening.' And Lucy wished for half her poise.

'Evening.' Lucy decided that must be what they all say around here and the conversation died because the lift doors opened.

'What floor?' the girl asked as she stood in front of the control panel.

'Nine.'

The girl's brow puckered a little and she glanced at Lucy more thoroughly as she pressed the button. 'I'm on nine, too. Haven't seen you before.'

Lucy studied the shiny white tiles of the lift floor. 'I'm just staying with a friend for tonight.'

'Oh.'

Lucy looked up at the change in tone. She saw the other girl digest her answer as she looked at Lucy's baggy scrubs and the unmistakable bulge of pregnancy at the front. Her eyes narrowed.

The tone wasn't unfriendly. 'I'm Chloe Kefes.'

Bingo. She had all the luck. 'Nick's sister.' Lucy tried to keep the resignation out of her voice.

'Yep.' Her gaze was drawn to Lucy's bulge. 'Would you be Lucy? His patient?' Chloe had a twinkle in her eyes that took the sting out of her next comment. 'The one the whole hospital is talking about with my brother?'

At least Nick's sister didn't seem to hate her. 'That would be me. And ex-patient. Actually, he's handed me over to Dr Donaldson.'

Chloe's eyes widened. 'I see. Good. I'd hate him to have to justify to people what he does naturally. He's the kindest man in the world and the best brother.' She raised her eyebrows at Lucy. 'Gets a bit over-protective at times.'

The lift arrived and Lucy had never been so glad to step out. 'I know. And I do understand. Nice meeting you, Chloe.'

'Interesting meeting you, too.' They walked down the corridor together and Lucy remembered Nick pointing out his sister's flat next to his. This just kept getting better and better.

Chloe's eyebrows rose when Lucy pulled the key to Nick's door out of her pocket but she didn't say anything. Before Lucy could turn the key Nick opened the door anyway.

'Hi, Lucy, Chloe.' He looked from one woman to

the other. 'Did you guys walk home together? That's a good idea.'

Chloe looked like she might disagree but didn't comment. 'We met in the lifts. I'll see you in the morning, Nikolai. Bye, Lucy.'

Nick held the door for Lucy and she closed her eyes as she ducked under his arm. This was becoming more complicated by the second. She should have just gone back to her own home. She'd tidied up the big house before work today and maybe she would have been fine.

'I don't think your sister is happy I'm staying.'

'Tough.' He looked supremely uninterested. 'I'd be more unhappy if you didn't. Who matters most?'

She had to smile at that. 'I guess she's worried the gossip will taint you.'

He looked more closely at her. 'Have you had a bad day or was it just Chloe?'

She sighed and allowed herself to be steered into a chair. He handed her a soda water and she took a sip because she hated the way, even without intention, Chloe had made her feel. 'I'm a scarlet woman, having an affair with the consultant.'

He shrugged and then smiled crookedly at her. 'I hope I'm the consultant concerned?'

'Stop it.' But he did make her smile despite the gravity of the situation. Not that he seemed to think it grave.

He sat down opposite her. Caught and held her gaze. 'You're new here. You're not used to it. The place thrives on gossip. Next week it will be someone else.'

'I don't want to be this week's juicy titbit.'

Nick couldn't stand it. She looked so forlorn. Juicy titbit. She was that indeed, but at the moment she needed comfort, not his sexual frustration, and he'd promised himself he would not sleep with Lucy.

It wouldn't be fair. What single, pregnant young woman, after giving herself, wouldn't be hurt when he walked away?

And he wasn't capable of the emotional roller-coaster ride needed to stay. He owed it to her to be strong for both of them.

So gently, like a brother, he stood, reached down and she put her hand in his without hesitating, and he held that thought as he stood her up. 'In that case, come here and get a sympathetic hug.'

Before she could pull away he'd folded her loosely in an embrace and just for a moment he felt her let the worries and stresses fall away. But only for a moment. Would she ever let him in? he thought ruefully, forgetting he'd agreed on keeping his distance, not thinking about his own walls that held them back.

A few more seconds and he'd have to let go. She felt too good, snuggled in against him, too rounded and lush and gorgeous. Maybe they should really give the gossipers something to moan about.

Lucy relaxed against Nick and tried to stop thinking. Just for a moment. Then she remembered the safe harbour last night, remembered the time he'd hugged her when she'd been frightened for her babies, remembered he'd kissed her once. She didn't want this for comfort, she wanted it because he desired her. Because all night while she'd waited for the clock to crawl around she'd hoped he'd do this, because she certainly desired him.

She just wanted him to sweep her up, show her the love she had no right to expect, because she had the horrible feeling she was reading too much into his kindness. Learning to rely on him too much. And he had a real life apart from being her shiny white knight in her fantasy.

She didn't kid herself he'd be dropping by with his paddleboard when she had two tiny babies to manage. What man would?

So she'd be the one doing the moaning if she let herself snuggle up to Nick for too long. She shouldn't have come here tonight feeling needy and emotional, and more than semi-sexually aroused at the thought of sleeping under Nick's roof again. She'd heard that the second half of pregnancy hormones could startle men. She smiled sadly to herself and prepared to ease back.

But she never got to take that step away because Nick lifted her chin with one long, caring finger, smiled into her eyes and kissed her. A soft and sweet and gentle kiss.

It was too much. Lucy despaired. The tragedy of this beautiful, too-perfect man, and the chance of him falling for her, nearly broke her heart. Something must have shown in her face because he gathered her even closer, whispered, 'Don't look like that, my gorgeous girl,' and kissed her again.

And then it was just like last night, under the streetlight, a long star-studded, sensation-filled path to losing herself in a place where no rational thought was allowed.

'Hold me, Nick.' She didn't know where the voice had come from, or even if she'd said it out loud, but she felt the floor disappear from under her feet as he lifted her into his arms and carried her carefully into his moonlit room.

Nick put her down gently on her feet beside the bed,

murmured, 'Far too many clothes,' and helped her pull off her purple scrubs so that she stood before him in her bra and panties. Then he pulled his T-shirt off and drew her back in against his chest. Skin to skin. Like a baby against its mother's breast. Her lace-covered breasts against Nick's chest.

She could stand like this for ever—his hot skin on hers, lean muscle against her soft curves. She pictured them in her mind's eye to save the memory, inhaled the scent of freshly showered man, leant into solid, muscular chest, lifted her hands to corded shoulders and slid her fingers along the rough growth of his unshaven chin.

Every part of him felt as wonderful as she knew it would and her body began to dance to his music as his hands slid slowly from her shoulders to her hips.

He made her feel wanton, desirable, for a moment even beautiful, and she tilted her head as he dropped feather-light kisses along her jaw.

She'd dreamt of this but it had never felt as magical as this.

Emboldened, her hands began their own exploration, the play of muscle and sinew and raw strength under her fingers, the bulge of biceps, and with a woman's smile she felt his breath catch as her thumb slid across his taut belly.

The sliding doors to the veranda were open and the sound of the surf washed over them as he drew her down gently onto his bed and with her eyes shut by his kisses, the soothing sound of the waves and the salty freshness of the breeze surrounded her, along with Nick's arms as he lay down next to her—and pulled her more fully into his embrace.

When he kissed her again she sighed into him. This was where she wanted to be. She had been fighting against the dream, fighting against the taboos of falling for a man who wouldn't be there for her always, but it was too late. She loved him for what he'd done for her, loved him for looking after her babies, loved him even when he undermined her independence, even loved it that he was so confused about his own feelings for her—but that didn't mean he loved her.

I love you, she said silently to him, and hugged him tighter because she needed this one night before she returned to the real world tomorrow.

He hadn't meant to get to this point. he held Lucy in his arms and she felt so right, so perfect that it scared him. Terrified him that this woman—his hands slid with gentle reverence across her satin belly—and these babies—his breath caught—could be his responsibility.

But was he ready for this? Did she think he was? Was he open enough emotionally, worthy? Could he be trusted to never let them down, like his parents had let Chloe and himself down? He hoped so but hope wasn't good enough. In his heart he knew that 'not sure' was unacceptable.

But still he couldn't stop because she pulled his hand back when he tried to leave, answered when he kissed her mouth with a molten response that undid his intentions, pressed herself against him until his need for her outstripped his brain's refusal.

But this couldn't happen while he wasn't committed. He owed Lucy that.

So, after a timeless journey of sensation, intoxicating kisses and the tender wonder of this woman's beautiful body, Nick drew back. Shuddered the demons back into their boxes and stilled his hand.

Lucy sensed the change. In some pathetic part of her a tiny molecule was glad that one of them had stopped because this had no future and she would hate Nick to regret it.

It was fortunate indeed that Nick had more control than she did.

But, then, he didn't love her.

He probably cared for her and was happy to be there when she was having one of her many crises, but for now he soothed her disappointed murmurings with, 'It's okay. We'll talk in the morning. Sleep and I'll hold you.'

And she felt like weeping as he gently rolled her onto her side until they were spooned together, slid his arm beneath her pillow and then cradled her breast in one hand and her belly in the other. And she sighed away the longing, acknowledged in some recess of her brain this was how it would always have ended, and that when she woke tomorrow this book would close.

For ever. Because she couldn't open herself to this kind of pain again.

Lucy closed her staring eyes with the unpalatable insight that Nick was being kind and unintentionally she'd asked too much of him.

It took Nick hours to go to sleep. Apart from his screaming frustration as he held her gorgeous body against him, it was the generous innocence of her response that tore at him. The innocence testified to her pre-

pregnancy inexperience and how low he'd been to even consider making love to this woman without a full commitment.

She was so different from the other women he'd been with. He hadn't understood, hadn't learnt what Lucy's kind of giving was about, so maybe he could cut himself some slack that he hadn't recognised what he was doing until almost too late.

But it had opened a deep well of wonder, and also great guilt.

He needed to rethink this whole Lucy world. Because that's what she was. A world. An amazing, generous, loving world that he wasn't sure he was ready for. Or deserved. He fell asleep wishing to hell he did.

When Nick finally fell asleep it was so deep he didn't feel Lucy rise before the sun. Or hear the blinds being drawn across to darken the room from the pre-dawn light before she slipped away. Or the rustle as she dressed herself in the lounge room with the new clothes she'd picked up yesterday. Or the sound of his front door closing as she carried everything she'd brought with her back to her own house.

Lucy knew she needed to go. Preferably before Nick woke up because, unless she wanted to be the Nikolai Kefes groupie of the year, she had to get out.

She wasn't sure if this was a final stab at the independence she needed to survive or the ultimate in self-protection. All she knew was that her babies deserved more respect and she needed more self-respect than the morning after an almost-affair from a man who had only ever been kind to her.

And most terrifying of all, she needed to go before Nick trapped himself into something she refused to see him regret.

Even before Nick woke up his hand searched for the warmth of Lucy. His eyes opened but the dent in the pillow beside his head only made him feel sad. He strained to hear the sound of movement in his flat but all he could hear was the relentless ocean, washing in and washing out across a deserted beach, and in his heart he knew she was gone.

He couldn't believe how empty, and deserted, his own life seemed, so different from yesterday when he'd bounded out of bed to make her a surprise breakfast. Today—it was just him. Like old times.

Times before Lucy. He couldn't believe how much he missed her.

Nick rolled out of bed, walked to the blinds and pulled them back. He wished he could share the sunrise with Lucy because she'd have enthused over it. He wished he could have seen her bathed by the golden light.

An ominous prickle under his skin asked the question. What if she never came back? If he never woke to Lucy beside him, ever?

He searched for a note but didn't find one. He resisted the urge to phone her. Had to give her space she'd silently asked for by leaving and take on board that it was time to sort out his own issues before he saw her again.

Tomorrow morning. At work. He could wait till then.

CHAPTER ELEVEN

LUCY TRIED SO hard not to think about Nick. About leaving his bed in the early hours like a thief.

But he was the thief. He'd stolen her heart and nobody was going to get it back for her so she needed to grow another one. And that wasn't going to happen unless she stayed away from Dr Kefes.

But it was so hard to pretend she didn't miss him. When she swept the path, she thought of Nick, and got hotter than she should. When she picked a frond out of the pool her stomach dropped as she thought of Nick. Opening her refrigerator even the water bottles reminded her of Nick.

But the worst, when she lay on her bed, she missed his warmth. His strength. His caring.

Could even hear him telling her to stay, the day he'd run all those errands for her, when she'd been scared she'd lose her babies. But she had to be strong.

For both of them. For all of them.

On Friday morning, Flora introduced Lucy to Dr Donaldson on his first day back at GCCH. He was a tall, smiling, stick figure of a man with very kind eyes, so it seemed strange, when Nick had endorsed the man to her, that Flora obviously wasn't comfortable with him.

Lucy's first antenatal visit with the new doctor was that afternoon after work. It had been arranged by Nick on Wednesday, with strict instructions not to miss it, and while she'd been steamrollered into changing doctors, it seemed now it was all for the best.

The shift was busy, but thankfully Flora was still allocating her non-Kefes patients. Lucy saw Nick twice in the distance, but ducked into a room each time before he saw her, and once she turned round when he'd started to walk towards her.

All painful, heart-wrenching choices she had to make, and at times she wasn't so sure she was doing the right thing. She had to face him some time but she was feeling too fragile yet.

Flora seemed preoccupied, and Lucy, hunting for distraction from thoughts of Nick, tried vainly for an opportunity to broach the subject of why she didn't like Dr Donaldson. If she wasn't having Nick, she wanted someone good.

Finally, at the end of the day as both were about to leave, Lucy caught up with the senior midwife. 'As far as Dr Donaldson is concerned, do you think he's a good obstetrician?'

'Of course.' Flora seemed a bit short, and Lucy still didn't feel any better.

I'm not reassured, Lucy thought, and tried again. 'Would you recommend anyone else?'

Flora stopped walking and sighed. She met Lucy's worried eyes with a strange expression on her face. 'David Donaldson is an excellent obstetrician. Very experienced with twin pregnancies and has a stellar reputation. You could do no better.'

Well, that was glowing, it just hadn't been said in an enthusiastic voice. But at least Flora wouldn't say something that wasn't true. And there was no doubt Flora would prefer it if Lucy dropped the subject.

So, reluctantly, she did. 'Thank you.'

Fifteen minutes later she was shown into the good doctor's new rooms and Lucy suspected that behind the twinkling grey eyes lay a very astute mind because he glossed over the point that Nick had handed her on for personal reasons and concentrated on her pregnancy.

After taking her blood pressure and weight, he helped her climb up onto the examination couch to feel her tummy. It just wasn't the same as doing this with Nick but she needed to stop thinking about that.

Dr Donaldson palpated the babies, and he must have been a little firmer with his hands than Nick because once or twice Lucy winced with discomfort.

He lifted his hands. 'Sorry. So you're twenty-four weeks, the babies are growing well, one is head first and the other breech today.'

She nodded. Wished she could tell Nick that one was breech at the moment.

The kind doctor smiled. 'You know they can swap and change for a few weeks yet?'

After he'd found and listened to their two different heartbeats he wiped off the gel and palpated one more time on the lower part of her abdomen.

Lucy winced again and he nodded to himself. 'I thought that was uncomfortable?'

She nodded and he quizzed her on her general condition. 'So you're well. No discomfort you didn't expect, babies moving as usual. Anything worrying you?'

Did he mean apart from tearing herself away from the man she wanted to spend the rest of her life with? She'd barely thought about her body—too obsessed with pining for Nick. 'Just a few aches and pains. But probably ligament discomfort or a mobile elbow.'

Dr Donaldson was more interested than she was. 'Show me where.'

Lucy pointed to the right side of her abdomen, the spot that he'd touched, and he nodded, and gently palpated the area again.

Lucy winced and his eyebrows drew together. 'Haven't had any temperatures? Sweats? Nausea?'

Well, actually… Hot and feeling sick? Lucy nodded reluctantly. 'Yes. I might have.'

He smiled kindly and helped her sit up. 'One or all three?'

To be honest? 'All three?'

He helped her down from the couch and directed her back to the chair beside his desk.

But she'd just thought the day was warmer than expected, the babies were growing and making themselves known, and the stress of moving back into her house, away from Nick, was making her feel a little rotten.

He sat back behind his desk and typed on the computer. 'I'd like you to go down to Pathology and have another blood test.'

Not again. But she wasn't having any unusual tightening of her belly. 'I've already been treated for a kidney infection.'

He smiled. 'I think it's more likely you have a grumbling appendicitis. Fairly unusual in pregnancy and quite complicated with twins on board, but we'll keep an eye on you.'

Lucy felt her mind go blank. Appendicitis? Where was Nick at this moment? What would he say about this? So it wasn't a baby elbow or knee. And it was still a bit achy from where he'd palpated. She couldn't afford a grumbling appendix. 'What happens if it gets worse?'

He smiled kindly. 'You have an appendectomy.'

Good grief. Why did this have to happen today? When she was being strong about not calling Nick? 'I didn't think I could have a general anaesthetic. What about the babies?'

Let alone the six weeks off work with no sick pay. And she wouldn't even have Nick to bring her healthy yoghurt and sympathise.

'Yes is the short answer. If necessary, your babies would be anesthetised as well, because the drugs do cross the placenta.'

Too scary to even think about.

'The babies would wake up when it wore off.'

This was a nightmare. And a hundred times worse because she couldn't share it with the one person she wanted to.

She needed him. But she couldn't have him. 'Don't tell Dr Kefes.' The words were wrenched out of her and were the direct opposite of what she really wanted. More than anything she wanted Nick with her. More than anything she knew she couldn't. This was the start of it. She had to push him out of her life.

This was her surviving the next crisis without Nick.

She'd already had two disasters he'd had to manage and she needed to sort this herself. The problem was, all she felt like doing was bursting into tears.

'You remind me of someone I used to know.' Dr Donaldson gave her a quizzical look. 'Determined to be independent. But I won't mention it if you wish. And your symptoms might go away. We can hope.'

He gave her his card and wrote his mobile phone number on the back of it. 'So take it gently. Phone me if there is a problem or the pain becomes severe. You must do that.'

She nodded, took the card and put it in her purse.

He opened his door for her and before she walked through he said gently, 'And don't forget to have that blood test done today.'

She stopped. Looked at him. He smiled blandly. Surely Nick hadn't told him she'd done that last time? She narrowed her eyes at him. She'd bet Nick had mentioned it. 'Thank you, Doctor.'

Nick found himself wondering how Lucy had gone with Dr Donaldson.

He'd woken so many times on Thursday night, wondering how she'd gone back to her house after the break-in. How she'd gone after leaving his bed. Was she thanking him for not seducing her or hating him? The jury was still out how he felt about that himself.

His eyes strayed to the clock again. She'd be in there now. He knew he'd miss Lucy but he hadn't realised how much he would miss his frequent interaction with Lucy's babies when he handed her on. And this was only the first visit. It was worrying how invested he'd become in her babies' well-being.

He'd been subtly trying to catch their mother's eye all day, without drawing the attention of the whole hospital, watching for developments, but it had been frustratingly difficult to even get close to speaking with Lucy.

He hated the distance he could feel between them and that was despite the fact he was ten rooms away. In the end he'd asked Flora how she'd gone at home, an innocent question, and had been told she was fine.

He'd have it out with her on Sunday, when they had breakfast, if she was still going to come with him. He didn't like to think how much he had riding on the assumption she would.

On Saturday morning Lucy felt well enough to work the early shift, despite the fact she'd been miserable all night, missing Nick, because the discomfort in her side remained constant but was no worse.

After work Flora was coming around late afternoon with some baby clothes and that was something she could look forward to. She needed more distraction like this if she was going to stay sane.

Baby clothes. She hadn't had a chance to do anything yet but her friends with their twins had promised to bring a load of things around next weekend. Lucy decided to ask Flora to come when they did and they could all have an afternoon together.

More distractions and moments to look forward to. Funny how her friends were all older now.

Her midwifery training friends were all far flung and busy partying. Finding herself pregnant on her first shift had made her less outgoing with her mind more on survival than on forming friendships.

Except with Nick. Always her thoughts came back to Nick.

He'd taken her under his wing from the first day.

But you couldn't be a pseudo sister when you fancied the big brother so she was doing the right thing to get out of that situation as soon as possible. Before he did.

Everything else was fine. Truly.

She wouldn't be as lonely when she'd had the babies, went to play groups and met other mums. But for the moment it was brutally lonely and not just because she missed Nick. Mostly that, but not only that. She just needed to keep reminding herself.

By the time she finished work at three she didn't feel quite so well.

At four o'clock, when Flora arrived with her freshly baked scones, Lucy was feeling pretty darned miserable.

Flora took one look at her and made her sit down. 'What's happening here?'

Lucy felt like crying. Or being sick. Or both. 'Dr Donaldson thinks I might have a grumbling appendix.'

Flora felt her forehead. 'Hot! It looks to be more than grumbling. You need to go to Emergency, my girl.'

'Dr Donaldson gave me a number to ring him on if I got worse.' Lucy pointed to her handbag on the table. She didn't have the energy to get up and get it herself.

Flora picked up the handbag and brought it over. She dug out Lucy's purse and gave it to her. 'And you haven't?'

Another urge to weep. 'I didn't like to bother him on a Saturday.'

Flora patted Lucy's shoulder and stood up. 'I'll pack you an overnight bag. What about Dr Kefes? Nikolai? Have you told him you're unwell?'

Lucy felt so miserable. And hearing Flora say it only made it worse. 'I'm trying not to lean on Nick. He's treating me like his little sister. It's not fair on him and I have to learn to stand on my own feet...' She put her face in her hands and squeezed her eyes to hold back the tears. She was pathetic.

'Hmph,' Flora said as she stood up. 'I don't think it's a sister he wants.' Flora spoke more to herself than to Lucy as she bustled around. 'And you are a very capable young woman so stop beating yourself up. Shall I ring him?'

Nick would take control again. And she'd throw herself on his chest. She knew she would. She needed to learn to rely on herself. 'No. Don't bother him.'

Flora sighed as she busily rummaged through Lucy's drawers. She held up a soft nightgown. 'This one okay? These underclothes?'

Lucy sniffed and had to smile. 'Nobody has ever packed a bag for me before.'

Flora glanced at her. 'Maybe it's time you let them.'

'Let you?' Lucy would have liked to laugh but she didn't have one in her. 'Could I stop you?'

'I doubt it.' Flora came back to Lucy and leant down, all elbows and awkwardness, and hugged her. 'Stop worrying about putting other people out. They wouldn't help if they didn't want to. Now, do you have a small bathroom bag?'

The pain was getting worse. 'No. I've never needed one. But my toothbrush is there.'

'Never mind. I'll put it in a plastic bag and bring you one later.' She stopped for a moment and sighed again. 'Give me David's card and I'll ring him.'

It all happened very fast after that.

Flora drove her to the hospital, a scary trip in Flora's big off-road vehicle, and with Flora's attitude that everyone needed to get out of her way because she had a medical crisis.

Lucy wanted Nick. Needed Nick to hold her hand. Say her babies would be fine after the anaesthetic. But it was too late now.

The emergency staff knew she was coming, Dr Donaldson was waiting, and before she knew it she was repeating her name to the gowned theatre nurse as she was being wheeled into the operating theatre.

When she came round, it felt like she'd been stabbed. Der, she had been, she thought groggily, and then she remembered her babies.

Her hand slid gingerly across her belly for reassurance and there they were. Probably asleep, like she wanted to be, and she glanced at the empty chair beside the bed and tried not to cry before she drifted off again.

Flora had arranged for Lucy to be cared for in the maternity section, and that meant she knew the people who cared for her. Except Nick didn't come.

In her groggy haze they all seemed genuinely concerned for her and maybe she wasn't quite as friendless as she'd assumed. Even Cass apologised for not knowing about the break-in, and her less-than-flattering comments that had caused the gossip storm.

Lucy brushed it away. She really didn't care any more but Cass apologised again when she brought Lucy jelly for breakfast before she went off. Lucy just wanted Nick but she knew she couldn't have him.

Down the road from the hospital Nick had gone round to Lucy's at eight o'clock as arranged for Sunday breakfast, but the gate had been locked and when he'd used the intercom she hadn't answered.

Late Saturday afternoon, when he'd got home from a function he'd promised Chloe he'd go to, he'd tried to confirm their date for today and just hear her say she was settled. But that hadn't happened.

He hadn't rung later, even though he'd wanted to, in case she was sleeping. He knew she was due to work yesterday to make up for the Thursday, that would be Thursday when she'd left his bed, but he pushed that thought away.

And he'd rung this morning but there had been no answer and now she wasn't answering the intercom. He didn't like that one bit.

He'd told himself she was probably doing something industrious around the mansion but this time when he phoned and it again went through to the message bank his skin crawled at the thought of Lucy unconscious or, worse, attacked by criminals in her own home.

Why on earth had he agreed she should come back here when he knew it wasn't safe? Three nights she'd been here alone.

Nick strode the long way round and peered over the rear beach fence but again he couldn't see any movement. He called out but there was still no answer and now he was seriously concerned.

It wasn't easy but he managed to scale the gate without impaling himself on the protective spikes. He could just imagine the headlines in the Gold Coast newspaper if he did. *Well-known obstetrician impaled during break-in.* Lovely.

No doubt Lucy would have a giggle about that one. After he'd strangled her for scaring him.

And no doubt the security firm would be haring to

the rescue by the time he got to Lucy's cabana. They'd better be, he thought grimly, or heads would roll.

When he reached Lucy's flat it was locked up. It seemed she wasn't lying on the floor unconscious from what he could see through the white curtains and the place didn't look as if it had been rifled.

He heard a car screech to a halt outside and the sound of the gate. At least that was slightly satisfying.

Maybe she'd just forgotten their meeting. Not good for his ego or his heart, but better than the alternative.

'Stop right there.' The burly security guard stood with his feet planted as soon as he got inside the gate.

Nick decided that attack was the best form of defence. 'Do you know where Miss Palmer is?'

Belligerent eyebrows shot up. 'And who might you be to her?'

Good question. What was he? He wasn't her doctor. He wasn't the father of her children. He certainly wasn't her brother or her father. 'I'm a concerned friend.' Certainly not her boyfriend—why was that? Because he didn't know his own mind!

It was becoming clearer by the second.

'Prove it.' The man's tone suggested he'd been lied to by experts in the past.

Nick didn't have time for this. He needed to find Lucy. 'I'm Dr Nikolai Kefes. I work at Gold Coast City Hospital.' He pulled his business card from his wallet. 'I want to know she's all right. I was here the other night when her house was broken into and she's supposed to meet me for breakfast today.'

The security guard took his card. Nodded. 'I can understand that, sir. But you will have to leave unless I get Miss Palmer's permission for you to stay.'

'As it seems neither of us knows the answer to her whereabouts I'll be leaving anyway.'

The man nodded. He stepped aside so that Nick had to leave first. At least the security seemed to be working, he thought.

The only other person who might know anything was Flora May. He'd try her first and then the police.

Flora answered on the first ring.

'Lucy is in hospital.'

Nick couldn't believe what he was hearing. 'She's where?'

'In Maternity, post-appendectomy.'

A sudden surge of anger took Nick by surprise and he forced himself to hold back the explosion he would love to have unleashed. It wasn't Flora's fault. Or only a small part of it. She could have rung him. Finally he managed, 'The babies?'

'Seem fine. No sign of prem labour. Lucy is still very sore and a bit dopey from the pain relief but she's fine, too.'

He was still having problems comprehending that he'd been excluded. 'Why didn't someone phone me? Why didn't you? Or David? I can't believe this.' After all he'd done. All the other crises he'd helped with.

There was a pause. 'She asked us not to.'

Nick couldn't believe that Lucy had deliberately excluded him. Had his friendship to her not meant anything? 'She what?'

Flora paused again. Reluctant. 'I'm sorry, Nick. She said she didn't want to bother you.'

The words chilled him. Iced his veins in a way he hadn't expected. 'Bother me?' Her precious independence. It hurt so much that he wanted to smash something. He thought of the state-of-the-art twin stroller he'd been looking at. All the times he'd been there for her. God, he was such a fool.

'Fine. Thank you.'

'Nick.' Flora at her most urgent. 'Listen. She's young, doesn't want to lose her independence, is used to looking after herself. She's not good at taking.'

This was about that all right. 'I know all about her independence, Flora. She can have it.' He would have been there for her. All she'd had to do was ask. Or include him when she told the rest of the world.

'Nick?'

'Gotta go. See you Monday.' Not that he was looking forward to that. Lucy would still be in hospital and he was hurting so much he didn't think he could talk to her.

Lucy didn't know what was wrong with her. Post-operative blues perhaps. She'd slept all night and through Sunday morning, her tummy was okay, the babies were waking up, and she had a beautiful vase of spring flowers from the staff. But she missed Nick.

She'd sort of thought he would have found out and visited by now. Maybe she should have asked Flora to ring him but it all seemed a bit needy now that everything was over.

Flora bustled in, on her day off, and brought a bottle of apple juice and a pretty glass instead of the usual foam cups to drink out of. 'My. Don't you look miserable.'

'Well, thanks for that.' Lucy stifled a weak laugh because even that hurt, and Flora looked contrite. 'No. You're right.' She guessed Flora knew that she and Nick were more than friends but less than anything else. You never knew what crossed the line with Flora.

'Um. Has anyone mentioned to Nick that I'm here?'

'He rang me this morning.'

Lucy had the feeling Flora was choosing her words carefully and her stomach sank. 'It would be fair to say he's upset we didn't inform him earlier.'

'Oh.'

Flora sat down and pulled her chair closer to the bed. 'I think you hurt him, Lucy. He was very—I was going to say upset, but I think angry and confused might be better words. And it's not something I've noticed before with our Dr Kefes.'

Lucy said, 'Oh,' again, in an even smaller voice, and wanted to hide under the pillow. 'I just didn't want to bother him.'

Flora sighed. 'So I told him. I think that upset him more.'

She pleaded with Flora but inside she knew really she was pleading to Nick. 'I don't want to be a nuisance. He's been so good to me. And I can't expect him to look after me.'

'Oh, don't I know that feeling,' Flora said softly, then she pointed her finger at Lucy. 'And why not? I got the impression he enjoyed looking after you.'

Lucy looked anywhere but at Flora. 'Because he has his own life. He won't want to be saddled with a silly young midwife who got herself pregnant with twins by another man.'

Flora snorted. She did it every well. 'You underestimate your attraction. Women do that. Why do you think he helped you? Allowed you to stay at his flat? Went to the trouble to hand you over as his patient?'

Lucy looked at Flora but maybe she had misread Nick's interest. 'Because he's kind? And I needed help?'

Flora shook her head. 'You have an inferiority complex. Not his problem if he didn't care. But he made it so.' She patted her hand. 'Do you remember me saying people wouldn't help if they didn't want to?'

Lucy nodded. Maybe she had been too prickly. Too determined she wouldn't be needy. Had too jealously guarded her independence and her ability to be hurt again by someone she loved.

'From what you told me, you did a lot for yourself growing up. I understand that. I'm not saying you should use people but you aren't very good at taking help from others. You might want to cultivate that skill.' She laughed. 'Especially with twins coming.'

Then Flora said something startling. 'Did I tell you I was an orphan?'

Lucy shook her head. Looked at this strong, powerful woman and tried to imagine her lost in a dormitory with motherless children. It was a heart-rending picture.

'Had to look after myself in the orphanage. I was the same as you. So when I grew up I found it very difficult to allow others to try to shoulder some responsibility for me. To the extent that eventually nobody tried any more.'

Flora chewed her lip. 'I lost a good man because I wouldn't let him in. He married someone else and I joined the army. Don't make the same mistakes I did.'

She squeezed Lucy's hand. 'Now I'll leave you to rest.'

Suddenly Lucy wondered, and maybe it was the loose-tongued side-effect of the pain relief or maybe her own emotional state but she blurted out the question before she put thought into it. 'Was it Dr Donaldson?'

Flora pursed her lips and didn't say anything for a

moment. Then her eyes twinkled. 'Could have been. And I have learnt my lesson.'

She narrowed her eyes at Lucy. 'So you need to learn yours.' Then she stood up. 'Now, let's get you tidy and I'll fix your hair.'

When his sister knocked on his door after work on Sunday and Nick answered it, he saw her eyes widen at the sweat that poured off him, and he couldn't have cared less.

'I'm about to have a shower.'

'Good.'

Nick didn't need this. He'd run about twenty kilometres and he needed to sit down. 'Not in the mood, Chloe.

'So I see.' Chloe pushed a curl behind her ear. 'Just thought you might want to know that your little friend had an emergency appendectomy last night.'

He grunted. 'I know.'

'Okay.' Chloe paused but Nick didn't offer anything else. She shrugged. 'Thought you might. Just checking.'

Nick wanted to shut the door but maybe he had been neglecting his sister lately for a certain someone who didn't want his attention. 'You okay?'

'Better than you, I think. Let me know if you want to talk, Nicky. It would be nice to be the one leant on for a change, instead of me relying on you.'

After his shower he felt better. And after fluids and food he felt almost normal. Much better for him than the bacon and eggs he would have had this morning. Which brought him back to this morning.

He'd really lost it when he'd realised he'd been excluded from Lucy's emergency.

He wanted to see Lucy. See for himself that she was okay. That her babies were okay. But now he didn't know if he could open himself up to offering her more support if she was going to turn him down.

He needed to re-evaluate his priorities. See his way to the woman he was beginning to think he needed more than he needed anything else in his life.

Should he talk to Chloe before he talked to Lucy? Because this was way outside his experience.

He didn't even know if he could do that. Be the one who needed help instead of the other way around.

Chloe opened her door and she shook her head. 'I don't believe it.'

'You said to come.' But now he wanted to leave. She must have known because she put out her hand and took his wrist. Pulled it.

'Sorry. You took me by surprise. Come in.' And she drew him into her flat and sat him down.

Nick wondered what on earth he was doing here. His sister was looking at him like he had something terminal and he wasn't used to being on this side of the fence—not being the one who sorted out the chaos.

'Nicky, you're a mess.' She shook her head. 'It's about Lucy. Isn't it?'

He looked across the room at the sea outside the windows. 'I lost it this morning.'

'You never lose it.' He could hear the surprise in his sister's voice and there was a certain irony in that. There'd been times when he'd been close to losing it while he'd been trying to make ends meet as he'd waited for Chloe to grow up.

He shrugged. 'She told them not to ring me when she

was sick. I would have been there for her. Why would she do that?'

He could read her sympathy. He didn't want pity. He wanted answers.

'I don't know.'

He knew it. Chloe had no more idea than he did.

When she said, 'Why do *you* think she did that?' he knew it was no good. He wasn't any good at asking for help.

He stood up and Chloe shook her head. 'I've never seen you like this, Nikolai.'

He hesitated and finally sat down again. Ran his hands through his hair. 'I've never felt like this before.'

'Lucky you,' his sister said dryly 'And poor you.' Chloe chewed her lip. 'So you've slept with her.'

Nearly. 'I didn't sleep with her.' Well, he had but that was all. He didn't get the response he expected.

Chloe looked at him like she didn't know who he was. 'Why on earth not? I thought you fancied her. And I'm pretty sure she's in love with you.'

'Of course I fancy her but she's having twins, for goodness' sake. And I needed to get my head around where we were going.'

'You're allowed to have sex when you're pregnant, Nicky.' Chloe shook her head. 'You knocked her back and she left.' Chloe looked out the window herself and thought about it. 'I'd have slipped away while you were asleep.'

He blinked. 'She did.'

'After a knock back like that I wouldn't talk to you again.'

How did she know this stuff? 'She hasn't. She's moved back home. Avoided me.'

'She's decided to go noble.' She looked at him. 'Your Lucy is a good woman, Nicky. But I'm not surprised she told them not to ring you now she knows you don't love her. She doesn't want to trap you into something you don't want.'

What was Chloe talking about? 'But I do.'

'Do what? Give me specifics!' Chloe wasn't letting him off without him saying it.

'Love her. Want her.' He thought about that. Repeated the words in his mind. Of course he knew that. What the hell was wrong with him? 'But she's so darned independent.'

Chloe laughed. 'But isn't that what draws you to her? You can't control her. Isn't that one of the things you secretly love about her? Why she's worth fighting for?'

He stood up. Hell. Of course it was. And of course he'd never said he loved her. He needed to do that. 'Wish me luck.'

Chloe hugged him. 'Of course I do.'

CHAPTER TWELVE

WHEN NIKOLAI ARRIVED at the hospital he didn't go straight to see Lucy. Running on instinct, he saw Flora May leave Lucy's room and followed her back to the lifts.

Flora turned when she heard him behind her. She smiled. 'So you came anyway.'

Nick shrugged and smiled ruefully. 'Wasn't going to.'

Flora sighed. 'It can be an awkward and difficult game.'

Nick knew what she was talking about. He wondered how long she'd known he was smitten. 'What game would that be?'

'Don't play with me, Nikolai. She's miserable. She's in love with you. Has no idea you're thinking long term.' She tilted her angular face at him and pinned him with a direct look.

'That is what you're thinking, isn't it?' Flora huffed. 'Because if you're not…'

Nick grinned. He liked this woman more and more, and Lucy could do worse when she looked for champions.

'Yes.' He held up his hands in smiling defence. 'I want to be there for Lucy. And for her babies. For ever.'

He shrugged and the liberation of just saying that out loud, hearing those words leave his mouth, filled him with a feeling of marvellous resolution. This truly was where he was meant to be.

'She makes me smile just watching her. I love everything about her, maybe even her independent streak, which, I guess, I'll just have to get used to it.'

Flora laughed. 'Afraid so.'

'I love her you know.' He shook his head. 'Besotted and I didn't realise it.'

Flora said again, 'It's not always a smooth journey.'

Nick straightened. 'Now all I need is someone to ask for her hand.'

Flora's face softened and she patted his shoulder. 'Have my blessing. You're a good man. And a lucky man. And Lucy is the one you need to ask. I just don't know if our Lucy has even allowed herself to dream there could be a happily ever after.'

She stepped back and pushed the lift button. 'She's just had more pain relief. You should go and fix that misconception before she falls asleep.'

When Nick entered Lucy's room she had her eyes closed and her red hair was plaited neatly at the side of her face. He remembered Lucy saying she couldn't do a good plait, had never been taught, and he bet Flora May had done that before she'd left.

He put the single red rose down beside her bed on the chest of drawers and sat down. He'd watched her sleeping before.

She was frowning in her sleep and he worried, with a pang, if she had pain. He hadn't been here and she must have been scared when they'd told her she needed to have the operation.

'I should have called you,' she whispered, and he saw that she was awake.

He leant over and kissed her forehcad. 'Yes. You should have.'

'I missed you. I'm sorry I didn't call you.' Her eyes glittered with unshed tears and his heart squeezed because she was upset.

'I'll let you off with it this time but don't do it again.'

She smiled sleepily. 'I only have one appendix.'

He smiled. She was so cute. 'I'm sure you'll find a new ailment some time in the next four months. And if you don't, there's always labour.'

Her eyes clouded. 'But you're not my doctor. You won't be there with me in labour now.'

He took her hand and held it between his. 'I'd very much like to be there with you if you'll have me. And I was thinking of a more legally binding arrangement than being your obstctrician.'

She frowned and he could see the drug was starting to work well.

'I'd like to be with you whenever I can.' He leant over and kissed her on the lips this time. Very gently. 'Go to sleep. I'll sit here and we'll talk about that when you wake up.'

When Lucy woke up Nikolai was still there. It hadn't been a dream. And as for the things he'd said before she'd gone to sleep, she hoped she hadn't dreamed that. He was playing with a single red rose, spinning it in his hand, and she drank in the sight of him until he noticed she'd woken up.

He smiled and the whole room brightened. She loved his smile. 'Hello, sleepyhead.'

Suddenly she felt very shy. Surely this tall and gorgeous man hadn't said what she'd thought he'd said. 'Hello, there.'

He was still smiling. 'How are you feeling?'

Nervous. 'Better.'

'Good.' He nodded and there was that little catch of accent she almost missed now because she was so used to him. Maybe he was nervous, too. The thought brought a little calmness.

He went on. 'And you are properly awake?'

She nodded and moistened her dry lips with her tongue. Nick's eyes darkened and he leaned backwards and picked up her glass of water and a straw from the pile Flora had brought. 'Would you like a sip of water?'

Well, she would, but the suspense was killing her. 'Only if you're quick.'

He passed the water and she took a fast sip before he put it back. He frowned over her words and then got it. Laughed out loud. 'Am I being too slow for you?'

'Maybe a little.'

'Lucy Palmer, I should have told you earlier.'

'Yes.' Lucy wanted to cross her fingers he wasn't going to ask her to be his patient again.

'I love you. With all my heart.' Words she'd never hoped to hear.

Her mouth refused to work. How did you answer that?

His brow creased. 'Is that okay with you?'

More than okay, but she still couldn't speak, so she nodded. 'I love you,' he said again, and she blew him a kiss.

Nick must have seen that as a positive sign because he took her hand and went down on one knee beside her bed. Stared into her eyes with an expression she'd thought she'd never see on his face. 'Lucy Palmer, will you marry me?'

Lucy felt the tears sting her eyes at her gorgeous man, down on one knee, looking into her eyes with the promise of loving her like she'd never been loved before. Fulfilling dreams she'd only dared to dream as she fell asleep in her lonely bed, and here he was, offering her the world. His world.

Waking up with Nick every morning. Sleeping in his arms every night. Her babies would be their babies and if they were blessed they would make more. A family with Nick. How had this happened to her?

Then she said something dumb. 'Are you sure?'

He shook his head. Pretended to frown at her. 'Flora May said you wouldn't believe me. You're supposed to say yes!'

Lucy blinked. 'You've already told Flora?'

'I had to ask someone for your hand.'

She smiled. Loved the idea of Nick asking Flora. Someone else who had really been there for her. Joy bubbled up with the sudden belief that this just might be true. Nick loved her. She loved him so much. Had loved him from the day he'd taken her to breakfast.

'Um, can you ask me, again? Please?'

Nick nodded, suddenly serious, and she loved that, too. Nick serious was Nick seriously sexy.

'Lucy Palmer, I love you. With all my heart. Will you marry me?'

This time she had the right answer. 'Yes. Yes, please.'

He leaned forward and helped her sit up. Then his

arms were around her and she felt as if she'd finally come home. Nick's chin on her hair. His arms around her. Home.

She was home with Nick. She'd found her man, who understood her, loved her and would be her family for ever.

And she would be the home he'd lost at too young an age, the love he could always be sure of. The life he could trust his heart to. She would always be there.

CHAPTER THIRTEEN

Lucy and Nikolai's wedding took place at sunrise on the beach at Coolongatta an hour south of the Gold Coast, two months after Lucy and Nikolai's twins were born.

As the sun peaked over the ocean horizon the bride walked slowly down the long silver carpet to the edge of the sea where her groom waited with love in his eyes and a swelling so great in his heart he could barely breathe.

Gold and red lights shimmered through her hair as she was blessed by the first rays of the sun, just like their marriage would be, and the trailing wildflowers of her bouquet danced and swayed in her shaking fingers as she closed the gap between them.

He glanced at the assembled guests, seated on white chairs in the sand, more wildflowers edging the silver ribbon that led her to him. To his baby daughters, Phoebe and Rose, being nursed at the moment by Callie Richards for the service.

To the attendants: his best man, David Donaldson, Flora May's new husband; his bridesmaid sister, Chloe, smiling beside Flora May, the Matron of Honour looking tall and gangly with joyful affection in her eyes when she, too, looked back at his bride.

Then his eyes were drawn irresistibly to his beautiful Lucy—the woman who had resurrected his belief in family, given him such joy—and healed his heart. His bride.

Lucy wore a ring of flowers in her hair and her neck rose from the circular neckline of her dress like a swan, and at the hem, her coral-tipped toes peeked out as she walked towards him. He'd always loved her bare toes.

When she put her slender fingers into his he linked her to him and finally believed this dream was real. He'd found the woman he wanted to spend the rest of his life with and he could barely wait to pledge his love, for ever.

* * * * *

A sneaky peek at next month...

Medical Romance™

CAPTIVATING MEDICAL DRAMA—WITH HEART

My wish list for next month's titles...

In stores from 1st November 2013:

❏ Gold Coast Angels: Bundle of Trouble – Fiona Lowe & Gold Coast Angels: How to Resist Temptation – Amy Andrews

❏ Her Firefighter Under the Mistletoe – Scarlet Wilson

& Snowbound with Dr Delectable – Susan Carlisle

❏ Her Real Family Christmas – Kate Hardy

& Christmas Eve Delivery – Connie Cox

Available at WHSmith, Tesco, Asda, Eason, Amazon and Apple

Just can't wait?

Visit us Online

You can buy our books online a month before they hit the shops! **www.millsandboon.co.uk**

1013/03

Wrap up warm this winter with Sarah Morgan…

Sleigh Bells in the Snow

Kayla Green loves business and hates Christmas.

So when Jackson O'Neil invites her to Snow Crystal Resort to discuss their business proposal… the last thing she's expecting is to stay for Christmas dinner. As the snowflakes continue to fall, will the woman who doesn't believe in the magic of Christmas finally fall under its spell…?

4th October

www.millsandboon.co.uk/sarahmorgan

MILLS &
BOON®
Book Club

Join the Mills & Boon Book Club

Want to read more **Medical** books?
We're offering you **2 more** absolutely **FREE!**

We'll also treat you to these fabulous extras:

- **Exclusive offers and much more!**
- **FREE home delivery**
- **FREE books and gifts with our special rewards scheme**

Get your free books now!

**visit www.millsandboon.co.uk/bookclub
or call Customer Relations on 020 8288 2888**